ALSO BY KRISTEN SIMMONS
FROM TOR TEEN

STANDALONES
The Glass Arrow
Metaltown
Pacifica

DEATH GAMES DUOLOGY
Find Him Where You Left Him Dead

ARTICLE 5 SERIES
Article 5
Breaking Point
Three

VALE HALL SERIES
The Deceivers
Scammed
Payback

"Bone-chilling. You'll be kept on the edge of your seat with your heart in your throat."

—Lauren Shippen, author of *The Infinite Noise*

"Crafted from pure nightmares—so twisted, so turny, that the second you hit the end, you'll feel compelled to start the whole book over again."

—Lish McBride, Morris Award finalist

"Kristen Simmons strikes the right balance between horror that sticks to your bones and friendships that pull at your heart. The kind of great horror book I can't put down . . . but that also won't let me sleep!"

—Chelsea Mueller, author of
Prom House and the Soul Charmer series

"Simmons crafts an interesting world brimming with unique takes on Japanese mythology, giving readers who know their stuff or do their research some unexpected treats. The fast pace, horror elements, and speedy action scenes will be a draw for many readers looking for some high-stakes action as the characters outsmart the yōkai and progress through the game."

—*The Bulletin of the Center for Children's Books*

SHE WAITS FOR YOU BEYOND THE DARK

KRISTEN SIMMONS

TOR PUBLISHING GROUP

NEW YORK

SHE WAITS FOR YOU BEYOND THE DARK

Copyright © 2025 by Kristen Simmons

A Tor Teen Book
Published by Tom Doherty Associates / Tor Publishing Group
120 Broadway
New York, NY 10271

www.torpublishinggroup.com

Tor® is a registered trademark of Macmillan Publishing Group, LLC.

EU Representative: Macmillan Publishers Ireland Ltd, 1st Floor,
The Liffey Trust Centre, 117–126 Sheriff Street Upper, Dublin 1, DO1 YC43

The Library of Congress Cataloging-in-Publication Data is available upon request.

ISBN 978-1-250-85117-8 (trade paperback)
ISBN 978-1-250-85118-5 (ebook)

Our books may be purchased in bulk for specialty retail/wholesale, literacy, corporate/premium, educational, and subscription box use. Please contact MacmillanSpecialMarkets@macmillan.com.

First Tor Teen Paperback Edition: 2025

10 9 8 7 6 5 4 3 2 1

For all the yōkai,
especially the KriSTANs

IAN

"What did you like?"

Ian's heart stuttered, heat rising in his cheeks as he met Owen's gaze. The light caught the lenses of Owen's glasses, then his eyes, making copper flecks stand out in his dark irises.

Ian gulped.

"I liked . . ." It was a simple question. It wasn't like Owen was asking him to do calculus, or how his chest looked when he took off his shirt.

Static filled Ian's brain.

"Um . . ." *Focus.* "I liked all of it?"

"All of it," Owen repeated with a skeptical smile, leaning back in the corner booth they'd always taken, ever since they were old enough to meet here alone. He scratched a hand down his smooth jaw, and Ian felt a new flush warm his cheeks. "I knew it. You didn't listen!"

"I did!" Ian sighed. "I love your playlist! I just don't remember the names of all of the songs. I liked the one with . . . the guitar? And the girl who sings that high part like . . ." He made a sound like an angry bat and Owen began to laugh.

"That was beautiful," Owen said.

"Shut up."

"I mean it. Put this kid on a stage."

"I hate you."

"That's not what you said last night."

Ian's face heated. Was Owen flirting with him? Since Ian had made it home last month, Owen had been polite. Cautious. Frustratingly attentive to whatever Ian needed. But now he was more relaxed, more confident. Nothing like the shy kid he'd been four years ago.

Ian liked it.

"Sorry, I was home last night," he said. "You must be thinking of someone else."

Owen nodded thoughtfully, his brown eyes glinting behind his wire-rim glasses. "You're right. There are *so* many people I spend *hours* curating the perfect playlist for. It's hard to keep you all straight."

With a laugh, Ian kicked him under the table.

"Drinks up, gentlemen."

Ian startled at the sight of the barista, a man with forearm tattoos and a lumberjack beard, who'd appeared beside the table. He was holding a wooden tray with their coffees and a buttery croissant.

"Iced coffee for you, sir," he said, setting the drink on the table before Owen. "And a cappuccino for my good friend Ian."

Ian stiffened at the title. They weren't friends; Ian hadn't even known the barista knew his name. But then, lots of people did now. He'd been missing since he was thirteen, and come back without a clear explanation of what had happened.

He glanced down at his hands in his lap, relieved to find his nails blunt and pink, not clawed like they were in his nightmares, and swallowed the knot in his throat.

"So what's on the agenda today?" the barista asked, setting the croissant down between them.

"I'm trying to educate Ian on good music, but he's resistant." Owen sent a mock glare Ian's way.

"I'm not resistant," Ian argued. "I just can't sit for that long. I need something else to do."

He didn't say why. That when he wasn't busy, his thoughts went places they shouldn't. That flashes of cold, dark places filled his mind. That he felt so lonely he could hardly breathe.

It was easier when he was with Owen. Everything was just better.

He didn't want to ruin it.

He reached for his cappuccino, but the first sip was scalding and tasted absolutely terrible. He tried not to make a face, but Owen noticed, and smirked. Ian set down the cup. He didn't even like coffee, he just didn't know what else to get and it was the only thing on the menu he recognized.

"You could listen while you play a game," the barista suggested. He motioned to the bookcase stuffed with board games against the wall. "We've got—"

"No games," Owen said quickly. A muscle in his jaw ticked as he stared down at the ice floating in his drink.

Ian tensed. Owen had been forced to play a game with Maddy, Emerson, and Dax in the place where Ian had been trapped for four years. *Meido.* Ian couldn't remember much of what had happened there, but he knew they'd almost died to save him.

And that Dax hadn't come back.

A surge of guilt filled him, as it always did when he thought about his old friend. He knew it wasn't true, but he couldn't help feeling like Dax's absence was his fault somehow. That the only reason Ian had been able to come home was because they'd traded places.

He wished it hadn't been this way—that they both had come back. That they were all here together. Dax's absence burrowed into Ian, a pit that couldn't be filled. Had the others felt that way when he was missing? He wouldn't wish this kind of emptiness on anybody.

"Well, we have puzzles too, you know," the barista said. He crossed his arms over his chest, and the hearts and cartoon characters inked from his wrists to his elbows stretched.

"We'll take a puzzle," Ian said when Owen didn't respond.

The barista smiled and retrieved a 150-piece picture of a ceramic teapot and cups. Ian wondered if all the puzzles matched the coffee-shop theme.

"Some people think I could pull off a sleeve," Owen said when the barista had returned to the counter. He still wasn't meeting Ian's gaze.

"A sleeve?" Ian dumped the pieces on the table and spread them out. "You mean tattoos?"

He imagined Owen with a tattoo. Owen wasn't the full sleeve type; he'd probably get something small. Hidden beneath his clothes somewhere.

Ian's mouth went dry.

"I can only assume you're surprised because my arms look so good without them."

"That, and I remember you crying for six hours after getting stung by a bee."

"I was *allergic*."

Ian smiled, sneaking a peek at Owen's slender arms. Arms that looked great in a T-shirt. Arms that gave amazing hugs. It occurred to Ian that Owen had seen him looking at the barista's tattoos, and this was why he'd brought it up.

"Maybe I'll get a big heart with Emerson's name in it," Owen went on.

Ian grinned. Owen and Emerson loved to pick on each other. Mostly because neither of them saw how alike they were.

"She'd love that. Where is she anyway?" She was supposed to meet them an hour ago, after she'd finished studying for her GED.

Ian still couldn't believe she'd left high school. She'd always been the smartest of their group.

"Doing something with Maddy."

That was good. Maddy had talked constantly when they were younger, but she was so quiet now. Sometimes, when they mentioned Dax, she'd stare off, and he could feel her sadness, and wonder if she didn't wish he had come back instead of Ian. It hurt, but he didn't blame her. From the way she talked about him, Ian could see that he'd missed a lot when he was gone.

Dax was Maddy's person. And without him, she was lost.

Ian and Owen lapsed into a comfortable silence, fitting pieces together. The border was easy enough, but the inside was harder. A jumble of shapes that didn't connect, and overwhelmed Ian to sort through. He made small piles of colors while Owen found a song on his phone and played it softly. It was the one Ian had liked, with the guitar and the high melody.

"This is it." Ian reached for the croissant they were sharing and tore off a chunk. The buttery pastry melted in his mouth, and he nearly groaned at the pillowy feel against his tongue.

"What can I say?" Owen said. "I have excellent taste."

"In some things."

"In all things," Owen insisted, giving a victorious smile as he fit two pieces of the puzzle together. "You didn't see me order a cappuccino like a forty-year-old soccer dad."

Ian tried to look offended, but broke down. "You could have warned me."

"I could have. But I didn't." Owen slid his iced coffee toward Ian. "Here. Try this."

Ian hesitated for only a moment before lifting the cool cup to his mouth. He wondered if his lips were touching the same place Owen's lips had touched. When he looked up, Owen was watching him taste the cool, milky coffee, and he forgot that they were making a puzzle, that they were in public at all.

But as he lowered the cup his heart gave a painful pang. His hand jerked. The episode was only a moment, but coffee had sloshed over his knuckles. He hoped Owen hadn't noticed. He forced a steady breath, and quickly wiped his hand on a napkin.

"See? Excellent taste," Owen said, motioning toward the drink.

"Well, you still separate your noodles from the chili," Ian said, remembering last week at Skyline when he, Maddy, Emerson, and Owen had all dared each other to eat cracker bombs with hot sauce and laughed so hard he'd almost cried. "And you don't even add the cheese." He found two puzzle pieces and connected them, and then two more, making the golden outer ring of the teapot.

Owen cringed. "Because it's disgusting. Because chili shouldn't have cinnamon in it. Because a metric *ton* of grated cheddar doesn't go with noodles. Would you like me to go on?"

Ian gave a skeptical shrug, fitting the cluster of pieces into the frame of the puzzle. "Ninety-eight percent of Cincinnati's population would disagree with you."

"You made that up."

"If I'm lying you can pour hot sauce all over my next three-way."

Owen sputtered. "To be clear, you're referring to the absurd regional specialty of chili and cheese on noodles."

Ian bit his lip so he didn't laugh. "Maybe I am, maybe I'm not."

Owen blinked. "What were we talking about? My brain just reset to factory settings."

"You sound like Emerson." With a little cheer, Ian connected another piece to the cluster Owen had been working on.

Owen blinked at him. "She's in my head. This is my worst nightmare."

Another rush of heat spread through Ian's chest as Owen slid out of the booth, crossed to Ian's side, and sat beside him.

Their shoulders touched. And their hips. Owen's heel bumped the toe of Ian's shoe.

Ian held his breath to focus and in the quiet, he heard a woman's voice.

I'm waiting.

The hair rose on his arms and nape.

He looked over his shoulder, but there was no one there.

"All right?" Owen asked. He was close enough Ian could smell his tea tree oil shampoo. His nerves settled. The voice wasn't real. It was anxiety, that's what the therapist Ian's parents had hired said. Breakthrough trauma. It would pass, someday. Hopefully.

"Yeah." His voice was shallow.

Owen frowned, but didn't push the issue as he lifted his phone and took a picture of them. He showed Ian. It was cute. *They* were cute. Smiling like a couple, their drinks and food and puzzle pieces strewn over the table before them.

Were they a couple?

He didn't know what people did now to make it official. Owen had been catching him up on all sorts of movies, just like he had with the playlists. Cultural education, he called it. But that was something any friend would do, right?

He doesn't want you, the woman's voice whispered.

Ian rubbed absently at his chest, wishing the voice would leave him alone.

"Puzzling pros . . ." Owen spoke as he texted. "See, Emerson? We're not just pretty faces." The phone made a little whoosh as he sent it to the Foxtail Five group text, a name they'd called each other when they were kids. Ian's phone dinged a moment later, and even though he'd already seen the picture, he looked again, grinning down at Maddy and Emerson's ID pictures beside Owen's and his.

Foxtail Five, they still called themselves, even though there were only four now.

The phone dinged again a moment later, and a new picture appeared from Emerson.

Not a new picture, the same one, zoomed in on the puzzle on the table. There were red mark-ups—pieces circled and then pointed into place with arrows.

"Is she solving it?" Ian said with a laugh.

Another ding.

"*Take a better picture*," Owen read aloud. He turned to Ian. "She says we're blocking the right side. She refuses to work under these conditions."

"Same," said Ian, gesturing dramatically toward the counter. "I can't even hear your perfectly curated playlist over the steamer."

"We could go somewhere else," Owen said.

Ian stilled. The noise of the coffee shop seemed to grow ten times louder around them.

"We could go somewhere quieter, I mean. So we can hear the music better," Owen said.

Ian was nodding quickly, as if this was the best idea in the world. "Your place?"

If they went to his house, his dad would sit next to Owen on the couch like they were pals and grill him about school, and his mom would barge in on them every five minutes with snacks. He loved his parents, but they hovered. It was bad enough they were tracking him on his phone and messaging every hour to check in.

Owen's house, on the other hand, would be empty. His mom was still at work. He'd said that when they'd first gotten here. They would have the place to themselves.

"Sure," said Owen, his voice a little rough. He cleared his throat. "Yeah. Sure. That works."

Was he nervous? That couldn't be right. Owen was . . . *Owen*. Cool, and funny, and always so at ease with the everyone and everything around him. Sometimes Ian envied that calm. Mostly though, he was in awe of it. If he could be half that confident, that stupid voice in his head would never speak a harsh word to him again.

A hum of anticipation seemed to fill the space between them.

"Let's go," Ian said, standing. "My dad gave me money for the coffee." He blew out an uneven breath, leaving the cappuccino on the table.

"Great," said Owen, then scratched his head. "Can I meet you at my house? I need to pick up my room."

"I don't care that you're a slob," Ian said with a grin.

"I'm not a slob," Owen retorted, standing across from him. Was he closer than he normally stood? It felt like he could lean forward and touch him at any moment. "I just need to . . . . make my bed and stuff."

Ian's throat went dry.

Owen needed to make his bed. Because they might be lying on it. Together.

"Yeah," said Ian. "Yes. You go make your bed. I'll pay, and meet you at your house."

"You're okay to walk by yourself?"

It was only a couple blocks, and it was light outside, the streets busy with people. But it was nice that Owen asked.

The truth was, Ian kind of wanted the challenge of walking alone. He needed to be more independent. He didn't want his friends worrying about him all the time.

"I'm okay. Go."

Owen nodded, and hurried out.

As Ian watched him go, his eyes caught on a shadow, sliding across the floor in his direction. His breath caught as it stretched, untethered to any object.

Just a trick of the light.

He tore his eyes away from the ground to focus on the barista behind the cash register, handing a cookie and a drink with whipped cream to a man in a navy suit. Outside The Bean, in Foxtail Alley, a moving truck was backing up. The loud *beep beep beep* ground Ian's teeth together.

He closed his eyes, picturing Owen's front door. He pulled the money out of his jeans pocket, wishing the guy in front of him would hurry up.

When he opened his eyes, the shadow under the counter had begun to pulse at the edges, the bottom moving slowly toward the man in the navy suit's shoes. The customer stepped back from the counter just before it got him.

Terror gripped Ian's chest.

"Closing out, Ian?" The barista smiled, twisting the end of his bushy beard around one finger.

Ian forced his eyes up off the floor and nodded quickly. He shoved the cash toward the barista.

"How was the drink?"

"Great," Ian muttered. "Thanks."

The shadow spread on the floor, joining the one by the door. He fought the urge to step back. This wasn't real. The shadow, the voice. He needed to get out of here. Go to Owen's. Everything was fine when he was with his friends. He was always safe with Owen.

So much for being independent. Maybe his friends were right to worry about him.

He couldn't think of that now.

The shadow grew thick. Turned glossy and liquid as it appeared behind the counter around the barista's feet. A bubble rose in the thick goo and popped, splattering black droplets on the barista's jeans. It seared through the fabric, bringing the rotting stench of burning flesh to Ian's nostrils.

The barista didn't flinch.

Ian's hands curled into fists over the thighs of his pants.

It's not real. If it was, the barista would feel it. He'd scream.

"Some people think it has too much milk. We can try an espresso next time if you're looking for a kick. Or a tea maybe. We've got a great selection. All fair trade, loose leaf—"

"I need to go," Ian interrupted as the darkness spread over the coffee machine behind the barista, inky tendrils painting black snowflakes up the wall. "Can you hurry?"

"My bad," said the barista, opening the cash register with a sharp *ding*. "I'm a talker. That's what my girlfriend always says. I met her here, you know. . . ."

His voice faded into the static in Ian's ears. A bitter taste filled his mouth. The man's casual tone was grating. He spoke to Ian as if they were friends, but they weren't friends.

Nothing more than a servant, the woman's voice whispered in his ear. He turned, but he knew he wouldn't see her. She was inside. In his head.

Shut up, Ian willed her. *Shut up.*

Ian's heart skipped painfully, a lurch in his chest. He rubbed at it, but it didn't ease the throb.

He was fine. He needed to find Owen. He needed—

The snowflakes expanded. Joined together at the edges to paint the wall behind the cash register black. A buzz filled Ian's ears as darkness covered the chandelier above.

"Hey, man," said the barista, not acknowledging the shadows. "You all right? You're looking a little rough."

Ian didn't have to look back to know the darkness had surrounded him, making him an island on a single tile of the coffee shop's floor. He tried to make himself smaller, hugging his arms over his chest, but he couldn't escape it.

Such a fragile little mortal you are, the voice whispered inside him. His heart slammed against his ribs.

"Shut up," Ian said out loud.

"Ian?" The barista's voice was far away.

Ian gasped. *Not real not real not real.*

The liquid darkness crawled up the man's legs, making a hungry slurping sound.

We are connected, you and I, the woman whispered in his head.

"Go away," Ian cried miserably. He wanted to run, but where could he go? He was stuck on this single tile, with nowhere else to step. Around him, the other customers had frozen in place, stuck in the dark like they were trapped in tar.

I cannot, she whispered. *I will not.*

The barista was leaning over the counter now. Ian tried to fight back the terror, but the voice was too strong, spreading through him like a fever.

"Please," Ian begged. Bile churned in his stomach. Every customer remained frozen in place. Held by the darkness. It was filling the room now. Covering them all. In moments it would cover him too.

I can protect you, the voice whispered. *I can keep you safe.*

He didn't want to listen. He needed to get out of here. To get away from her. But where could he go when she was lodged inside him?

"Okay," he said miserably. He was weak. He couldn't help it. "Yes, make it stop."

The darkness froze. The buzz silenced in his ears.

Cold. In his chest. In his head. In his mouth and his bones.

"Hey." The barista placed a steadying hand on Ian's forearm. Ian covered his ears to drown out the sound. It didn't help. She wouldn't be silenced. The barista's forehead wrinkled with concern. They weren't at the counter anymore, but in a storeroom of some kind. Boxes of tea and coffee lined the shelves. Paper cups and sleeves were stacked in rows. The man must have led him here. Ian didn't remember it happening.

"Take a breath. You're all right," the man said.

Ian's arm lifted of its own accord, as if he were a marionette puppet, controlled by some other force. His eyes examined the pale, feeble knuckles of his hand. The clipped nails. The common, pink hue of his skin.

Fear burst inside him. His body was moving without his consent.

"Remove your hand, mortal." The woman's voice was no longer a whisper in his mind, but its own force, spilling from his mouth.

"Mortal?" The barista gave a strained chuckle, but withdrew his hand. "I've been called a lot of things, but that one's new."

Ian inhaled, the man's scent—fresh meat and blood—filling his nostrils. Panic seized him, but he didn't tremble. His body remained perfectly still.

He could see through his eyes. Hear through his ears. But he couldn't control any of it.

He was not in control of his own body.

He tried to scream, but his lips didn't move.

Cry, said the voice in his head. *Weep, like the pitiful creature you are.*

His eyes burned. Filled. Before he could stop it, a tear ran down his cheek.

"Hey," said the barista. "You sure you're okay?"

Ian's hand reached to his face. He gathered the tear on his fingertip, then examined it. A tiny bead of water, catching the dim light from the overhead bulb with a rainbow's reflection.

He reached across the space, and let the tear drop on the man's wrist.

The barista's face contorted with pain. A whimper slipped from his throat. Ian tried frantically to help him, but the force was too great.

"Where are you?" the woman crooned in Ian's voice. "You said you would come when I called for you, Emperor. You have been summoned."

The barista gasped. Crimson tears dripped from his eyes.

"Come to me, my love," she sang, using Ian's mouth. "Save this pitiful creature before I take him. Hear my voice and find me."

She gripped Ian's hand into a fist, and punched the barista. The man was thrown against the shelves, knocking a bag of plastic lids to the ground. His mouth opened wide, as if he might be screaming, but no sound came out.

You're hurting him, Ian shouted in his own mind.

In response, he felt the woman's sick wave of pleasure.

A wave of fury invaded Ian's body, and with a flick of his wrist, the woman snapped the barista's right arm above the elbow. It made an awful right angle to the shelf, pointing outward.

"Izanami," the barista groaned.

"There you are," Ian's mouth said. "You know I do not like to be kept waiting, husband."

Confusion shook through him. Ian knew that name . . . *Izanami.* His friends had talked about her—the cursed empress from the game they'd begun four years ago. The one they'd brought back to life with the body-part prizes from seven challenges, and escaped to make it home.

"These mortals are not yours to toy with, Izanami." The barista's voice had changed—his words were a deep bellow, richer than any Ian had ever heard. They teased over Ian's skin, bringing pleasing goose bumps to his exposed arms against his will.

She hummed thoughtfully. "Isn't this amusing? Both of us, confined to mortal hosts. Tell me, do you find it hard to stay within the boundaries of their paper skin? It is an exercise in control not to burst free, isn't it?" She sighed.

"What do you want, Izanami?"

"You know what I want."

"The tomoe is broken. You will never find the pieces."

An image filled Ian's mind of a circle split into three swirling commas, each piece equal in size. One black, one silver, one gold.

"This sounds like a challenge."

"One you will never complete." The barista's eyes rolled back to a sea of white. "The pieces of the tomoe are protected. They can only be gathered by a willing mortal."

"You and your precious mortals." She tutted. "You underestimate my charm. I can be very persuasive." Ian's fingers raked through the barista's hair, pulling him straight. His broken arm hung limply at his side. "I'll use this mortal right here to find them."

"None under your control may play this game, Empress. Only one pure of heart and intention may seek the pieces of the tomoe."

"So it *is* a game!" She giggled in delight.

"It is assurance that you will never again wield the power of a god. No willing mortal would help you, even in that body."

Ian's heartbeat thudded, sending another frigid dose of poison into his blood. Cold fingers pried into his private thoughts, fishing for memories.

They paused on Owen.

Ian tried to hide him, but it was impossible. The empress saw everything.

"I would not be so sure, my love," she whispered.

The barista's lips pulled back over his teeth. "You are arrogant as ever, wife. Even if you do find a mortal to help you gather the pieces, you will not remake the tomoe before that body fails. Your soul has already begun to tear it apart. That body will reject your heart by the end of the night."

"Then I'll have to finish the game before then," she answered, and Ian could feel the arrogance her husband spoke of, even as it warred with his own skittering pulse. "The next time we face each other, Izanagi, your living world will look quite different. I suggest you enjoy it while you can."

With her dismissal, the emperor was gone. Ian could see the light leave the barista's eyes, how they rolled back in his head as he fell unconscious. Izanami released his body then, and he dropped to the ground in a heap.

Ian's spine bowed as Izanami shuddered. Dizziness had her gripping the shelf for support. She would have to pace herself. Not exert too much energy. She needed this mortal's body to last until the tomoe was rebuilt.

That body will reject your heart by the end of the night.

Urgency rippled through her. She had returned to the land of the living, but the body she possessed was limited—her husband was right, it could not bear her power without eventually dying. To re-create her empress form, she needed the tomoe, but to get it, she had to find a willing mortal to gather its three pieces.

She did not have much time.

Turning toward the door, she strode out, the darkness lapping at Ian's feet with each step. No one noticed as she crossed the coffee shop and stepped into the light of day.

A new game had begun, and this time, she would not lose.

EMERSON

Emerson had packed for the party with all the necessities: spray paint, a shovel, a knife, and a box of Holtman's doughnuts. They'd gotten a little smashed in her backpack on the streetcar, but Maddy wouldn't care.

Smiling at the last message from Owen—a middle finger emoji—she tucked the phone into the back pocket of her baggy pants, and strode down the manicured path at Smale Park. It was a night-and-day difference from the last time she'd been here, a month ago. The flowers had bloomed in a riot of color. The playground was teeming with kids and their sticky, juice-box fingers. The hum of cars on the Roebling Bridge mingled with the buzz of the bees, and the air smelled fresh after last night's rain. Like spring and hope. Like all the shitty things they'd been through had finally washed away.

Ahead, the Ohio River came into view, brown and gleaming in the afternoon sun. Even its lazy current seemed unworried as it reflected the steel-and-brick city rising behind her.

She ran a hand over the soft tips of her short hair, the warmth soaking through her palm.

Home.

She didn't know how much she loved it until it had nearly been taken away forever.

She picked a shady spot on the fence, hidden from the main path, and climbed over onto the steep rocky shore. As her feet hit the ground on the other side, her heartbeat quickened. She had not been here since they'd brought Ian home.

Since they'd beaten the game.

She sucked her lip ring between her teeth. Thumbs digging under the straps of her backpack, she picked her way through the chunks of shale and debris toward the water. She wished Maddy had come with her—they could have ridden the streetcar together—but her friend was coming from school, and Emerson's flexible home education plan allowed her the privilege of arriving early to set up.

She pushed on. The game was done. They'd won it. The empress was dust and now she and Maddy would eat a goddamn doughnut to celebrate.

After they blocked the entrance of the cave.

Her steps quickened as it came into view. She almost missed it at first—the black recess was covered with green vines. The foliage had been dead before, yellow and thin, but now it was fresh and alive like everything else in this world.

She set down her bag, and began to unpack.

The shovel was a fold-out tool—not as strong as one with a straight handle, but she hadn't wanted to attract unnecessary attention on the streetcar by cruising around like some teenage gravedigger. The steak knife was from her kitchen—an excessive precaution, maybe, considering they were safe now, but she wasn't about to come back to this place completely unarmed. She set it in the dirt beside the shovel, then placed the neon green spray paint and two yellow CAUTION signs beside it. She'd even brought pink nail polish as a joke—a color called Glitter Me Baby that she'd sooner set on fire than actually wear. A throwback to their Meido slumber party when she and Maddy were going to paint their nails and smash the patriarchy.

Maddy was going to die laughing.

She placed the dented doughnut box on a rock beside the makeshift weapon wheel and grinned, then took a seat on a nearby stone to wait for Maddy.

Time passed.

She checked her phone. She'd come early, but now Maddy was officially late. With a scowl, Emerson opened their text chain to check the time and date, but she'd been right that they were meeting today. They'd set it up last weekend, when they'd decided they needed to mark this shithole before anyone accidently stumbled inside and found themselves in Meido.

Emerson started to type, *On your way?* But stopped and deleted it.

Maddy would be here.

She waited another ten minutes, but no one came walking down the path.

Her nerves prickled. She stood and walked to the river, tossing in a few stones before heading back. She checked her phone again, but no word from Maddy.

Giving in, she texted, *@ worst place in this universe, c u soon!*

She held her phone for the next five minutes, but there was no reply.

Worry began to gnaw at her. What if something had happened? Maddy could have been in a car accident, or gotten in trouble with her parents. She sent off another message: *U ok?*

Nothing.

Hellllllllo?

No response.

Minutes stretched into an hour, and Emerson's worry grew teeth. Where was she? Maddy hadn't texted her in three days. Emerson hadn't wanted to seem needy, so she'd given her space. It wasn't like Emerson had to know her every move or anything. Maybe Maddy had a big test she hadn't mentioned, or some family thing, but she could have at least sent a heads-up. This wasn't like her.

Or was it?

She and Maddy had only really been friends again for the last month. They hadn't spoken for *four years* before that. The Maddy she knew—that she'd fought beside in Meido—never would have forgotten something this important, or worse, blown her off, but the girl from before, the dean's list swim champ with her designer clothes and highbrow friends . . . she might have.

No, she *would* have.

A hot droplet of sweat slid down Emerson's back.

It wasn't true. Maddy would be here.

Another ten minutes passed.

Wandering down to the shore, Emerson caught her reflection in the muddy water. Her brows, drawn in worry. Her cheeks, soft and rosy from a month of eating actual meals her parents made rather than chips and cereal during gaming marathons. She looked away, awkwardness prickling inside her. Sometimes looking at her own face felt like looking at a stranger's. Objectively, she looked fine. But the person staring back never felt like her, not even after she'd buzzed her hair.

She kicked at the water, distorting her image, then marched back up over the rocks toward the cave. Tore open the dented box and snagged a doughnut. Surviving the nightmare called for the best doughnuts in the entire city. The Cap'n Crunch cream-filled had been for Maddy, but Emerson tore into that one first, her hands getting sticky with the glaze.

It was fucking delicious, and she hated it.

She lifted her phone again, her thumb leaving a coat of sugar on the screen as she swiped across it.

Are you coming or not?

She finished the doughnut.

Maddy did not respond.

The doughnut sat in Emerson's gut, too heavy, too sweet. She thought of Owen and Ian, hanging out at The Bean, having the time of their lives with that stupid puzzle. Maddy probably giving in to her mom's wishes to hang out with the "right crowd" and shopping at Kenwood Mall with the popular girls from her school. She probably didn't even eat doughnuts anymore; she was always ultra health-conscious when she was preparing for a swim meet.

Emerson grabbed the second doughnut—the Oreo-topped chocolate cake one she'd gotten for herself—and hurled it toward the river. It landed with an annoyed splat against a rock and was soon mobbed by birds. Then she stuffed the nail polish back into her backpack.

It had been a dumb idea anyway.

Extending the shovel to its full length, Emerson turned and got to work. She hacked at the vines over the mouth of the cave. Maddy didn't want to come? Fine. She would do this herself. The stringy vines fell to the ground, revealing the uneven rocks over the entrance, and a space wide enough for Emerson to climb through. She snagged the spray paint.

Heat seared through her as she shook the can, the click of metal only making her more irritated. She'd thought Maddy was different now. They'd gone through Hell together. They'd saved Ian, and each other. They were fucking sisters in battle, and now Maddy couldn't even be bothered to tell her she wasn't going to show up?

Emerson was an idiot.

She should have seen this coming.

Just because they were friends in one world, didn't mean they were friends in every world. Just because Owen and Ian were inseparable now, didn't mean that Maddy and Emerson would be. Hell, Maddy had always been closer to Dax anyway—her stupid, back-stabbing, yōkai *husband*.

Emerson gripped the can harder, remembering the blank look on Dax's face when he'd stood beside the empress. How his eyes had gone black and glossy.

Maybe he'd been their friend once. Maybe he'd helped them escape in the end. But he was a creature of Meido, and he belonged there. Emerson had told Maddy as much.

Her heart panged.

Maybe that's why Maddy hadn't shown up today.

Why she wasn't returning any of Emerson's texts.

"Shit," she muttered, insecurity crashing through her. Of course Maddy didn't want to hear that Dax belonged in Meido, even if it was true.

She shook her head, shaking the spray paint can harder. This wasn't her fault. If Maddy had a problem, she could have an actual conversation about it, rather than running back to her boring, predictable life.

CAUTION, Emerson sprayed in giant letters on the rocks over the cave's entrance.

She thought of the green mist in her game, *Assassin 0*. The Choke. How it killed anyone it touched. She should have brought a smoke machine, rigged it to go off when anyone passed through the threshold.

Hot with anger, she stepped closer to add: DANGEROUS FUMES. Maybe people were stupid enough to come exploring here when they saw the caution signs, but no one wanted to inhale toxic gas.

As she leaned closer to the entrance, cold air prickled her skin, as if an invisible hand had reached through the air and grabbed the thin material of her T-shirt. She gritted her teeth. This place would not scare her again. She'd beaten it.

But she'd been with her friends then, and now she was alone.

Her stomach twisted. How fast they'd all become necessary to each other in that world. But here, they simply weren't. They could go back to being strangers. Go back to hating each other.

"*Emerson.*"

The whisper came from inside the cave. She jolted backward. Stumbled. Dropping the can, she caught herself on a boulder beside the entrance, then picked up the knife off the ground for protection.

"Hello?" she called, hardening her voice.

Nothing.

She was hearing things. The game was over. The cards were gone—they'd looked for them while they'd waited for Ian's body to be remade as human in the dark cave. Her senses were playing tricks on her, that was all.

"Emerson."

She gripped the handle of the knife harder. The voice was rough, as if coming from the earth itself. A thin, shallow sound of pain.

"Maddy?" she whispered.

It couldn't be. The vines outside the entrance hadn't been disturbed when Emerson had come here. No one had been inside in a long time. She should get on with the task she'd come here to do—post the caution signs, and close up the entrance with as many rocks and shovelfuls of dirt as she could carry. Still, her heart stammered with uncertainty. What if Maddy hadn't blown her off at all, but had arrived early, and gone inside the cave? She could have gotten sucked into Meido again.

She could be in danger. Hurt.

Emerson shook her head, her breath coming faster. Maddy knew better than to go into the cave alone. She wasn't a fool.

Unless she was *trying* to find the game again.

Because she'd come here searching for Dax.

"Dammit, Maddy," Emerson hissed.

She stepped through the threshold into the cave.

"Hello?" She turned on the flashlight on her phone, but it didn't penetrate the darkness. The cold seemed to blow straight through her, stealing her breath.

She pushed on.

"Maddy! You better not be in here!"

Dark surrounded the blunt beam of her flashlight. A crack behind her made her jump. She peered back toward the entrance.

There was no movement.

Her hearing sharpened. From ahead came the strained sound of breathing. Shallow gasps of pain. Her boots slid on the dirt floor as she charged forward. She kept her head low so she didn't hit the rough ceiling of the tunnel.

"Maddy!" she shouted. She gripped the phone light in one hand, the knife in her other, ready to fight. The scream of blood in her ears covered the gasps.

Maddy was nowhere to be seen.

No one was here.

She slowed, trying to get her bearings. The breathing still came from up ahead, but it was deeper than before. Slower.

Not human.

She should have run. Called her friends for help. But something was pulling her deeper into the darkness. She had to look, to see that it wasn't real. To prove that Meido was behind them.

Her gaze lowered, the rough walls and ground unfamiliar. She'd passed the place where the game had pulled them into the earth. Stepped over the once-quicksand like it had never grabbed her feet and pulled her under. This was deeper in the cave than she'd ever gone.

Her pulse raced as she neared the source of the sound.

The tunnel widened around her into a space the size of her town house. The ceiling stretched into darkness, but based on the echo of dripping water it couldn't have been more than two stories high. The walls were uneven and lined with trickles of moisture, and the cold air reeked of iron and rot.

Emerson gripped the knife tighter. The tunnel had been tight, had made her claustrophobic, but it had left little room for things to be hiding. Here in the open, anything could be waiting.

"Hello?" Her voice wavered with uncertainty.

She stepped deeper into the room, and stretched the light out as far as she dared.

Before her, a boulder blocked the path forward. The sound of breathing came from behind it, as if the deep gasps were siphoning through some unseen crack between the blockade and the wall. Her eyes traced the broad width of the rounded stone. It was as if it had been rolled here to stop anyone from going forward.

Or anything from getting out.

The knife slid out of her hand, implanting with a *thud* blade down in the ground.

She didn't waste time searching for it. Turning on her heels, she ran for the exit. When she was outside, she heaved every stone she could lift to block the entrance of the cave, and didn't stop shoveling dirt into the cracks until blisters on her hands broke open, and she was dizzy from the exertion.

Then she sent the emergency signal to the Foxtail Five group text. The code they'd agreed they would only use if any of them were in trouble:

5

MADDY

Maddy set her gaze on the woman before her. The familiar scowl—Dax's scowl—on someone else's face gave her a very bad feeling in the pit of her stomach.

"I'm going to find him," Maddy told her. "And I'm going to bring him back."

The woman's dark eyes pinched around the corners. All Vera had said since Maddy's arrival were two words, repeated over and over.

My fault.

"Vera," Maddy said, leaning forward in the velvet armchair. The wooden floor beneath her sneakers creaked as she shifted. "Did you hear me? I said I'm going to find your son. I'm going to find Dax."

Gently, Maddy touched the back of Vera's hand, finding it cold.

Vera flinched. When her gaze landed on Maddy, she blinked, as if surprised to find her there.

"I'm Dax's friend. My name is Maddy."

Vera pulled her hand back, pressing a thumb between her brows.

"I'm sorry, you must be mistaken. My son . . . he died. A long time ago."

Maddy leaned closer.

"What if I told you he wasn't dead?" she said. "At least, not in the traditional sense."

Vera huffed. "I'd say you need to be here more than I do."

Maddy pressed her teeth together. She hadn't known what to expect when she'd made the drive from Ohio to upstate New York. Whether Vera would be willing to see her, if she knew anything about what had happened to her son after the fire that had killed him. . . . The old report Maddy had found archived online hadn't said much, only that Vera had accidently knocked over a candle while trying to protect Dax from his father—a ghost, she claimed, trying to take their child to Hell.

Once, Maddy would have thought the court right to deem Vera incompetent to stand trial. Now she knew better.

Ghosts—*yōkai*—were real.

"You're here because they didn't believe you about the ghost that came after Dax," Maddy said quietly. "But I believe you. I've seen them too."

Vera stared at her a long moment before shaking her head. "Is this a test? Are you from the court? Did the judge send you? Because I've done all my therapy. I've done everything on my treatment plan."

"No," said Maddy. "I'm just a friend."

"My dead son's friend."

Maddy's cheeks heated. "I know it sounds impossible."

"You have no idea what's possible." Tears glazed Vera's eyes. "I . . . I can't do this. I can't have this conversation. It's not healthy for me."

She made to stand, but Maddy reached out to touch her knee. "Please. I just want to talk."

Vera stared down at Maddy's hand. Maddy pulled it back.

"My son is dead." Vera's voice was louder now. "I was there. I saw it. How could you come here and say these things to me?"

Maddy swallowed, her throat suddenly dry. She glanced over her shoulder, but the attendant, Raul, had left the room, and the other residents didn't appear to be listening.

"I've seen him," she said. "He's different, but he's still out there. And he needs my help."

Vera stilled.

"You've seen him?"

Maddy nodded.

"He helped me escape a terrible place." Maddy closed her eyes for a moment, seeing Dax hold back the horde of split-faced players so she, Emerson, Owen, and Ian could get through the waning green fire gate. "He was very brave."

"He always was," Vera said, pride mixing with grief. "What do you mean he helped you escape?"

"From Meido," Maddy said. "The game."

Vera leaned back. Her gaze chilled. "No one gets out of the game. Only yōkai." Her shoulders rose as her breath quickened. "What are you?"

"A friend. I promise."

Doubt flashed in Vera's eyes. She reached for the guitar from the wall where it had been leaning. The strings plunked against her open hand as she gripped the neck. Maddy's pulse spiked. She lifted her hands in defense.

"Please," she said. "Please listen."

The woman didn't believe her. She thought Maddy was a yōkai.

"Carol made banana bread!" Raul returned, holding a plate of freshly sliced and steaming bread, which he set on the coffee table beside the couch. Several residents stood to make their way over, but Vera remained perfectly still.

"I'm not one of them," Maddy said quickly. "I'm not yōkai."

"Lies," Vera hissed, one hand still on the guitar. "He came to my house. He tried to take my son. There was a fire." She bent forward, as if punched in the stomach. "My fault."

Maddy flashed to Meido. To the woman in the brush, punctured by thorns. *My fault my fault my fault.*

She was sure that woman was Vera, Dax's mom, but she was different there. A creature of Meido. The woman before Maddy was human in every way, from the silver strands of her hair to the bright fear in her eyes.

"It wasn't your fault," Maddy said.

"I couldn't protect him." Her throat worked to swallow. Slowly, she released the guitar, looking out the window beside her armchair to an old, red barn and the silver lake behind it.

"I know this is hard," Maddy said, feeling the woman's pain like a vise around her chest, "but I need to get back to Meido. Did Dax ever mention any cards to you before the fire? Did he ever talk about the cave, or . . . or the ghost that came after him?"

"He was a *child*."

Maddy sucked in a breath. Whatever help she was hoping to find here was sliding out of her fingers. But she'd come too far to give up. There had to be a way back to Meido. Another way to enter the game. That stupid cave was no use, they'd already looked for the cards when they'd brought Ian home.

The cave.

"Oh no." She was supposed to go to the cave with Emerson to-day. They'd set up a time to ceremonially block off the entrance—there were going to be doughnuts.

She reached to her pocket to grab her phone, before remembering that she'd left it in her car. Had Emerson called? She'd silenced her notifications, knowing that her parents were eventually going to figure out that she wasn't at an away swim meet like she'd claimed.

Her chest tightened. When she'd figured out where Vera was, she hadn't hesitated. She'd gotten in the car and driven to New York. She hadn't even told her friends where she was going—Owen needed to stay home to look out for Ian, but Emerson would have demanded to come, and how could Maddy tell her that she was trying to get back to the place where they'd almost died? She couldn't bring Emerson along, no matter how close they were. Last time, they hadn't had a choice to go, but now, it was Maddy's decision. She wouldn't let her best friend be dragged into it just to watch her back.

She would call Emerson as soon as she left.

"Hungry?" Raul approached with a smile. He handed them both a slice of banana bread on small napkins. The warmth of it soaked through the paper to Maddy's cold fingers. The sweet scent of it filled her nostrils. She smiled to Raul so he would leave, but didn't take a bite, and neither did Vera.

"Look," Vera said quietly, but firmly. "I don't know what you are, but you won't find the answers you're looking for here. The mirror's broken. I can't see him anymore."

Maddy grabbed the banana bread too tightly, smashing it in the napkin. Crumbs spilled over her thighs.

"What mirror?" she asked.

"The one his father gave me."

"His father," Maddy said carefully. "The yōkai."

Vera didn't answer.

"You can see Dax in this mirror?"

Vera stared out the window. "I told you, it's broken. He's gone."

The word echoed through Maddy with finality.

Gone.

She took a slow breath. Her fingers closed over her opposite wrist, where a dark scar carved by a jagged fingernail glared up from her brown skin.

It is a promise that cannot be undone. Even in death your souls will belong to each other.

She felt that pull now, every fiber of her body dragging her toward Dax. She had felt it since the moment he'd said goodbye.

"Where is it?" Maddy asked. "The mirror. Can I see it?"

Vera lifted her brows, the wrinkles in her forehead betraying her age. She had been a young mother when Dax had died, and while Dax's aging had suspended until he'd met Maddy and the others, Vera's had not. She was near sixty now, if not older.

"I threw it into the lake," she said.

"What lake?"

Vera couldn't see Dax through this mirror, but maybe Maddy could.

"How's it going over here?" Raul was walking back toward them now, a gentle smile creasing his face.

"I'm tired," said Vera, cradling the slice in her hands. "I need to go lie down."

Raul nodded. "Sounds like you're taking care of yourself. That's what I like to hear."

"Wait—" Maddy started, but Vera had already stood and was walking away. Maddy raced after her, ready to beg for more information, but Raul was suddenly between them.

"A little stimulation can feel like a lot when you're not used to it," he explained.

"We weren't done talking. Please, I just need to—"

"Give her some time," Raul said. "Why don't you go check out the property? The barn is open. The goats are real sweethearts, but watch out for the llama. He's . . . still working on his social skills."

The man's firm tone told her she wasn't getting any more from Vera right now.

"Thanks." Her shoulders sagged.

Before Vera left the room she paused, turning back. Her eyes were pinched at the corners, her cheeks pale. She looked like she might say something, but instead took a slow breath, and bit off the corner of the slice of banana bread she was still holding.

Then she walked away.

Maddy's hands shook. She wanted to push Raul aside, make Dax's mom talk, but what good would that do? The conversation was over, and pressing her too hard would get probably get Maddy kicked out before she got a single answer.

She turned, catching another glimpse out the window of the red rickety barn, and the lake in the pasture beyond it.

I threw it into the lake.

Maddy was striding toward the door before she had time to question herself. If there was a chance something here was going to bring her closer to Dax, she had to find it.

The door squeaked when she opened it, and she was greeted by a rush of cold air as she stepped outside onto the wraparound porch. She jogged down the wooden steps, out of the shadow into the fading afternoon sun. The scent of livestock and grass grew stronger as she sloshed over the muddy ground toward the barn. Her teeth pressed together as a white llama poked its head out from the open sliding door.

She steered wide around the paddock, her pulse growing faster as she headed toward the pasture lake near the woods.

It had been a month since she'd seen Dax. Since she'd left him in a palace on the brink of collapse, surrounded by cut-faced players and giant spiders. He might really be gone now, like Vera had said.

No. Maddy refused to believe that. Dax was strong. He was *yōkai*. He'd defeated monsters in the living world, he could defend himself in the land of the dead.

Her nails pressed into her palms at the thought of him facing any number of horrors alone. Knowing he was there, that he'd been there for the last month without help, scratched deep beneath her skin. Most nights she could hardly sleep, dreaming of him being torn apart by tengu.

Or worse, changing, his eyes black from lid to lid, his mind empty.

She shivered.

At the edge of the lake, the muddy ground gave way to an old wooden dock, and the boards creaked under her feet as she walked out over the flat water. It was clear to the sandy bottom.

The sun was setting behind her, the last of the sparkle on the glossy surface disappearing with the cool evening air. The scent of fresh pine from the trees across the water sharpened her senses. She crossed her arms over her chest, hopelessness making each step heavier. What was she doing here? She'd no sooner find a mirror in a lake than she'd find a game card floating on the small waves. Vera wouldn't help. The woman had accepted that Dax was dead. Every hour Maddy had wasted coming here was one more that Dax was alone in Meido, fending for his life.

A scream was rising up inside her, pressing out her ribs, scraping her throat.

She wanted to call Emerson, but she'd left her stupid phone in the car.

Far off the edge of the dock, something caught her eye.

A glow from beneath, like a flashlight. Her gaze locked on it.

Her heart seized.

She moved to the last plank, leaning over the water. The sunlight was going quickly, the sky an apricot haze, but she could still see the bottom.

Nestled in the reeds was a jagged piece of glass the size of her palm. It reflected the sky above, but was dimming with the failing light.

Without taking her eyes off of it, she tore off her shoes and socks, then stripped off her sweatshirt so she was wearing only a tight black tank top and ripped jeans.

Clasping her hands, she dove.

The cold shocked her, but her body knew how to move in water, how to cut through it with grace and power. She kept her eyes open, not letting the mirror out of her sight for more than the blink it took to pass the surface.

Bubbles slipped from her nose, from the corners of her mouth, as she kicked down, her arms in a streamline position over her head. The water dragged at her clothes but it only made her push harder.

Deeper she went—the clarity of the water made the depth deceiving, and the pressure grew in her ears. Reeds tickled her hands, and she pushed them aside, reaching out for the glass.

Her fingers skimmed the smooth surface.

A jolt shot through her palm up her arm. Her blood felt electric and raw, the pain biting through every nerve as the reeds began to spin around her. The pond circled like in a drain, but Maddy did not release the mirror. Not when the dizziness made her lose her sense of up and down. Not when the last of her air pressed from her lungs, and the shadows leaked out between her fingers and fanned through the water like ink.

Show me Dax, she willed it.

It was the last thought she had before darkness invaded her mind.

OWEN

Owen had never cleaned his room so fast in his life. He straightened his books on the nightstand. Shoved his history homework into his desk. Made sure his dirty clothes weren't half hanging out of the laundry basket. He wasn't a slob, like Ian had suggested—his room was mostly clean. But he did want to change the sheets, just in case he and Ian decided to sit on his bed to listen to music, or lie down and watch a movie.

Or in case other stuff happened.

Which he wasn't anticipating or expecting because Ian had just been through a traumatizing situation that defied all imagination and Owen was not about to take advantage of his vulnerability.

Unless Ian was looking to forget himself for a little while. In which case Owen would be happy to accommodate.

A laugh burst from Owen's throat. What was wrong with him? This was Ian, but more importantly, he was Owen. He had moves. He had fucking lines—good ones too. But with Ian, that all went out the window.

Damn, he was *nervous*.

He could never tell Emerson about this.

He scratched a hand through his hair, smoothing the side that stuck up with his fingers, then ruffling it again to bedhead. People he'd dated, even hookups, always commented on his hair. It was one of his best features—smooth and soft, but messy enough to look like he'd just rolled around with someone. He'd worn it fluffy to The Bean earlier, but Ian hadn't said a word about it. He hadn't even attempted to smooth it down when Owen had sat next to him to take that picture.

Bastard.

Turning back to his bed, he shook out the wrinkles in the blotchy green watercolor comforter on his double bed under the window. Ian would be here any minute. In a surge, Owen grabbed a book and threw himself on the bed, trying to look like he'd been waiting.

A minute passed.

He tossed the book onto his desk and leaned against the wall beside his full-length mirror. Folded his arms over his chest. Crossed his ankles.

"Shit," he muttered.

He didn't know how to be. He *always* knew how to be.

Owen thought he'd been picking up signals that Ian was interested, but the truth was he'd been gone for four years. He might just want to come over and hang out the way he used to when they were kids. Had Ian ever even kissed anyone? Not before he'd gone to Meido, Owen knew that much. And the chances were slim he'd found a partner who wasn't, well, homicidal, in that hellish place.

A puff of breath escaped Owen's lips.

He might be Ian's first kiss.

He turned to sit on the edge of his bed. He wanted to kiss Ian—he'd wanted to basically as long as he'd known him. But also, he just wanted to hold him.

Owen had been so careful around him since they'd come back. He didn't want to push any boundaries, or make him uncomfortable. But when he laid in bed—*this* bed—at night, he wasn't thinking of tearing off Ian's clothes. He was imagining the weight of Ian's head on his chest, and the feel of his fingers woven through his own. How their socked feet would touch at the end of the mattress, and their knees would bump, and the shadows beneath Ian's eyes would disappear when he laughed at something dumb Owen had said.

He just wanted Ian to feel safe.

His phone buzzed with an incoming text. Worry spiked through Owen as he stood and grabbed his phone from his back pocket— maybe Ian had gotten held up at The Bean. Or something had happened on the walk over. Owen knew he shouldn't have let him go alone.

It wasn't Ian. It was Emerson.
She'd been texting for ten minutes.

> *5.*
> *5.*
> *5.*
> *WHAT FUCKING GOOD DOES THE CODE DO IF*
> *NOBODY ANSWERS IT? 5 5 5*

The numbers glared back at him, sinking his gut. It was a code they'd decided on when they'd returned home from Meido—a number from the name Ian had given their group, the Foxtail Five. 5 meant they had to meet. That something catastrophic had happened. And after their return from Meido, they all knew just how bad catastrophic could get. He must have missed her messages in his hurry to get home and clean up.

His plans changed in an instant. So much for hanging out in bed. When a 5 came, they were supposed to meet at The Bean, but since Ian was already coming here, he crafted a quick reply to meet at his house instead. Before he could press send, his phone buzzed again with another message from Emerson.

> *5 5 5 5 5*

Perspiration dampened his palms. He was already walking toward the door, but stopped short when a figure blocked the threshold of his room.

"Ian!" He jumped back. "I didn't hear you come in." Usually Owen locked the front door. He must have spaced in his rush to clean up.

Owen's gaze flicked down the hall, seeing the footprints of Ian's shoes on the beige carpet. He grimaced. They always left their shoes by the front door. His mom was not going to love that.

"Hello, Owen," Ian said in a strange voice. He stepped into the room.

Owen followed him with his eyes, taking in the familiar hooked scar on his chin, and his blue T-shirt and jeans, his sneakers on the rug. He looked down at his own socked feet, then stuffed his hands in his pockets. Ian was moving stiffly. Was he nervous? It made Owen nervous just watching him survey the room through his narrowed stare.

"Did you knock? I didn't hear. I'm sorry."

Ian stopped at the full-length mirror across from the bed and startled, as if he didn't expect to see his own reflection.

"The handle on your front door is broken," he said simply.

Owen glanced back toward the hall. "Seriously?" This was the city, and you didn't just leave your house open. He needed to check it out, but something stopped him from leaving the room. "Is everything all right?"

Ian lifted his hand, touching his chin, his eyebrows. Still staring at the mirror with a tight frown.

Heat rose up Owen's neck. "It was a prop in *West Side Story*. Maria's mirror. You know, 'I feel pretty'? The prop manager let me take it home." The gold frame was gaudy but Owen loved it. At least, he had before Ian had started glaring at it that way.

"I definitely do not feel pretty," Ian said, disgust in his tone.

Owen's shoulder blades drew together. Something was wrong. Something must have happened.

The phone was still in his hand. He hadn't sent the message to Emerson to meet here. Pressing the send button, he stuffed the phone into his back pocket.

"Did something happen?" he tried.

Ian's gaze tore away from the mirror, bouncing from the bed to Owen's desk, to the tickets and signed Playbills wallpapered over the dresser. His eyes landed on a ceramic bowl on the wooden surface. Owen had made it in art in middle school, and for years it had held his lucky rock—the half-heart prize Ian had given him years ago in the cave. Now it was where Owen put his wallet at night.

"Everything looks a little different, I guess," Owen said, clasping his hands together.

"So do I," said Ian.

Owen wasn't sure if he meant from when they were kids four years ago, or from when he'd been an oni in Meido, with fire-red skin, horns, and teeth like knives. *I definitely do not feel pretty.* Owen's jaw tightened. Ian had self-esteem issues. After everything he'd been through, how could he not? Owen should have seen it sooner.

"You're right," he said. "You get any hotter, I'm calling the fire department."

Ian leveled him with a stare.

Owen coughed into his fist. Something was clearly wrong. That one always worked.

"Talk to me," Owen said, regrouping. "Something happened, I can tell."

Ian breathed in slowly.

"I hurt someone."

Owen gave a half smile.

"In the last ten minutes since I saw you at The Bean? That's quick work."

"The man who makes the coffee."

A warning buzzed at the base of Owen's skull.

"Okay," he said. "Is he all right?"

Ian shook his head. "His arm is broken."

Owen froze. "How . . . how did that happen?"

"It snapped, and the bone broke."

Owen clasped his hands behind his neck. "Ian, if this is a joke, we seriously need to work on your delivery."

Ian lifted his chin.

"It isn't a joke," he said. "I dislike jokes. Games, on the other hand . . ."

Owen flashed to the challenges in Meido. The stones they collected as prizes, each a petrified part of the dead empress's body.

The hair rose on his arms.

"Ian, what's going on?"

Ian walked to the bed, reaching out to spread his fingers over it. Turning, he sat on the edge, his posture straight. "*Ian.* Such a soft soul. Gentle enough to shatter under just a little pressure."

Owen's gaze narrowed. He took a step closer. This wasn't good. Was Ian having some kind of anxiety attack? Hell, Owen was still having nightmares about Meido, and he'd been there a fraction of the time Ian had.

"What are you talking about?" he asked.

Ian met his gaze, his stare cold. "Do you care for him?"

"Him?"

"Ian."

Owen swallowed. "You're Ian." He reached for his phone. "Look, maybe we should call your parents." He thought of the barista Ian had supposedly injured. Was that true? He glanced down at the screen, but all he saw were the messages from Emerson.

"I asked you a question, Owen."

Owen put his phone in his pocket. "Of course I care about you."

"If he needed you, would you be there? Would you do what he asked?"

"Why are you talking in the third person?"

"Why is it so difficult to answer?"

Owen glanced to the door.

Ian raised his fist, and with a twist, the bedroom door slammed shut.

An alarm blared in Owen's head.

Not real, he thought. What he was seeing wasn't possible.

But it was.

This wasn't Ian.

This was something else.

"Okay." Owen scrambled backward, bumping into his desk. "So we're doing tricks now, huh?" He reached slowly for the door handle, but it didn't turn. The metal was locked in place, unshakable.

He lowered his hand, stomach tight.

Ian stood. "I asked if you would help Ian if he asked."

"Yes! Yes, okay?"

Horror lanced through him. This looked like Ian. Sounded like Ian. But he had been tricked by yōkai before.

Ian stalked toward him, his feet gliding over the carpet. Owen turned, yanking the door handle with both hands. It didn't budge. He spun back toward Ian, and with a shaking hand, he reached for his phone again. The screen was flashing on and off, flickering faster the closer Ian came.

When he was within reach, it shut off.

Slowly, Ian lifted his hand, and Owen flinched as his cold fingertip trailed down his cheek.

"So fragile. I could hurt you, you know. I could break you."

"You're scaring me."

Ian smiled, his teeth gleaming. "I'm scaring him too. I can feel it. The panic in this mortal body. The desire he has to keep you safe."

This mortal body.

"Who are you?" he whispered.

Ian tilted back his head, his nostrils flaring. "Come now, you don't remember? You stole my heart. You and Emerson and Madeline and your little yōkai friend. *Dax.*" Ian's voice ground over the last name.

Invisible bands tightened around Owen's ribs.

I was wrong when I said you weren't brave. I was wrong about a lot of things.

Owen shook his head, but Dax's last words to him were just as clear as ever.

"I would think that I would have made more of an impression," Ian continued.

The room felt like it was tilting.

"Izanami," Owen murmured.

Ian's eyes narrowed. He grabbed Owen by the throat, pinning him against the door. His heartbeat pounded in his temples, the air cut off from his lungs. Desperately, he scratched at Ian's hand, trying to break free.

"I am an empress," he whispered. "And you will show me the proper respect, or I will slice you to threads and use them to bind my clothing. Do you understand?"

Owen gave a frantic nod. As Izanami released him, the air seared down his throat. He fell to the floor on his knees, gasping.

"You're dead," Owen said, forcing himself to look up into the face he'd memorized every line and freckle of. "We watched you die. You turned to dust."

Izanami laughed. "Such a narrow, mortal view of existence. Death is not an ending, it's simply the next chapter. Do not be afraid to turn the page."

Quaking, Owen pushed himself to a stand. "Where is Ian?"

"He's in here." She tapped the side of Ian's temple.

Owen's chest seized. This wasn't a shape-shifting trick. Ian was here. The empress was *possessing* him.

"I want to talk to him."

"To what end?"

"To make sure he's okay."

"He is a prisoner inside his own body. What makes you think he is okay?"

Owen shuddered. "What do you want, Empress?"

"I want to play a game." Her fingertips glided over Owen's shoulder. He fought the urge to jerk away.

Memories speared to the front of his thoughts. The dark sky. The putrid smell of the wind. Dead-eyed players with mouths cut from ear to ear.

"N-no," he stammered. "I can't go back there."

"That's a shame," she said.

Izanami inhaled slowly, and Ian's eyes filled with terror.

"Owen?"

The vulnerability in his voice made Owen's chest seize. This wasn't Izanami, it was Ian.

Owen wanted to tear Ian free from whatever hold the empress had over his body. He pulled at his arm, but it was stiff, and held firmly to his side. He reached for Ian's face, finding his skin was clammy and cold.

"Ian!"

"Owen, you have to run. Get out of here!"

Ian's body began to convulse. A cry of pain pressed through his locked jaw.

"Stop!" Owen grabbed Ian's shoulders. "Empress, *please.*"

"Owen, it hurts!"

Terror blended with the rush of cold over his skin. His damp palms slid up Ian's twisting throat. Grabbing Ian's face in his hands, he stared into the dark pools of his eyes, searching for recognition.

"You have to run. You have to get away from me." Ian's spine gave a series of cracks.

"I'm not going anywhere. I'm going to fix this. You're going to be fine, okay?"

Ian slumped forward, his body heaving in heavy gasps.

Owen held him close, shaking. But when Ian lifted his head, his green eyes were filled with a strange brightness, and Owen jerked back at the low laugh that rumbled from his lips.

Izanami had returned.

"Swear it," she said. "Swear on this mortal's life you will help me play this game."

The pressure built between Owen's temples. He recalled the heavy feel of Ian's head on his lap when Izanami had nearly killed him in Meido. The way his body had been rebuilt from the dust in that cave. He didn't know what this new game entailed—more challenges? More body-part prizes?

He needed Maddy and Emerson. Dax.

But it was just him.

"I swear it," he said.

Izanami pressed Ian's palm to his own mouth, as if she might be stopping herself from speaking. An awful tearing sound filled Owen's ears, and when she pulled back Ian's hand, it was pooling with dark blood.

"What are you doing?" Owen said. "I said I'd help. You don't have to hurt him!"

"I will do whatever I please." Izanami stalked to Owen's dresser and lifted the glazed ceramic bowl. Holding it in the palm of one hand, she made a fist with her injured one, squeezing until blood dripped into the gleaming basin. "Disgusting, isn't it? I admit, there was a time I would have been repelled by such filth. But time has changed me. Meido has changed me. We all must evolve, after all."

"Stop," Owen begged. This wasn't right. It wasn't clean. It wasn't *safe*. "Please!"

Downstairs, the doorbell rang. Owen's heart skipped.

"Owen? Are you all right? The door handle's broken off!"

Emerson.

"Where are my eyes?" Izanami murmured, as if not hearing Emerson. Owen followed Izanami's gaze to the filling bowl. Horror pierced him as she leaned closer, staring at the blood—*into* it—as if she could see beyond the dark surface. "Come to me, eyes. Come to your empress."

Owen wanted to shout for Emerson. To bang on the door until

she busted through. But he couldn't do anything that might endanger Ian.

"Ah, there we are." Izanami opened Ian's fist, and the blood stopped dripping from his hand. Then she stepped back.

The bowl remained in the air—*floating*.

It wasn't just the shiny ceramic anymore. There was a crunch, and a crack, and then a reptilian hand extended from the underside of the bowl. The claws on each finger fanned out like hooked blades, reaching toward the floor.

"What is that?"

From outside his room came the pounding of footsteps on the stairs.

"Owen!" Emerson's voice called down the hall.

"Have you never seen a kappa? They are quite obedient creatures." Ian smiled, a look that chilled Owen to the bone. "If you feed them."

The arm beneath the bowl extended through the air, long gray-green scales covering a thick mass of muscle. Two legs followed, feet unfurling toward the floor until the creature's long, dirty toenails gouged into the beige carpet. Owen's nose crinkled at the foul stench that arose as the monster's body spread, a bulbous, shifting balloon of peeling skin lined with rivulets of blood, as if it wore its veins on the outside of its body. By the time the head emerged below the bowl—a moon with yellow eyes and a turtle's mouth— Owen was pressed so hard against the desk, the back of his legs had gone numb.

"Empress," the kappa hissed, rising to its full height, just above the corner post of Owen's bed. The floating bowl of blood had become a recess in its forehead, and it balanced carefully, not spilling a drop.

Disgust rolled through Owen.

"A kappa needs blood the way you need air," the empress said to him. "If the bowl spills, they perish. They're fragile that way. Like mortals."

A wave of nausea climbed Owen's throat as the creature's eyes blinked wider, yellow saucers in a sea of gray.

"Owen?"

The sound of Emerson's voice made him jump. He looked back to the door, now shaking on its hinges.

"Ian, are you in there?" Emerson knocked faster.

"Do you have them?" Izanami asked the creature, ignoring the interruption.

The kappa rose, a thin line of pink saliva dripping down its chin. "Yes." Its voice was a hiss as it coughed up a corner of yellow paper, dripping with red-speckled phlegm.

Owen's knees turned to water as the kappa drew the paper from its mouth with its clawed hand. One piece, then another, and another, before wiping away the spittle and blood to reveal the ancient kanji marks on each.

Cards. Like the Karuta games he and Ian had played as children, but so much worse.

He knew what the hard corners would feel like if he touched them. The weight of them in his palm. The flash as they dissolved into a prize.

His vision was blurred by the pounding in his temples.

The game had restarted. He could feel it in the churning in his stomach and the pull of his blood toward each awful piece of paper. He felt suddenly sick that he hadn't spent the last month reviewing his kanji. It seemed impossible in that moment that he was ever destined to do anything but return to the game.

He gripped the back of his desk chair for support.

"Did he give you any trouble?" Izanami asked the kappa.

"The cardmaker's madness has consumed him," the kappa said. "He lives in the prison of his own mind."

Ian's mouth curved into a dangerous smile—one that wasn't Ian's at all.

"Good," Izanami said. "Let him rot there."

Owen didn't know what they were talking about. He couldn't take his eyes off the worn cards as the kappa passed them to Izanami.

"Owen!" shouted Emerson. The door banged again, but didn't open.

Near the bed, the kappa gave a strangled moan. The creature dug its sharp nails into its belly, cutting downward in a slow, jagged slice that spilled the liquid contents of its body onto the pale carpet below. Black bile infused with strange, gleaming organs and entrails.

Owen gagged.

He spun toward the door, grabbing the knob. He tried to turn it. It wouldn't budge.

"Emerson? Emerson!"

"She can't hear you," said Izanami.

Dread surged down Owen's neck as Ian's hand closed around his shoulder, yanking him hard backward. He slipped on the blood on the floor, his arms wheeling. His wrist smacked against Ian's forearm, knocking two of the cards from his hand. They flew through the air, landing just outside the bloody puddle on the floor.

"Foolish mortal!" Izanami hissed.

The kappa's insides squished and slurped, smashing beneath his weight as Ian's possessed body lunged over the bloody mess to grab the fallen cards, but it was too late. Ian jolted, as if shocked, arching back. Blood sloshed beneath Owen's shoes as he reached out but grasped only air. A second later, scalding heat shot up Owen's legs, through his chest, straight to his fingertips and his prickling scalp.

His last sight as blood rained over his vision was of Emerson's shocked face as she broke through the door.

DAX

The path down the shale cliffside was treacherous, a jutting lip of rock barely wide enough for Dax to scale sideways. Below, the river raced by, white-tipped rapids over steel gray water. The farther down he went, the louder the river became, its rush a lonely groan that tightened the muscles between his shoulder blades. It echoed off the far cliff, drowning out the screams of the monstrous black birds that circled the dead woods above, and the hordes of old players who searched mindlessly to complete challenges for a game long over.

At the bottom of the ravine, Dax stepped onto the rocky shore, picking his way through the branches and debris from upriver. The stench had stopped bothering him, but he was sure it was still there, popping in green steam from foam bubbles that lapped near his feet. The skeletal bones of a tengu blocked the entrance of a shallow cave ahead, the white arching ribs jabbing skyward. He'd dragged them here from a carcass rotting downriver.

"Home sweet home," he said, tucking his thumbs into the obi fastened around his waist. It was punctured with ten-inch thorns he'd shorn off a razor-sharp bush, dull end up for an easy grab, and a small satchel where he kept his pocketknife.

He frowned at the rib entrance. A potted plant would have gone a long way. Maybe a welcome mat made out of spider fur. He could make a white picket fence out of the bones of old players. That wasn't weird, was it?

With a sigh, he scratched a hand through his hair. It had grown ragged in the last month—he'd kept the days tallied on the wall of his cave since his friends had finished the game and left Meido. He didn't know why he did it—if he was going to be here for eternity, he'd eventually have to find a new canvas—but the ritual made him feel somewhat more human.

Not much else here did.

He glanced up, searching the hazy sky for tengu, and scowled at the shape of the eye above the horizon. It wasn't exact science, but Dax thought of dawn as when the eye cracked open, and noon when it was at its widest, a glowing white orb in the sky. Now, the giant's lid sagged at the top. Night was coming.

In the dark, everything was worse. The spiders were hungrier. The players were more ruthless. Even the river's howl was more desperate.

A crunch of footsteps over sand brought his attention to a fine point.

He ripped the pocketknife from the satchel on his belt. The lucky engimono was stronger than any blade he could whittle—powerful enough to make him remember who he was, even in this place.

Someone was inside the cave. They must have replaced the ribs over the entrance to surprise him. That kind of higher-level thinking pointed to human. At least, something that *had* been human. Probably an old player, rooting around mindlessly for a prize that would get them to the next level. He cringed, hoping they had all their skin. Since the game had ended, Keneō, or Cannibal Keneō as Dax liked to think of him since he'd tried to serve them a player's meaty ass for dinner in the woods, had gone a little overboard preparing for his new Spring Line of flesh attire.

Gently, Dax moved aside a bone near the edge. His pulse jumped at the small fire that had been lit in the circle of stones inside. Behind it, a creature huddled on the sandy cave floor in the shadows, its exact size disguised by the way it bundled its arms around its bent legs. Anger punched through Dax. This cave was the last place he'd been with his friends before everything had fallen apart at the empress's palace. They'd circled this fire and talked, and when Emerson, Owen, and Maddy had slept, he'd watched over them to keep them safe.

No one came here without permission.

"Dax?" a pained voice whispered.

His breath caught. His hand holding the knife went damp.

This was a trick. His mind playing games. He scratched at his chest to dislodge the knot within.

"Dax isn't here right now," he said, tension weaving through his tone as he slipped through the narrow opening. "But if you'd like to leave a message, he'll get back to you when he's available."

The visitor unfurled to a feminine silhouette. A shape Dax had studied, and would recognize for all of his doomed eternity in this place.

"Maddy?" His voice broke over her name.

"Dax."

She came into the light, her braids parted over her shoulders, her smile brighter than the giant's eye. Hope exploded in his chest as she extended her arms toward him. Shoving the knife into his obi's satchel, he closed the distance to her in two steps, his hands ghosting over her shoulders to her wrists, up to her cheeks. He wanted to touch her everywhere at once but couldn't decide how to start.

"You're here?" He couldn't believe it, but the proof was just before him. Her small grin renewed his bravery. Her dark eyes punctured his shield, making him weak in the way that only she could. Until this moment, he'd refused to allow himself to believe he'd ever see her again.

"I've been looking all over for you," she said.

Her voice soothed his raw nerves.

Maddy was here.

Maddy had come back.

It hit him a moment later. The fear, a brick in his gut.

"What are you doing in Meido? You shouldn't be here." His heart was swelling, too big for his rib cage. He lifted his hands to her face, but something stopped his thumbs from grazing her cheeks. As if doing so would reveal that this was a dream, and she wasn't really back. The scent of burned rice came in a wave before receding, and he wondered what she'd been through to get here. He moved closer, their chests inches apart.

His breath came out in a huff.

"I came for you," she said, a whisper that shook through him.

"You shouldn't have come," he said, even as he longed to pull her close and never let go. Emotion clogged his throat. "What were you thinking? You got out. You . . ." Another cold splash of terror. "What happened? Something's wrong. Is it Ian? Did he make it?"

After the others had left Meido, Dax had wandered the wreckage of Izanami's palace for a long time, numb from his fingertips to his empty thoughts. Then, in the water that had risen from the cracks in the ground, he'd seen a reflection off a glowing piece of glass—one like the mirrors he'd seen in the palace where they'd been confronted with their dishonorable acts. In it, just for a moment, he'd seen Ian. It was a strange, distorted image, Ian's eyes black and his smile hungry, but enough to show he was alive.

"Ian," Maddy repeated, her mouth pulling into a flat line. "Ian is in trouble. He needs your help."

He still couldn't look away from her eyes. She was cold, he could feel that now, even though they didn't touch. Her skin was chilled enough to make his hands cool as they curved around her arms. How long had she been here? She wasn't like him, immune to the frigid air. He looked down, realizing for the first time what she was wearing. A black kimono, tied at the waist in a ratty knot. Something about it looked familiar.

"What happened?" he asked.

"He needs the cards."

A muscle ticked in Dax's jaw.

"Maddy, they're gone. They changed when we beat the challenges, remember?" He could still feel the thick board in his fingertips, see the ancient kanji mocking them as they moved from one terrible test to the next.

Each of them had turned into the prizes they'd needed to complete the game.

"You must have more," she said, her voice turning a little desperate. "How did you get your first set?"

"I don't know," he said. "I don't remember getting them. I didn't even remember . . ." He swallowed thickly. He didn't remember putting them in the cave for Ian to find, starting a game that would drag him and his friends back to this nightmare. If not for the mirrors in the empress's palace showing his past, he never would have known what really happened.

"Try." She knelt, and he followed, mirroring her on the sand. With the light closer, he could see beads of moisture in her dark brown curls, and again the strange scent of burning rice wafted over him. "Try to remember, for me."

There was nothing he wouldn't do for her.

"I wish I could," he said, shaking his head. He wanted to help her—to help Ian—but that part of his past was missing. Every time he tried to look closer, he could feel only emptiness. "Maddy, why do you need the cards, what happened?"

"You've been looking all over Meido, and you haven't found anything?"

"I haven't been looking for cards, I've been—"

He stopped.

"How did you know I was looking for something?" He glanced around the cave, tearing his eyes away from Maddy's imploring gaze. The giant's eye had just been opening when he'd left—he'd made it all the way to the Keneō's bridge and back, dodging spiders and players along the way.

Doubt pressed through him.

"I missed you," she said.

His heart lurched.

The scent of rice grew stronger—the burn of it making his throat dry.

She leaned in quickly, grabbing the back of his head to drag him into a kiss. Shock dragged a gasp from his throat. Her lips were wet and cold, and . . . not solid.

Anxiety tripped through him.

He knew the feel of her kiss by heart, the sound of her sigh, the skim of her nose along his. He reached for her wrists, seeking the scar Kuchisake had cut with his jagged nail when he'd married them, but the skin was permeable. Like pressing through a wet cloud.

Shoving back, his gaze met her gaze. White and empty. No iris.

"No," he whispered, as something inside him, something that had been reforged, shattered all over again.

"Where are you hiding the cards?" she asked with a flash of teeth.

Her movements were strange, he could see that now. Fog rising up from her forearms and shoulders. From the top of her head, as if she were turning to steam.

He tried to gather the pieces, but fumbled. Stupid. *Stupid.* He knew better. Of course Maddy wasn't here. She would never be here again.

"What are you?" he said through a locked jaw.

"I'm what you want," she said, dragging a fingertip over his collarbone. It was lighter now than a human touch should have been, the tip of her finger dissipating into smoke as it touched his skin. He jerked away.

"I'm Madeline."

Madeline.

Maddy hated when he called her that.

A bitter laugh fell from him. The fun in this place never ended.

"Nice try," he said.

Burned rice. Of course. He cringed in recognition.

The sour stench of over-brewed tea.

Before he could register what it meant, Maddy changed before him. The vibrant colors of her hair and clothes and skin turned gray and muted. What remained of her defined lines softened. As he sucked in a breath she rose off the ground, hovering for a moment, before disappearing in a cloud of steam.

A low chuckle came from the darkness, and Dax shot to his feet, his lucky knife drawn. An old woman appeared, someone he hadn't seen since he'd first arrived in Meido. A cracked teapot sat in the cradle of her wrinkled hands, the last of the steam drifting into the dim cave light.

"Shinigami."

She stepped forward, her laughter silencing. Her skin sagged with age. Her dark hair was peppered gray, straight strands of it pulled loose from the low knot on her neck to fall over the shoulders of her tattered black kimono. He pointed his pocketknife at her and her mouth flattened in anger.

His mind flashed to the first time he'd seen the old woman in her shack in the woods. How the steam from her enchanted tea had told the story of Izanami's betrayal by the oni. He'd been foolish enough then to think she'd be on their side. Emerson had even called her a NPC.

She had only ever been in this game for herself. To help her beloved empress.

"Where are the cards?" With a tilt of her chin, a new burst of steam shot from the small spout and lashed at him, a burst of cold, damp air throwing him to his back. He dropped the knife in the dirt, kicked out as the pressure crushed his windpipe. He scratched at the steam, but his hands went straight through the white cloud to his own skin. She couldn't kill him—a fire had already done that—but that didn't stop the human panic from flooding his brain, or his body's automatic response to fight back.

"They're gone," he ground out, shocked by her desperation. She'd been so nice before—for an ancient ghost, anyway. "Maybe you missed the memo, but the game's over. Izanami's dead."

"She is not dead, she is death itself," Shinigami whispered, striding closer to lean over him. "My empress never dies like some common mortal. She needs us."

A new fear tainted Dax's thoughts. He'd been all over Meido looking for the one person who might explain why he was here—a man he'd seen in the mirrors before the empress's palace had imploded. Monsters and madness were abundant, but nothing he'd seen had led him to believe Izanami still existed, dead or not.

"Sorry to be the one to tell you," he said, "but all Izanami needs now is a gravedigger and a shovel."

"You disrespectful fool," Shinigami said. "A new game has begun. I can feel it."

His gaze flicked toward the entrance of the cave, where a dull, white light seeped through the opening in the brush. The giant's eye was closing, but it did that every night.

"Sure you can," he managed. "What's wrong, Shinigami? Been too long since a player fell for your tricks?"

She leaned over him, close enough that flecks of spittle spattered on his cheeks. "I need the cards. The gate to the land of the living must be opened."

Not on his life. Or . . . lack of life. He wasn't about to let Shinigami or any of the monsters here out of Meido. Not when Maddy and his friends were safe on the other side.

He kicked out, striking her ankle. Thrown off balance, she loosened her steam hold on his throat momentarily. It was enough for him to shove one hand in the dirt beside him. His probing fingers closed around the handle of his knife. He hid it in his fist. Not yet. Not until she was closer.

"Why don't you just snag some cards from a failed player? They're crawling all over this dump." His gut twisted with the fear that she might be right—that new challenges would begin. New opportunities for players to be tortured. But to what end? The empress was gone. What was the goal now?

"Foolish half mortal," she said, moving above him, out of the reach of his legs. Her face hung over him now, upside down. "Those cards are spoken for. Each game has its own set."

"Well I'm sorry to break it to you, but I don't have any cards." Her steam squeezed his throat tighter, and he bridged up, his heels digging at the ground.

"Then who made the current games?"

"Um . . . not me?"

She leaned closer. Almost close enough. "You are a cardmaker, like your father before you. It is in your blood. And since he is gone, you are the only option."

Dax went still.

"What do you know about my father?"

Shinigami growled. "I know he is a coward, hiding from his honor and his empress."

"Where?"

"Somewhere not even I will go to find him."

Dax was reeling. His father was missing. He was a cardmaker. Dax was a cardmaker too. What did that mean? He had led players into the cave to start the game before. Had he made the cards that they'd found as well?

"You're out of luck," he said, and she bared her gums at him. "Even if I did whip up a new batch of cards, I wouldn't give them to you."

She shrieked in anger as he arced his knife through the air. The blade caught Shinigami in the temple, bumping hard against the ancient bone of her skull before sliding heavily through. The sharp edge dug down to the handle, spraying black blood like a fountain into the air. Shinigami let out a primal scream, her mouth growing impossibly wide. The darkness of her throat enveloped her face, as if she were turning inside out on herself. It spread over her eyes, her hair, down her throat and over her tattered kimono, blending with the black cave ceiling above her.

Then she was gone, her steam whip and teapot with her, her scream still echoing in his ears.

A slow clap filled the cave.

In an instant, Dax was on his feet, the bloody knife extending from his fist.

The figure sauntering toward him was wearing green satin, the gold obi glimmering in the firelight. A lithe build led to a smooth, elongated neck, adorned with onyx jewels, but as he moved, the necklace slid across his skin, and Dax realized each ornate piece was a small, gleaming spider. They shifted along the lines of his throat, one climbing over his jaw to his mouth, which had been cut from ear to ear in a jagged, bloody line.

"That was impressive, my friend!" Kuchisake bellowed, exaggerating his grotesque smile. "I especially enjoyed the finale!" He mimed the stabbing with a flourish.

Dax shivered. The last time he'd seen this man he'd been forced to play a shamisen for a crowd of split-faced players. He kept his knife raised. Kuchisake did not look like he meant him harm, but that didn't mean he could be trusted.

"How long have you been standing there?"

"Long enough to feel the heat from that kiss." He waggled his slender eyebrows. "I thought your type was more corporeal, but it seems I have been mistaken. Do not be ashamed. I have had many lovers here, of all different shapes and consistencies."

Dax grimaced, then spat on the ground, ridding himself of the last of the steam kiss. With the back of his hand, he wiped away the dampness on his face. Shinigami's black blood stained his wrist.

"Thanks for the help," Dax said.

"I did not want to interrupt."

"What *do* you want?"

"I long only for your company!" Kuchisake said, injured. "A new game is afoot!"

"So I've heard."

"I thought we might partner up. Be heroes together."

Dax groaned, finally lowering the blade. First Shinigami, now him? Did everyone want to play this stupid game? "Only mortals can play, pal."

Maddy had changed the card with her fear. Emerson with her honor, Owen with his bravery. Even Ian's loyalty had earned a prize.

Dax had thought he was playing too, but he wasn't even living. All he'd done was put his friends in more danger.

"A new game has new rules," Kuchisake said.

Of course it did. "How did you find me?"

Kuchisake giggled. "Can you keep a secret?"

"Does it involve you trying to kill me?"

"Not today it doesn't!"

Dax huffed. "All right then."

Kuchisake reached into the wide neck of his kimono, withdrawing a small bag that looked suspiciously fleshy. He stepped forward and opened the drawstring, revealing a shimmer of green fire within.

Dax gaped. He had seen this before, a door between challenges called the passage. It had transported him and his friends from one part of Meido to the next.

"How do you have that? I thought the flames went out when her royal highness turned to dust and the game ended."

"I have a few tricks left in me still," said Kuchisake with a wink. "Only mortals can call the flames, but look! I used a mortal stomach and captured the last of the passage. I can use the fire, I just can't hold it. Wonderful, yes?"

"Wonderful," Dax repeated.

"I thought of you, and the flames opened a gate, carrying your voice across the distance. It is fated that we find each other again, my friend. The music at my parties has been so dull since you left."

Dax recalled the way the crowd had swayed awkwardly when he'd sung, and cringed.

"What do you want for that?" If the flames had brought Kuchi-sake here, maybe they would take Dax somewhere too.

"Well, if you are offering a trade, a set of cards would be nice. I hear you have certain . . . abilities."

Each group of players must have their own set.

Was this going to become a thing? All of the old ghosts looking him up for something he couldn't deliver? He needed an address change, stat.

"I'm . . ." he stopped himself. "Sure, okay. You want a card, no problem. But first, I want you to take me somewhere. Since we're teammates and all."

Kuchisake beamed. "Where do you want to go?"

Dax lowered his knife, but kept it firmly in his fist.

"I want to see my father," Dax said, remembering the man's familiar face in the black mirrors from the hall of truth. How he'd seduced Dax's mother like a common mortal. How he'd come for Dax, and when his mom had resisted, a fire had started, and Dax had died.

Dax set his feet, and gripped the engimono. "I need to talk to Aka Manto."

EMERSON

Owen and Ian were gone. The blood on the floor, that awful monster near the bed, gone. Emerson's gaze shot back to the door, now open wide as if it had never been locked.

The pound of her heart felt like a detonation on repeat.

Ian came over. Meet here.

She swiped the sweat from her brow. Dropped her backpack still holding the shovel and empty can of spray paint on the floor. She'd run just over a mile from the river to Foxtail Alley, nearly making it to the Bean Coffeehouse before getting Owen's message and rerouting to his house. She hadn't been fast enough.

Her gaze dropped to the pale blue ceramic bowl on the floor in front of the closet—she'd made a similar one in art class in middle school. Light from the window glinted off the shiny glaze. Lunging toward it, she snatched it off the ground, but dropped it with a cry.

On the carpet beneath the bowl were two cards.

Game cards.

Her pulse hammered in her temples.

The rectangular shape of the hand-sized paper was too familiar. The kanji, condemning. Hating how she'd had to rely on Owen to translate in Meido, she'd taken it upon herself to learn as much as she could, but she didn't recognize any of these characters. She stumbled backward.

"No," she said, shaking her head. This wasn't happening. They'd beaten the game. They'd destroyed the empress.

But she'd felt Meido waiting, just behind the boulder in the cave. Calling to her. Pulling her back.

A sob raked up her throat. The cards wavered in her vision behind hot tears.

Owen and Ian. The monster. The blood.

The game had restarted.

She wiped the back of her hand over her wet eyes. Before, they'd gone into the game through the cave, but her friends had just disappeared right from Owen's room. Maybe that bloody monster had dragged them back. Maybe they had other cards. Before, the game had been composed of seven challenges. Owen and Ian could have dropped these two, or purposefully left them behind for her to follow.

If she touched them, would she be dragged back to Meido too?

"Emerson."

The voice came from far away, and she turned to face the gold-framed mirror on Owen's wall.

A scream burst from her as wide, panicked eyes stared back.

She was back in her bedroom, back to the night the game had begun, when Ian had appeared to her in the mirror, teeth broken, skin wrapped tight around his bones, summoning her to find him before dawn.

Only she wasn't at home, and this wasn't Ian.

"Maddy?" Her voice broke over the name.

Her gaze flew over Maddy's skintight tank top and ripped-knee jeans. Her mouth spewing tiny bubbles of air as she screamed. Her box braids floated around her head as if she were underwater, but beyond her, the reflection showed Owen's room—his green and white comforter on the bed. The dark wood nightstand. The corner of the desk.

"Emerson!" Maddy pounded against the glass, her legs kicking in the waves. "Help me!"

Emerson clapped her hands over her ears. This wasn't Maddy, just like the yōkai she'd seen in the mirror in her room hadn't been Ian. This was something else.

But Ian had really been in Meido, waiting for them. And Maddy had been quiet for days. What if she hadn't shown up at the cave because, somehow, she was already in Meido?

Forcing her hands to her sides, Emerson stepped closer to the glass.

"How do I know you're really Maddy?"

Maddy scratched at the glass frantically. Punched at it, her legs pedaling through the air as if treading water.

"Get me out!" Maddy screamed.

A trick. It wasn't Maddy. It couldn't be Maddy.

Emerson jerked back, looking for a weapon, something to defend herself with. All Owen had was the stupid bowl.

She grabbed her backpack, ripping out the shovel, and extended it to its full length with shaking hands. Her palms grew damp around the handle.

"Emerson, *please*." Maddy's movements were slowing. Emerson glanced down at the cards. If Maddy really had gone back to Meido, Emerson would need to pick up the cards to join her. She'd need to restart the game.

She'd have to go back.

Owen and Ian might already be on their way with that monster.

Blood roared in Emerson's ears as Maddy's hand slid weakly down the opposite side of the glass.

"Maddy!" she shouted. "Where are you? What happened?"

The last of the bubbles slipped from Maddy's mouth as she twitched.

Emerson pressed her hand to the cold glass, but it didn't give. "Maddy, wherever you are, you have to go! Get out of there! You're going to drown!"

Maddy bowed back. Her eyes bulged. Her lips turned white, then blue.

They were out of time.

"Okay, goddammit!" She snagged the cards off the ground, gripping them in her fist. Hoping they would take her to her friend. "I have them. I have—"

The carpet beneath Emerson's feet softened. It squished as she lifted one foot, then the other, marching to keep from sinking too fast. Before her, the closet changed. The clothes parted, making uneven rock walls. The carpet became the dirty ground. A hole in the center stretched into darkness.

A cave.

Panic raced through her. It was happening again. She was going back to Meido. *Alone.*

Fear sizzled down her spine.

"Emerson."

She tore her gaze away from the black recess to see Maddy's head loll back on the other side of the glass.

She twitched again, then went still.

"No! Maddy? Maddy, where are you? I'm coming, but you have to move!"

Maddy floated lifelessly.

Emerson shoved the cards into her back pocket and gripped the shovel handle with both hands. Resetting her feet, she swung hard, but the ground pulled at her, and the metal handle slipped, chipping the golden frame of the mirror.

Her teeth pressed together as the carpet pulled her down to the ankles.

"Wait, wait, wait!" She tried pedaling out, but was dragged deeper.

Before her, in the mirror, Maddy's head tipped down.

A frenzy took Emerson by storm. She threw herself forward, grabbing the rock wall beside the closet's cave-like entrance with one hand to anchor herself. She twisted until one leg came free. The clothes that had not yet changed to boulders fell over her as she swung the shovel upward, banging against the outside of the cave.

She thought of Maddy, falling through the mirror in the empress's palace when they'd played the game before. Of how Emerson had reached through the glass and pulled her out. She would do it again. Save her friend again.

Would she save you?

The question had teeth, and she faltered. Maddy had missed their date at the cave. She hadn't come to The Bean with Owen and Ian yesterday. Whatever she'd been doing, whatever trouble she'd found herself in, she hadn't thought to include Emerson in it.

Her trapped foot sank another inch.

It didn't matter what Maddy had or hadn't done. She needed Emerson *now.*

Siphoning in a breath, Emerson heaved the shovel into the glass. It connected, sending a spiderweb of cracks outward.

The floor swallowed her halfway up her shin.

"Break!" she commanded the mirror, and hit it again. Fragments of glittering glass exploded around her, but the mirror didn't give.

"Stupid fucking goddamn piece of—" She swung again, and a sliver of the mirror came free.

Water leaked from it down the surface and over the frame to the floor. It echoed in the cave. *Drip. Drip. Drip.*

"Maddy!" Emerson dropped the shovel, and leaned forward with all her weight, punching through the glass. It was cool, like the mirrors in the palace, sharp enough to cut her skin. She pushed through with a scream, until her hands plunged into cold water. Gripping Maddy's arm, she yanked back.

They fell in a heap, Emerson sinking into the too-plush carpet, a sopping Maddy over her. Maddy coughed hard, her body seizing as she expelled the water over Emerson's shoulder.

Bracing up, Maddy looked down at Emerson.

"How . . ." she asked between gasps, "did you do that?"

Emerson didn't have time to answer. The closet cave was extending over them, uneven rock covering the ceiling and the overhead light in Owen's room. The broken mirror vibrated, falling with a crash as the drywall behind it turned to stone. Her skin chafed against the hard pebbles that took the place of the carpet. Then she was falling, sucked under a suffocating wave of earth, aware only of Maddy's arms hugging tightly around her chest, refusing to let go.

OWEN

Owen was in a freefall. He flipped through the air, shirt billowing up over his eyes, glasses lost in the tumble. He couldn't catch his breath. As he twisted, his shirt flattened against his chest just long enough for him to make out the dizzying circles around him, and a flash of blue jeans against the bright white below.

Ian.

The surface grew closer in an instant. Owen braced for impact, but instead of hitting something hard, his speed decreased, suddenly enough to give him whiplash. His stomach flip-flopped. He was still falling, but slowly. The thick air swallowed him in a cloud, so hot it burned his skin.

"Ian!" he shouted, squinting his eyes against the heat and sudden brightness. "Ian!"

"He is here," gasped Ian's voice. "And so am I."

Izanami.

Owen rolled in the air, clawing for a something solid to grasp. A small, hard object struck him on the shoulder. His glasses. They bounced off, sliding into the mist near his hip.

He caught one arm of the frames, but the plastic was already growing soft from the heat. His glasses sagged on his face when he shoved them on.

His vision didn't become much clearer. The foggy air hid everything beyond an arm's reach. Still slowly dropping, he swam toward a fuzzy Ian, reaching for his arm.

"What's happening?" He coughed on hot air.

Izanami grabbed his throat with one hand, still bloody from where she'd bitten it to call the kappa. He sputtered, his airway choked off. She was close enough now that every angry line on Ian's flushed face was in sharp focus.

"You . . ." His stomach lurched as they dropped another few inches. ". . . lost the other cards!"

"Why did you knock them from my hand?" They twisted in the cloud, sinking in heart-stopping spurts. "What did you . . ." Izanami gasped as they fell again. "What could you possibly hope to accomplish?"

"I . . ." Owen bucked in the air, pushing back against Ian's chest. Panic seared through him. From the heat. From the fall. From the hatred in Ian's face.

Not Ian. *Izanami.*

"I didn't mean to . . ." he managed.

"What am I supposed to do with one card?" She flashed it before him, the kanji half hidden behind Ian's white knuckled fingers.

Owen grew frantic to tear Ian's hand free. Pain sizzled up his spine. "We'll solve it," he groaned, his stomach dipping as they fell. "We'll play the game."

"Then do it now," Izanami said. "Before we hit the bottom."

At her words they began to fall faster, slipping through the steam. Ian's hair ruffled from the wind.

"What's at the bottom?"

Owen glanced over his shoulder downward. The whisps of cloud were thinner, but he still couldn't see what lied below.

"My nightmare," Izanami said, Ian's lips thinning with fear.

It wasn't real. The empress wasn't afraid of anything. Not even falling to their deaths.

"We don't have time for drama," Owen shot back, then kicked out of the way before Izanami could grab him again.

"If you don't solve the card before we break through the steam, we'll . . ."

They both gasped as their speed increased.

"We'll what?" Owen asked.

"Shatter."

Owen's heart skipped. "What does the card say?"

Izanami glanced at it and roared in frustration. "Benevolence."

"So we have to help someone? In a goddamn cloud?" How were they supposed to do that?

"We're caught in the steam."

"What steam?"

"The steam from a coil. Look around, mortal. This is Jigoku! The horrors made by my mind while my body lied in pieces for your game. Where did you think we were?"

"I thought we were in Meido!"

"Does this look like Meido?" Ian's arms circled, but Izanami's efforts to stay afloat were in vain, and she sank another foot. "Does it *feel* like Meido?"

Owen's chest lurched as he rolled through the scalding air, so opposite the frigid bite he remembered from the last game. The light was nearly blinding, but it came from around him. A circle. A *coil*. Not the single eye of the giant.

He stared at her, seeing the fear flickering in her gaze. "This is your *actual* nightmare?" What had he done? Meido was not somewhere he would have willingly returned to, not in a million years, but here he was, in an infinitely worse place, with the most dangerous being in the universe.

Izanami growled. "Solve the card."

They fell faster.

"How?"

"You're a player!"

"You made the game!"

"My husband made this—"

Izanami's words broke off as the last of the steam dissipated. Owen looked down just in time to see the gleaming golden earth careening toward them. His heart lurched into his throat. His thoughts scattered. He couldn't breathe to scream.

He hit the ground so hard his bones shattered, just as Izanami had predicted. Pain tore through him, as bright and hot as the steam. He couldn't cry. He couldn't find the air to gasp. Through one fuzzy eye he could see his arm, broken in many places. Ian's head, tilted backward, neck snapped. Waves of heat, rising from the ground.

His heart beat loud and fast. Uneven.

Then it slowed.

Don't die, he willed himself. *Don't die.*

Searing heat spread through his arms and legs, his ribs and back. His lungs filled with a gasp of hot air.

He was . . . unbroken.

Shaking, he sat up, pulling his knees to his chest. He touched his shins, his shoulders, his face. Soreness throbbed through his body, but he seemed to be in one piece. He shook with adrenaline. Reached for his glasses, still mending the way his body had. The ground beneath him was as hot as the steam, and glimmering. *Sand.* He was on some sort of beach. He looked up, pushing off the ground to stop the uncomfortable warmth from pressing through his clothes.

The building around him was the shape of a cylinder. The floors circled him like a spring, each coil climbing at an angle to spiral steadily upward. On the bottom story, people crawled across yellow sand, their clothes tattered, burned away from the heat. They moaned and cried, fought to push past each other. They all seemed to be going the same direction, clockwise around the ring, toward a stone wall with a circular door that was closed to keep them from moving past.

The second layer continued beyond that blockade, and expelled clouds of heat—steam. He could see people caught in it, their descent slowed momentarily like Owen and Ian's had been.

Ian.

He turned to search for his friend.

"Ian?" he whispered, squinting to block the light. Through a break in the steam, he could see a wooded third level with its pine trees thrusting out into the center, and the fourth coil, where amber liquid gushed over the rounded edge like a waterfall, evaporating into the cloud. The light came from above it, in the fifth ring, where a raging orange fire circled the coil clockwise, spitting flames into the center. Every level was blocked by a wall with a closed door, trapping people behind it.

This was definitely not Meido.

"Empress!" Owen shouted. She'd been right beside him when they'd fallen. He'd seen her. Seen Ian's neck, snapped.

Sickness rocked through Owen.

Was Ian dead?

Had Owen died?

The impact had broken them beyond repair. He'd felt his heart stutter. And then . . .

Then he'd been okay.

"Ian!" he screamed, spinning to search for his friend through the bodies raining down from the steam above.

But it wasn't Ian he found, but a guy in a familiar costume. Brown tights. A blousy tunic. A sage hat with an ostentatious feather.

"Dante?" Owen blinked. He hadn't seen Dante Salvaro since a week after *Midsummer Night's Dream,* when the actor who'd played Oberon had cornered Owen to ask why he'd run off stage in the middle of their production.

Dante looked just as furious now, though both his legs were broken at the ankles. He glared up at Owen, his teeth bared.

"Why?" he groaned. "Why did you bring me here?"

Owen gaped.

"I . . ." He didn't understand. Why was Dante in the game? Did he have cards too?

The ground began to shake, and Owen dropped low so he didn't stumble.

"Get out of the way, you fool!" Izanami grabbed Owen's shoulder from behind, and shoved him away from the center of the ring. The yellow sand there had begun to rise, parting and tumbling over itself like a giant anthill punching up from beneath the surface. In moments, Dante was buried.

"Wait . . ." Owen turned back, but Izanami pushed him on. "I know him. I have to—"

"It's a dream, mortal!"

"But—"

The top of the sand hill broke open, cut through by a shard of white bone. Another joined the first, then more, until a pointed skull split the surface.

A skeleton, Owen realized in horror. The head alone was the size of Owen himself, pointed tips molded into the bone encircling the top of the skull like a crown. Its sharp shoulders broke free from below the sand next, nearly as broad as the circular room. Bony arms followed—one pair after another. Dozens of hands reached into the levels of the corkscrew tower to drag people out and throw them to the earth below.

Leaving Dante behind, Owen raced after Izanami toward the bottom ring. The sand there extended outward into a shimmering mirage, the path packed with people, all running clockwise up the incline toward the next level.

"Hurry!" Izanami cried, leaping out of the way as another set of skeletal arms crested the ground. There were too many to count now. The skeleton's hollow groan rebounded off the walls as it grew into the endless space above. Its body was draped in living shadows, which swarmed against its pale spine, ribs, and pelvis like maggots.

"What is that?" Owen dodged out of the way of a punching fist.

"Gashadokuro," Izanami answered. "A monster that feeds on bone dust."

"*Bone dust?* Did you dream that up too?"

Fear flashed in Izanami's gaze as someone at their feet was sucked into the sand.

"Move, mortal, or you'll be next," Izanami told him.

Owen dove under the high, pale white ceiling of the first winding floor, Izanami beside him. The ground heat was blistering, burning Owen's hands and cheek. He was up in a shot, taking in his surroundings. The sand stretched infinitely into the distance away from the center of the room, packed with struggling people. Someone half-naked grabbed his shoulder. His eyes and cheeks were so sunken, the outline of his broken teeth pressed through his skin.

Owen's heart stammered. Mike Tran. He'd been in the last play too—Lysander. Owen could barely recognize him. How long had he been here?

"He's coming," Mike cried. "He'll make you start again. We have to go up. Up is out!"

Owen shook Mike free. "What are you talking about? How did you get here?"

A moment later, Owen understood.

A bony arm plunged past him, over the desert sands. Gashadokuro reached into a crowd of people, blindly grasping at anything that moved.

"Get up, get up!" Owen chanted as one of Gashadokuro's sharp, white fingers hooked around Ian's ankle. Owen grabbed his friend's shoulders, pulling him free. They scrambled up a dune just as one of the skeleton's fists closed around Mike Tran's leg, snapping it like a twig. With a scream, Owen's castmate was dragged out onto the main floor where he was raised, then slammed down against the ground with others who Gashadokuro had pulled from higher levels. They cracked and broke as they hit the sand, like watermelons dropped from a rooftop, some of them re-forming in seconds, others sucked into the earth to feed the giant skeleton.

"Mike!" Owen shouted.

"Forget him!" Izanami hissed. "This place took him from your mind."

"What does that mean?" Owen was shaking. "He . . . he isn't real?"

"Of course he's real! Everything here is real! But he is a replica. A nightmare creation."

Owen gave a quick nod. This place was reading his thoughts, pulling people he knew out of his mind. As he looked around he saw others. A few kids from his year. A woman who looked like his mother. His chest grew tighter.

Nightmare creations. *Tricks.*

"It burns," Izanami hissed. "Quickly. Play the game."

Burning fabric singed Owen's nostrils, blending with an awful stench of baking flesh. He looked down to find that his feet, clad only in socks from his room at home, were smoking, and the knees of his pants were charred from the sand. There were people ahead, some of them in modern clothes, some dressed in rags or kimonos from Izanami's time, all of them running up the dune. Burns marred their skin. The soles of their bare feet had been ripped away, and they were leaving bloody footprints on the gold ground.

Owen glanced out of the edge of the desert, to where Gashadokuro's arms, still stretching from the elongated trunk of his body, were reaching through the pack to drag more people out. The skeleton's monstrous legs had emerged from the ground, but one was weighed down by a thick chain, links as big as car tires circling its ankle.

As they ran, others joined them, their frantic cries and groans of pain spiking Owen's adrenaline.

They had to get out of here.

Play the game.

"Last time we had challenges. You completed the challenge, you got the prize." Owen spat out the words quickly, nausea rolling through him as he dodged around a burned body on the ground.

"The tomoe," Izanami said.

"What's a tomoe?" Owen asked.

"A pendant made of three connecting sections," she said quickly. "Flat stones, shaped like commas. Each part must be a prize. Without the tomoe, I won't be able to—"

A girl ahead of him fell with a cry, rolling down the back of the dune. Owen recognized her face—she'd played Hermia in *Midsummer.*

"Won't be able to what?" Owen asked.

"It doesn't matter now. Just solve the card." She flashed benevolence at him. "Help somebody!"

Help somebody.

"It's not that simple!" he said, staring at the girl he knew as she struggled to stop her momentum. "If I do the challenge wrong, if I help the wrong person . . . the game will punish me!" Last time when they'd screwed up, they'd forgotten Ian. What if it happened again? He couldn't risk it.

"This is my husband's game, you fool," Owen said. "The lord of life would not punish a mortal for a mistake."

Owen gritted his teeth, still unsure. "That's just you, huh?"

She flashed a wicked grin. "That's just me."

He looked again at Hermia, still rolling, sand flying around her. He hoped the empress was right.

Owen lunged for his old castmate, but Gashadokuro got there first, dragging the girl away. As Owen watched in horror, the hot surface burned through his socks, scalding his feet. He ran on.

"How can we help them if we can't stop?" he asked.

"You're the player, you tell me!" She swiped a hand over Ian's forehead, smearing blood over his skin from the bite she'd made to call the kappa.

They couldn't slow down without burning. They could barely reach anyone before Gashadokuro dragged them away.

A woman in an eggplant-colored pantsuit stumbled in front of them, and Owen stopped long enough to hoist her up.

"Thank you," his sophomore history teacher groaned.

Half her face was melted off. Owen released her at once, swallowing a cry. She raced away.

"Ungrateful," Izanami spat.

Owen's gaze shot to the card in her grip, but it didn't burn into a prize. Maybe he hadn't helped the woman enough. Maybe it wasn't the right person. At least he still remembered Ian—there seemed to have been no consequence to doing the first challenge wrong.

If this even was the first challenge.

"What did the other cards say?" he called as they raced toward a clustered group halfway around the coil.

"Does it matter? If we don't have them, we can't get the pieces of the tomoe!"

Owen's jaws gripped together. She was right. Even if they completed a challenge, they needed the physical cards to change into prizes.

If the cards were lost, they couldn't finish the game.

They would be stuck here, forever.

His feet slowed, then burned. Panic overtook him as a man in the lead tumbled, screaming as his bare chest hit the hot ground and began to cook. The smell of his flesh made Owen's nostrils flare. Others were climbing over the fallen runner, using his body as a stepping stone.

Beside him, Ian's cheeks were red. Bright, dizzying colors raged around him. The scent of fresh blood filled the air. Owen's shirt clung to his chest. His thighs and lungs pumped as they climbed the dune, and at the top, he could see a black spot through a break in the stampede.

An exit.

Up is out.

The top of the coil had to be a way out of Jigoku.

"There!" he shouted, grabbing Ian's wounded hand. It was slick in his grasp. "That's our way out!"

They raced toward it. Owen's glasses clouded from his own per-spiration. A sob escaped his lips as the heat bore through the pads of his feet, tearing up his shins. People tripped and stumbled in front of him. He followed Izanami onto their backs and chests, hopping from one island to another to save himself.

They neared the threshold, a wall hosting a large black portal. A quick glance out onto the main floor revealed that they were no longer level with the main floor, but higher than before.

"Move!" Izanami shouted, but the throng of people corked the exit, blocking their path.

"Step aside for your empress!" she screamed.

They did not clear.

Pain shot up Owen's legs. He didn't dare look down at his feet.

Izanami extended Ian's hands like claws, reaching toward the crowd. A man in singed hakama pants was lifted from the ground as if by an invisible stage harness and tossed aside. A high cry echoed off the glinting sand as a woman's spine bowed in pain. She fell to the ground, convulsing before them, darkness surrounding her body like a pond of ink.

Horror raked through Owen. "What are you doing?"

Another man was knocked out of the way. Izanami glared down at her victims, lips curling into a small, wicked smile. Ian's shoes were smoking from the heat as she moved toward the black portal exit.

"Stop! We're supposed to help them, not hurt them!" Owen grabbed Ian's shoulder, tearing away her focus. The temperature was oppressive, burning him from all sides.

Izanami blinked at Owen, then wavered.

Owen caught her before she fell.

"Ian!" Owen wrapped one of Ian's arms over his shoulder. The people Izanami had whipped around with her shadow power were now still and smoking on the ground. Whatever she had done to them had weakened her.

"Ian, wake up! *Empress!*" Owen dragged her toward the hole in the wall, but Ian was bigger, and his dead weight slowed them too much. Owen limped on, his eyes set on the exit, a path now cleared to the next level.

The empress muttered something Owen couldn't make out.

"What?"

"Damn this fragile, mortal body," Izanami said, blinking in exhaustion.

Owen's slash of worry for Ian was overwhelmed by panic as he reached for the portal and found it blocked.

The recess ahead was like the cave's entrance, the darkness unending. But where the cave had always dragged them in, this exit had an invisible barrier, stopping them from passing through.

"No," said Owen. "No, no, no." He slapped his hand against the black wall.

They were going to burn.

"We can't get out." He pounded a fist against the dark exit, but it was hard and unyielding. He fell forward on his knees, the sand's heat tearing up through his thighs. Exhaustion stole his breath. Pain made him writhe.

Around him, the crowd gathered again, pressing close, screaming their demands to be let out. He was crushed against the portal, Ian's weak body beside him. He couldn't breathe. Panic overtook him. Hot, gritty sand pressed between his bloody toes. Into the wounds on his knees and shins.

"What do we do?" he whispered, as the bodies crawled over him.

"Die," Izanami breathed.

And then, he did.

⸻

Owen's breath came in a hard pull. His eyes snapped open. He clutched his chest. His head. Sat up to look down at his legs, and found them where they should be.

He was alive.

"Ian?" He choked on the name. The air was too hot. Too cloudy. *Steam.*

He was back in the thick cloud of it. No, that wasn't right. He wasn't falling. He was sitting on hard ground. Someone bumped him from behind, a knee to the back of the neck, throwing him forward. Footsteps resounded around him, the crunch and slide of feet on gravel.

He rolled to the side, bumping into a large rock. He huddled under it as the horde ran by, disappearing into the bright foggy space. His glasses clouded in the steam, but were still on his face, somehow unbroken. Thin strips of fabric from his socks surrounded his ankles, but the rest of the fabric had been burned away, along with the knees and ends of his jeans. Even his shirt was charred, and hanging in straps over his chest.

But his body was unburned. His skin was pink from the heat in the air, but not stripped away.

"How . . ."

"Are you alive?" finished a voice behind him. He spun to his knees to find Izanami crouched against the side of the bench behind him. She trembled, her breaths uneven and rough. "It is a mystery, since you were dead mere moments ago."

"What did you . . . how did you get me here?" The steam shifted with a hot breeze, and the sounds of screams cut through the air. To his right, he could make out the first level across the coil below them, packed with frantic, burning souls. A moment later, the scent of tea permeated the air, and pale yellow liquid poured down from above, hissing as it hit the steam and sent a new cloud of hot air into their coil.

Owen scrambled back away from it, emerging on the other side of the rock, beside the empress.

"I did nothing," Izanami said quietly, huddled beside him. "The last thing I remember is your pitiful attempt to save us."

Owen's jaw tightened as someone banged into the bench, fell over it. The man's red skin was marred with heat blisters.

"Do you still have the card?" Owen asked.

Izanami lifted it, blood smeared over the kanji on the surface.

"Your hand," he said quietly. "It didn't heal?" He could make out shadows moving in the steam ahead in the coil, gray patches in the white clouds, but whether they were people or more of the giant skeleton's hands, he didn't know.

"Why would it heal?" She extended Ian's fingers, revealing the deep wound, still oozing with dark blood. "Do Jigoku's rings look like a hospital?"

"We're not burned anymore."

She considered this with a frown. "Perhaps it still bleeds because the cut was made before we got here."

Was made, she said. As if she hadn't been the one to bite Ian.

He jerked as a crash sounded behind them, heart banging against his ribs. They jumped up, racing into the fog, squinting against the white light of the steam. He couldn't see past his outstretched hands.

"Maybe we accessed a health pack or something." Where was Emerson when he needed her gamer brain? He thought of her breaking through the door of his room. Had she found the other cards?

Would she follow?

Heaviness slowed his steps. The cards could have been sucked into this world with them, gotten lost somewhere in the sand. They might have been ground into the bone dust that fed Gashadokuro.

The steam thickened.

"What is this level, anyway?" he asked.

"How should I know?"

"It's your nightmare."

"Do you remember every dream you have?"

He growled in frustration, looking away. He told himself it wasn't Ian, but it was Ian's mouth saying the awful things. Ian's face twisted in bitterness.

The sooner the empress was out of him, the better.

"The ground is rocky," he said, avoiding her gaze, and instead focusing on the pool of boiling water he'd nearly stepped into. Carefully, he skirted around the outside of it. "There's water. A hot spring, maybe? I can't see where the coil ends through the steam."

"The steam," she said, then nodded. "Yes. An onsen. There was one near my palace before . . ." she moved closer as a shadow in the steam loomed toward them.

"Before you created the passage fire that landed you and your crew in Meido."

She straightened with an indignant *hmph.*

"We need to help someone," Owen said.

"You tried that. It didn't work, remember?"

He recalled his old teacher with the half-melted face that he'd dragged off the sand. "Maybe it wasn't enough."

Izanami's gaze pinched.

"What?" Owen asked.

"I said nothing."

"But you're thinking something. I can tell."

"You may know this body, mortal, but you do not know me."

Owen's hands fisted at his sides, thinking of how he'd made his bed for Ian and thought of lying in it with him.

A shadow was moving to his right, probing through the steam. Its skeletal fingers unfurled, feeling around the rocky ground for something to grab.

Gashadokuro.

With a crackling twist of its bony wrist, it snagged someone within the white cloud—a shadow shaped like a woman—and pulled her, screaming, over the ledge of the coil.

Owen and Ian pressed against each other, taking tentative steps forward.

"If you've got any ideas," he managed, "now would be a great time to share."

"Benevolence was my husband's favorite virtue," Izanami finally told him, hopping over a body, prone on the ground, passed out from the heat and barely breathing.

Owen glanced at her. "The husband who made the game."

"Yes." She coughed in the thick air. They rushed past the edge of the pool, farther up the coil. The air was hotter there, but it was easier to hide in the dense fog. "Benevolence was his gift to mortals. A value he wished them to possess. It is not just helping each other, but doing it with intention. Giving without expecting anything in return. Knowing that what you give may leave you bare, with nothing left for yourself."

Owen pulled at the collar of his shirt, now stuck to his skin with sweat. "How'd you two hook up exactly?"

"You have an insolent tongue. I should cut it out."

"So we need to help someone with pure intentions," Owen said quickly, not wanting to linger on that thought. "Help them because they need it, not because we want a reward."

"How can we possibly help anyone? All these mortals want is to be free from this nightmare, but there is no escape. The coil reaches up endlessly. The doors between levels are locked."

"They can't be locked completely. We made it through."

"In death."

Owen shivered. He hadn't died. People didn't just come back from death like one of Emerson's video games.

But he remembered falling from the steam onto the hard sand. Breaking.

Re-forming.

And when he'd gotten to the portal at the end of the first level, he'd been crushed, then woken up here.

"No," he said. There had to be another way to get through. "We have a card. We have to play the game. It says to help, so we put our heart into helping someone, then we go to the next level."

She groaned as another puff of steam came their way, moving the air enough to show the blistered, red face of someone bumping into them as he hurried ahead.

"There is no help here," she said. "Did it not occur to you that is the point of my husband's game? To send me on impossible errands in an unending coil? To mock me?"

"So it was a good breakup, then."

"Mortal, you have no idea."

A new cloud of steam covered the screams from below with a loud hiss, and soon all that could be heard was the crunch of their steps against the pebbled ground. Owen's glasses clouded, and he swiped a hand over them, smearing the condensation. When he glanced over, Ian's eyelids were drooping closed. It looked as though the Empress were falling asleep standing up.

"Keep moving," Owen said, fighting back his own fatigue. "We'll never make it if we stay here. Everyone's trying to get to the top of this thing. Maybe that's where the challenge takes place."

Izanami nodded, slapping Ian's face with one hand with a growl of frustration.

Owen bit back the urge to tell her not to touch him.

He tripped, catching himself against the boards on the ground. It took an effort to push back up. He blinked back the dizziness.

The heat was affecting him, but not like it was Ian. His friend's body was stumbling, his face gaunt. He looked as if he hadn't slept in a week. Whatever the empress was doing to him was taking a toll. They could not stay here much longer.

"There," said Izanami. Ahead, a black circular exit appeared in the white steam. A portal, two feet off the ground, surrounded by stones. As they drew closer, Owen made out a pile of people hunched just below it, their clothing stripped off, their bodies red with heat.

"Up is out," Owen recalled, remembering how Dante had been on the bottom floor trying to get free. Owen was so overheated he could barely think straight. The steam pressed on him like a weighted blanket, suffocating and wet. He squinted at the people, moaning on the ground just below the exit. Their skin was bubbling, as if they'd been boiled alive.

His heart sank. He knew, even before his fingers touched the portal, that it would be as unyielding as the last.

"We can't get out," he said.

"Not like that," Izanami said. She had slipped behind Owen. He flinched as a dark shadow curled around the sides of his head.

"Wait," Owen said, realizing a moment too late what she meant to do.

The next sound he heard was his neck snapping.

—•—

Owen startled awake.

He was lying on the forest floor, the sun beating down on him.

Not the sun, a fire, coming from another level in this nightmare—a coil, two levels above. Somewhere close, a woman was crying. Bawling. *Someone help her*, he thought. The pained sound of it raked over his nerves. From around him came a stampede of steps. As he curled into a ball to protect his body, he could feel the ground beneath him shift.

The forest floor was moving.

The pine needles, too yellow to be real, were sharp as ice picks, poking him as he rolled. The leaves sprouted legs, the gleaming emerald catching the light of the fire to blind him.

In an instant the bugs were on him, biting him. *Devouring* him.

He opened his mouth to scream, but they crawled over his face, into his mouth. Hundreds of spiny legs tickling the insides of his cheeks and tongue. He gagged, then choked.

"Up is out," he heard Izanami groan weakly, somewhere nearby. The shadow covered him again, and his heart stopped.

"Goddammit!" He roared awake to find himself sitting on a dry tatami mat that crackled under his legs. "Stop killing me!"

Izanami, across a low wooden table in the new coil, laid forward, passed out on the wooden surface. The coil was filled with tables just like it, a ringed restaurant of tables topped with bronze teapots and small cups. His gaze shot to the center of the coil, where the giant skeleton was reaching toward a monstrous kettle the size of a car, set atop a pile of flaming wood. As one of its hands knocked into the bronze body, it tipped, spilling amber liquid over the edge of the coil.

It passed the forest coil where Owen had just been eaten by bugs, and hissed, evaporating in a cloud of steam on the level below.

Three levels up. How many more were there?

Up is out.

Was it truly an escape from this hell? Or was that where the first challenge for Izanami's terrible game lay?

"Don't play possum now," he said, reaching across the table to give Ian's shoulder a firm shake. "I know any second you're going to pop up and off me again."

"Owen?"

Izanami's voice had changed. It was softer. Higher.

"Ian?" Owen lurched forward, knocking into the table and spilling a bit of tea, which hissed from the pot onto to the tabletop. Behind them, two women tipped their table over, hiding behind it from Gashadokuro's hands. Hot tea sizzled as it fell to their mat, burning straight through the tattered weave. Other people were running for the exit, another circular portal behind the giant, tipped pot of tea.

"What . . . what's going on?" Ian mumbled sleepily.

Owen yanked him into his arms, squeezing him so tightly, Ian groaned. Tears prickled Owen's eyes.

"It's a long story," he said over the brick of emotion in his throat. "But you're back, and she's gone. That's all that matters."

Ian's hands circled Owen's waist, the press of them too light. His head sagged against Owen's shoulder.

Owen pulled back, a new worry inside him.

"Ian?"

"She's not gone," Ian said, his eyes blinking heavily. "She's using too much power. She's . . . worn out. Weak."

"That's good. It's good, right?" He pushed Ian's hair out of his eyes. Shit. Ian didn't look good. He was pale, his gaze unfocused. He could barely hold himself up. A man in tattered clothes who looked like Owen's old acting coach dodged by.

Recognition seized Owen's chest.

Nightmare creations.

"Don't drink it," he warned them. His fearful eyes darted to the tea on the table before he ran on around the loop. Owen followed him for long enough to see other people leaving their tea sets untouched. Was it poisoned? The hiss of the amber waterfall hitting the steam below stabbed through the roar of blood in his ears.

His eyes caught on a woman in a plain kimono, kneeling before a table two over from theirs.

That place had been empty just a moment ago. It was as if she'd appeared out of nowhere. His chest lurched as he realized he must have come here the same way. Dead in one coil, alive in the next. She flopped to the side, as if drunk, then roused suddenly and ran.

Clockwise, toward the exit, just like everyone else.

Defeat lodged in his gut. He could already see the people crowding behind the giant spilled tea kettle. Gashadokuro's hands were picking them off, one by one.

"Ian?" Owen shook Ian, who had slumped against his shoulder. His skin was too warm. Feverish. His hand, still gripping the card, was a bloody mess from his previous wound at Owen's house.

"I'm here," Ian said weakly. He blinked. "Owen. Owen, listen, she's making some ultimate weapon."

Owen's stomach went tight. "A tomoe, I know."

"She's going to use it to open the gate from Meido to the living world."

The weight of his words pressed Owen deeper into the crumbling mats.

"The three pieces of the tomoe can do it—break the wall between worlds. She wants revenge for being kicked out of the living world. She sees it as hers, and she's going to take it back."

Owen fell back on his heels. *Drip, drip, drip* went Ian's blood on the floor.

"But what about you? She'll leave you alone when she has what she wants, right?"

Ian closed his eyes tightly. "She'll have everything, Owen. Once the gates are open, everything in Meido will be set loose on the world."

"I don't care!" Owen said. "She can do whatever she wants just as long as she finds a new body!"

Ian opened his eyes, the grief there nearly too much for Owen to bear.

"The cost is too high." He placed the card he had gripped in one hand on the table.

The screams, the hiss of steam, the footsteps, all faded behind the throbbing of Owen's heart.

"Don't say that," he told Ian, tucking the card into his pocket. "Don't talk like that."

Ian lifted his wounded hand to Owen's chest, but a moment later seemed to realize that it was still bleeding and pulled back. Owen caught his fingers and pressed Ian's palm against his heart. For once he didn't care about the mess it made.

Ian was dying.

He could feel it in Ian's trembling hand. See it in his broken stare. Not the kind of dying where he would come back again and again like in this terrible place, but permanent. Ian could not survive the empress, and the empress could not survive without Ian—not unless they completed the challenges to get the three pieces of the tomoe.

But they only had one card. One challenge they didn't even know how to solve.

Ian knew that he would not last much longer like this, and now Owen did too.

He tore the end of his shirt, already tattered, and knotted it around the wound. Any other time, he would have been proud of that move—real leading man shit—but he found himself suddenly wobbly.

In Meido, they'd played the game to win their freedom, only to learn that raising the empress meant setting her army of demons and yōkai loose on the world. They'd managed to outsmart the game and return home, but to what end? Now he was in another game, and to save Ian, he had to give the empress what she wanted.

Three prizes, and a ticket to his world.

His hands were shaking as he finished the bandage.

Ian, or the empress.

Ian, or the world.

It was too big a responsibility to hold alone. Why couldn't Emerson and Maddy be here with him? He would have even taken Dax, yōkai or not. They would have known what to do. He wasn't clever enough for this. He wasn't brave enough alone.

He looked at Ian, at the strange expression on his face and the moon-shaped scar on his chin.

It didn't matter if he was brave or smart.

He'd left Ian before. He would not do it again.

Up is out.

He didn't know how to solve this challenge. All he knew was that they needed to get out of here.

"Ian," he said, a desperate resolve shaking through him. "Can you wake the empress up?"

Ian's eyes widened. "What? Why?"

To kill us.

Because there's only one exit in these coils, and it's not through a door.

He couldn't say it.

He cleared his throat.

"She can get us out of here."

Ian's gaze darted around. He shuddered, as if noticing for the first time where they were. Horror filled his eyes as he shoved closer to Owen's side.

"I . . . I can't wake her up. I don't know how."

"Okay," said Owen, trying to be calm.

The portal out was blocked—he could see the people trying to get through, picked off by the skeleton's hands. More people were appearing in the seats around him. Waking, just to run for the exit. People who had died, like he had, on the previous level.

His gaze dropped to the table. To the copper pot of tea.

Don't drink it, the man had warned. Owen remembered how a few spilled drops had burned through the tatami mats. Surely a cupful would kill you.

"Okay," he said, resigned. If the empress couldn't kill them, he had to find another way to move up. Another way, and another way, and another way, until they reached the very top.

He steeled himself. Put on a gentle smile. He was Puck, dancing through the trees, playing his *Midsummer Night's Dream* tricks. He was an actor, and a goddamn good one.

He looked at Ian, felt him trembling against his side, and his dedication wavered.

A breath, and Owen focused.

"We have to drink the tea," he said.

"We . . . we do?"

"Yeah, it's part of the game. Weird, right? Everyone's avoiding it, but that's how we get out of here."

Ian gave the copper pot a strained look. "You're sure."

No.

He smiled, like Puck. Like everything would be just fine.

He reached for the copper kettle. The handle burned the shit out of his palm, but he barely flinched. He couldn't let Ian see him falter. He poured one cup, then another. It bubbled, like it was still boiling.

"Don't look at it," he said quickly, as Ian's eyes darted down. "It probably tastes like shit. But we'll do it quick, all right? Together?"

Ian's doubt was evident, but he gave a firm nod. When he met Owen's eyes, the trust shone in his gaze.

It almost broke Owen.

"On three?" Owen's voice cracked. Screams echoed around them. The scrape of Gashadokuro's bone fingers against the mats. The deafening hiss of steam. He kept his gaze on Ian's.

It was just them.

They were getting out.

Ian reached for the cup, but drew back when it burned him.

"It's hot!"

"I know." Owen shrugged, as if this wasn't a big deal. "We'll drink it fast though. Barely feel it."

"Owen—"

"On three?" Owen said again.

Ian's hands circled the cup. His jaw set with determination. Trust in his eyes. Owen almost faltered. What if he was wrong? What if this only hurt them? What if it did kill Ian, and he didn't return, and Owen was stuck here alone?

His head was pounding.

He grabbed his own cup. It burned his hand. He didn't let go.

"One, two, three!"

He lifted to the cup to his lips, but didn't drink. He had to know it worked, that Ian wouldn't be left here alone. He watched as Ian drained the cup. Choked, and sputtered, a trickle of blood coming from the corner of his lip. Ian screamed then, and Owen grabbed him against his chest and held him. Held him until he stopped shaking. Until his head lolled against Owen's shoulder.

Until he was dead.

Owen was wrong. He wasn't Puck. He was goddamn Juliet, holding her Romeo, knowing there was only one option left.

"I'm sorry," Owen sobbed, feeling something unhealable break inside him. "I'm going to fix this, okay? I promise."

Ian disappeared, as if he'd never been there.

Owen drank his cup of tea.

It burned all the way down. Melted him from the inside. He fell back on the tatami mats, staring up at the ceiling of this coil, hating the empress for doing this to him, to them.

He would make her pay for it.

But first, he had to die.

DAX

Travel by fire was a lot more convenient than dying by it. In one breathless, frigid moment, Dax was standing in the dark, on a sloping bed of wet, musty straw with the poster boy for plastic surgery mistakes.

"Hello," Kuchisake said. He was standing uncomfortably close. Dax eased a step back. "Hi."

"You sweat like a mortal." Kuchisake licked his elongated bottom lip. "It smells delicious."

"If I had a nickel for every time I heard that." Dax put some more distance between them, keeping his eye on the green flames still dancing in the drawstring skin pouch open in Kuchisake's palm. Dax had moved by that fire before—from one challenge to the next when he'd played the game with Maddy, Emerson, and Owen. But he hadn't realized the flames could be used to move someone to a place of their choosing.

If he could get that fire away from Kuchisake, it could come in handy.

"I wish I were able to sweat. If I could, I'd let you lick it off." Kuchisake wiggled his eyebrows.

"The disappointments just keep coming." Dax's fingers closed around his knife.

"You aren't full yōkai," Kuchisake said, giving him another sniff. "Fresh blood runs through your veins."

In a punch, he saw his mom, not like he'd remembered, but in the mirrors at Shinigami's palace, absently plucking a guitar in Tricounty Wellness Center.

It was supposed to have been him there, charged with starting the fire. Him, playing that guitar, But it had gotten mixed up in his mind. She'd been sent away and he'd . . .

He'd died.

"Why don't we leave my mother out of this," Dax suggested.

"Ooh, why?" Kuchisake's dark eyes turned greedy. "Is there mal-content? Did you murder her? Did *she* murder *you*?"

Dax sighed. "You guessed it."

"I bet it was gloriously grotesque." With a giggle, Kuchisake turned, lifting the pouch of green flames in the palm of his hand. Dax peered into the gloom. They were in a room of some sort, with four walls and a ceiling.

Attached to the ceiling was a table and a single chair.

He looked down. The steep layer of straw under his feet looked like the thatching of an old roof.

Was this house upside down? Or were they?

"Where are we?" he asked.

"You said you wanted me to meet your father, Aka Manto. Is this not where he resides?"

"I said *I* wanted to see my father . . . you know what, never mind." Kuchisake was going to hear what he wanted, despite what Dax said.

"Have you brought many of your best friends home, Dax?" Kuchisake crawled up the straw incline to a wall, standing on his tabi-covered toes to peek out a small, square window. The passage flames cast a greenish glow on his pale skin and his curious, cocked brow.

"You're the first," Dax muttered, heading toward him to see what was outside.

"Such an honor." Kuchisake pressed his free hand to his chest. "It will not be forgotten in all our eternity together."

Dax laughed shallowly, his feet slipping on the damp straw as he gripped the edge of the window. He'd been right about the house being upside down—everything was. Outside, the ground was up, the pewter sky was below, and blackened, burned trees were rooted above. People—probably old players—were clinging to the scorched branches for dear life.

"Well, this is new," Dax said, his nose curling up against the harsh scent of burning wood.

"New indeed," Kuchisake agreed. "Perhaps it is a challenge in the game. Can you make a card now? I would like to try my hand at playing!"

Dax cringed, remembering the promise he had made in exchange for their travel to find his father.

"Not yet," he said. "I haven't seen Aka Manto."

Kuchisake scowled. "He might have fallen into the oblivion outside."

"This doesn't make sense," Dax said. "The passage fire brought you to me, why wouldn't it bring us to Aka Manto? It's not like he can die in Meido, right?"

"Under the usual circumstances, that would be correct," Kuchisake said, sliding down the straw to the center ceiling beam, which he walked across like a tightrope act, hands stretched out to the sides. "But I'm not entirely sure this place is even Meido."

Dax turned, his eye catching on the sliding door on the opposite side of the room, now visible in the glow of Kuchisake's bag of flames.

"What do you mean?" Dax asked.

"The giant's eye was still partly open when we left your quaint cavern. But now, it appears to be closed tight. Either the giant has gotten sleepy quite quickly, or we are somewhere else."

He was right. Dax had been so thrown off by this upside-down house that he'd forgotten it had been light outside moments ago.

"And then there is the matter of our downside-upness," said Kuchisake. "That is nothing I have seen in Meido. And I have lived there a long time." He smiled. "But then again, it could just be a new challenge in this game." He pet the spiders around his neck fondly, and a few climbed onto the back of his hand.

"So if we're not in Meido, where are we?"

"Somewhere of the empress's design, I would guess," Kuchisake answered. "I'm afraid my little passage flame does not respond to my desire to cross over into the land of the living as it did our friend Madeline and her companions." He frowned, and with a pull on the satchel's drawstring, extinguished the green fire. "I have tried."

Dax crushed the thought of going home before it kindled in his mind. Even if he could go back to the living world, he wouldn't. He was yōkai—the reason his friends had come to Meido in the first place. If he hadn't planted those cards in that cave, they never would have been in danger.

"Bummer," he said, glad for the dark so that Kuchisake couldn't see him falter.

"Indeed. It seems we are confined to the dark lands until the empress sets us free."

Dax scratched a hand through his greasy hair, frowning.

Was it possible Shinigami had been right, and the empress wasn't dead? If players were working to put her back together again, she could open the gates to the living world.

Maddy and his friends would be in danger.

He shook his head. He'd seen the empress reduced to dust. He'd watched Owen pull the heart from her chest. Whatever game was going on now, it was different than before.

Doubt needling him, Dax slid down the straw, fearful now that he might break through and tumble into the sky below. He followed Kuchisake along the ceiling beam, then cut up the opposite straw slope to the door. The sliding panel was framed with wood, but made of thick paper.

Was Aka Manto here after all?

Apprehension spread through his chest. The roots of his hair prickled. He had been waiting for this moment for what felt like his whole life—since even before he knew that Aka Manto was his father, when he was just a kid, seeing other kids with their dads and wondering why his mom never spoke of his.

He gave the door a shove, but it didn't open. He tried again, but it held solid. It was as if it had been sealed shut.

Frustration had his teeth pressing together. He hadn't come this far only to be shut out by a closed door. He punched at it, but the paper held strong. Taking his knife from his pocket, he flicked open the blade, reached up, and stabbed the door.

The blade slid through. He started to saw downward.

"You still carry the engimono, I see," Kuchisake muttered.

Dax grinned, recalling when he'd buried the lucky blade in the side of Kuchisake's neck when they'd last played the game. "Just in case you get any ideas."

His smile faded. He didn't just keep this knife because it scared the bad guys. Ian had given it to him, and whatever magic existed inside it made Dax remember who he was, and who he wasn't.

"Oh, you do have spice in your young bones, don't you?" Kuchisake chuckled, then crawled up the wall like one of the spiders that made up his necklace. His kimono billowed open below, giving Dax a clear view of his bare ass.

"Maybe try some underwear," Dax muttered.

"I have, and it is not for me," said Kuchisake. "I prefer a cool breeze and easy access for all."

Dax grimaced.

"How are you doing that?" He motioned to Kuchisake's position, crouched over on his feet and hands as if gravity were no issue at all—except for his kimono.

Kuchisake looked confused, then laughed. "Have you never explored what you can do, my friend?"

"Been a little busy." He'd been searching for his father, trying to keep away from roving bands of players or whatever else might try to tear him to pieces, but now he regretted not using that time to hone his skills. He was strong—he'd knocked down the pillars in Izanami's palace when the horde of slit-faces had attacked, but that was kind of a special occasion, the lives of his friends being at risk and all.

"You can do many things," Kuchisake told him. "You can go upside down if you wish." He skuttled to the ceiling, the ends of his kimono now hanging down over his head to fully reveal his package.

Dax blocked the sight of it with a raised hand. "Seriously, dude."

"You can dance here!" Kuchisake swung his hips, and everything swung along with them. "Have you never taken a lover on the ceiling? Oh Dax, you have so much ahead of you! When you slit their throat from above, the blood streams down in such a beautiful way. Like a waterfall. It goes right up their nose!"

"How romantic," muttered Dax. He placed a foot on the wall beside the door, but it slid free. "Maybe it doesn't work because I'm half mortal." His shoulders slumped. He might only have some of the powers other yōkai did.

"Maybe it does not work because you do not believe it will work!"

With his hands overhead, Kuchisake cartwheeled through the air until his sandaled feet landed on the thick ceiling beam below. "Try again. But know that you can do it. That is just a wall, made of wood, but you are made of the fury and iron of an empress."

Dax snorted. "In another world, you would have made a great motivational speaker."

Kuchisake beamed. "Perhaps if we win the game, there is still time."

Dax's gut sank.

He refocused on the wall in front of him, and stuck his knife back in his pocket. Maybe Kuchisake was right. Dax could try at least. He was part yōkai. Immortal. Maybe. He wasn't really interested in testing that.

He placed one foot on the wall, imagining it sticking there. When he tried to adjust its position, he felt a strange magnetic sensation, as if the sole of his shoe would actually cling to the wood.

"Here goes nothing," he said, then, after a couple hops with his base boot, stepped his left leg up to join the right.

He slipped, but then held steady.

"Whoa."

He was standing on a wall.

He was goddamn Spider-Man.

With a whoop, he raised his hands, but a sudden sear of pain from his left wrist took him by surprise. He was used to the cold now, but this was white hot, burning just below the heel of his hand.

With a cry, he fell back to the ceiling below, holding his arm before him. The puckered scar on his wrist was bright red and angry. He could feel his pulse beating in the veins beneath.

"What is it?" Kuchisake asked, hurrying beside him. "Do you have a splinter?"

"My wrist," he said, grinding his teeth together against the pain. "Something's wrong." The pain was already receding, though, sending prickles through his fingertips.

"I remember when I gave you that mark," Kuchisake said fondly. "You, and sweet Madeline. Her blood became yours. Yours became hers. You are bound by kegare—by the blood and filth that defines our world."

"Even in death your souls will belong to each other," Dax whispered, recalling the wedding vows Kuchisake had bestowed upon them.

He stared at the mark, the ache moving to his chest. Kuchisake was wrong. He and Maddy weren't bound by anything filthy. They weren't bound at all.

This mark was all he had left of her.

The pressure of gravity now weighed against him, pulling at his hair and clothes. The pain was almost gone, but it had left behind uneasiness. What had just happened? He hadn't felt anything like it since the Kuchisake had first delivered the cut.

"A love across worlds." Kuchisake sighed. "How romantic."

"If you say so," Dax muttered, as a putrid scent came through the cut in the door. "Do you smell that?"

He leaned closer to the cut. Even if the air always smelled rotten in Meido, he still grew queasy at this scent.

"Yes," said Kuchisake, his eyes flaring with excitement. "Someone is bleeding inside."

"Aka Manto?" Dax asked. The old man better not be dead.

"Perhaps!"

Dax threw his weight against the tear in the door. The impact reverberated through his shoulder; it had definitely been reinforced by something magic.

"Together, on the count of spleen!"

"What?"

"It is my favorite mortal organ. A delicacy over rice."

"I'm sure." Dax aligned his body against Kuchisake's, a little closer than he would have liked.

"Brain!" Kuchisake counted. "Lung! Spleen!"

The paper broke as they shoved through. Dax lost his bearings inside, tumbling onto the thatched ceiling in the next room. He was up in a shot, taking in the long hall, and rough, bowed wooden walls. The air was filled with floating paper, rectangles marked with red ink. They flew without gravity, as if they'd been tossed into the air and were falling in slow motion.

Cards.

Dax bent to a crouch, muscles coiled.

The cards were the size of his hand, weighted enough to clack against each other as two collided in the air nearby.

The smell was stronger in here—the sour rot of it made his nostrils flare.

Blood.

Dax's shoulders laced together.

In the back of the room, a man sat on the overhead floor at a desk. His black kimono bloused around his knees and his long hair hung toward the ceiling beneath their feet.

Dax recognized the shape of his face and his long limbs, once covered with black tar as he crawled out of the toilet of the coffee shop.

His fists clenched.

"Your father is here!" Kuchisake said. "How should I present myself? Should I look demure? Fearsome? Perhaps you would like to present my severed hand as a token."

Dax didn't look to Kuchisake. He couldn't look away from the man sitting upside down at the desk. "Just be normal."

Kuchisake smiled broadly, the insides of his lips turning outward with the strained effort.

"And don't touch anything," Dax added, when Kuchisake reached for a card, dancing slowly through the air.

Kuchisake busied his hands in his obi.

Dax gripped his knife tighter—this wasn't his first run-in with Aka Manto, and he knew what to do if things got nasty. But that didn't slow the sprint of his heart as his feet found the central beam along the ceiling below. He tried to keep his steps steady, but his mind was reeling. He could handle Aka Manto as a yōkai, but now he looked like a person.

Now, he was Dax's father.

"Aka Manto," he called, his voice low.

The man didn't look up.

"I'm talking to you!" Dax said.

Anger flared through him. In the hall of mirrors, Dax had seen himself plant the cards for Ian and his friends to find in the cave. Where else would Dax have gotten these cards than from his father? The *cardmaker*? Aka Manto must have given them to Dax.

His friends had come to Meido because of those cards.

Ian had been stuck in the game for four years because of them.

Before he knew it, he was charging down the wooden ceiling beam, the blade sticking out of his fist. Cards bounced off of him, twirling through the air, smearing wet ink on his dirty kimono and exposed arms. Behind him, he could hear Kuchisake's sandals clattering against the narrow plank.

"Aka Manto!" Dax roared as he neared the desk on the ceiling. Aka Manto was old—Dax could see the wrinkles on his face now, and the thinning patches of hair. He was muttering quietly as he painted a stack of cards. Rapid sweeps of a delicate paintbrush with soaked, bloody bristles. There was no ink pot on the table, only the stack of papers and the brush in his hand.

He was so consumed by his task, he didn't seem to notice Dax or Kuchisake.

"Aka Manto!" Dax shouted. "*Dad.*"

Aka Manto paused.

"His brain may be rotten," Kuchisake said. "I like him already!"

"Look at me," Dax said between clenched teeth. Instead, Aka Manto hunched farther over his work, his thin forearms sliding free from his kimono.

"Look. At. Me." Dax growled. They were nearly eye to eye— Dax walking down the ceiling, Aka Manto suspended above on the floor.

Slowly, the yōkai raised his gaze. He blinked rapidly.

"You recognize me, don't you?" Dax said. "You know who I am."

Aka Manto's gray gaze softened. His throat worked to swallow. Then he dropped his chin again. "Go away."

"I don't think so," Dax said. "We're going to have a chat, and I'll be damned if you're going to work through it."

Without thinking, Dax jumped. He spun through the air, and would have kept spinning if he hadn't caught himself on the edge of the desk and planted his feet on the floor above. He glanced back at where he'd been, shocked that he was now upside down. His hair hung from his head, his kimono jacket and loose pants bloused from his body.

Below, Kuchisake cheered silently, fists in the air.

Dax wished Maddy could see him.

He leaned over the desk to look Aka Manto in the face.

"Why'd you do it?" Dax demanded. "Why'd you haunt my mom? Why'd it have to be her?"

Aka Manto kept writing.

"Why didn't you leave us alone?"

His father stopped. Closed his eyes.

"I never wanted your stupid cards," Dax told him. "I never asked for any of this!"

In his mind, he saw the fire that had consumed his apartment. The orange flames gobbling the curtains, licking the ceiling, leaving black slashes behind on the white paint. *Get out of here*, his mom had told him. But he was a kid, and he was scared, and he couldn't leave without her.

He'd run into his room.

He'd hidden.

But the fire had chased him there.

"You killed me," Dax said, his voice shaking now. "You almost killed her."

"I did not light the flames."

Dax slammed his fists on the table, making it jump.

"She only knocked over that candle because she was trying to get away from you!"

"You are not real." Aka Manto shook his head. "A nightmare creation, nothing more."

Dax snapped, memories of Aka Manto, fearsome and inky black, tumbling through him. Had this been the real man the whole time? A feeble cardmaker, so obsessed with his work he couldn't even look at the person talking to him?

"You stole my life," Dax said.

If he'd had a different father, he would have been normal. He would have been living.

He could have met Owen, and Emerson, and Ian and Maddy, like any other kid. They could have had a real friendship. They would still be together.

But Dax was alone.

Shoving the knife into his pocket, he reached forward, swiping his hand over the tabletop. Cards flew weightlessly through the air. He was strong now—he didn't need a magic blade to defend himself. There was enough power in him to knock this asshole into the darkest corner of this cursed kingdom.

Aka Manto stared down at the cleared wooden surface, his brush still in his hand. Dax leapt onto the table, grabbing his father by the front panels of his kimono. The old man went limp, his arms hanging over his head, his messy, gray hair swinging. The stench of old blood wafted toward Dax.

"Fight back," he told Aka Manto. "You weren't so scared to do it back home, were you? Didn't seem to mind crawling out of toilets to scare the living hell out of me."

"Yes!" Kuchisake cheered. "May I help, Dax? Do you want me to take his leg off?"

"You are not real." Aka Manto's voice was only an echo of the formidable boom it had once been.

"I am real!" Dax shouted. Something broke open inside of him. Since his friends had left, Dax's only goal had been to find Aka Manto. To confront him about what he'd done. But this wasn't the fight he'd longed for. The surge of victory he'd imagined as he pummeled the yōkai into oblivion.

This was nothing but a sad old man, alone at his desk.

Tears burned Dax's eyes, another painful sear of heat like the burn of his wedding scar. He blinked them back. He didn't know why his chest was so knotted, why his throat was so thick. He wasn't going to cry. He absolutely was not going to cry.

He dropped Aka Manto, who fell unceremoniously back into the chair.

"What's wrong with you?" Dax demanded, his voice wavering.

"Look at his arms," Kuchisake said. He was standing behind Dax, too close, like always. "Oh, such lovely paint!"

Dax cringed as he registered the dozen cuts up Aka Manto's biceps. His kimono flung open, more incisions stretched across his chest, all leaking black blood.

Slowly, the old man plucked a blank card from the air to set on the table, then he dipped the paintbrush into an open wound below his clavicle. When it was wet, he painted the card.

Disgust rose in Dax.

Aka Manto was making the cards with his own blood.

"This one says pain." Kuchisake stood beside him, holding one of the cards that had been floating. "They all say pain."

"I told you not to touch them," Dax said.

"We must do what it says, correct? Isn't that how we win?"

Wariness bubbled up in Dax. "Leave them a—"

Kuchisake stabbed one of his bladed fingernails into Dax's side. It cut through his shirt. Through his skin and flesh. It hit a rib— Dax could feel the clunk of it, and then the fiery turn as it sliced deeper.

He threw himself sideways, knocking the table free from the floor. It spun through space.

"What the hell?" Dax gripped his side. Black blood spewed free through his fingers. Each shallow breath seared his lungs.

"Does it hurt?" Kuchisake asked. "Oh look, it must! That is the mortal in you! You still *feel*."

A spasm took Dax as he staggered toward the wall. He gritted his teeth. It was fire. Agony. *I can't die. I can't die,* he told himself, but damn if it didn't feel like he might.

"It's happening! We have beaten a challenge!"

Kuchisake leaned down before him, shoving the card in front of his face. It was burning now—glowing orange embers consumed the paper. Dax didn't have time to consider what he'd done, because in the ash that gathered in Kuchisake's hand, a small plastic triangle formed.

"What a strange, delightful treasure," Kuchisake said, holding it up. "What do you suppose it is? A tooth for a flat man?"

"It's a guitar pick," Dax managed, crawling to his knees. The pain was already receding. The bleeding had stopped. When he glanced down the wound was knitting closed.

"Not real," the cardmaker said. "Not real, not real, not real."

"You idiot!" Dax told Kuchisake. "You just made us players!"

"If we are players, why has the gate to the next challenge not appeared?" Kuchisake asked, examining the guitar pick from each side. "Shouldn't the passage flames take us to a new part of the game?"

"Not the game." Aka Manto had clapped his hands over his ears. "Not every card has to belong to them."

"Not the game?" asked Kuchisake. "That's disappointing."

"Who's them?" Dax asked, but Aka Manto didn't answer.

The other cards floating through the room had begun burning. They were turning into . . . *toys*. Broken train sets. Baby books with ripped out pages. Splintering blocks.

"All the cards said pain?" Dax asked weakly.

"Tremendous." Kuchisake clapped his hands. "Such an easy challenge! Why did it take the mortals so much time to revive the empress? I could have done it in moments!"

Above them, the strange, broken toys were rolling through the air. Dax's eyes caught on a tiny ukulele. He'd had one just like it when he was little, only his had strings that didn't look like razor blades.

His gaze bounced from toy to toy. They were all his. The train set. The books. The blocks. Every pain card had changed to a twisted version of something he knew.

How was this possible? He looked again to the cardmaker, who was now huddled in his chair, his arms wrapped around his knees.

"Not real," he whispered.

"What is this?" Dax asked as Kuchisake tucked the guitar pick into his kimono.

The old man shook his head rapidly.

"Why are these toys mine?" Dax asked, but Aka Manto was staring at the wall. Dax froze, listening, and soon heard the crackle of flames.

"Fire?" he asked, leaping toward one of the windows. In the dead trees where the people had clung to the branches, a fire was raging, hopping from one blackened branch to the next until the only escape was for the people to drop into the sky below.

"How did that start?" Kuchisake wondered aloud. "Is this the next challenge, do you think, Dax?"

"I don't know!"

The flames were drawing closer. The scent of smoke filled the air. Had one of those people outside started this? Or was it part of the game, like Kuchisake said?

The air grew hot.

Dax's vision wavered.

For a moment he was back in his apartment. Ten years old.

Run, his mom screamed, as the fire spread up the curtains. Ate up the carpet. Blackened the walls.

He shook his head. He was not a child. He was not even alive. This could not hurt him.

Aka Manto looked up at him, his face wet with tears.

"My boy," he said. "My fault."

Emotions crashed inside Dax. What was that supposed to mean? Aka Manto was not capable of remorse. This was the yōkai who had haunted Dax to his own death. Who was the reason his mother was stuck in some wellness center in New York.

Dax didn't want to be here anymore. He never should have come.

A boom came from outside, and then the house began to shake. Dax crouched, watching Aka Manto turn away from the wall the sound had emanated from.

"Gashadokuro," he said. The screams intensified outside. The fire roared through the trees, so bright it made the walls of the shack glow a pale yellow and sweat dew on Dax's cool skin.

"What does that mean?" Dax could barely hear him over the flames. "What is Gashadokuro?"

"It will destroy us all," Aka Manto said, clapping his hands over his ears.

Dax's eyes widened. "Kuchisake, what is he talking about?"

"Who," Aka Manto said, fear creasing his brows. "Gashadokuro is a who, not a what. He is . . . a child of bones. A large child. Fit for tantrums, as the story goes."

Another crash came from outside.

"What does that mean, a child of bones?"

The fire had caught the shack's thatched roof, sending black smoke into the room. Hungrily, it ate across the ceiling, forcing them to cling to the walls. It was so bright Dax had to shield his eyes.

"It means we are not in Meido," Kuchisake said.

"What?"

"I have always wanted to see the great skeleton," Kuchisake said. "They say he can rip a man in two using only one hand."

Outside, the screams grew louder. The sound of trees, crackling as they were ripped from their roots, cut through the roar of the flames.

"As fun as that sounds," Dax said, "I think it's time for us to get the hell out of here."

"What about your father?" Kuchisake lifted one hand, the skin bag of passage flames open to flicker between his fingers.

"Forget him," Dax said, but the old man's twisted expression made him pause. Why had Aka Manto made those toys to look like Dax's? What had he meant when he'd said, *My boy, my fault?*

"Goddammit," Dax said.

Kuchisake's green flames swelled, turning the air to a mirage before them. The space widened to a portal, large enough to fit through. Biting the inside of his cheek, Dax lunged toward his father and dragged him by the arm toward the passage.

The last sound he heard was the roar from outside the house. The crack of wood as the floorboards gave way and crashed down on what remained of the burning roof, tearing it free into the sky below.

Dax glanced back one last time, seeing the burning remains of the upside-down house in this new hell. Another home where he didn't belong. Another place charred to ashes.

MADDY

Maddy's scar on her wrist was burning.

She sat bolt upright, covering it with her other hand, pressing down on the puckered brown skin from the cut Kuchisake had given her in her wedding to Dax. A bright light had her squinting, sunspots blocking her view of her immediate surroundings. The pain in her wrist cleared, but left behind a dull ache at the base of her skull and a bitter taste at the back of her tongue.

"Maddy!"

Before she could take in her surroundings, she was wrapped in a tight hug, soft, short hair tickling her cheek. *Emerson.* She breathed in her familiar rainy-day scent, and squeezed back.

"What happened?" she asked, rolling onto her knees. Her fingers dug into soft, powdery ground. Ash. It covered her braids, streaked her skin. The smell of burning filled her nostrils.

"The usual Meido bullshit," Emerson told her. "You were drowning. I pulled you through a mirror. Owen's closet turned into some kind of cave, and ta-da. Game, reactivated."

"Owen's closet?" She didn't follow all of that. "Where's Dax?"

Emerson pushed back, her face scrunched in annoyance. "How should I know?"

"The mirror was supposed to show him to me." Maddy stood, recalling the glimmer of the glass at the bottom of the pond. The shock in her body as she'd grabbed it. She'd been so sure she would see Dax—that's what Vera had claimed she'd seen before it had stopped working. But instead of seeing him, Maddy had seen Emerson.

One minute they'd been on the floor of Owen's room, the next, she was falling, her stomach in her throat. Then they'd landed here.

"What mirror are *you* talking about?" Emerson asked with a frown.

Maddy searched the ground for the black shard of glass, but it wasn't anywhere in sight. It could have slid out of her grip when they'd fallen here, or sank into the ash, or she might have dropped it in the lake or Owen's room. Standing, she turned toward the source of light, lifting a hand to guard her eyes. A gaping hole in the ground beside them, more than twice as wide as her house, shot light into a black sky. From inside, she could hear faint screams, and an inhuman roar.

Carefully, she inched toward the edge, the soft surface compressing under her feet.

The heat hit her first. A punch that rocked her back on her heels. As she blinked, a strange sight came into focus. It was like looking at the inside of a hole made by a screw, each layer its own vastly different environment—one filled with pine trees that stretched branched fingers toward the center of the spiral, another belching fire in an unending loop around the floor. There were lights flashing from one and a waterfall pouring over the edge, spreading out into a cloud of steam near the middle, and something that looked like a cross-section of an ant farm, with intersecting tunnels. It was too much to take in all at once. People charged around the rings clockwise, but were blocked at different places by circular gates, as if they couldn't pass through to higher levels.

In the center, through a bed of steam, three giant skeletal hands reached upward. They seemed to only be able to stretch as far as the ant farm, leaving the top two levels alone.

"What did I tell you? Usual Meido bullshit," Emerson muttered beside her.

Maddy's knees bent slightly, muscles bracing. Her hands fisted at her sides. She rolled back her shoulders, a shimmer of determination running down her spine as her feet planted in the soft ground.

She'd needed the mirror to show her Dax, and it had shown her the path back into the game. This was exactly where she was supposed to be.

She wasn't unafraid—she wasn't that stupid. No doubt horrors waited in that coil that she couldn't even imagine. But she wasn't the same girl who'd played this game before, jumping at her own shadow and hiding behind the others. She had already abandoned one friend to Meido, she would not leave another.

This time, she was here of her own choice.

"Stop that," Emerson said.

Maddy turned to face her. "What?"

"Being all . . ." She waved her hands at Maddy, the light from the hole setting one side of her face aglow and highlighting the ashy streaks over her jaw. "*Excited.* Looks like you're about to do a double axel flip off the ledge. Not instilling a lot of confidence in a strategized approach, if I'm being honest."

A small smile tilted Maddy's lips. "There's no such thing as a double axel flip."

"Wonderful," muttered Emerson. "I'm glad that's the takeaway."

"Think it's Meido?" Maddy asked. "It's hotter than I remember. And more . . ." She made a corkscrew shape with her finger. "Spiraly."

"I don't know about Meido, but it's definitely the game." Emerson pulled two cards from her pocket. "Found these in Owen's room, just before some monster took him and Ian."

Maddy faced her fully, her stomach dropping. She knew those cards. The shape of them. The thick feel of the paper. The faded ink of the kanji.

They were the same cards they'd used to play the last game.

"You couldn't lead with that?"

"I'm sorry. I was busy saving your ass from drowning. I thought you were a champion swimmer, by the way."

Maddy sucked in a breath. She remembered the burning in her lungs when she'd been stuck underwater. The moment she'd gone from uncomfortable to panicked. She'd always respected the water, known what it could do. But it had never scared her before then.

"I went to see Dax's mom."

"*What?*"

Maddy grimaced. "It's a long story."

"Did she make Dax a yōkai? Is she even human?"

"Yes." She glanced back at the hole. "She is. But Dax's father may not be." She cringed. "It's a whole thing."

"*That's* where you've been? Finding Dax's mom?"

Maddy gave a guilty shrug. "I didn't want to tell you in case it was nothing."

"How very fucking thoughtful of you!"

"You didn't tell me about Owen and Ian restarting the game!"

"That's because I found that out thirty seconds before you did!"

"Owen," a voice hissed in the darkness outside the light of the hole. "Owen restarted the game."

Maddy stopped cold. Beside her, Emerson shoved the cards into the hip pocket of her pants.

"Do you hear that?" Emerson asked, backing up quickly to stand shoulder to shoulder with Maddy at the edge of the pit.

Maddy nodded. "Who's there?"

"Owen." The voice hissed again, but it wasn't Owen. It was something else. Maddy peered into the dark, making out a creature near the edge of the hole. It was hunched over, and appeared to be stuffing its guts back into its stomach. How they'd fallen out, Maddy didn't want to know, but as they approached, it lifted its reptilian face toward them, wide-set eyes glaring.

"That's it." Emerson cringed. "That was the thing I saw in Owen's room."

Maddy's gaze flicked to the edge of the hole, placing the creature between the ledge and her in case it tried anything funny.

"Where are they?" Maddy demanded. "Owen and Ian."

"Thirsty," the creature moaned. "Can you spare a little blood for my bowl? I have dried out." It tapped its head, where its concave skull contained a few drops of blood.

"Tell us where our friends are, and we will," Emerson said, but the glance she sent Maddy's way told her she had no intention of following through on that promise.

"They fell into the coils of Jigoku," hissed the creature, pointing toward the hole with one long, deadly claw. "Had you landed just a few steps to the right, you would have followed."

"They're in there?" Maddy asked, her gaze again finding the edge. How far would they have fallen if they'd tumbled into that hole? A thousand feet or more at least. She couldn't even see the bottom past the steam.

The breath turned cold in Maddy's lungs.

If Owen and Ian had fallen down there, were they even still alive?

She shook the thought free from her head. Owen was smart, and Ian, even if he didn't remember, had survived worse than this before. The two of them would find a way to get through this.

If they were among those people running around the rings, they would need Maddy and Emerson's help.

"How do we get inside?" Maddy asked.

"Jump," said the creature. "But if you do not want to break apart, there is another way."

"Of course there is," said Emerson. "But let me guess, there's a cost. What do you want, my skin? Get in line. Been there, done that, pal."

The kappa smiled widely, and tapped its head again. "Just a little blood. I am so very thirsty."

Emerson leaned closer to Maddy's side. "I say we hold him over the edge until he tells us how to get down."

Maddy's teeth pressed together. It wasn't a terrible idea, but what if it didn't work? What if it was stronger than it looked and tossed one of them over? For all they knew, it wouldn't talk.

"Just a little blood," she said. "And you'll tell us how to get down?"

"Yes," the creature hissed.

"Maddy." Emerson grabbed her wrist.

"We don't have time," Maddy told her. "Owen and Ian are down there. They need our help. We can't waste any more time."

Emerson grimaced, then stepped back. "What's the play?"

Maddy turned back to the kappa. Sucking in a deep breath, she stepped closer, motioning toward its clawed hand.

The kappa made a chuffing noise, then extended one sharp talon, and sliced a cut into her open palm.

Pain sizzled up her arm. No doubt she'd need some of Owen's disinfectant after this. As the creature withdrew its arm, Maddy reached over its bowled head, and squeezed her fist. After a moment, a few droplets splashed into the dish.

"A little more," the creature hissed.

"No," said Emerson, pulling Maddy back. "You got what you wanted, now tell us how to get down."

The creature hesitated only a moment, then, with a deep growl, stepped aside. Where it had been standing a moment before, a small stone staircase appeared, winding down into the dark.

Maddy started toward it, but Emerson stopped her.

"Could be a trap," she whispered.

"Could be," said Maddy. "But unless you want to jump, I don't know that we have any better options."

With a sober nod, Emerson moved aside, and Maddy stepped down onto the first stone step. It held solid. She took another step, then a third, hearing Emerson follow. The muddy ground came into view in the dim light below, and she was blasted by a wave of heat.

"It's clear," she called back.

A few more steps and the top of the stairs sealed over, making it impossible to climb back out.

"Hey!" Emerson shouted back up at the creature, but it either didn't hear, or didn't care to respond.

There was no way to go but down.

Step by step they descended until they'd reached the bottom. Through the mist came the quiet lapping of water against the shore, and a trickle of a stream. Squinting, Maddy could make out small waves moving past two torches at the edge of an underground river. It circled the level, a pool-length away from the ledge, before disappearing into the mist.

"Where is everyone?" Emerson asked, glancing back to where the stairs had been moments before. Now there was only darkness.

"I don't know," Maddy said. Every floor had held people, but this one appeared empty.

"Eyes open," she said, thinking of the skeleton's giant hands.

They sloshed through the mud, away from the river and the torches. The mist made the distance deceiving—they might have walked the width of a street, or just a few steps. Uneasiness rooted inside Maddy. There had to be a way down to the next level, but if there was, why hadn't anyone come this way?

"Listen," Emerson whispered.

Shouting sifted through the fog before them. Screams. The gray brightened; they were approaching the light near the center of the ring. Crashes of rock and clangs of metal filled Maddy's ears. It sounded like a battle was raging just beyond where they could see.

"I think this card says wise," said Emerson. "I don't know about this one, though."

Maddy turned, finding her friend looking at the cards.

"You learned kanji?" She was delighted. This would definitely come in handy. Even if she didn't know both, one was a good start.

"Oh, my bad. Did I forget mention it?" Emerson's tone was sharp again. "Guess it slipped my mind."

Maddy winced. Emerson was mad that she hadn't told her about going to New York to find Dax's mom. She would have told her eventually, she just hadn't yet, because . . .

Because if she'd known that Maddy would try to go back to Meido, Emerson would have tried to stop her.

"Why are there only two cards?" she asked, awkwardness prickling between them.

"I don't know. Ian might have had others. I didn't get a good look before he and Owen disappeared."

"So no idea which is first?"

"Nope."

"But if we accidently do . . . whatever the challenge is wrong, then we're probably going to be punished by losing an important memory."

"Yep. If the game's the same as last time, anyway."

Maddy wasn't convinced it would be. This place had a way of screwing up all her expectations.

"We need an NPC," she muttered. Not Shinigami—she'd helped

them figure out the rules of the game last time, but forgot to mention the whole "Empress busting out into the living world" thing.

Emerson's gaze glanced off Maddy before returning to the muddy path in front of them. "Maybe Dax can fill us in."

Maddy flinched.

"He's not part of the game."

"I don't know," said Emerson. "He's a yōkai, isn't he?"

"He wouldn't try to hurt us."

"You mean like he did the last time we were here?" Emerson bit on her lip ring. "I don't know, Butterfly. People are full of surprises these days."

Maddy's shoulders drew together. She hated when Emerson called her that.

"If you have something to say, maybe you should just say it," Maddy said.

Emerson stepped up to her. "Or I could send a vague text and then ignore you for three days."

Maddy's fists bunched. "I can't let him stay in Meido."

"Apparently."

"You don't understand."

"I understand that a monster showed up at Owen's, and he and Ian disappeared right in front of my face like *that*." She snapped her fingers. "I understand that the cave at home has a boulder in it that looks like the only thing stopping Meido from breaking through."

"What?" Maddy fell back a step.

"If you'd have showed up when you said you would, you could have seen it for yourself."

"I—" Maddy tried to swallow, but guilt was a knot in her throat. "You went into the cave alone?"

"Silly me thought you might be in trouble inside." Emerson had stopped, and was staring at her. "But no, you were out who-knows-where, hanging out with the mom of the *yōkai* who dragged us into this shitty universe in the first place." She jabbed a finger at Maddy's chest. "For all we know, Dax is the reason Owen and Ian got sucked back here!"

"No . . ."

"You remember what he was like when he dropped that knife. He wasn't the Dax we knew, Maddy. There was no humanity in him."

The mist felt hotter than before, closing in around her. "That wasn't him."

"But it was," Emerson insisted. "You don't get to pick and choose which parts of him you want. He's dangerous. You can't be sure he's still our friend. What if we do find him here and he tries to kill you?"

"What if we don't find him, and he's alone like Ian was?" she shouted over the roar of a fire from below, through the gray smoke that drifted up in plumes.

Desperation had her doubling over her knees. It hurt Maddy, losing Dax, more than it had hurt Emerson. Because he wasn't just a friend to her.

She had loved him—*still* loved him. And that was a wound that would never heal.

"I had to do it," Maddy said. "I'm sorry you got dragged into this. I didn't mean for it to happen."

Emerson pushed her hard in the shoulder.

"That's your problem," she said. "You should have meant it. You should have trusted me!"

Maddy straightened, her throat hot. "Of course I trust you."

"Then act like it."

Maddy stared at her, the guilt and anger deflating. She had been wrong not to tell Emerson her plans. She hadn't given her friend nearly enough credit.

Emerson's bottom lip was trembling. Her eyes were wet. *I'm sorry,* Maddy wanted to say, but something stopped her. It felt like she was being pulled in two different directions—to Dax and Meido, and to Emerson and their home. Why couldn't they just be the same place, like when they were younger? Everything had gotten infinitely more complicated.

"Look," said Emerson. Their movement had stirred the fog and smoke, clearing the way ahead to reveal a dark, circular portal before them. The outside of it was smooth stone, not like the cave at home, but with the same blackness within.

"That's got to be the way down to the next level," said Emerson.

They ran toward it, and with only a brief look back, Maddy stepped through. A blast of hot air, and they were on the other side, blinded by the sparkling lights from the high ceiling.

People charged toward them, trying to get out the way the two of them had come. A big man grabbed Maddy's wrist on the way by, giving her a firm shake. Tattoos snaked up his exposed forearms to the burned ends of his sleeves.

"What are you doing? Up is out! *Up*, not down! The river is so close I can hear it!"

Maddy shook him free, choking on the heat. Though the room was open to the center of the coil, the air was like the inside of a closed oven.

"Was that . . ." Emerson started, frowning after him.

"The barista?" Maddy finished. It couldn't be. What would the coffeemaker from The Bean be doing here?

Her thoughts turned to the river, circling the level they'd just come from. Was that the way out?

"We're looking for our friends," she said as another woman ran to the portal, now behind them. She pushed beside the barista look-alike, banging her fists on the barrier.

It looked the same as it had from the other side—circular, dark, lined with stone like the view looking down a well—only this exit was solid.

People crowded around it, pushing against the recess in the wall, but it didn't give. It was as if an invisible film covered it, stopping anyone from getting through.

Maddy shuddered.

Up is out.

Down was a one-way street.

"Maddy," Emerson whispered. "What is this place?"

Maddy scanned the faces of those pushing past to crowd around the closed door. They must have been players in this game—their ragged clothes, gaunt forms, and empty eyes were familiar from those who'd attempted the challenges in Meido last time they were there. Dozens of them pushed around the long black nets, hanging decoratively like old spiderwebs from the ceiling, Maddy and Emerson forgotten. But behind them, in the dark, others were *dancing*.

Linking her arm in Emerson's, Maddy stepped cautiously forward into the path that descended down the coil. The hot air brought a sheen of sweat to her skin. The music—if that's what it was—made her want to cover her ears to drown out the cacophonous whines and bell tones. It felt like the inside of a hellish club, shattered pieces of a mirror pressed into a misshapen sphere on the ceiling above them, slowly rotating.

"Is that a disco ball?" Emerson muttered.

Maddy didn't know what to say.

Skin flayers, oni, and monster birds she expected.

But a dance?

"Look for Owen and Ian." Maddy almost added Dax, but stopped herself, the topic still too tense between them.

"Is that . . ." Emerson dodged out of the way as a strange, monstrous man with a smooth, gray-green head and a crossbow swinging from one hand twisted around one of the draped nets. He raised his hands, jumping like the best song he'd ever heard had just come on. When he turned, Maddy drew back sharply.

His face was drawn. *Animated.* Slivers of nostrils and black beady eyes over a mouth of sharp teeth.

"N00bki11er87," Emerson whispered.

"What?"

"He's an orc."

"This place has orcs now?"

"No. The orc is a player I've gone up against on *Assassin 0*. His avatar, I mean. What's he doing here?"

Behind him, a man in clothes that looked as if they had been burned away was caught in a net, twisting as though he couldn't stop dancing while an old woman shoved cookies into his mouth. Emerson and Maddy stepped around him, and pushed aside another sheer curtain to pass a woman bobbing to the beat, so tired her eyes were closed, while a man in modern street clothes yelled at her.

"Those are my neighbors," said Emerson.

"No way," Maddy said, as she caught a group of girls dressed in tattered swimsuits swaying to the uneven beat of an unseen drum.

As one turned to shoot a dirty look at them over her shoulder, Maddy's heart stuttered.

She recognized the girl from her swim team.

"Did you see her suit? Her ass is practically falling out."

Maddy's chest heaved at the girl's familiar voice.

"Why else do you think Coach K bumped her up to varsity?"

"Couldn't have anything to do with those one-on-one training sessions after the pool closes."

Old humiliation scalded through her. She glanced to Emerson, but couldn't meet her eyes.

"It's not real," Maddy said, pushing past. But the fact that the game had gotten into their head, accessed their memories, filled her with fear. "This place must be pulling things from our lives." She glanced back at the old woman with the cookies, and the man yelling as his partner danced.

As they rounded the bend, the swimming girls were there again. A buzz filled her head.

"Did you see how big her swim cap is?"

Shame heated her. She could drown out the voices in the pool, the water filling her ears. But here they were louder than the music.

"Keep going." Emerson was pulling her now. Maddy felt as if she were shrinking.

"I feel sorry for her. It's not like she has any other friends. Why else do you think she's in the pool all the time?"

"Shut up," Maddy said. She couldn't even tell which girl was talking—they all looked the same, their mouths slightly flapping open and closed like hand puppets. A curtain was closing on the edges of her vision. The music filled her ears.

She slowed.

Her hips moved from side to side with the music.

"What are you doing?" Emerson was shouting, though Maddy could barely hear her over the music.

"She's not that good, anyway." The girl's voice was louder now. More insistent. *"Twenty bucks says Coach K is shaving her times."*

"It's trying to get in your head," Emerson told her. "This is a trick, okay? This is Meido we're talking about."

Meido.

She staggered back as the awful, discordant music roared in her ears.

Her heart was pounding. This was a test. A challenge. She tried to remember the cards. She wished she knew what they said.

"*Suck-up.*"

"*Coach's pet.*"

"*No friends.*"

Maddy covered her ears.

She closed her eyes.

She was dancing again. Swaying her hips, lifting her arms. The light from the disco ball cut through the nets and her closed lids, but she didn't stop. The music reached some deep part of her, called to her in a way she couldn't refuse.

Stop, she told herself. But she couldn't.

A scream had her eyes shooting open.

Emerson's back was to her, but in the blinding sparkles of the rotating mirrors, Maddy saw her heave a weapon over her shoulder like a bat. It was a crossbow—the strange, animated piece the avatar from her game had been holding. She swung it toward the girls in their swimsuits, then lifted it to her shoulder like she was about to shoot them.

"Shut," she said slowly. "The fuck. Up."

Their mouths stopped moving. In the silence, they gathered together.

"Another word about my best friend and you're all going over the edge, got it?"

The girls vanished.

Maddy's heart thudded hard against her ribs, and then the music released its grip. She stopped dancing, the spell broken. A gasp brought cool air down her throat. She was okay. She was herself, in control of her body again.

Emerson had saved her.

Maddy leapt forward, wrapping her arms around Emerson's shoulders from behind.

"I'm sorry I didn't show up at the cave."

Emerson lowered the crossbow and patted her hand. "I brought doughnuts."

"Holtman's?"

"Obviously."

"They have a new one with Cap'n Crunch on it."

"I got it for you."

"Damn."

"I ate it. It was fucking delicious."

Maddy grinned, then squeezed her tighter. "I should have told you about Dax's mom."

"I'm sorry I wasn't there." Emerson's shoulders lifted in a sigh. "I only had time to learn a little kanji. I wanted to, just in case."

Long late-night conversations filled her mind. Maddy, reliving every moment with Dax in Meido. Emerson sitting silently, holding her hand. "You were there."

Survivor's guilt, Emerson had called it, but it was more than that. It was knowing that every glittering possibility she'd glimpsed in her brief time with Dax was now extinct. They would never talk all night, or hold hands in a car, or kiss in her bedroom. Their future had been stolen, just like he had been stolen. And it had punched a hole in her chest that she could not fill.

"I don't suppose that move with the crossbow changed either of the cards?"

Emerson pulled them from her pocket as Maddy rounded to her side. They were still in one piece, the kanji frustratingly unreadable.

"No such luck," said Emerson.

"We don't need luck," Maddy said. "We've got Captain Carroway."

Emerson grinned at the reference to her Foxtail Five comic name, hooking her little finger around Maddy's. "And Queen Kickass."

Maddy didn't let go of her hand as they dodged through the nets and raced around the coil for the next portal. She'd meant it when she'd said she couldn't lose Emerson. She refused to let this place tear them apart again, but the harder she gripped Emerson's hand, the more she could feel it slipping out of her hold.

"Wait," she told Emerson as they neared the portal at end of the level. They were under another disco ball, this one low enough to jump up and touch. "Let me see that crossbow. I've got an idea."

OWEN

The first thing Owen noticed when he revived was that there was a stick jabbing him in the ribs. The second was that the ground was a long way down.

In fact, he couldn't see it at all.

He jolted back in a spray of splinters and crackling wood, the basket-weave of branches that held him bouncing as he pushed against the blackened trunk of a tree. Soot stained his hands. The air reeked of burned wood, the scent so strong it burned his eyes. His gaze darted through the trees, landing on a boy in jeans and a blue T-shirt at the end of the branch, smeared with coal.

"Ian!" Carefully, Owen crawled toward him, trying not to look down. The last time he'd climbed a tree the branches had been papier mâché and he'd been wearing tights. What he would have given for this to be an act.

Ian pushed up on the branches, moaning. Then, in a burst, he seemed to notice there was no ground beneath him and gave a screech.

"Don't move!" Owen ordered, as the branch cracked beneath him.

Ian froze.

His stare, bright with fear, turned to Owen.

"Don't look down," Owen told him. He reached out.

Slowly, Ian put his hand in Owen's.

"Drop me, mortal, and we won't have the luxury of dying to advance. We will fall forever."

Owen flinched at Izanami's tone. Disappointment flooded him. He didn't want her. He'd been foolish enough to think that she might not wake back up.

"Where is he?" Owen asked. He didn't have to say who.

Izanami ambled over the branch, resting against the tree trunk beside Owen. She was breathing hard, as if she'd just run miles. Dying was wearing on them.

"He is locked away," she said. "For safekeeping."

Bits of burned bark filtered down on their heads. Owen glanced up for the first time since they'd arrived on this level, seeing a man perched over them in the branches, hugging the trunk tightly. The ground not far above him.

They were upside down.

Or rather, the level was upside down. He peered down into the sky below them, just inside the rounded lip of the floor. It stretched into clear blue, clouds hundreds of yards below, moving lazily around the coil.

If they fell, there was nothing to stop them.

"Ian's tired," Owen said, watching as Ian's hands began to shake. He was paler than before. "We need to rest." He checked his pocket, finding the benevolence card still there from when he'd taken it from Ian at the tea table. He quickly placed it back inside.

A crackling in the dark drew their attention, and Owen's skin flushed as the air surged with heat. He turned to where the sound had come from, finding a bright orange wall of flame was crawling their direction, looping around the coil. It chased people through the branches. Some could outrun it, hopping nimbly from one tree to the next like monkeys. Others seemed to accept their fates, and were either consumed by the flames with blunted screams, or jumped to escape them.

"There is no rest here," said Izanami.

Owen started to pull her up to the next branch, but she caught his arm.

"If we run, we only delay the inevitable," the empress said. "Death is the only way to advance."

The thought of burning to death made his teeth chatter. It made him think of Dax, dying by fire as a child, in his apartment.

"You're sure in a hurry to burn to death," he muttered.

"If the fire doesn't kill me, this body will."

Owen stared at her—at Ian's pale face and shaking hands. Owen was tired. His head and body ached. But he could go on.

Ian looked like he might pass out if forced to stand.

A buzz filled Owen's ears.

"What do you mean?" His voice didn't sound like his own.

"A mortal's body was not meant to support the heart of an empress. It will fail. Soon, if we don't hurry."

"Then get the hell out of him!"

"This was not my choice," she said between labored breaths. "If you recall, it was you who placed my heart in this chest. The moment you did that, his time began to wane."

Owen jerked back.

What have I done?

When he'd put the empress's heart in Ian's body, he'd been too desperate to think of the consequences. But now, with the empress draining Ian, with Ian telling him that the cost was too great to save him, Owen wondered if he'd made a mistake.

He'd kept Ian alive just to kill him again and again in this awful game.

"No," said Owen. "You're not going to kill him. I won't let you." But even as he said the words, despair coiled through him. He couldn't stop the empress from doing anything, and if they somehow found a way to get her heart out of Ian, what then? Would he die permanently?

"Then we must continue this game," she wheezed. "The tomoe is an item of great power. If we can get the three pieces, and combine them to make it, I can save myself, and salvage what's left of your Ian."

Owen was shaking.

I'm sorry, he wanted to tell Ian, but even if his friend could hear him, an apology didn't even begin to cut it. Owen didn't know what to do. He couldn't save Ian without helping the empress get the pieces to make her tomoe. He couldn't block the empress's plan without hurting Ian. And if they somehow won this game, and Ian was free from Izanami, what would she do then? She'd have her full power. She'd be unstoppable.

Their time was ticking, and if Owen didn't act soon, his friend would die.

A crash across the circle drew his attention, and he turned to see the back of Gashadokuro's exposed spine, covered with dark, translucent shadows, rising up against the far side of the coil. As its bony arms reached overhead, it attempted to climb the coil like a ladder, dozens of hands gripping the curved floors to pull upward like a centipede moving across the ground. It rose ten stories, until the back of its pelvis came in view. Then it stopped.

With a roar loud enough to shake the entirety of the coil, Gashadokuro fell to the bottom, as if some force had pulled it back. The coils trembled at the impact, branches giving way around Owen and Izanami to dump people into the sky below. Their screams filled the air, stabbing terror into Owen's chest.

"Hold on!" he shouted, grabbing the upside-down tree trunk with one arm, Izanami with the other. As the quake stopped, he leaned closer to the center of the coil to see over the ledge. The skeleton's fall had cleared a space in the steam, revealing its landing place, seated on the yellow sand below. With another angry roar, it pulled at its leg, and again Owen caught sight of the thick metal links fastened by a wide lock around its left ankle.

"It's chained to the ground," he said.

"Yes," Izanami agreed, following his gaze. "Gashadokuro is as trapped here as we are."

"He doesn't look happy about it." As the skeleton rose, its hands shot skyward in a rage, grabbing twice as many people out of each floor as before. Then it straightened, its head tilted back, jaw snapping like a hungry shark.

Owen felt his own frustration rise. The need to escape consumed him. The chains, keeping them all trapped here, felt like a vise around his throat.

For a moment, he understood the giant skeleton's desperation.

He forced his gaze back to the fire, ripping through the woods across the coil. Burning was one thing, but if they fell, they wouldn't advance, and if Gashadokuro threw them down to the bottom, they'd start over.

Or he'd grind them into dust and eat them.

"We've got to move," he said. The fire had moved forward a quarter of the circle, now only twenty trees away. He could feel the heat of it drawing the moisture from his skin. His throat was parched, his skin, burning. He couldn't look at it without being frozen in terror.

But he could feel its approach, like a wave, eating everything in its path.

They climbed up to a sturdier branch. There, Owen led them along the edge of the coil, crawling and tightrope walking from limb to limb until they reached a place where the trees began to thin. There, locked in tangle of burned branches, he thought he could make out a house clinging to the earth above, but it was difficult to tell. The roof was gone, and the sides were blackened with soot and still smoldering.

They tried heading toward it, farther away from the center and Gashadokuro's hands, but the trees were too far away to jump without risking a fall.

"How many more coils before we reach the top?" he asked Izanami.

She squinted up the center, where Gashadokuro's hands had pulled free a tree and everyone within it. They peppered to the ground, screams swallowed by the flames.

"Three levels?" Izanami guessed. "Maybe more."

Three more deaths. Then they'd be at the top.

Would the challenge be there?

He blinked as the light from the fire grew brighter.

He was missing something, he could feel it. Before it had been clear when a challenge began, but they'd been in Jigoku for five levels now, and they were no closer to earning a prize than they had been when they'd fallen down this coil. If they didn't hurry and figure it out, Ian's body would give way, and Owen would be stuck here forever, like one of the wandering players in Meido with the split faces, but dying again and again in the heat of this nightmare.

Desperation made him shake.

"We need to get to the top," he said, though doubt chased him faster than the flames. Maybe Izanami was right, and this was an awful trick from her husband. There was no opportunity for benevolence in this place. He couldn't help the people. He couldn't help himself or Ian. The benevolence card might not even be the first challenge.

Hopelessness circled his throat like a noose.

He looked out into the center of the coil, the air shimmering from the heat. Above them, he could make out the strange rise and twist of brown earth, like mole holes pushed up from below. Above it was a dark level, lit by a thousand shimmering lights.

His gaze stopped.

His heart tripped.

Hanging over the edge of the dark level was a black net. A banner, draping into the center of the coil. Crudely fastened to it were shards of mirror reflecting the brilliant orange of the fire just behind them.

The pieces of glass formed a number.

"Five," he said aloud.

"So?" Izanami asked.

WHAT FUCKING GOOD DOES THE CODE DO IF NO-BODY ANSWERS IT? 5 5 5

"It's Emerson." It had to be. She'd seen him in his room before the kappa had dragged him and Izanami to Jigoku.

She'd used their emergency text code.

"Emerson!" he shouted, though it was impossible for anyone to hear him over the flames. How had she gotten so far above them so quickly? She must have figured out that you needed to die to move up faster than they had.

"What are you—" Izanami started, but a moment later the flames reached their tree. The fire started at the tips of the branches, moving toward them like the entire thing had been doused in gasoline.

"Hold on," Owen muttered, pinning them both to the trunk as they began to burn. He couldn't let them fall.

They had to die. Then they'd find Emerson, and get the hell out of here together.

DAX

Dax raised his knife as his father spread his bloodstained fingers on the dusty floorboards and unfurled to his full height. The air was cold again, the room, shades of gray and black. *Meido*. They had returned through the green-flame passage from the skin-bag to Kuchisake's house, but Dax barely registered the tattered shoji sliders that lined the length of the main hall, or his unhinged companion standing somewhere behind him.

His eyes were on Aka Manto.

"Easy," Dax warned. His skin itched from the cold fire that had slashed across his body as he'd stepped through the passage. Aka Manto paused at his words, then rolled his broad shoulders back. His nostrils flared as if he was breathing in a fresh sea breeze, and not the spoiled, dead air of Meido. It was an upgrade, Dax supposed, from wherever they'd been before.

"You freed me," Aka Manto said. His bony chest was revealed through his threadbare kimono. Cuts from the blood ink he'd used on the cards stained the fabric, but his wounds were already healing. They closed like small mouths.

Dax crouched, ready.

"I didn't know you were trapped," Dax said. "If I had, I might have left you there."

Aka Manto blinked, and the black of his eyes shrunk to pupils, surrounded by chocolate irises.

He looked . . . *human*.

Dax adjusted his hand on his pocketknife. He would not let his guard down.

"I should leave you to talk to your father," said Kuchisake. "I will be just outside the door eavesdropping if you need me."

Dax's teeth clenched as Kuchisake exited the hall through a

side door, leaving him alone with the cardmaker. It wasn't that he thought Kuchisake would have his back in a fight—the man had stabbed him in the side just moments ago to activate the pain card. But better the evil he knew than that he didn't.

"Is it you? Truly?" Aka Manto stepped forward, but halted as Dax jabbed the point of his knife his way. The man's lips parted in surprise as he stared down at the steel. "You still have the blade."

The floor creaked as Dax moved in a slow circle around the cardmaker. When Dax had been here before with Maddy, there'd been a room full of people with split faces—people who swayed and danced as he'd played a shamisen at Kuchisake's demand. Tables of rotten food lining the walls. But now the room was empty.

"You remember, huh?" Dax smiled grimly. In the living world, Aka Manto had attacked many times, unfolding like an inky spider from the coffee shop's public toilet. More than once, Dax had gotten him to flee by stabbing him with the blade.

"How could I forget the engimono?" Aka Manto whispered. "It was I who gave it to you."

"Nice try," Dax glanced down at the pocketknife Ian had given him years ago outside the burned remains of his apartment. Holding it had changed Dax into more than a yōkai. It had restarted his life, allowed him to age with his friends—something he hadn't realized until he'd come to this place and learned what he truly was.

"This was a gift from a friend," he said. "My memory may be a bit spotty, but that I can remember, old man."

Aka Manto slid sideways into a harsh beam of light coming through a rip in the paper wall. It was a grim reminder that the giant's eye was slowly closing, and that whatever new game this place had cooked up was being played.

"Yes. A friend," Aka Manto murmured.

Dax's gaze narrowed on the man's face. His skin was wrinkled with age—though if he was fifty or one hundred, it was hard to tell. There was a tired look in his eyes that said he had seen many lifetimes, but the proud lift of his shoulders said he would not back down from a fight.

"Ian," Aka Manto said, as if pulling the name from deep in his memory. "Ian gave it to you."

Dax flinched at the name. It wasn't unusual for yōkai to know things, though—they had a way of getting inside your head.

"Am I supposed to be impressed?" he asked. "So you know his name. Big deal."

"I know all of your friends' names. Ian. Emerson. Owen." He paused. "Mad—"

"That's enough."

"I've upset you." There was no taunting in Aka Manto's tone, only mild curiosity. It pinched the base of Dax's neck. He needed the yōkai's wrath. His lust for blood and death. That, Dax knew how to fight.

This calm, like Aka Manto was a normal guy capable of rational conversations, just pissed Dax off.

"Now why would I be upset?" he asked. "It's not like you made me into a yōkai or anything."

Aka Manto's hands fell slowly to his sides, the fingers of his right hand drawn together, as if he were still holding a blood-dipped brush. "Yūrei."

"Is that your new name or something?"

"*Yūrei*," he repeated, touching his chest. "We are yūrei. You. Me. Your friend Kuchisake. My friend Shinigami." Her name made Dax flinch. "We are not yōkai."

"And the difference is . . . ?"

"We were living once. Now we are not."

"So we're ghosts."

"Ghosts." Aka Manto nodded. "You have always been half mine, half yūrei. A child with his foot in both worlds, living and dead."

"I'm not even a little bit yours, old man." Dax's voice was weak, though. He hated how he desperately he clung to this information. He tried to keep his expression neutral, but he wanted to know more about himself. *Everything.* There were so many blank spots in his past, and this was the only person who could fill them in.

Aka Manto took a slow step closer.

"Yōkai have always been yōkai. The giant with his heavenly eye. The tengu who roam the skies. They were made here, not in the land of the living."

Heavenly eye? Sounded like someone had a little crush.

"If I'm already dead, why'd you try to kill me in all those toilet-side chats?"

Aka Manto dipped his head. "Not kill. Just talk."

Dax scoffed. "Maybe I misread your vibe, but something about the whole how-do-you-want-to-die line of questioning didn't exactly scream 'father-son bonding time.'"

"Red or blue," Aka Manto muttered.

Dax laughed coldly, stepping closer, so that his father had to edge back to avoid the blade. He was nearly even in height with Dax, his shoulders just as broad. Even though Aka Manto was thinner, there was a similarity in their build—the same long, lanky legs and tapered waist. The same high cheekbones. Dax and his mom both had tawny eyes, but the rest of his face had always felt like a stranger's until now.

It infuriated Dax to see the connection.

"Red or blue," he repeated. "Most of my friends' dads talk to them about keeping their grades up, or learning to drive, but not mine! No, sir. My dad only asks me if I want to be painted red with my own blood, or choked out until I turned blue."

Aka Manto frowned. "I did not want to hurt you."

"And yet."

"Crossing over changes us. Makes us different. In looks. In intent."

"How convenient."

"I only wanted to bring you here. Where you belong. You were never safe in that world." Aka Manto lifted his hands, his blood-stained fingers stretched toward Dax in pleading.

It was wrong. This yūrei who'd threatened him dozens of times did not show weakness.

"Safe?" Dax asked, an edge rising in his tone. "What do you know about safe?"

"I can protect you."

"The only real thing I needed protection from *was* you."

"You're my son." Aka Manto's voice boomed across the hall now, but Dax refused to back down. In the hall, he heard the shuffle of footsteps. True to his word, Kuchisake was listening in, though he didn't interrupt.

Dax squared his shoulders. Aka Manto wanted to scare him? Go ahead, try. Dax had come a long way from the guy who played gigs in coffee shops and trembled when monsters jumped out of the commode. "There is much you do not understand. That your mother—"

"Nope." Dax leapt forward, closing the space between them. He pressed the small blade of his knife against his father's throat. "You don't get to talk bad about Mom. You don't even get to say her name."

Aka Manto's eyes flared with challenge. "Vera," he whispered.

Teeth bared, Dax flinched, the knife cutting a small line into the skin of his father's throat. Blood beaded on the blade, black as ink. Aka Manto blinked once, and in a flash was across the room, standing near a tear in the sliding paper door.

The breath whooshed from Dax's throat as he tipped forward, his balance thrown off in the sudden absence of his father.

"I know your heart," Aka Manto said, his voice low and taunting. Raising his finger, he dipped it into the last open wound on his chest. When it was wet with blood, he pressed it to the paper slider. "I know what you feel."

He drew a line with his blood. The start of a kanji mark.

"You have no idea how I feel," Dax countered. Fury warred with a desperate thirst for information. He didn't want to hear anything this man said—to be in the same space with him at all.

But at the same time he wanted Aka Manto to explain everything. What it meant to be a yūrei. What he was supposed to do here now, for the rest of his life.

If he was a cardmaker too.

He was torn. It was as if his insides were swelling, too big for his body. Like he was on the brink of exploding. Like if he did, everyone would see what he was underneath. Not yūrei. Not human.

Not enough.

A fraud in every world.

He wanted to scream, but his mouth stayed shut. He wanted to tear himself apart, to be free of the curse of his own existence. The ache pounded through him, coiling his muscles, making curtains of rage around his vision. Aka Manto had done this to him. He had ruined him. Cursed him.

And now he would pay for it.

Dax raced across the hall toward his father with an inhuman burst of speed. A roar ripped from his throat. His vision compressed to slits.

This was what he was—what he was meant to be. A creature of rage. A monster.

Maddy would have been afraid.

His shame only made him stronger, and he swung the knife in a wide arc as he landed at Aka Manto's feet. Just before the blade connected, the kanji mark his father had drawn on the wall was eaten by smoldering orange embers—the same way the cards had changed for each challenge—and became a long, rectangular shield. Aka Manto grabbed it, thrusting it in front of himself for protection.

Dax's blade pinged off of the shield, the handle nearly torn from his grasp as the metal-to-metal contact reverberated up his arm.

"Is this what you want?" his father asked, holding the shield high. The same mark that Aka Manto had drawn on the wall was scratched roughly into the metal. "Will this change anything?"

"It might." Dax swung again, a spark flashing as the blade was blocked by Aka Manto's quick parry.

"A yūrei cannot die twice," his father growled.

"Let's test it."

He stabbed at Aka Manto, his knife pitiful in size against the tall shield. Dax didn't care. He attacked again and again, each deflected blow driving more frustration through him.

Aka Manto fell back a step. Then another.

"What did you write on the wall to get that shield?" Dax forced a cold laugh. "Deadbeat dad? Because I've never seen a card change to a prize that fast." Dax leapt over Aka Manto, onto the wall. With his opposite hand he punched down, his fist connecting with the metal. It cracked in the center, sending a rush through him.

"I wrote fear." Aka Manto snapped his shield in half against his knee, and tossed the broken shard aside. He leapt to the wall beside Dax, so that they were both hanging sideways, and braced the remaining piece before him.

"You're afraid now? Maybe I should jump out of the toilet and see how you like that."

Aka Manto reared back before Dax could attack again, and slammed the shield against his side. Pain sang through Dax's shoulder and chest. His feet went out from under him and he flew through the air, off the wall to the floor, where his temple smacked against the splintering wood.

He gripped the knife in his fist, refusing to let it go, even as the room spun above him.

Aka Manto walked down the wall toward him.

I can't die twice, he told himself, but in that moment, he wanted to. He wanted out of this house and this world. He wanted to go home. He wanted his friends, and his mom, and a life where he didn't spend every minute waiting for something else to attack him.

He wanted Maddy.

The rage inside him was too big to breathe.

Aka Manto's brows pinched together. With a wince, he tossed the remains of the shield aside. It clanged off the floor.

"Your fear changed the mark," the cardmaker said, peering into his son's eyes. "Not mine."

They stared at each other. Dax on the floor. Aka Manto above him.

Dax refused to look away, because if he did, his father would see that he was right, that he was afraid. That the fear was bigger than the giant with his bright eye. If he wasn't angry, that terror would eat him alive.

The spell was broken by footsteps, and a quick tapping against the floor.

Dax glanced toward the side exit to find a creature scuttling toward them, eight hairy legs clicking against the wood in quick succession. Dax bolted up to face one of Kuchisake's monstrous spiders. More waited in the hall, crowding the narrow space with their bulbous, hairy bodies and glowing red eyes.

"I am here with reinforcements, Dax!" announced Kuchisake. "Shall we murder your father now, or do you have more issues to work through?"

Dax glanced back at his father, watching the heave of his shoulders, and how his back rounded, as if he were aging decades before Dax's eyes.

Dax couldn't look at Aka Manto another second.

He strode out the door at the back of the hall, away from what his miserable life had become.

— · —

Dax climbed to the top of Kuchisake's house. Since the upper rooms were filled with spiders and webs as thick as cotton candy, he decided to take the less conventional route, scaling the outside of the building.

It was simple when he didn't think about what he was doing—climbing the crumbling walls of a decrepit building with only his fingertips and the soles of his shoes. And he wasn't thinking about what he was doing, because he couldn't stop thinking about everything else.

The room filled with broken toys.

His father making a weapon from a word—*fear*—drawn in blood.

The pain in his eyes when he'd said he'd known Dax's heart.

Aka Manto knew nothing about him.

And yet with each story Dax climbed, he ached more for everything he'd left behind.

Was his mom still stuck in Tricounty Wellness Center? Did Owen have a new play coming up? Was Emerson obsessed with a new game?

How was Ian?

Maddy's face appeared in his mind and his grip wavered. He slid back several feet in a cloud of dust. He readjusted his hands and moved faster, trying to outrun her memory. He couldn't go fast enough. She was always in his mind. How many times had he kept fighting because that's what she would have done? More than he could count.

This was the true haunting. Not the dead of the living, but the living of the dead.

He crawled over the tile awning of the fifth floor, the highest roof, and stood upright on the cracked tile. The light from the giant's eye made him squint—the beam was harsh and direct, even if it was only three quarters open. It was as if the big guy was staring directly at Dax alone.

He lifted both hands and flipped him off.

Somewhere in the distance, a tengu flapped its monstrous wings and screamed.

Dax lowered his arms, turning to take in the horizon. A shiver crawled up his back from the cold. Murky gray fog blanketed everywhere he looked, except for the silver river twisting like a snake from the giant's feet. Dax's breath slowed as he stared at it. He followed it to a bridge that arched from bank to bank, remembering how he'd fallen off of it with his friends, and how Maddy had dived in to save him.

A river in the dark.

Twisting. Rolling.

Your hand in the water.

Reaching. Holding.

A melody played through his mind, catching him off guard. He didn't sing the lyrics aloud. Music had been dead to him since the last game had ended, but now the fingers of his right hand pressed gently against his palm, miming chords for a guitar.

On the other side of the wall around Kuchisake's, Dax could see a horde of old players in a clearing of mist, moving mindlessly through the trees. He was glad Maddy and his friends were gone.

You won this game.

Playing. Fighting.

Now you're free.

Living. Dying.

He sat on the edge on a patch of tiles, imagining Maddy sitting beside him. For a moment, he thought of taking her up here for a picnic, but what would they eat? Spider legs and rotten eels?

"May I join you?"

Dax's eyes shot open. Aka Manto stood at the edge the roof beside him.

"Do whatever you like."

Aka Manto frowned. After a moment's hesitation, he sat several feet away.

Dax hadn't realized his knife was back in his hand until his father's gaze lowered to it.

"What do you want?" Dax asked.

"Only to talk."

Dax snorted. "If you're going to ask how I want to die, I choose purple this time. Death by a big dumb dinosaur sitting on my chest."

"You liked dinosaurs when you were young."

"Yeah. Well. I liked lots of things."

He shifted a few more inches away. How had his father known what he was into? What toys he'd had? Had his mom told him? Did Aka Manto spy on him?

"You are angry."

"No kidding."

"It is my fault."

"You don't say."

"I am sorry," his father said.

Dax ground his teeth together. "For which part? The fire? The toilets? Or maybe we should go back even further, to how you haunted my mom."

"I cared deeply for your mother."

"Oh." Dax laughed. "Now that's an exciting twist."

Aka Manto shifted, as if uncomfortable. He sat cross-legged, and rested his hands on his knees.

"She was meant to play the game, but . . ." His shoulders rose with a harsh breath. "She was difficult. She did not scare easily."

"No. She didn't." Once he'd come home after school, terrified by some insane clown rumor going around on the bus, only to have his mom laugh and tell him if he saw it, to send it her way, because she would make sure it never came out of the sewer again.

Man, did he miss her.

"I tried many times to drive her toward the cave, but she was not affected by me like others were."

Dax thought of the hall of mirrors in the palace, where he'd seen images of himself leading people into the cave. Over and over, he'd done it. One group after another. They always followed, like kids after candy.

He didn't even remember doing it.

"I should have let it go. There were many mortals in other lands that could have played. The gate to Meido should have moved to a new location."

"The gate? You mean the cave?" Dax interrupted, recalling the dark, creepy recess that had transported his friends and him into the game. "It wasn't always in Cincinnati?"

"The cave is just a temporary house for the gate. A hiding place from . . ."

"Who?" Dax asked.

"The emperor," Aka Manto finished gravely. "The one who locked the empress in Meido in the first place. Let me begin again." He gestured to the land below them. "Meido lives, do you understand? It has a spirit. Kami."

"Okay," Dax said. Owen had told them about kami once. The living spirits in everything.

"Meido changed itself for each player, so they had a better chance of winning and setting the empress free."

Dax recalled that—how the challenges seemed to adapt to their needs, like with Emerson's NPC player, Shinigami, and the truth or dare game in the woods with their younger selves.

"The gate is the only weak spot between our worlds—the land of the living and the land of the dead. Meido moves that gate, so that the emperor cannot guard it and keep new players out."

"Why would he keep new players out?"

"Because," said Aka Manto. "The emperor protects the living, just as the empress rules the dead."

"But the gate's been in Cincinnati for years. All my life," said Dax. "It hasn't moved."

"No, it hasn't," said Aka Manto. "Because of me."

I tried many times to drive her toward the cave, but she was not affected by me like others were.

"Because of my mom?" Dax asked, the pieces still unclear.

Aka Manto dipped his chin. "As the cardmaker, I could influence the location of the gate. If many players were coming through, and the emperor had not discovered us, Meido would keep its entry in one place. If the players stopped coming, or the gate was found by the emperor, it would move to a new location, where more mortals could be brought in to help free the empress."

"But you couldn't get my mom to play."

He sighed. "I made sure others would come in. A steady stream of mortals to keep Meido satisfied. And while they played, I used a new strategy on Vera."

Dax flinched at her name. He did not like Aka Manto using it.

"I seduced her," Aka Manto said.

"Seriously?" Dax cringed. "Spare me the details."

An ashen blush rose in the cardmaker's cheeks. "At first, I was just trying to get her to go to the gate—to find the cards I left, and to play. But it was different with her. *I* was different."

His father had tried to send his mom here? How messed up was that?

"Different, how?" He opened and closed the knife in his hand.

"When yūrei cross into the world of the living, they are changed. Corrupted. We are kegare itself, you understand?"

"Pollution?" Dax asked.

"Yes. But with Vera, I was myself. I became as I was before. When I was mortal."

"Which was . . ."

"In the beginning. After the empress and the emperor created the sky and the earth, and the mortals to fill it."

"Damn," said Dax. "You're older than I thought."

"I was honorable. I was the empress's historian. Her scribe. They called me Jun then, not Aka Manto."

Dax tried to picture the man in a tattered kimono beside him serving in a palace. It was less of a stretch than he wanted it to be. As much as Dax hated admitting it, he was different here than he was in the living world, or in Jigoku. He had a certain dignity about him. *Jun.*

Dax shook his head. He was Aka Manto, and always would be.

"When the empress made the passage—the green flames that transported us here—we rallied around her, ready to protect her from any who may have meant her harm in this grim world. But we did not expect that threat to come from the one she trusted most—Izanagi."

"The emperor," Dax clarified.

"The emperor." Aka Manto's back straightened, his jaw bulging. "He came to find her in Meido, only to be disgusted by her ravaged form. Death had already marked her, and for all his love, he could not see past her ugliness. So he locked us in Meido. He took every-thing from us."

Maddy had told them this story before, but it sounded different now. He almost felt sorry for his father.

"So she made the game so she could escape."

"Yes," said Aka Manto. "The cards were once a favored pastime of the emperor and empress. They were not attached to such quests. I could make a card for joy or love, and she would solve it for a trin-ket. I once made the emperor a card for humor, and he could not get the prize—his favorite meal—until he made the empress laugh."

"The pain card Kuchisake solved," Dax said, feeling a little awk-ward. "Those weren't attached to a game then."

"No, those weren't attached to a game." Aka Manto rubbed the back of his neck. "Neither was the fear card—or wall panel—downstairs."

"So what's this new game, then?" Dax asked, looking up at the giant's eye.

"That requires a longer story." Aka Manto took a slow breath. "When the empress and the emperor decided to make the living world, they created a divine artifact to aid in their task. An object to magnify their abilities. It was blessed with the three values they wished to bestow on all living beings—wisdom, valor, and benevo-lence. They called it the tomoe."

"Like a power-up?" Dax said, thinking of Emerson and her video games.

"I do not know what this power-up is."

"Forget it," Dax said.

Aka Manto sighed. "When the empress started the fire that brought us to Meido, the emperor used the tomoe to guide him here to find her. But when he did, he was so frightened by what had become of her that he fled. He broke the tomoe so that she could never use it for her dark desires, and locked us here for eternity. But he lost one piece before he left. The piece they'd infused with valor."

Dax could see it. The emperor running through the dark woods here, trying to escape Izanami and her army of yōkai. Breaking his magic power-up. Dropping it on the ground.

"I took that piece, and hid it."

Dax's brows rose.

"The empress had lost her mind," Aka Manto explained. "I had to guard it."

"Aren't you noble," Dax muttered.

"For many lifetimes I kept the piece safe," Aka Manto went on. "But there were rumors that the emperor would return to Meido while the empress slept to take it. If he could rebuild the tomoe, he would use it against us, I was sure of it. Burn away Meido completely, or create more and more until the living world burst at the seams." He sighed. "So I did the only thing I could think of to do. I returned to Vera, to give the piece to my only son."

Dax turned to face his father fully. "I'm sorry, you tried to give me what now?"

"A piece of the tomoe," said Aka Manto. "Valor. The root of all honor and bravery, made by the empress herself, before she went mad." He sighed. "It would be safe in your world as long as the emperor thought it was in mine."

"Right," Dax said slowly. "But I don't have any special tomoe pieces in my possession, so something must have gone wrong."

"I was . . . not myself," Aka Manto said roughly. "I was too harsh. Desperate. My yūrei state magnified those emotions. I went to Vera and begged her to take it. It was the only time I succeeded in scaring her."

"The fire," Dax said, flames ripping through his mind. "You were trying to give her the artifact, and she knocked over a candle."

"Her home burned, you in it," he finished.

Dax said nothing for a moment, staring blankly into the hazy sky beyond.

"So . . . you weren't there to hurt her?"

Aka Manto's head fell forward. "Not her. Not you."

Dax tried to absorb this new information, but it didn't fit.

"And the piece of the tomoe?" His voice was gruff.

"Was nearly lost. But it did find you, eventually."

Dax frowned as his father motioned to the knife in his hand.

"This?" Dax asked, almost disappointed that this story couldn't be true. "This is a pocketknife."

Aka Manto's lips tilted at one corner.

Dax brought it to his face, examining the oval base and the small three-inch blade. His eyes caught on the hooked mark at the bottom of the base. A silver comma. "*This* is what the empress and emperor used to create the world?"

"What do they say? *Appearances can be deceiving*. Has it not aided you? Has it not given you strength?"

Dax supposed that was true. It had protected him from his father, after all, and Kuchisake, and even Ian when he was an oni. He stared at the small comma in the handle. *The root of all honor and bravery, made by the empress herself.*

"People call it an engimono."

"A charm for luck," said Aka Manto. "Yes. It is that and much more."

Dax's fingers closed around the knife, feeling the familiar weight in his hand. Was Aka Manto right? This was one of the three broken pieces of the tomoe? Sure, it had helped him out—it had even made him remember who he was—but did that mean it had the power to create the world?

"Maybe you're thinking of a different knife," he said. "This was Ian's."

Aka Manto nodded. "After the fire at your mother's house, I was sent to Jigoku, the nightmare prison, for my failure to move the gate. But I had made cards for Vera, games to entertain her while I was away. One of them found its way into the path of a mortal boy—one who walked by the burned remains of your home."

Aka Manto adjusted his obi around his narrow waist, tucking his kimono into the belt in an almost nervous manner. "I doubt the boy remembered picking the card up later. But when he looked into that field, he saw you, a yūrei, and the paper in his hand turned to a small knife."

Dax blinked in shock, then looked down at the weapon.

"What did the card say?"

Aka Manto smiled at his sandaled feet. "*Friend*. It is what I wanted your mother to know me as, but when Ian held the card and saw you, it changed to a prize for him."

"The knife."

"I wanted this piece to find you, and it did."

His father had hidden a piece of the world's greatest power-up as a prize in a card that Ian had found.

Dax didn't know what to say.

My boy. My fault.

"All those toys in that shack," Dax finally said. "They were my toys."

Aka Manto was quiet.

"In Jigoku, a moment can seem like a lifetime. I suppose I wanted to spend that lifetime thinking of my son."

My son.

The words made Dax raw inside. He scratched absently at his chest.

"How do you do it? Make the cards?"

Aka Manto beamed then, in a way that made Dax uneasy. He reached into his obi for a small piece of paper—a stiff, blank card. Dax tucked the knife into his pocket and wiped his damp palms on his jeans.

From the side of his obi, Aka Manto removed a slender wooden paintbrush, and passed it to Dax.

"You know your kanji?" he asked.

Dax shook his head.

Aka Manto gave a small, disappointed hum, then shook his head. "It doesn't matter. The game bends to the player's will. It will bend to that of the cardmaker as well."

"So it's true," Dax said, looking at the paper Aka Manto set before him. "I'm a cardmaker." Shinigami had certainly thought so, and so had Kuchisake.

"We will see," said Aka Manto.

"Don't I need ink? I'm not using blood." Dax was suddenly nervous. He gripped the paintbrush like a pencil, but his father slowly adjusted his grip to a looser hold, with a more graceful curve of his wrist. His father's fingers were cold, but the chill that pressed through Dax's skin was not unpleasant. It had been a long time since someone touched him without meaning harm.

"You do not need it," Aka Manto said.

Dax pressed the brush against the paper, and a black spot of ink appeared.

Excitement vibrated through him.

"What do I write?"

"Here lies the test," said Aka Manto. "You must imagine the thing you wish to see, while writing a task for the reader to complete."

Dax nodded. He understood the general concept. When he'd played the game with Maddy, Emerson, and Dax, they'd had to show fear, or loyalty, whatever the card said, in order for it to turn into a prize.

"Could I make a car?" he asked. "An airplane?" His mind shot to Maddy. "A person?"

"Not a person," Aka Manto said quietly. "Not fully. I have tried."

Dax thought of the toys floating in that shack and shivered. Had his father tried to make him as well? Dax wiped Maddy's image from his mind. He didn't really want to bring her here anyway, much less accidently create some distorted version of her.

"A living creature is too complex to replicate," his father added. "Try something inanimate. Something small. Imagine a stone. A pebble. And as you hold it in your mind, write a challenge for me to complete."

He thought of the words he'd seen on cards before. Bravery. Wounded hearts. Honor. His father had used *friend* with Ian, and in the shack, the card Kuchisake had played was *pain*.

He looked at Aka Manto, then, picturing a small pebble, wrote the only word that mattered.

Truth.

He handed the card to Aka Manto, the paint still damp.

Aka Manto read it slowly, and nodded. "What would you like to know?"

"If it's true. What you said about the knife. About the fire. All of it."

Slowly, Aka Manto nodded.

Dax looked down at the card, expectation rising in him. His fingers gripped the paintbrush so hard they turned white at the knuckles. He was so focused on the card, he could barely breathe.

Change, he willed it, still thinking of that pebble. *Change.*

The card did not change.

Dax settled back, his spine rounding as creases formed in his father's forehead.

"Well," he said. "It was a good story, I'll give you that."

He stood, and tossed the brush in his dad's lap. He was at the edge of the roof when he stopped, staring out over the ground, sixty feet below. He didn't know where to go, or what to do. Since his friends had left, he'd been searching for answers only his father could give, but now that he'd found them, he only felt more empty.

A song slipped into his head. "Welcome to Paradise"—one of his favorite Green Day tracks. He started humming, the sound watery. He didn't realize he was crying until a tear hit the back of his hand.

They didn't even have a real guitar in this dump.

"The sudden fear has left me tremblin'," he sang quietly. "'Cause now it seems that I am out here on my own. And I'm feeling so alone."

He tilted forward, dizziness taking him as he leaned over the edge and prepared to walk down the wall.

"Dax," his father said.

Dax turned.

Aka Manto was holding a card in his hand—or at least, the remains of a card. Had Dax done that? *Made* it? The marks on it weren't letters, but musical notes, which quickly disappeared as the card burned. Orange embers met black ash that swirled through the air in a dark snowstorm to the roof below.

And when it cleared, there was a guitar sitting in his lap.

It wasn't perfect. The body was too big, the neck warped to the side. There were at least five too many strings, and not all of them connected. But it was real, and when Aka Manto plucked a string, a high note sung through the air.

"An excellent start," his father said, his brows arched in pride.

Dax's tears cleared, and for the first time since his friends had left Meido, he smiled.

EMERSON

The mouth of the tunnel was jagged with sharp rocks, and big enough to drive a semitruck into. It blocked the way, the earth over the top stretching to the ceiling of the new level Emerson and Maddy found themselves in. The only path.

"Remind you of anything?" Maddy muttered.

Emerson pressed a hand against her stomach, where nerves had started buzzing. The tunnel wasn't unlike the cave they'd gone into to start the game, but it wasn't exactly the same either. This one was brighter, the packed dirt speckled with obsidian that caught the light from the fire, circling the level below them. It was bigger, every part of it, from the boulders lining the ground around the entrance to the cavern itself.

"It's like our cave on steroids," she said.

"I don't love the term *our cave*," said Maddy.

"Fair point." Emerson nodded. "It's like that hellhole where we almost died a couple times on steroids."

"Better."

People were running toward them, past them, to the portal they'd come through moments before. Through the thick film over the exit, the sharp beams from one of the rotating disco balls could be seen, but like last time, no one could get out.

They could only move freely down the coil. She still didn't know how people came up.

"You think they're in there?" Maddy asked, rolling back her shoulders.

She glanced back to the exit, but couldn't see the net they'd hung over the edge with the five they'd made from the broken bits of mirror in the disco ball. If Owen and Ian were somewhere in this corkscrew like that bowl-head creature had said, they would see it, and try to move upward. Everybody else was—with the exception of her and Maddy.

If Owen and Ian were climbing the levels, they would run into each other.

If they hadn't already been killed by the giant skeleton.

Her palms itched, empty at her sides. She wished she still had that crossbow, but it had disappeared as soon as she'd crossed the threshold.

"I hope so," Emerson said, as one of the giant's hands reached blindly over the edge and grabbed a man banging on the round exit with both fists. He looked like Maddy's swim coach, his warm-ups dirty with mud, and Emerson watched Maddy flinch as she recognized the same. With a scream, he was dragged over the edge and into the steam below. "It's better than being out here."

Maddy grabbed Emerson's hand, and they charged into the tunnel. The rocky ground was uneven—down, up, down again. Shadows drowned out the light, but only for a moment before they came to a punctured skylight.

"Watch out!" Maddy shouted, as the earth gave way below them. Another tunnel extended under their feet, and people were standing on each other, trying to climb out.

With a nod to Maddy, they jumped down, this tunnel smaller than the one above, wide enough that Emerson could touch both sides if she reached out her arms. Sweat dripped in her eyes; the heat was oppressive, each breath thick with the scent of mold and fetid water. It was so like the smell of the cave in Cincinnati it made her stomach turn and her memory flash glimpses of cards on the ground. They bumped against people as they ran, all of them heading the opposite direction. Their desperate grunts and heavy breaths filled her ears. She searched their faces for Owen and Ian, but none were familiar.

The tunnel veered right, then left. It cut up sharply, then branched into two. They took the path where the most people were emerging, though Emerson couldn't be sure it was the correct choice. Long patches of darkness and the echoes of footsteps and echoing screams made her lose all sense of direction. She was about to suggest they turn back, take the other side of the fork, when the side of the cave was punched inward with a spray of rock and dust and a huge, skeletal hand shot toward them.

With a scream, Emerson threw herself backward, knocking Maddy to the ground. As her eyes adjusted to the sudden, bright light, she watched the bony fist close around a runner coming down the tunnel in the opposite direction, and drag him, sobbing, out into the coil.

Emerson helped Maddy back to her feet, and they ran past the gaping hole. Panic sang through Emerson's blood. She didn't know how far around the coil they'd run, or where the end of this level was. As she swiped the sweat from her eyes, another skeleton hand came through the gaping hole behind them. Its white bone fingers clawed into the ground, leaving trenches a foot deep behind.

"Go!" Emerson cried, skirting by the fingertips.

They scrambled up the steep incline, toward another fork. The path to the right was bottlenecked with people heading toward them. The left side was half blocked by a boulder.

Her feet slowed as she stared at the giant rock. The divots in it. The way it looked as if it had been placed there to block something behind it.

"What is it?" Maddy asked.

Emerson trembled.

"I've seen this before," she said.

She stepped toward it.

And heard the whispers.

Her breath staggered. She was back in the cave at home, the boulder looming before her in the dark. The breath that came from behind it raised the hair on her arms. She could hear it calling to her, the way she'd thought Maddy had called to her at home. Her hand curled, as if still holding the knife she'd dropped into the ground, just before it.

"*Emerson*," a voice murmured.

"What's going on?" Maddy stepped closer to her side. She faced the boulder, her hands lifted, ready to fight. A moment later, she stiffened.

"Do you hear that?" she asked. "I heard my name."

"Something's in there," Emerson said.

She moved closer, stepping out of the way of a woman in rags running past. In the space between the boulder and the tunnel wall, she could see a glimmer of gold, and her breath came faster.

"Emerson, wait," Maddy said. "No one's coming from that direction. It could be a trap."

"It could be the way down," Emerson said. The last time they'd gotten close to the side that was exposed to the coil's interior, she'd been too distracted by the skeleton's hand to see how far around the ring they'd gone.

"I don't like it," Maddy said.

Emerson didn't either, but there was something to this. Call it gamer's intuition, but she could feel the challenge upon them.

She reached into her pockets for the cards, tracing the hard ridges with her fingertip.

"I'm going to take a look," she said.

Maddy gave a somber nod, and they walked closer. As they peeked around the edge of the boulder, she could make out a closed room, the back wall less than twenty feet away. A flat, gleaming black stone, not unlike the slab Izanami's body had been laid to rest on in Meido, had been placed in the center, and on it was a key.

Her knees weakened.

It was two feet long. Slender. Dark gold. Light pulsed from it in heated waves, like it had just been forged. At the top was a ring big enough to circle her waist. At the end that would go into a keyhole, two knife-thin prongs stuck out.

"Is it . . ." Maddy started.

"A prize?" Emerson finished. They looked to each other, confused. The prizes they'd gotten for the challenges before had been the empress's petrified body parts—an eyeball, a tongue—this looked like a more typical RPG prize, though what the key was for, she didn't know.

"Did either of the cards change?" Maddy asked.

Emerson pulled them from her pocket, but they were no different from before. The same unreadable kanji. The same unbendable paper.

"I wish I knew what they said," she told Maddy.

Maddy nodded, glancing over her shoulder. The room was quiet, eerie and calm compared to the chaos of outside. No voices called their names. No breaths whispered around them. The heat intensified as they moved closer to the key. Sweat ran in tear tracks down her temples.

Emerson put the cards back in her pocket, then wiped her damp hands on her ripped pant legs. Carefully, she reached over the key, feeling heat pulsing from it.

"It might be how we get out of here," she said, wetting her lips.

"What about the river?" Maddy said. "One of the people we passed said that's how we got out. Up was out."

"There was no one by the river," Emerson said. Either that meant that it indeed was an exit, or that no one had been able to breach that level. But with the number of people they'd seen on every other level, an escape that way felt doubtful.

"We should take it," she continued, thinking of the crossbow on the previous level. That had come in handy, hadn't it? "In games, you never turn down loot. We might need it later."

Maddy cringed, then nodded. "All right. Okay."

Emerson grabbed the handle of the key.

The heat of it was shocking, but manageable. The metal was smooth beneath her fingers. As she lifted it, her arm bobbed—it was heavier than she'd expected, and she needed both hands to pull it off the slab.

But before she could, a loud groan cut through the air.

"Emerson, the door!" Maddy screamed.

Emerson turned to find the boulder rolling closed over the entrance. Pebbles shot out from beneath the weight of it, peppering them with instant bruises.

Maddy dove toward it, clearing the rolling exit by inches. Emerson was just behind her, but the door was closing too rapidly. She lunged, extending her body toward the narrowing opening.

Her shoulder collided hard with the boulder and she fell to the ground, the key still in her hand.

"Maddy!" she screamed.

A cry came from outside, and then a roar loud enough to shake the walls. Fear pummeled Emerson. The skeleton was back. Had he gotten Maddy? She couldn't see.

She scrambled up just as a slender fingerbone wedged into the crack. The boulder stopped, leaving a gap four inches wide.

The finger squirmed.

"Maddy?" The room was dark now, but for the glow of the key. Her heart was pounding. The air was thicker without the ventilation. She could barely breathe in the heat.

"Are you okay?" Maddy asked. Emerson could see half her face through the crack.

Emerson's hands began to shake. She dropped the key. Stupid of her to grab it. Of course it was a trap. This was a classic luring method. Now she was stuck, and unless they found a way to move this boulder, she would never get out.

She swallowed thickly.

"I'm fine," she said, jumping back as the finger below her wiggled. "Is that . . ."

"His arm got stuck around a bend in the tunnel. Figured he didn't need that finger so I broke it off. He's got enough."

Emerson tried to laugh, but it came out hollow.

"Push on three?" Maddy asked.

Emerson braced her shoulder against the boulder. Below her, the key pulsed light, mocking her.

Maddy counted her off, but though both of them pushed as hard as they could, the rock would not budge.

They tried again to no avail.

"Maybe it's a challenge." Emerson's voice shook. She pulled the cards free, but though she was pretty sure the first card said wise, she still couldn't read the second. "Are we supposed to be wise, here? I don't know how that's even possible!"

"It's okay," Maddy said quickly. Her voice was farther away when she spoke again. "Help! Someone help us! Please!"

Emerson's blood crashed in her ears. She'd screwed up. She'd gotten herself trapped.

"No one's stopping," Maddy said a moment later. "What do we do?"

"I don't know." Hot sweat prickled on her neck. "But there's an answer. There's always an answer. I just . . . I just need to think." She turned around the room, but it seemed to be growing tighter around her. *Breathe,* she told herself. *Focus.* But it was so hot, and the walls were so close. Panic was coursing through her.

"It's okay," Maddy said, deliberately making her voice light. "If I can get more bones, maybe we can wedge it open."

"Wait!" Emerson swallowed her cry. She didn't want Maddy to leave.

There was no other way out.

No way out.

The key glowed brighter. Maybe *it* was a way out of this room. She searched the walls for a keyhole. Scanned the ceiling. Kicked away the soft dirt of the floor.

Outside, the skeleton howled loud enough to send dust raining down on her head. She coughed as it coated her throat.

"I'll be quick," Maddy said. "Just . . . just stay here."

"Like I can do anything else!"

Silence.

Maddy was gone.

"It's fine," she told herself, but the trickle of panic had turned to a rush. She kept searching for someplace to use the key, but there was no hope.

"Maddy?" she called.

Maddy didn't respond.

"Maddy!" she screamed.

Terror flared in Emerson's chest.

Tears seared her eyes.

She was alone.

Just as she'd been at the cave at home.

Seconds turned to minutes. Maddy could have been taken by the skeleton. Fallen off the ledge into the center of the coil. Been trampled.

"Maddy?" Her voice was watery.

More time passed. She remembered waiting at the cave by the river for Maddy. Remembered how Maddy had never come.

She was stuck here, and no one would ever find her.

She turned her back against the boulder and lowered to the

ground. Her head fell into her hands. Why had she been so stupid? Why had she—

"Emerson!" Maddy shouted through the gap. "Can you hear me? They're here. Owen and Ian . . . they're here!"

MADDY

"We have to roll the boulder back," Maddy told Owen. When he and Ian had come around the bend in the tunnel, she'd never been so happy to see anyone in her life. "If we push at the same time, we can move it."

"Perhaps this is the help we need to give," Ian gasped. He was curled on the floor of the cave, his eyes pinched closed, sweat dripping from his temples.

"Ian?" She stepped toward him, but Owen was already kneeling at his side. "What's wrong with him?" Another crash down the cave had them all spinning in that direction. The skeleton must have punched through another part of the tunnel.

"It's a long story," Owen said, standing. "Come on."

Maddy gave a curt nod. They didn't have time for stories, short or long. Emerson was trapped, and they weren't leaving without her.

Owen braced against the bottom of the rock just above the segmented squirming fingerbones. His clothes were torn and burned to black ends, but he seemed otherwise all right. Whatever had happened to Ian, Owen seemed to have escaped.

Maddy took her place over him, shoulder pressed against the stone.

"Ready, Emerson?"

A soft "Yes!" came through the crack.

"Push!" Maddy ordered.

She threw her weight against the stone, feet pedaling through the loose dirt below. Owen slid out, landing on his chest and knocking her feet out from under her. She fell over him in a heap.

"Again!" She jumped up.

They pushed and pushed, but the stone did not move.

Anxiety tightened her chest. Her breath came in hard rasps.

"Stop," Owen finally said, sliding down the rock to sit on the ground. "This isn't working."

"It has to work," Maddy said.

Owen dug his thumbs into his temples. "The card says to help someone, but we can't help anyone."

"The card." Maddy reached into the gap. "That's it! Emerson, give me the cards."

"You have the rest of the cards?"

"We have two, but we only know what one means."

Emerson passed the cards through the gap, her fingertips brushing Maddy's. Her hands were shaking.

"That says wise," Maddy said, pointing to one.

"Wisdom," Owen said. "The other is valor." Beside them on the floor, Ian groaned. Maddy glanced at him, worried they'd have to carry him out.

"There are three challenges." Owen pulled another card from his pocket. "This is benevolence. We're supposed to help someone, but every time I try it doesn't work."

"You did the challenge wrong?" Emerson asked through the crack, her voice higher. "Have you been punished? Do you know who I am? Do you know Maddy?"

"This game doesn't work that way," Owen said, his gaze darting off of Ian. "Nothing happened when I helped the wrong person."

"But we could have been doing the challenges in the wrong order," said Maddy. "Maybe there's no consequence for screwing up benevolence. But what if the current challenge is wisdom? Or valor?" She looked from Owen to Ian, to Emerson, whose eye was only clear through the fissure. She knew her friends. She knew she was here for Dax.

"Maybe the punishment is getting trapped behind that boulder," said Ian.

Maddy swallowed.

"There's a key inside with Emerson," she said. "It looked like a prize, but when we touched it, the boulder rolled over the exit."

"You must need the key to get to the next level," Emerson said through the crack. "You can go down through the portals, but not up. This must be how you advance to get out of here."

"That's not how you advance," Owen said quietly.

"Well, do you see any other locks around here?" Maddy asked.

Owen shrunk back at her words. His gaze darted to the wiggling finger stuck in the gap between the boulder and the tunnel wall.

"Gashadokuro," he said.

"Gasha-what?"

"The skeleton," he said.

Maddy shivered. She could still hear the crack of bone when she'd grabbed the hand and torn the finger free.

"Gashadokuro has a chain around its leg," Owen said grimly. "It's stuck to the floor."

"Benevolence." Emerson's voice came through the crack.

Maddy moved closer, reaching again through the crack so that her fingers skimmed Emerson's.

"That's the challenge," Emerson told her. "You said we're supposed to help someone. Maybe . . . it's that skeleton."

"The one that's killing everyone?" Maddy said, one hand jutting toward the sound of screams.

"It's pretty on-brand for this game, don't you think?" said Emerson. "To complete this task you must help the bad guy do bad things."

"She's right," said Owen. "This is it. It has to be. Remember the last game? We had to match what the card said. If it said fear, we had to show fear. If it wanted us to be loyal, we had to be loyal, whatever the cost."

"Yeah, but what if Emerson's the cost?" Maddy whispered to Owen. "Handing that key over doesn't necessarily mean this boulder will roll back." Even if they completed the challenge, Emerson could still be stuck there.

Another crash had the floor trembling.

"She might have to die," said Owen.

"*What?*" Maddy couldn't believe what she was hearing. "You'd let her die?"

"Kind of?" Owen winced. "But not permanently." He stepped

closer. "Look, it's going to sound bad, but the only way to move up here is to die, again and again on every floor, until we're out. The key won't do shit for the doors between levels, and I haven't seen any other locks. The only way we're getting out is to die."

Maddy looked again to Ian, barely conscious on the floor. That's what was wrong with him. He'd been dying.

She couldn't fully grasp what that meant.

"If you set that thing free, none of us will get out of here," she said. "It'll climb straight to the top and kill everyone in its path."

"Then he'll save us the trouble of doing it ourselves," Owen said grimly, gripping the cards in his fist.

"All right," Maddy told them. She didn't have to be clear on the details to trust Owen with her life. They'd been in worse spots before and survived. "Emerson, can you get the key through?"

She passed it through the gap, tip first. Maddy took the end, the metal hot against her hands. The prongs at the end were as thin as blades, and the ring at the top got stuck a little, but she could maneuver it free.

"All right?" Maddy asked her, holding the key in her arms. The glow of it had attracted some of the runners. A woman in a black kimono stopped, and was hit from behind by a man who sent her spinning around.

"Yes," said Emerson, her voice quivering. "But it's dark now. Hurry."

"I will," said Maddy.

"They have a key," the man said, a spitting image of her father. "They have a key! We're saved!"

Shock nearly buckled Maddy's knees, but Owen pressed tight to her side.

"Nightmare creations," Owen said. "That's not your dad. Not the real one, anyway."

Mouth dry, Maddy nodded. This wasn't her father, just like the man who'd looked like Coach K wasn't her real coach, and the girls in the club level upstairs weren't really her teammates. Still, she couldn't meet the man's eyes.

A woman with matted black hair stopped behind him. Then two more.

Maddy's heart tripped.

"Ready?" she asked Owen. "Once I hand this over, we might not have much time to move."

"Go," Owen told her. "I'll stay with Emerson. Go!"

Maddy charged through the crowd past the man who looked like her father, holding the key tightly to her chest. Hands grasped at her, pulling at her braids and clothing, but she didn't stop. Head down, she ran down the branch of the tunnel, bouncing off of those who hadn't yet seen what she carried. A bright light appeared ahead—the hole the skeleton's fist had punched through, where she'd grabbed the monstrous hand and ripped free a finger. Two hands were now there in its place, feeling their way up the opposite wall. They couldn't go much farther than that, though. The chain must have stopped the creature from reaching any farther into the tunnels, or around the fork where the boulder waited.

"Hey!" Maddy slowed her approach. She didn't know why she yelled, the bones couldn't hear her. But maybe they felt her, because both hands flattened against the floor, patting the ground in her direction.

"Here goes nothing," she muttered, setting the key within reach of one hand.

The hand froze, and she did too, thinking that this had been a mistake. The skeleton didn't want the key. It couldn't even see the key.

Then it bent back at the wrist and grabbed the golden offering, ripping back so fast it knocked a section of the tunnel wall out in its retreat.

She took two steps closer to the edge, peering out into the center of the coil. At first, she saw nothing below but the billowing steam. No hands, no giant skeleton skull. It was as if the creature had disappeared completely.

Then it laughed.

The deep boom of it knocked her back into the far wall of the tunnel. Made her body vibrate like the hard hit of a bass and the dirt and pebbles bounce at her feet. Runners stepped on her as she passed. She barely had time to guard her body before a bare foot collided with her stomach.

Get up.

She rolled against the wall, used it to help herself up. Merged with the crowd and ran. In twenty steps she was back at the fork in the tunnels, where Owen, propping a hunching Ian against his chest, was waiting beside the boulder.

It hadn't rolled back.

"Maddy, *look.*"

Owen was cupping a card in his free hand. She recognized the edge of the kanji for benevolence. The rest of the card was burning to ash.

Changing.

They'd completed the challenge.

The other two cards had fallen to the ground at Owen and Ian's feet, jumping with the pounding laughter of the skeleton. Her gaze darted behind Owen, to where a green gate of fire grew on the boulder trapping Emerson.

Her heart leapt. She'd seen those emerald flames before.

The passage.

That gate would take them to the next task.

"We've done it," Owen said as the last of the card burned away, revealing a gleaming onyx stone shaped like a curving tadpole, round and wide on one side, narrowing to a pointed tail at its end. It was flat, and no larger than his palm.

"Run!" someone cried, drawing her attention from the prize. "Gashadokuro is coming!"

"Emerson!" Maddy hurried to the sliver of darkness between the boulder and the wall. She snatched the two cards off the ground, then threw herself against the boulder. "Come on," she told Ian and Owen. "Maybe the quake has loosened the ground enough to roll it."

"The gate," Ian murmured.

Maddy glanced back to find the green passage flames already dipping at the top, the sides collapsing. Fear roared through her.

Owen, still holding Ian, tried to help Maddy push, but it was no use. He looked to Maddy, terror in his face.

"No." Maddy shook her head. "I'm not leaving her."

"It would not," heaved Ian, "be the first time you abandoned someone."

Maddy swallowed a sob. He wasn't wrong. They had left him in Meido. For four years they had left him.

She would not make that mistake again.

Maddy shoved the cards into her pocket, ready to throw herself against the rock again.

A deafening crash came from outside the tunnel. They had only a moment to take cover before rock and dirt exploded inward, knocking them against the edge of the alcove. The blast covered them in inches of earth. Maddy shook it off and pushed up, her ears ringing.

Horror gripped her.

One of the skeleton's pale hands shot forward, punching through the tunnel's center-facing wall, just before the fork. The earth gave way in a landslide, dragging Maddy down two feet toward an open tunnel below before she dug her heels in to stop her descent. Dirt filled her ears, gritted in her teeth. She clambered back toward the boulder just in time to see Ian and Owen disappear through the closing gate.

"Owen!" she screamed.

They were gone.

They'd left her and Emerson.

The shock was shaken free as the skeleton's hand retracted back through the hole it had made, swinging wide, just over Maddy's head. It collided with the boulder, knocking it free of its place to roll down the level below. Blunted screams filled her ears, followed by the awful squish of a body.

Maddy swallowed a harsh breath as the severed finger tumbled after it.

"Maddy!" Emerson climbed over the debris toward her. Before them, the tunnel was open to the coil, giving a view of a body falling past the exit. "What's happening?"

"If I had to guess, the skeleton used the key," she said, as an enormous foot, crackling with all the bones that made it up, shoved into the hole the fist had left. They watched as the skeleton heaved itself up, the top of its foot taking out the tunnel ceiling near the ledge just before them.

Stones and discordant music poured through the gaping cavity above them. One of the swim team girls came tumbling down the landslide, rolling between Emerson and Maddy, right off the ledge into a freefall.

"Come on," Maddy said. She led them toward the drop-off, glancing down over the chaos below for one dizzying moment. Levels had been broken through, people and debris sliding from one to the next. The skeleton's other foot kicked at the steamy level, knocking over a teapot the size of a van. It fell over the edge into the center, hot amber liquid spilling into the air before the bronze pot crashed to the sand below.

"I think he's pissed," Emerson said.

"You think?" Maddy grabbed her shoulder, yanking her up the incline. They climbed through the stones, dangerously close to the ledge, until they reached the party above. Chaos had erupted there. The nets fell from the ceiling as the skeleton's jaw opened wide to bite a chunk from the siding. It laughed again as a person rolled into its mouth, banging like a rag doll from rib to rib all the way down to its pelvis.

"There!" Maddy shouted.

A waterfall from the river above streamed from the broken ceiling. They raced toward it, jumping over people and rocks, until they came to a mountain of stone the creature had knocked free. Maddy ascended first, pulling Emerson over the avalanche until they reached the top.

"There!" Emerson shouted. Two torches appeared beside the river's edge, marking the shoreline. They sprinted toward them, the ground trembling beneath their feet.

Please be an exit, Maddy thought. *Please be an exit.*

"Jump," Maddy told her, as the skeleton laughed again.

They leapt off the shore. The hot water scalded her, soaking through her clothes. A current flipped her through the waves, dragging her deeper. She held fast to Emerson's hand, and put her feet in front of her to protect her body from any rocks.

Around the coil they went. Maddy swam hard to keep them to the outside, away from the treacherous funnels where the river bottom had been punched through to the level below. Emerson, not the strongest swimmer, grabbed at her, dragging her down, but she kept them afloat.

The way ahead turned dark. She looked back, her gaze landing on the skeleton's empty eyes, staring at her as her head bobbed under the surface.

The next time she came up to gulp a precious breath, the monster was gone.

OWEN

Owen's hands fumbled over the gray, cracked wall. Old plaster crumbled beneath his fingers. The wooden beam held solid. He scanned for the green passage flames but they were gone.

His friends were *gone*.

"Where is she?" Izanami gasped, frantic. "*Madeline*. Did you get the other cards from her?"

"My friends are stuck in your nightmare, and all you care about is this stupid game?"

He searched for a flicker of jade fire. Even a charred bit of wood.

"The game is all that matters!" Izanami pushed off the floor beside him, staggering into the wall. She snatched the onyx stone out of Owen's grasp, the end curving around Ian's palm in the shape of a comma. "Did you get the cards or not?"

"I did not." He glared at her, the chilled air a shock after the heat of the coils. "I must have forgotten to grab them before you pushed me through the gate!"

"It was closing. We were running out of time!"

"Time doesn't mean shit if we don't have the next card!"

She growled and pushed off the wall, muttering sharply. "Why would Madeline not follow? Leave that bald creature behind? The exit was right there! What mortal has no sense of self-preservation?"

Owen turned to find Izanami at the back of the room, bathed in eerie yellow light. Tension braided through him. He recognized the flat stone table behind her immediately. They'd returned to Meido—to the throne room of Izanami's palace. Their battle with the split-faced army and the giant spiders had left the back wall punched through, half the floor torn up, and the ceiling removed entirely, but he'd always remember the place where he'd watched

Ian's heart ripped out of his chest. Where Dax had changed to a yōkai, then back into a friend.

Was he here now? Was Dax still *Dax*?

"That bald creature's name is Emerson," Owen said as a new tremor tore through him. "And she has hair. She just keeps it short."

"In my time with the living, long hair was a sign of beauty," Izanami snapped. "I had the most radiant hair. Like a river made of midnight. It was the envy of all."

"Well things have changed in the last thirty trillion years," he tossed back. "Now it takes a lot more to be pretty than a trendy style."

"Such as?"

"I don't know, common human decency? Intelligence? Emerson's the smartest person I know."

"Then why did she get trapped behind that boulder?"

"It was a *trick*."

"Only a fool falls for tricks."

"Says the empress who's renting a body because she lost her own."

Izanami bared Ian's teeth, pushing herself off the wall with a sudden wave of fury. "And what of you? Are you intelligent, Owen? Are you brave? Interesting?"

His jaw flexed.

"Pretend you aren't vain all you like, but we both know you do not look that way by accident. You polish your physical body like a shield, because you know its gleam will deflect any arrows." Her smile was cruel. "But you will age, mortal. You will bruise and scar and *burn*. And when you do, no one will want you."

"Whatever you say," he told her, but he would have been lying if he'd said he didn't make an effort—okay, sometimes a colossal effort—to look good. Before they'd gone to Meido the first time, he'd been veering dangerously close to shallow, but he'd changed since then.

He adjusted his glasses higher up on his nose. Despite the cold, his palms were sweating, and he wiped them on his ash-stained pants.

Brand-name pants, perfectly fitted before the knees and hems had been burned off in Jigoku.

Doubt crept through his mind. Ian would have been better protected by Maddy's strength, or Emerson's brain. But instead, he'd gotten Owen. An actor. A guy whose finest quality was pretending to be someone he wasn't.

How could he have let them get separated, after they'd found one another in that hellish spiral? What was happening to them now?

How was he supposed to finish this without them?

He looked up, out the torn-off roof to the hazy gray sky. In it, a giant eye crested above the horizon, a sliver, the points up.

"It will be night soon," said Izanami, following his gaze. "We must get the remaining cards."

Before Ian's body fails, Owen realized. He looked to his friend, hating the soul inside it. Fearing what would happen if they didn't succeed.

"How are we supposed to do that?" Owen asked. "You have a way back to Jigoku I don't know about?"

"No," she admitted.

"Then I guess we're stuck waiting for my friends to show up," he said between his teeth. Maddy and Emerson were strong. Resourceful. They'd find a way out.

He hoped.

If they didn't, Ian would not survive.

"Your friends," she said slowly, in a way that made Owen very nervous.

She slid the first prize into Ian's pocket. Ian's hand was red where she'd been holding it, as if it had given him a sunburn. Owen didn't like that one bit.

"Come with me," said Izanami. "There may be another way to find the cards."

--◆--

The palace looked like earthquake remains he'd seen on news broadcasts. They had to pick their way over chunks of stone and jagged boards that thrust up from the remains of the staircase that hugged the mountainside. Dead leaves swirled at their ankles in a cold wind, bringing a rotten scent. His feet, still bare but healed from the coils, grew numb against the frigid ground.

"You keep looking over your shoulder like someone is following us," said Izanami, without glancing back.

The last time Owen had seen Dax, it had been at this palace. He'd helped Owen carry Ian to the passage gate that would take them home, but had stopped.

They're lucky to have you in their corner. I was lucky too. Luckier than that damn knife ever made me, anyway.

Owen's chest ached.

"I'm fine," he said gruffly.

The empress skirted around a gaping hole in the ground. It must have led to a room deeper in the palace—one now buried by debris.

They climbed up a boulder splattered with dried black streaks that might have been blood. Meido unfurled before them, a haze of gray blanketing a dead forest, cut down the center by a twisting river. In the distance, black birds dotted the sky. Tengu. They must have been circling the arena and picking off the players.

Beside Owen, Izanami gave a wistful sigh, almost as if she were fond of what she saw. He recalled the stone in Ian's pocket—Ian's red hand when she'd held it, and how his body was wearing down—and wanted to shake her.

This was no time to get sentimental. Ian's life was on the line. But there were so many things he didn't understand. This game was different, and he couldn't afford to make mistakes, especially without Emerson and Maddy here to take the lead.

"You said your husband made this game. Why?" Owen asked.

She climbed down the backside of the rock, and he hurried after her.

"Because he has a twisted sense of humor," she said.

"He broke the tomoe and set up challenges to protect them. Things you need a mortal to do."

"Correct."

"Why? If he wanted to stop you from getting the prizes, why let you have a partner? Why set up a challenge where the object is to help a bad guy? That's right in your wheelhouse. You probably help bad guys do bad shit all the time."

"What are you saying?"

"I don't know," Owen told her. "It's just that . . . Okay, if your husband really wanted to stop you from getting the jewel, wouldn't he have made you help someone, I don't know, nice? Do something against your nature? Instead he's giving you a teammate and a task to free a guy who eats bones for lunch. It's almost like he *wanted* you to complete that challenge."

Izanami hesitated before climbing down a section of stairway still intact.

"You underestimate his grudge," she said. "If he had wanted me to succeed, he would not have had me face my nightmare at all."

He supposed she had a point.

"What happened to you two, anyway?"

Ian's back stiffened. Owen felt the sudden urge to place his hand between his shoulder blades. Owen was a physical person by nature—comfortable with hugs, with the buddy arm squeeze, or a flirting skim of his fingers. But it was different with Ian. Since he'd come back from Meido, Owen had practically measured how close their knees were when they sat, and if he was walking too close, and how long to hold on to his hand when he helped him up from the beanbag in his room.

He wanted so badly to touch Ian now, but this wasn't Ian.

Izanami's pace quickened, and she hurried down the last stairs toward the back of the palace, smashed between the wreckage and the shale mountainside. Sandwiched in a pit of brown puddles were the remains of the hall of mirrors. Massive shiny black stones, taller than Owen and twice as wide, jutted out at odd angles. Some of the mirrors were cracked. Others shattered completely. Dust coated them, dulling their shine.

Chills rose on Owen's skin. This was the place where he, Maddy, and Emerson had witnessed their most dishonorable acts. Where he'd watched Dax spreading the cards in the cave when they were kids—the game that would lead to Ian being lost for four years in Meido.

Owen's gaze shot from stone to stone, searching for Dax now, but nothing moved here. An eerie quiet settled over them, the cold bringing a chill to Owen's skin. As he stepped closer, a hum of dread filled his veins.

"Do not touch the mirrors," she warned. "They have a way of drawing you in."

He stiffened, remembering how Maddy had fallen through the glass in the hall of mirrors, and they'd barely managed to pull her free.

Carefully, Izanami continued on. "If your friends survived Gashadokuro, we should be able to see them here."

Owen's pulse quickened.

A flickering of light on one of the glossy surfaces ahead caught his eye, and he stared up at the dark tinted mirror. But instead of seeing his friends in the glass, a man appeared, close enough that he seemed to be looking straight into Owen's eyes.

Owen jumped back, banging into the mirror behind him. It flashed white, then showed the same man, this time from the side. He was young—college age, and masculine, but not in a bro-ey, unapproachable way. His dark eyes were settling, calm, even if his jaw could cut glass.

He wasn't from their time. His pale blue kimono was plain but heavy, and fastened around the waist by a thick obi. His long black hair was tied in a knot at the base of his neck.

Wariness tightened Owen's throat as the man's dark beard framed a gentle smile.

"Who is that?" Owen asked as Izanami came beside him.

"The emperor."

"Your husband?"

She turned, striding through the ruins of the mirrors. They flickered to life around her, the way the lights came on in the freezer section of a supermarket when you passed. The emperor was everywhere then, his gaze tracking her with a fondness that made Owen feel like he'd just stepped into something very personal.

"He's not what I expected," Owen said.

"Did you expect horns and pointed teeth?" She ducked under two mirrors that had fallen against each other at the top, forming an A. "Not all demons look like monsters."

"Sometimes they look like Ian," he muttered.

She gave a snort.

"He's young," Owen said. When she hummed, he added, "I just thought you two had been around awhile, that's all."

"There is no need to age when you live forever."

He caught up with her. "Do you see Emerson or Maddy?"

She shook her head.

"What about Dax?"

Izanami paused. "Hoping for a reunion?"

"You sound surprised."

"He did betray you, did he not?" She blew some dust off a jagged mirror, looking away when the emperor appeared in it.

He frowned. "It's complicated."

"No," she said. "It isn't. One is either a friend or an enemy. There is no in between."

"Not much for forgiveness, are you?"

"Forgiveness is for cool tea and late arrivals. The rest falls to vengeance."

"Cut me in on the royalties if you ever print that on a bumper sticker," Owen muttered.

Ahead, the flickering mirrors changed to a different scene, and Owen hurried toward them, searching for some sign of his friends. A shoreline appeared, golden sands meeting ocean waves with white foamy tips. On a sparkling dune, two people stood. The emperor, barefoot in his kimono, and a smaller woman in a matching outfit.

Owen knew who she was before she turned toward them.

"That's you," he said.

Her long, loose braid hung over her shoulder beside a necklace bearing a heavy charm. A circle, cut in into three identical, curving sections.

"Is that . . ."

"The tomoe," she finished. "Wisdom, benevolence, and valor."

Izanami's expression was almost wistful as the young woman in the mirror turned and lifted her hands. At first, nothing seemed to happen, but as the seconds passed, the sand before her shifted, rising up to the sky.

In seconds, the two people were standing at the foot of a mountain.

"Whoa," said Owen. When he breathed in, he swore he could smell the freshly turned earth. "Did you . . . make that?"

"I made everything," she said quietly. "*We* made everything."

He squinted again at the pendant around her throat. It glowed on her skin, pulsing with light. One of the three sections gleamed black like the jewel she was now holding.

"The tomoe's energy was so raw, so eager . . . and I could direct it in any way I chose." Her voice sagged.

His gaze shifted to the necklace's other sections, which were gold and silver. "And you couldn't make less matchy outfits?"

She huffed. "For all the complexities he gave you, you remain so obtuse."

"He?"

"The emperor."

"That guy made me?" Owen pointed to the man in the glass. He had placed the tomoe around his own neck, and was now slowly swirling his hand to make a leaf. "Funny. He doesn't look like my dad."

"*That guy* is the lord of life," she said, her voice harsher than before. "The father of all fathers. Creator of the living. He is the reason you *exist.*"

Owen's brows rose as the leaf in the emperor's hand turned into a tree that sprouted skyward. As it took root, a forest spread, painting the mountain deep green. Fallen needles painted the ground, yellow and soft, a home for the insects and squirrels. Springs turned to streams, fish fed at the surface of the water. As the emperor blew the dust from his hand, a flock of white cranes flew over the water, their talons skimming the surface.

This was nothing like the tales of yōkai his mom had told him growing up, or the Bible stories he'd heard from friends who went to church. Watching Izanami and Izanagi work was wondrous. Proof of his being—of the *world's* being.

He shrugged, not wanting her to see how it moved him. "It almost sounds like you respect the guy."

With a growl, she turned, striding deeper into the wrecked maze. She passed a glowing red dawn. A den of foxes. A burst of white and magenta orchids. Emerald vines yielded fruit and crops. People in primitive clothing appeared, bowing deep before the empress and emperor. In the next mirror they were seated at low tables, sharing tea from bronzed kettles, poured by a woman who looked suspiciously like a young Shinigami.

"Wait," said Owen. The teapot was familiar—smaller, but the same he'd seen in Jigoku. The tables. The tatami mats beneath it. "That's one of the levels in your nightmare!"

No one looked upset here. No one was dying from drinking the scalding hot liquid. He spotted the emperor and empress at the front of the room, lifting cups to their lips. They looked . . . *happy*.

He glanced back to the first mirror, where the golden sand beside the sea glimmered back. His feet ached at the sight of it, memories of the way the hot ground had burned through his soles too close. "And that's the bottom floor. The hot sand." He turned until he found the forest, remembering how he'd been swallowed by the sharp pine needles and insects in Jigoku. "Your nightmares are real places?"

Izanami walked on, ignoring him. He ran to catch up.

"I thought the mirrors showed your dishonorable acts," he said. That's what had happened the last time they were here.

"It shows what you need to see."

"Why are we seeing the past?"

"I don't know." She crossed Ian's arms tightly over his chest. "Perhaps it is my husband's influence on the game. He means to torture me with what he took away when he locked me out of the living world and threw away the key."

Owen swallowed tightly, thinking of how Emerson had been locked behind that boulder, Gashadokuro's key their only salvation.

"Where are Emerson and Maddy?"

Izanami didn't answer.

"Is that the palace?" he asked, pointing ahead to an ancient house, stacked two-stories high by flaring roofs. It gleamed in the sun, simple but pristine, each beam and board sanded to a shine. Instead of being smashed against a cliffside, it stood on the mountain itself, overlooking endless miles of forest.

"Yes," she whispered. "Before it moved."

He remembered the tale from the last time they'd played the game. She'd created the passage to take a person from one place to another, but had accidently transported the entire palace and all inside it to Meido.

He could see inside one of the open sliders at the side, where a party was taking place. Long tables of food lined the walls. Mirrors hung from nets across the ceiling like stars. Musicians played in a corner while people in the center of the room danced.

Her entire life had become a nightmare.

He almost felt sorry for her.

A hiss came from up ahead. He ducked through two mirrors, hurrying toward the sound.

"Empress?"

Before him, the mirror was white with steam. It beaded against the glass, droplets of moisture covering the surface. The steam seemed to be all around him then, filling every glass wall, until only the sky above and the earth beneath him were not white and cloudy.

"Watch where you are walking!" Izanami shouted.

He stepped back, narrowly missing the mirror just before him. The steam cleared with his sudden movement, as if he'd been the one to cause it, and revealed a man sitting on a large, smooth stone, tan skin slick with perspiration. A woven towel rested on his lap, hiding his nakedness.

Owen cleared his throat, glancing back for Izanami, but she was not behind him. He looked again at the emperor, taking in the thick cords of muscle in his arms and thighs, and his impressive rippling abs. He had large hands, which he lifted to wipe the sweat from his brow.

Not Owen's type, but he could see the appeal.

"You look pleased, Emperor."

More steam cleared, and Owen made out Izanami, stretched out on the rock beside him.

She . . . did not have a towel covering her.

His cheeks heated. He felt like he should look away, but he couldn't. She was beautiful. Brimming with confidence. She rested on her side with one arm over her head, knees slightly bent and overlapped, like a person who was absolutely comfortable in their own body.

Propping up on her elbows, she smiled. Her face lit up, eyes bright, hair cascading over her back and waist.

Okay, she did have great hair.

The emperor chuckled, as if he found her too adorable for words, then pulled her higher and ravished her mouth in a kiss that had her fingers digging into his bare back.

She gasped, and the sound clenched Owen's chest.

He thought of the onsen in Jigoku. The bench they'd hidden behind that looked just like the one in this mirror. Had she been thinking of this moment when they were there burning? Talk about a mindfuck.

"Izanami," the emperor breathed. His hand worked down her waist and over her hip.

He stared at Izanami's throat, the long arching column that hummed with her pleasure. His gaze lowered to her collarbones, where the tomoe hung from a braid of seagrass, glowing with power.

The stirring of attraction warred with Owen's sense of reason. He didn't want the empress, but something about the lazy way she toyed with her hair in the steam made his heart trip. Her laugh was music, and sent warm shivers over his body. She pulled at Owen. He could see why the emperor had loved her.

"We cannot stay here all day," she said, her voice husky.

"We make the days," the emperor answered, trailing a finger down her throat. "We can stay here as long as we wish."

She kissed him again, but when she pulled back her eyes were wet.

"What is it?" he asked.

She smiled, and he dabbed a tear from her cheek, examining it on his finger as if it were precious.

"My joy is too great. It can only end in sorrow."

"Why do you say that?" He pressed the tear to his heart.

"I feel it," she said. "Like a wave coming to shore. We have made this world too perfect to last."

He kissed her closed eyes. One, then the other.

"I love you," he said. "Infinitely. Impossibly." He kissed her forehead. Her chin. "Enough that if you said the sky should be sea, and the sea, clouds, I would make it so, just to see you smile." He pulled back. "Your tears will call me across the universe, Izanami. And if there is sorrow, I will undo it, and you will feel joy again."

She smiled, and then laughed, the sound of it making Owen's breath catch.

"Enjoying yourself?"

He spun to find Izanami standing before him, Ian's arms crossed, jaw set in anger.

"Sorry," he mumbled. "I just . . . I wasn't . . ." He sidestepped, dropping his eyes to the ground.

"Thought you'd take in a little show?" she asked. "Bear witness to my humiliation?"

"No, I—"

"Is it so hard to believe I was once wanted? *Loved?*"

Owen felt something inside him crack.

"Of course not," he said.

She reached toward him and he jerked back, misunderstanding the shock in her eyes for anger, and the thrust of her hand for an attack.

He tripped, bumping into a panel at his side. The glass was cold against his shoulder, and then gave way. He tried to grab her outstretched hand for balance. It was too late. He fell back, through the mirror, landing on the hard ground in the dark. Dead branches from the trees crackled under his hands and feet as he scrambled up, and the scent of decay filled his nostrils.

"You found me." The woman's voice was rough, strained. Sickly.

He jumped to his feet, spinning to see who was talking, but there was only darkness. His breath came out in a wheeze. He touched his forehead, finding the skin cold and clammy.

"My love." A man's deep baritone came from his opposite side. He carried a small torch, lighting his grim expression. *The emperor.* "I'm here."

The woman groaned in pain.

Owen trembled in the dark.

"Turn around," the man told her as he approached a shadowed figure in rags. "Look at me, Izanami."

She turned, sending a shock through Owen. She was not the blinding beauty she had been before, but a rotting corpse, her flesh greened with disease and peeling off over her cheeks and collarbones.

Maggots feasted on the flesh there, and on one eye, which had grayed and was leaking pus.

"What is this?" The emperor stumbled back. "Who are you, demon?"

Owen's vision grew blotchy as he breathed faster.

"Your Izanami. Please. Please, my love."

"This is a lie," he growled. "What have you done with the empress?"

Blood dripped from the corner of her pale lips, but though the wounds looked excruciating, she did not cry. She seemed almost to revel in them. "It is me. I swear it. I am Izanami."

The emperor leaned slightly closer. "Izanami?"

She nodded. Her hair, once beautiful, was falling out in clumps. "I have brought death upon us. Kegare."

Dread curdled inside Owen. The emperor stumbled back, agape.

"Not us, Izanami. You have brought it upon yourself."

"My love?"

"I am not your love," he spat. "You have reached too far with your emerald flames. You always reach too far."

"That is not true," she said. "That is not . . ." She tried to touch him, but he jerked away.

"I will not be polluted," he said, hardening. "I have made too much to see it tainted by your obsessive need for more."

"You have made? You? Not we? Not me?"

He shook his head.

Izanami straightened, revealing the holes in her kimono and the bruised skin beneath. Owen felt himself straighten too.

Felt his breathing slow.

"You dare to speak to your empress with such venom," she whispered, her voice a frightening crackle. She spread her hands and orange flames leapt from them, circling them, around and around in a dizzying loop. The fire lit the blackened, leafless trees in the woods beyond them.

"I do not know you," the emperor said, horrified.

She laughed, high and forceful. Owen felt himself drawn closer to her, but the fire held him back.

"You will regret this day, Izanagi. I curse every living thing you have ever made with the poison of death. I curse it all to fade and fail with the same great force it took to come alive. I curse you to watch it, and suffer, knowing that none of your great creations will thrive into eternity, but will be destroyed like your fragile love for me."

Owen gasped, and was back on the cold ground of the hall of mirrors. His head was pounding, the words still echoing in his mind. He looked up into Ian's face, hard with Izanami's rage. She was laboring to breathe, one hand still fisted in his shirt.

She'd pulled him free from the mirror.

"I told you not to touch the glass."

Owen felt his face—the warmth, the softness of his skin, bringing a wave of relief. He looked up to Ian, to the empress, his chest aching with emotions he didn't understand.

"He left you," Owen said, standing. His mind echoed with what he'd heard. With what she'd said before they'd come to these mirrors. *But that body will age, mortal. It will bruise and scar and burn. And when it does, no one will want you.*

Izanami didn't answer.

"I—I'm sorry," he said.

I will not be polluted. The emperor had thought she was dirty. Disgusting. Ruined. He'd abandoned her because of how she'd changed. No wonder she thought no one would love her if she was ugly. No wonder she hated everything and everyone they'd made together.

It wasn't her who was polluted. He'd tainted life by his betrayal.

Owen grabbed her, and pulled her into his arms.

It wasn't just for her—he needed it too after what he'd felt. But as her frozen stance curved against him, he felt something twist inside him, fray with new emotions. She didn't hug him back exactly, but she rested a cheek against his shoulder. He squeezed her tighter, and she shuddered, and he could feel her give. Her vulnerability. Ian's vulnerability. It all braided together.

Slowly, he pulled back, and then they were kissing.

He wasn't sure how it happened. If he leaned in first or she did. All he knew was that he was pulling her closer, slowing the quiver of Ian's lips against his own, wanting to erase what had happened. Her abandonment. Ian's fear. His own ragged pain.

Izanami sighed, and the sound pummeled him. And as she raised a hand to his chest, his hold on Ian's face tightened.

Ian.

Owen staggered back.

"I'm sorry," he said, wiping his mouth with the back of his hand, as if that would get rid of the memory of her kiss.

She cocked a brow at him. *Ian's* brow.

"I'm sorry," he said again, though he wasn't sure if he was sorry for kissing her, or sorry to Ian for what felt a whole lot like cheating.

He didn't know what had come over him, only that he didn't feel like himself. His body wasn't working the way he wanted it to. She was smiling at him now. Smiling with Ian's mouth.

He hadn't meant to kiss her, hug her even. But even if he wanted to unsee the memory in the mirrors, he couldn't deny the feelings it had left behind. The need, still coursing through him, to ease her pain. The pity he'd felt when she'd reached for the man who shunned her. Even now, he could feel the jagged edges of his anger for her soften.

He bit the inside of his cheek, desperate for focus. The empress had taken over Ian, had hurt him—*was* hurting him. The only thing he should have been feeling for her was hatred.

She walked away, and he stumbled after.

"Your friends are here," she said harshly, stopping at the final glass. The frothy, steel-colored waters of a river filled the stone. At first, he didn't see anyone, but after a moment he caught sight of a head bobbing up above the surface.

"Emerson!"

Maddy joined her a moment after, arms churning through the water to keep afloat.

"We have to find them!" Owen said. "They need our help!"

"The river comes from depths beneath this land and runs all across Meido," said the empress. "By the time we reach this place they could be miles downriver. No. We'll intercept them somewhere else."

"Where?"

"Where would they go in Meido?" she wondered. "Where would your friends look for you here?"

He caught sight of Maddy, pulling Emerson around a sharp, gray rock jutting out from the river. He remembered sitting on the shore, shivering in the cold while their clothes dried by the fire. Him, Emerson, Maddy, and Dax.

"They won't look for me," he said. "They won't know where we are. If we're here, even. They'll go to Dax for help."

"Ah," said Izanami, in a way that made Owen feel like he had just said something very wrong.

"Show me the half-mortal, Dax," she said with a wicked smile. "Show me the cardmaker's child."

She stared into the black mirror, the reflection flickering to a dark building, the black ground around it slipping from side to side like a rug.

Not a rug. Spiders.

They covered the floor. The walls. The ceiling. Some as giant as cars. Others no bigger than a fingernail.

And in the center of them stood Dax.

DAX

Dax strummed a D chord, grinning to himself. It had taken fourteen tries, but he'd finally made a playable instrument. The prototypes were in a pile against the wall, some barely recognizable with their deformed bodies or uneven strings, but each a step closer to an actual guitar. He could still see how the songs he'd sung had painted notes on each card, feel the strain of holding that perfect six-stringed image in his head as the paper burned away to create what he envisioned. Now, he had the exact guitar he'd always wanted.

He was a cardmaker.

Lying on his back, the familiar weight of the instrument on his chest, he stared up at the glow worms that dripped from the cavernous ceiling of Kuchisake's basement. Their neon color lit the rough stone walls, and reflected off the hot spring near his feet. It wasn't awful down here—especially once he'd cleared the gazillion spiders out with some card-made insect repellent. The single entrance made it hard for someone to sneak in without his knowledge, and the quiet was a welcome break from his father and Kuchisake.

His grip slid down the fret. The strings pressed back against his calloused fingertips.

His smile faded as his gaze dipped to the gleaming surface of the hot spring. When Kuchisake had brought him down here, he'd made a point of telling Dax that Maddy had bathed there before their wedding.

He imagined her there now, and his whole body tightened.

He cleared his throat and stared back at the ceiling.

Strumming a C chord, he inhaled the scent of mildew.

"If I was stuck to anyone," he sang.

"I'd be stuck to you.

"I wouldn't let you slip away,
"My peanut butter glue."

Beside him, one of the cards he'd taken from his father shimmered with black ink. A music note appeared, dancing across the page, then bleeding out like watercolor. The edge of the card began to smolder. He hadn't yet figured out how to set a challenge like his father's cards—something that the card holder had to do in order to get the prize—but that was something Aka Manto had promised to teach him in time.

Setting the guitar gently on the pillows, Dax reached for the paper, and laughed as it burned away to a jar of creamy peanut butter. It was a little misshapen, but close enough.

"*Yes.*" He unscrewed the lid and dipped his finger inside. When he shoved it into his mouth he let out a moan that echoed off the low ceiling. He fell back again, kicking out his legs. He didn't need to eat to live—food wasn't much of an option in Meido anyway—but the taste of it reminded him of home. His new jeans fit perfectly. The Green Day shirt he'd made for himself stretched across his chest as he took another finger swipe.

Peanut butter. New clothes. A guitar he never would have been able to afford in the real world. He could have anything he wanted here. He could make his own damn mansion, and have fifty boxes of pizza a night, and no one would be able to stop him.

"You won't believe this," he said, imagining he was talking to Maddy. "But I met my dad. He's not a total dick after all."

Silence.

"He kind of looks like me. Or I look like him. Which is weird." He slung a hand around the back of his neck, massaging a tight muscle at its base. "Tomorrow, we're going out into the woods to practice cardmaking. Bigger stuff, I think." He laughed quietly. "Maybe I'll make a TV. Or a car? Not a lot of roads here." He sighed. "I could make those too. I could make anything I want."

He grew heavy, the words weighing him down.

Not anything.

Not a person, Aka Manto had said. *Not fully.*

His friends could be at The Bean now, the coffee shop down the street from Maddy's. Owen would have gotten some fancy drink.

Emerson, a double shot of espresso to keep her awake for a night of gaming. He imagined Ian laughing as he sipped a smoothie through a straw in the center seat of the booth they'd always gotten when they were kids. Maddy would be on the side by Emerson, drinking one of those Italian sodas with the whipped cream. They were probably talking about one of Owen's plays, or a movie they all wanted to go see.

Did they ever talk about him? Did they even remember him? For all he knew, they might have forgotten all about the yūrei kid they once knew. He could have faded from their minds, the way the peanut butter card's ashes disappeared into the dark.

His palms grew hot. Then his throat. A clench beneath his collarbones had him sitting up fast, and he hurled the jar of peanut butter against the wall. It shattered, leaving a sticky mess of glass shards oozing down the rough stones.

His shoulders heaved with each harsh breath. The rush of air in his lungs was a reminder that he was still half human. Kuchisake didn't have to breathe. Aka Manto never got winded, or needed to rest.

Dax wasn't like them. He would never be like them. Just like he'd never been like his friends at home.

He scrambled up, grabbing the neck of his guitar. He swung the instrument over his shoulder. Who cared if he smashed it? He could just make another. And another. And a billion more, because that's what he could do. He could make things.

"Where is your son now?"

A low, familiar voice came from upstairs, prickling his nerves.

"He is enjoying his newfound skills," answered Aka Manto.

Dax set the guitar down quietly and crept around the hot spring. At the end of the room, crude, rocky stairs led to the corridor outside the main hall. Kicking aside a few scuttling spiders the size of his fist, Dax crept up the steps, his lucky knife—the valor piece of the tomoe, according to his father—blade out.

"He has embraced his true calling, just as you hoped," the low voice said. "How fortunate you are here to teach him your ways. I thought you might never return from Jigoku."

With a scowl, Dax flattened himself against the wall outside the room and glanced in. Near the empty throne, an old woman hunched beside Dax's father, the ragged sleeves of her black kimono waving as she reached to pet one of Kuchisake's many giant spiders.

Shinigami.

Dax cringed, remembering the steam kiss from the last time they met.

"If not for Dax, I would still be there," said Aka Manto gravely.

Dax flinched. Aka Manto had said that he and Shinigami were friends, but seeing them together, especially after Shinigami had tried to seduce Dax via a steam Maddy for cards, didn't exactly make him feel all warm and fluffy inside.

"We need the tomoe, Aka Manto," said Shinigami.

"The plan is already in motion," Dax's father replied quietly. "The cards have been made. The game is being played." He swept his arm toward the giant's eye, visible through the broken paper walls. The lid slumped, a third of the way closed.

"We cannot count on players to handle the pieces of the tomoe. Not after last time. We must open the gate ourselves."

"The emperor has forbidden it. The challenges must be completed by mortals."

Shinigami shoved the spider away. "The emperor will do everything he can to keep us out of our rightful home."

"He will fail," Aka Manto responded, with a certainty that made goose bumps rise on Dax's skin. "The players already have one prize. They will come here for the next."

"Valor," said Shinigami. "You still have it?"

Dax froze. He looked down at the knife in his hand, at the small, worn comma in the handle.

"I promised the empress I would guard it, did I not?" Aka Manto's grin was chilling.

A buzz filled Dax's ears.

"We may not be able to complete the challenges ourselves, but if we control the players, we control the game," his father continued.

"And we can open the gate to the world of the living ourselves," said Shinigami.

Dax flinched. The world of the living. *Our rightful home.*

They were trying to cross over, the way the empress had wanted to in the last game.

Panic beat through his temples. *That's* why Shinigami had wanted cards? To cross over? Izanami wasn't even around anymore.

"How long has it been since you have seen the sun, Shinigami? Since you ate food that wasn't spoiled and drank tea that wasn't cold?" Aka Manto mused.

Shinigami chuckled. "Old friend, you are full of surprises. Soon, we will be reunited with all we love. And punish all those who kept us from it all these long years." She shot him a knowing glance. "I suspect your mortal lover will be glad to have you home."

Dax's mouth went dry.

He pictured his mom rocking in a chair in her scrubs at Tri-county Wellness Center, unaware of the danger she was in. If Shinigami got her wish, and they went to their *rightful home*, Aka Manto would find Vera.

Dax couldn't believe he'd been so stupid. Aka Manto had been using him from the start—since he'd first tried to put this stupid knife in his possession.

To think Dax had almost fallen for that father-son bonding bullshit.

He gripped the knife tighter, the metal imprinting in his fist. He could deal with his father later. Now, he had bigger problems.

Players were coming here for his knife.

His father and Shinigami planned on taking it for themselves.

If they got it, Dax would forget who he was. He'd sink into the evil of this place, forgetting his friends and his mom, his life in the land of the living. He would become a full yūrei, and then nothing would stop him from haunting Maddy the way Aka Manto had haunted him.

He might hurt her. Kill her.

He could try to protect the knife—but his father and Shinigami were stronger than he was. They could take it if it came to a two-on-one fight. For all he knew, this piece of the tomoe might be stripped from his possession as soon as the valor card in this stupid game was solved.

He couldn't let this piece get into the wrong hands.

There was only one answer. He had to get rid of the knife. To hide it somewhere even he couldn't find it.

His wrist burned suddenly, as if he'd pressed a flame to his wedding scar. He hissed out a breath. Looking down, he found the puckered mark red, and hot to the touch.

"You still feel her." Dax spun to find Kuchisake leaning against the wall behind him, his jade kimono tied loose around his waist, one shoulder protruding from the open collar. How long had he been there? Dax hadn't heard him sneak up. From behind him came a slow tapping of spider legs, and the thick, hairy body of one of his many spiders.

"Kuchisake." Dax pressed on a smile. "What are you doing here?" He quickly stepped away from the door, but from the sudden silence in the hall beyond, he was sure his father and Shinigami had heard him.

"I found these cards," said Kuchisake, the stretch of his elongated mouth releasing a droplet of blood down his left cheek as he held out a stack of unmarked paper that had been tucked inside the obi tied around his waist. "I thought we might try to make our own game. I would so like the chance to earn a human head as a prize."

"Ah," said Dax. "Can't make people. Or . . . parts of people."

Kuchisake frowned. "That's a shame."

"Sure is. But I don't make the rules."

He backed toward the door, the knife still in his fist. Kuchisake followed.

"Then a doll, perhaps? With poison on its lips? So when little children kiss it they instantly go mad."

"That's . . . creative." He took another step back. "What do you mean, I still feel her?"

Kuchisake's gaze dropped to the knife in his hand.

"That mark from your wedding night. The blood we spilled."

"*You* spilled," Dax corrected, still moving backward as Kuchisake stalked closer. "But yeah. I remember."

"It binds you for eternity. You and your sweet Maddy."

Dax didn't like him talking about her, not after what he'd just heard in the other room. "She's gone."

"But not out of your body. Just as you are not out of hers." Kuchisake tapped his own wrist. "She sings to you. A song of fear."

Dax went still. "What do you mean, fear?"

"That is where terror lives—in the blood. You feel hers. She feels yours."

Dax's heart began to race.

"Hold on," he said. "If Maddy's afraid, that means she's in trouble."

"Indeed," Kuchisake said, fingers trailing over his living spider necklace. "What is it like? I did not share my blood with her, as much as I may have wanted to." He smiled, a hungry look filling his dark eyes. "But if you cut yourself now with that blade, perhaps I will still have a little taste of her."

Dax's muscles coiled as Kuchisake's gaze lowered to his knife, his steps quickening, like he was suddenly moving in fast forward.

"I'll pass. But thanks for the offer." Dax backpedaled quickly as the spider climbed the wall beside its master.

In the shadows at the entrance of the hall, Aka Manto appeared. He narrowed his eyes on Dax.

Kuchisake frowned. "Are you certain? I could do it. I think I would like to touch the blade that has brought such great fortune." He was getting close enough that Dax could smell the rotten flesh on his face. "I think I would like to hold it awhile."

Alarms blared between Dax's temples. Kuchisake was in on Aka Manto and Shinigami's plan. For all Dax knew, they'd been working together from the beginning.

"Maybe later," Dax said, catching his father's cold gaze down the hall for just a moment, before tracking the spider's quick approach, upside down, on the ceiling of the corridor. "But I've got a hot date with a tengu, and you know how those birds get when you're late. Don't want to ruffle feathers, if you know what I mean."

He turned, and ran.

"Stop him!" shouted Shinigami.

The spider caught up with him at the end of the hall, one long, hairy leg jabbing down to block the sliding door. Dax swung his knife, cutting through the end of it. The spider's mouth clicked loudly, close enough to Dax's arm to make him retract his wrist in terror. As he reached for the door, the spider shot ropes of webbing to seal the exit.

Dax used the blade to cut through the sticky mess, slowed, but not stuck. It clung to him as he pushed through, and, with a grunt, rolled to the ground outside.

Small spiders scattered, or were crushed beneath his body. Aka Manto grabbed his ankle. Dax kicked free of him only to find Shinigami blocking the path through the house's broken outer wall into the forest behind.

From a fold of her black kimono she removed an old ceramic teapot, the tip already spouting steam.

"Shit," said Dax.

A puff of white air grew into a cloud, and in an instant he was surrounded by a dozen Shinigamis, each as realistic and solid-seeming as the real thing. They took on various offensive stances, some with hands raised for a fight, others baring their teeth or crouching low to pounce.

"You don't want to leave, Dax," said Aka Manto, his voice more like the yūrei Dax remembered crawling from the toilets than the man who'd smiled with pride when he'd made his first card.

"You're right," said Dax, betrayal chased by another bolt of rage as he stood. "I'd rather stay and kick your ass, but you know. Places to go. People to see." He flinched as Kuchisake approached on his other side. He was still holding the cards in his hand. For a moment Dax considered trying to use one to make some sort of weapon, but no music filled his head.

"Steam," he said to himself. When Shinigami had created the tea-steam Maddy in the cave, she hadn't been solid—he'd reached through her. These Shinigamis couldn't hurt him.

But as he stepped forward, one attacked, planting a kick in his gut.

He heaved out a breath, stumbling backward as the steam woman dissipated into the air. In her place on the outside of the ring, another Shinigami appeared, smiling wickedly.

"Nice trick," he managed.

"Stay long enough, and you may learn some too," all of the old women replied as one.

He shivered.

"Put down the knife, son," said Aka Manto from his left side.

Son. The word burrowed into him. He gripped the knife tighter.

"I don't think I will."

"You don't need to be difficult."

"You don't need to be an asshole."

"Such a mouth!" Kuchisake cheered. "That is our Dax, is it not?" The Shinigamis drew closer, cutting off his view of the wall and woods beyond. There was only the cold steam of their bodies, and the harsh scent of over-brewed rice tea.

"The knife," they growled. "Put it down, or we will take it from you."

"You can try," Dax told her.

He crouched, then pushed off the ground with all his strength, flinging himself into the air into a backflip. With a crash, he landed on the sloped roof of Kuchisake's house. Clay tile sprayed through the air as his foot punctured a hole into a great hall below. Scrambling up before he fell through, he dodged out of the way of two spiders who'd emerged from one of the rooms on the second floor. The hairy body of one brushed the side of his face, its clicking teeth loud in his ears as he rolled down the slope toward the ground.

One of the Shinigamis leapt to the roof to block him, her wrinkled hands outstretched, her gums bared in fury. With a grunt, he swung the knife, connecting with her shin. She evaporated just before the blade made contact, another appearing in her stead to elbow Dax in the chin. He fell back with a grunt, head slamming into the tile. White spots scattered across his vision before a sandaled foot pressed against his throat.

Another Shinigami looked down at him, grinning, her steam eyes black. Puffs of smoke came off her shoulders, her bound hair. He twisted, loosing himself from her hold, and sliced at another of her warriors with the knife. She disappeared before he made contact.

Backing up, Dax ran, and launched himself over the yard to the broken bricked wall surrounding the property. He glanced back for just a moment, long enough to see Aka Manto's narrowed gaze.

Without looking back, Dax ran into the forest. Trees slashed at his clothes and skin as he raced by. He could hear the chatter of spiders behind him, the scream of Shinigami's rage as she ordered her steam selves to follow. In the sky, a dark cloud blotted out the giant's eye, but when he looked up, it was only a monstrous tengu, searching for prey.

He ran until the woods were so thick he could barely see beyond the dead, knotted brambles. Then he fell to his knees, gasping for breath.

His scar was burning. Maddy was in trouble. To help her, he'd need to remember who he was. He'd need to keep ahold of the knife—it was the only way he could stay himself and not a yūrei.

But she wasn't in Meido. She was home, and he couldn't help her.

He closed his eyes, willing his frantic thoughts to slow.

If he gave up the valor piece to Shinigami and Aka Manto, Meido would spill out into the living world. Whatever trouble Maddy was in now at home, that would be worse.

Wouldn't it?

Curling his fist, he punched himself in the thigh.

He couldn't help Maddy if he kept the knife—whatever trouble she was in in her world, she would have to handle it on her own. She was the most brave and capable person he knew. The only way he could keep her safe was to keep the gate to Meido closed.

"I'm sorry," he told her.

He tore a piece of bark from a tree, then knelt and set it on the ground before him. It wasn't a card, but he knew it would still work. It had to.

As he held the knife to his chest, a dry sob built in his throat. He cleared it away with a cough. This was no time for grief. Shinigami and her steam guard, and Kuchisake and his spiders, would be here any moment.

He needed to make to make a card—a real one, with a challenge. An impossible task. It was the only way he could help her.

He closed his eyes, his voice uneven as he summoned Maddy's smile one last time into his mind. He held her there, and it was easier than imagining the perfect guitar. She was already burned into his memories, never far from reach.

It's been you from the day we met.
You who I'll love through it all.
Only you have the valor to hold what I hold
Let it stay out of sight till you call.

Was it enough? Was he doing it right? The things he'd made before felt so trivial all of a sudden. Guitar. Clothes. Peanut butter. They were party tricks. This had to work.

He opened his eyes to watch the notes dance across the smooth underside of the gray bark canvas. His tears fell onto it, blending it into the wood.

A spark lit in the center, burning a hole into the makeshift card. It worked outward like a spiral, bits of ash flying into the air as the orange embers ate their way around and around.

He knew the moment the knife was gone. He didn't have to look into his empty hand. His palm turned cold, his fingers numb. The chill spread down his limbs, across his chest, swallowing him in gulps, until his mind, too, was cold.

Cold, and sharp, and hungry.

Yūrei.

A crackling came from behind him, and he smiled, turning slowly, hopeful for a fight.

"Dax?"

He blinked. The name was familiar. *Dax.* Yes, his name was Dax.

The boy before him was also familiar. A player, likely. His clothes were burned and torn. His hair, dark. He wore glasses that magnified his mortal look of surprise.

"Hello," Dax said. He stepped closer, sensing the boy's fear. Tasting it on the back of his tongue.

Bitter.

Delicious.

The boy wasn't alone. There was another beside him. Tall. Slender. Weak and stumbling, but somehow still powerful, even in its lessened state.

A strange presence.

Dax turned back to the boy with glasses, breathing in his wariness. With a smile, he stepped forward. A predator, ready to chase his prey.

"What happened?" the boy asked. "Dax, it's me."

Dax held open his hands. "I see that."

"Wait," said the boy. "He's changed. He—"

Dax moved faster than the boy could anticipate. He wrapped his hands around the mortal's fragile neck, squeezing just enough to make him terrified, but not enough to kill him. He wanted to make this last. He was very hungry, and nothing tasted sweeter than mortal fear.

The boy tried to knock his arm free, but failed.

"Dax, listen to me. It's Owen, it's your friend."

Dax laughed. He had no friends. He smacked the boy—Owen—to the ground. Owen was up fast, and stumbled back. Dax sniffed the air with a groan. The scent of his terror was stronger now. Dax could taste it. He wanted more.

"That's enough," said the companion. "We do not have time for this."

Dax stopped, compelled by some deeper voice within him. He turned to the companion with a sneer, but the look melted from his face. There was a weight in this being's command, and through the taste of mortal decay in the air around him—skin and sweat and pulsing, living blood—he could make out the undeniable scent of death.

With his yūrei ears, Dax listened. An uneven heartbeat filled his ears, not quite mortal, but not immortal either. Like his, but heavier, a punch of thunder. He peered at the boy's chest, past the coat of flesh to the organ that drew him, and he traced its hard black outline with his eyes, noting the bulging veins around it that seemed to writhe with objection to every pump.

He dropped to his knees, commanded by this heart that was not his own. He felt his will strip away, his mind remade to a creature of compliance. It was not an unfamiliar state; he'd been like this before.

He was a weapon of the empress, protecting her from the players who meant to keep her from returning to the living world.

He belonged to her.

"Empress," he murmured.

He bowed until his forehead touched the rocky ground, and his mind was empty.

"We're looking for some mortals who call you friend," she said. But he didn't understand. He didn't have friends. "They will come to you with something I need."

He lifted his head and met her dull, mortal eyes.

"Then I will take it," he said.

She patted his head and smiled.

EMERSON

Exhaustion burned through Emerson's muscles as she crawled up the bank of the muddy river. The water had flipped her through the current, and smashed against the rocky shore. Every part of her felt bruised and scraped. It was a wonder she hadn't drowned.

Beside her, Maddy was laid out face down, one cheek pressed to the rough sand. Her feet were still in the water—she'd lost a shoe at some point, and her ankle sock was covered with mud.

"Where are we?" Emerson gasped, searching the boulders and fallen trees that lined the shore for signs of danger. Before them, dull gray woods blended into shadows. White and black grains of sand seemed to absorb the sunlight above, rather than reflect it. A shiver raked through her. The air was cold, fogging in front of her mouth. Not the oppressive heat from before.

"As long as we aren't where we were, I don't care," Maddy groaned, still flat against the sand.

"Aren't you a swimmer?" She moved closer to Maddy's side. "That should have been cake for you."

"Cake?" Maddy sat up, sand stuck to the side of her face. "*Cake?* That wasn't swimming, that was white water rafting, only *I* was your raft."

To keep her head above water, she'd had to cling to Maddy like a frantic cat.

"I navigated."

"You steered me into a rock. Multiple rocks."

"Did you complain this much on the swim team?"

Maddy's jaw tightened. "I never complained."

Emerson quirked a brow. She remembered the girls in their swimsuits in the top coil, talking shit about Maddy. Had that really happened? It seemed wrong. Maddy was an all-star athlete. She'd placed at state competitions. She was *popular.*

Wasn't she?

"Is that . . ." Maddy's eyes lifted over Emerson's head. Emerson turned, looking over the dead trees that lined the shore to a sliver moon, resting on its back.

Or a giant's eye.

"Meido," Emerson said, laces tightening between her ribs.

"Dax." Maddy pushed herself to a stand. She gripped her opposite wrist, her thumb pressing to the scar she'd gotten in her wedding ceremony.

"Hold on." Emerson climbed up after her. "What about Owen and Ian? We need to find them."

"Dax can help us find them."

"We don't even know where Dax is!"

"The palace," said Maddy. "Maybe he stuck around there, found shelter."

"With the spiders? And tengu? And the horde of players? Maybe you forgot, but the last time we were there it was basically the end of the world."

Maddy was smiling.

Emerson slumped. "Why? Why do you look so happy?"

"We're here. We made it." She gripped Emerson's shoulders, squeezing them tightly. "Don't you see? We escaped the last challenge without going through a portal. We found a cheat code!"

"That's not what a cheat code is."

"A glitch in the game, then. We got past the skeleton, and now we're going to find Dax, and Owen and Ian, and we're going to all get the hell out of here for good!"

Emerson exhaled a puff of steam. "That easy, huh?"

"Come on, Captain Carroway." Maddy leaned closer. "You can celebrate a tiny bit. I won't tell anyone."

Emerson's fingers pressed against her temple. She didn't feel like celebrating. Where was the next challenge? The last time they were here each gate had led them to the next task. Now they were separated from their party, the first prize with Owen and Ian, while she and Maddy held the two remaining cards.

Emerson shoved her hand into the wet pocket of her pants for the cards, but felt only a clump of cold sand. "Oh no."

"What?"

She turned her pockets inside out. "They're gone. The cards are gone."

"Where are they?"

"If I knew that they wouldn't be gone!" Emerson spun toward the water, her wet shirt clinging to her chest and shoulder blades. "I . . . I must have lost them in the water."

The river was as wide as a four-lane highway, deep enough that she'd never touched the bottom. The current was fast. The waves that slapped the protruding stones spewed up white foam. She'd lost track of how long they were in the water—minutes? An hour? The cards could be anywhere.

"Okay." Maddy's breaths grew faster. "Maybe they washed up on shore."

"Where?" Emerson's voice was higher.

"I don't know, but we can find them. You found them in Owen's room, right? The game wants us to play. It wouldn't make us do it without cards."

"Okay," said Emerson. She was right.

They began to look along the shore, staying close. They picked through the rocks, dug under the sand. She looked to Maddy, wet hair tied in a knot at the back of her neck, her face set in concentration. Her confidence, even now, made Emerson envious. Ever since they'd returned from the first game, she'd been more herself, comfortable in her own skin in a way Emerson wished she could be.

Except for when she'd faced her teammates in the party coil.

"What happened on the swim team?" Emerson asked.

Maddy looked up. "What do you mean?"

Emerson went back to her search. She felt suddenly like she was reaching out to touch a cactus. "You always seemed so happy in the pool."

Maddy had joined the team freshman year. She'd had new friends to sit with at lunch. Her name had been posted in the hall under Academic Athletes.

She'd gone from middle school weirdo to someone everyone

in high school knew. And that had happened *before* Emerson had dropped out. She could only imagine how Maddy's rep had grown when she'd gone to regionals, then state.

"I was happy," said Maddy. "When I was swimming."

Emerson stiffened—an automatic defensiveness. There was a lot of time between entering a locker room and getting in a pool.

"And when you weren't?"

Maddy shrugged.

Emerson's neck muscles drew tighter.

"You haven't talked about practice in a while."

"I haven't gone in a while."

Emerson looked up. "You quit?"

"I was busy."

"Looking for Dax, you mean." She didn't mean her tone to sound so hard, but it just felt like another thing she'd hidden from Emerson, like looking for Dax's mom, and planning her return to Meido.

"That was your ticket to college," Emerson said. Maddy had great grades, sure, but she was the full package. Dropping out of a team sport senior year didn't exactly look great on her college apps.

"Things change."

"I know you're not telling me you're throwing away your future for a guy."

"Thanks, Mom."

"I mean it."

"I know," Maddy said. "I love him."

Emerson paused. It was so simple the way she said it. So factual. Like someone saying water was wet.

Jealousy flared inside her. Not of Dax, and not because Emerson wanted anyone to love her that way. But because love, whatever that really meant, was so simple for Maddy. She could feel something, and act on it, without a hundred different disaster scenarios playing through her mind. She could say, "I love him," like it was a good enough reason for doing anything, while Emerson could barely sputter the words to her own parents.

Why did emotions have to be so stupid?

"They hated me." Maddy went back to her search for the cards. "My teammates. They never liked me."

Her quiet tone put Emerson on guard.

"Why?"

"Because I'm good. Because I don't look like them. Because I'm getting scholarship offers and they're not. Because the coach likes me. Take your pick."

Heat prickled on Emerson's skin. "That stuff they were saying in the coils, that really happened?"

Another shrug, this one stiff. "They messed with me sometimes. It wasn't a big deal."

"Bullying is a big deal. Did you tell anyone?"

"You. Now."

"That's not what I meant. A teacher? Your coach?"

"What would they do that wouldn't make everyone hate me more?"

Emerson supposed she had a point. "And you never told them to go fuck themselves?" She couldn't imagine Maddy taking shit from anyone.

"I own how good I am, and they think I assume I'm better than them. I downplay it, and I'm lying to get attention. And god forbid I actually tank—then I'm just letting down the team." She gave a half-grin. "I did rip the seam on Angela Lacey's suit before regionals junior year."

Emerson smiled. She'd seen that before, when the black mirrors in the empress's palace had shown them their least honorable acts.

"She deserve it?"

"That, and then some."

"I would have lit her suit on fire."

"Subtle."

"Effective."

"I'll visit you in prison someday."

"Make sure to sneak me in a shank."

"Make one out of your toothbrush. I'll bring you cigarettes that you can trade for commissary credit."

"Sounds like you've thought a lot about this."

"I have known you since the fourth grade."

Maddy grinned.

Emerson grinned back.

After a moment, Maddy nodded. "I'd rather go through Hell for someone who loves me than stay anywhere else with people who don't." She shrugged. "So the way I see it, I'm not throwing away anything."

The heat that had been climbing Emerson's throat went suddenly cool.

She was here because of Maddy, and she would come here again without a second's hesitation if her friend needed her. If that's what Dax meant to Maddy, then he would mean that much to Emerson too.

They had to search for him. Maddy was right. People you cared about—that you trusted—were few and far between. When you found them, you didn't let them go, even if it meant ending up here.

"Forget about your teammates," said Emerson. "You think stupid Angela Lacey could survive what we just went through? Not a chance."

Maddy took off her shoe, examining the broken laces before tossing it aside. "You would have drowned her in the river."

"*On accident.*" Emerson made air quotes.

Maddy laughed. "I see a gold star for Inmate of the Month in your future."

Emerson posed for the make-believe mug shot, and after Maddy took her pretend picture, Emerson sighed.

"We should split up, we'll cover more ground."

"I'll go downriver, you go up?"

Emerson didn't like the idea of splitting the party, but they didn't have time to delay. The giant's eye was closing. She didn't know if it measured their time in this game like the last, but she didn't want to see what happened if they failed to finish the challenges before dark.

"Stay near the water, don't go in the trees," she said. "Take one hundred paces, then come back to check in."

Maddy grabbed a stick off the ground, and wedged it between ragged boulders to mark the place. "If you run into trouble, call out. I won't be far."

They shared one last glance, then Maddy rushed downriver, keeping her gaze on the shoreline.

Goose bumps rose on Emerson's skin as she watched her go—

the cold blending with a sinking sensation that planted her heels deeper in the wet sand.

She forced herself to turn upriver.

"One. Two. Three." She counted her steps aloud under her breath to make sure she didn't go too far, her gaze darting from the shore to the shadowed trees. "Four. Five." The cards could be anywhere. Owen and Ian could already be facing the other challenges, waiting for one of the cards they didn't have to turn into a prize.

"Fifteen, sixteen, seventeen." She turned over a rock with her hands, finding a pocket of wriggling black eels in the shallow pool below. Her breath grew choppy. She kept searching.

"Thirty-two. Thirty-three." She thought of Ian and Owen, going on to the next level without them. Leaving her behind, like they'd left her behind in Owen's room before the game had started. Getting out of the coils had been the right choice, but that didn't make her feel any better about it. She wouldn't have left them.

At sixty, she glanced back over her shoulder, but Maddy was out of sight. The river had curved—maybe she was behind the bend. Emerson thought about calling out, but she didn't want to risk drawing attention unless she absolutely had to.

She turned back, and a person was standing before her.

His face was strange. Distorted. A mask of different faces crudely sewn together.

She opened her mouth to scream, but before the sound left her lips the intruder's cold hand was there, blocking the sound. She stumbled backward, but was caught by a branch that stretched from the nearest tree, sending prickly pine needles down the back of her shirt. In an instant, the branch had forked into vines, trapping her body in a wooden cage.

"No need for that, my dear. No need." The low voice was warped with age. Emerson fought the urge to retch at his fetid breath—it smelled as if he'd eaten something rotten.

As he tilted his head, the light caught his mask. It was skin—she could see that now. Layers of peach and brown and beige. Wrinkles on some pieces, bushy brows and beard hair on others. The strips were stitched together by strands of hair.

His patchwork kimono blushed as he stroked his hand down his chest.

Keneō.

The skin tailor of Meido.

Dread balled in Emerson's gut. She had to scream for Maddy, but the old man's grip was like iron—she could barely turn her head, he had her smashed so tightly against the branches.

"You have returned to me," said Keneō. "I was hoping you would. You do have such beautiful cheeks. They will make a fine obi. The stretch is just right." He clucked in excitement.

"Let me go," she muffled against his hand.

"What's that? It is hard for this old man to hear you."

"Let. Me. Go!"

With a chuckle, he pulled back his hand. The branches around her tightened as she filled her lungs the scream, allowing only a wheeze to come out. Her thoughts grew frantic as he reached for a knife tucked in his belt. The blade caught the gleam of the giant's eye as he lifted it, momentarily blinding her.

Wisdom. Valor. Was this one of the challenges? She didn't have the cards to change even if she succeeded.

"The light dances so nicely across your skin," he said. "I should tailor a one-of-a-kind piece from it when I finally see the sun."

Emerson struggled, but her branch prison held solid.

"In a hurry to get started?" Leaning heavily on his cane, Keneō lifted the knife to her temple. "Now, this works easier if you hold still. But it is not completely necessary."

Keneō's skin mask began to slip. Blood dotted his forehead where it had been stuck to his own face. As it sagged, the hole for his right eye drooped, blocking his sight. He shoved it back up with his forearm before extending the knife toward her face.

"You don't want to do that!" she blurted out as the tip of the blade touched her jaw.

"Do not worry, I will let nothing go to waste." He tucked his cane under one arm and squinted at her, as if trying to find the perfect point to puncture her face. His tongue squirmed from the corner of his mouth in concentration.

"We're playing the game!" she confessed.

Keneō stilled.

"We already have a prize."

"So it's true." Keneō lowered the knife. "The benevolence card has been solved. Two more pieces and the tomoe will be complete."

Her heart stalled. "What's the tomoe?"

"An object of great power." He leaned closer. "I should like it in my possession."

"Then let me go. I'll get it for you."

He laughed, a low menacing sound.

"I am not a fool, pretty thing. If I let you go, you will run away like you did last time you were in my home, and I will be no closer to having the first prize."

The old man raised his blade again.

"My friends cannot complete this game without me!" she shouted. "They need me to solve the challenges. You think they can do it on their own? They'd still be here from last time without me."

It felt wrong to say the words, but they weren't a lie. She was a crucial part of this team.

A crucial part, which they all had left behind at one point or another.

His hand stilled. Slowly lowered.

He tucked his knife away.

"You will come with me," he said. "And if what you say is true, your companions will come for you, and bring the prize with them." He laughed again. "The empress will be so pleased when I present her with it."

Emerson went cold. "She's . . . still around?"

"Of course she is," snapped Keneō. "She's close now. I can feel her. A change in the air." He sniffed it like a dog. "Once she has the tomoe, her full power will be restored, and she will open the gate to the living world." He sighed, pointing to the sky. "By the time that eye closes we will have returned to the land of sunlight."

The sun. He'd mentioned it earlier. She thought he'd meant the giant's eye.

Of course. The game had changed, but the object was the same.

The empress wasn't dead—she was still here, trying to open the gates of Meido. To spread death to the living world.

If Owen and Ian had known about this tomoe, why had they restarted the game? Did they know how it was meant to end? Had that reptile with the bowl head forced them to play? Why?

She had too many questions and not enough answers.

Keneō sighed. "And if your friends do not come, well, I can always offer the empress your skin."

Keneō placed the end of his cane on the ground. The branches around her legs began to retract with a wave of his hand. "Come with me. It's time we visited my old friends." He smiled, the mask rising only on one side. "And before you think of running, know that the branches of my trees will catch you, wherever you try to go."

Keneō ambled up a path on the shore toward the trees, turning back when she didn't follow.

"Are you coming?"

She searched one final time for Maddy, and when she didn't see her, dropped down to pick up a sharp rock. It was small enough to fit in her fist. Not a great weapon, but better defense than nothing.

As they crossed the tree line, the smell of rancid meat grew strong enough to make her gag. The shadows grew long around her. Swatches of skin hung from the trees, blocking the giant's eye. She had seen them last time she was with Keneō in the woods, but now there were so many more. A dozen times as many pieces of arm and thigh and back. Small scraps of faces were piled in bowls against the trunks of the trees. The ground was littered with eyeballs and other pieces that could not be used—broken bones or burned and scarred skin.

"I have had many visitors since you left," Keneō told her, looking back through his sewn mask.

Emerson could only nod.

She glanced back, but Maddy was not following. Would she know where she had gone? For all Emerson knew, she could have found her own trouble.

She could have gone for Dax.

No. Maddy would come for her.

Her fist tightened around the rock in her hand. Turning it so that the sharp end protruded, she slowed her steps until Keneō had a comfortable lead. Then she lunged toward a hanging piece of stomach, and scratched a 5 into the flesh above the belly button, thinking of the five they'd made in the net in the coils.

The skin turned red and angry, but the mark remained.

"Hurry, Maddy," she said under her breath, then scratched another 5 into a flap of leg.

MADDY

Why did it have to be Keneō? Monstrous birds Maddy could take. Dead-eyed players wandering the woods, fine. Even giant spiders, sure, okay.

It had to be the cannibal.

Maddy followed the path of 5s through the woods, the scratches on the skin still pink and irritated, like they'd been marked recently. It was their sign, like the mirrored net they'd left for Owen and Ian in the coils. After Emerson hadn't shown up at their designated meeting spot, Maddy had begun searching the surrounding area, finally stumbling upon a long strap of skin bearing the mark. She'd been following the trail ever since.

As Maddy's socked feet flew over the cold ground, she felt for the cards in her hip pocket. Wisdom and valor had been on the shore downriver—damp, but undamaged, as if waiting for her to pick them up.

Her gaze lifted to the giant's eye, tying another knot of anxiety beneath her collarbones. Was it already closing more? It was less than half open now.

The hanging skins disappeared as the trees thinned. Ice hardened her damp clothes, made her teeth chatter and her fear sharp. Thick webs appeared in the trees, skeletons and half-rotten corpses trapped inside them. Her skin began to prickle with the feeling of being watched. Soft, quick clicks filled her ears, but every time she turned she saw nothing.

That didn't mean the spiders weren't there.

Slowly, she lowered, picking up a sharp, sturdy stick. It would work as a spear if she had to defend herself. Ahead, a wall appeared through the trees. The stones were broken and covered with webs, and through the gap of what had once been a gate, she could see a house lined with broken paper sliding walls. The higher, uneven stories were covered with spiders. Some were small enough she couldn't see them individually, moving like a wave of black over the siding. Others were as big as she was.

Kuchisake's house.

The scar on her wrist had been warm and itching since she'd dragged herself from the river, but now it prickled. Memories of her wedding flooded her mind. The dress that seemed to have come straight from her childhood dreams. Dax's gaze, bright with worry when Kuchisake had cut her wrist with his razored fingernail.

It is a promise that cannot be undone. Even in death your souls will belong to each other.

Movement caught her eye from inside the main hall. Beside a throne she made out two people—Kuchisake in his green kimono, flanked by a hip-high spider and an older man, bent over his cane. She shifted her position for a better view, keeping low behind the broken outer wall.

Keneō. What was he wearing on his face? Another face? *A lot* of faces? It was like he was competing for the Most Disgusting in All Meido prize.

Beside him stood Emerson, her wrists bound before her with thick, white webbing.

The three of them disappeared behind a still-intact panel.

Fear tightened Maddy's chest.

The courtyard was empty. Maddy scanned for the split-faced players that had been here last time, but they were absent. Stick in her hand, she dodged across the hard dirt, wary of the watchful spiders above. When she reached the side of the building, she skimmed along the outside, making her way toward the back.

The exit of the house had been torn open, the tattered slider left discarded on the ground. She remembered this part of the compound well—the hall led to a throne room on one side, and a stairway on the other. The steps descended into a basement—she'd bathed there in the hot springs before her wedding.

She adjusted her grip on the stick, then felt again for the cards to make sure they were firmly tucked in her pocket. One breath. Two. *Hold on, Emerson.* She crept inside, her socked feet quiet on the rough wooden floor.

Voices were coming from upstairs.

She stilled, but they continued as if they hadn't heard her.

"Emerson?" she whispered.

The quick clicking of a spider's feet came out from the hall into the throne room. She ducked into the stairway, flattening against the wall. The black, furry creature passed slowly, then stopped, ten paces past. It turned, eight red eyes the size of fists scanning the area. Maddy held her breath, pulling her stomach in tight, feeling the boards of the wall press against her spine and the backs of her legs.

The clicking steps receded, heading up the steps to the next level.

She exhaled. Wiping her damp palm on her thigh, she readjusted her grip on the stick and stepped back into the hallway. On the walls, she found the same sexual paintings she'd seen before of the people with split faces, but the frames were askew, the canvases damaged. When she reached a doorway, she slid beside the wall, taking a quick glimpse inside.

The room was in rough condition—the sliders ragged, a ceiling beam lying on the floor in a heap of web and dust. Kuchisake's wooden throne was still on the raised platform at the front of the room, but it was empty now.

Her gaze rose.

On the far wall, behind the throne, a giant web stretched from the ceiling to the floor. At the top of it, suspended sideways, was Emerson.

Keeping low, Maddy sprinted across the room. Emerson's mouth had been covered by webbing. Her arms were trapped at her sides, legs pinned together.

"Don't move. I'll cut you down!" Maddy told her.

Emerson's muffled cries pressed through her bindings.

Maddy raced around Kuchisake's throne. Setting the stick on the seat, she dropped low and pushed it with all her strength toward her trapped friend. Her muscles strained against the chair's weight, but it slid, making a screech against the floor.

The ceiling creaked. Someone was moving upstairs.

Maddy held her breath.

No one came.

She gave the throne another shove. When it was close enough, she climbed onto the left arm, her toes curling around the wood. Using the stick, she began carving away the fat white threads of the web over Emerson's body

Emerson bucked inside her bindings, making it harder to get her free.

"Hold still!" Maddy hissed. But Emerson didn't stop. She was shouting something Maddy couldn't make out. But Maddy couldn't release her mouth. Even standing on the throne, Emerson's face was too high to reach.

The footsteps were moving toward the stairs.

They were running out of time.

Finally, she got Emerson's arms free. As Maddy moved to her legs, her friend tore away the web over her mouth.

"Maddy, duck!" Emerson shouted.

Maddy dropped in the throne, spinning just in time to see a hand cut through the air. A fist crashed against the back of the throne, shattering the top into splinters that clung to the bouncing web.

Maddy blinked up, and the face staring down at her stole her breath.

"Surprise," said Dax.

With a cry, she shoved off of the chair, throwing herself down the raised platform. He lunged for her at lightning speed. For a moment, she thought he would catch her. That the brightness of his eyes meant disbelief. That the curve of his lips meant he was happy.

But his hand reached for her throat.

She twisted as his fingers caught in the collar of her shirt, and when he jerked back, the fabric tore. She fell to the floor with a gasp, panic searing through her as she scrambled back over the floor.

"Leave her alone!" Emerson screamed, one leg still caught in the web, the other foot precariously balanced on the arm of the broken chair.

Dax stepped calmly off the stage toward her.

"Dax." Her voice quivered. "It's me. It's Maddy."

This wasn't happening. He wasn't yōkai. He was her Dax. *Their* Dax. The Dax she loved.

Only he wasn't. He was sharp edges and wild eyes. Quick, frantic movements and sallow skin. His Green Day shirt and jeans were the clothes she remembered, but that was all that remained of her friend.

She'd known this was possible. Emerson had told her it would happen. But she didn't want to believe it. When she'd left, Dax had still been human. When she imagined him here, he was suffering. In pain. *Lost.*

Not like this.

"You're terrified," Dax whispered. "I feel it. I *smell* it."

He inhaled, then flinched, reaching for his wrist as if he'd been stung there by an insect. He hissed, lips drawing back in pain.

"Dax, wh-where's your knife?" she asked.

"Is that how you wish to die?" he asked. "Cut into tiny pieces?"

A sob raked up her throat as he stalked her. An animal and his prey.

"Dax, stop," she begged him. Behind him, Emerson was shouting his name. The footsteps pounded on the stairs.

Keneō and Kuchisake were coming.

"Ahh," Dax said. "You have them."

She followed his gaze to her hip pocket, where the corners of the two cards stuck out.

"Maddy, run!" Emerson screamed. "They want the cards! They're going to use the prizes to open the gate to our world!"

She stared at Dax's face. At his black, bottomless eyes. She'd walked into this house with the cards unprotected. He could take them—use them against her. He could hurt her without a second thought.

What have I done?

She flipped, feet sliding across the dusty floorboards as she ran to get away. Dax grabbed her around the ankle, and flipped her over. She kicked him in the jaw, but he only grinned.

Pushing up, she ran. He caught her against the back wall. He pressed against her, his body hard as he heaved her arms overhead and pinned them in place with one hand.

Slowly, the other reached toward her pocket.

"Dax, stop!"

She kicked again, but he stepped on her feet, his weight like lead.

"You know me," she said quickly. "You remember me. I'm Maddy. I'm your friend!"

She needed to find his knife. If he had his knife, he would be okay. He would be himself.

He leaned closer, his breath cold as he laughed. "I have no friends, mortal."

She turned her head, and her gaze caught on the angry red scar on his wrist. The one that matched her own.

"You have a wife," she said.

He flinched.

Hesitated.

It was still him. Still Dax. She just needed to find a way to reach him.

From behind her came a clicking, and she turned to find a giant spider at the entrance of the room. Behind it, a line of people had filed in. Her gaze landed on Kuchisake first, in his luxurious green kimono and shifting necklace of black bugs. He petted the spider's head fondly. Keneō followed Kuchisake, his skin mask blushing in delight along with his human coat. Behind him was the old woman who had once given them directions in this cursed world, Shinigami. She was still wearing her worn black kimono, but her gray hair was in a messy knot, strands of it sticking out from the sides.

And then, Ian.

On the stage behind the throne, Emerson's struggle went silent.

"Easy." Owen stepped out from the shadows behind Ian, his hands outstretched. "We just need the cards."

Maddy sucked in a breath, her chest colliding with Dax's. It was hard, unforgiving.

"Owen?" she whispered.

He was a prisoner. Kuchisake, Keneō, and Shinigami were holding Owen and Ian captive. That was the only explanation for what she was seeing.

"The cards. Quickly," said Ian. His back was bent, his voice harsh. Beads of sweat dripped down his face. Maddy's jaw tightened. His voice was strained and low. Wrong.

"What's going on?" she asked. Behind her, Emerson was struggling again to get free.

"We need to finish the challenges," said Owen. "It's the only way to save Ian."

"What are you talking about?" Maddy jerked, but Dax held fast. "Ian's right there."

"This isn't Ian," said Owen, taking another step closer. "Just like that isn't Dax." He waved a hand toward them. Maddy's exhale felt like broken glass, slicing her throat.

"What are you talking about?" said Emerson.

"Mind your tone when you're talking to your empress," said Shinigami, the long, tattered sleeve of her kimono swinging as she motioned to Ian.

Maddy's fingers prickled with numbness from Dax's grip.

That wasn't the empress. That was Ian. The empress was gone. They'd beaten her.

Doubt wormed through her veins.

"That's Ian," she said, twisting against the wall. "Izanami's dead."

Ian's laugh was husky. "Death is not a permanent state, I'm afraid."

Owen's cheeks darkened. "I wanted to tell you before, but there wasn't time. When we gave Ian the empress's heart, we gave him part of her. He brought it back with him to our world. She's been living inside of him this whole time."

"If living is what you can call it," Ian grunted, then fell to one knee, gripping his chest. Owen dropped beside him, one hand on Ian's arm for support. His breath was coming in quick, shallow gasps.

She shook her head. This was wrong. Owen was *wrong*. But she could see it all, replayed before her eyes. Ian as an oni, a hole in his chest. How they'd placed the empress's stone heart inside him. How the fine tendrils of skin had closed over it, locking it in place.

Ian had Izanami's heart.

Ian *was* Izanami.

The empress wasn't dead.

Maddy sagged in Dax's arms. Owen looked pained. Shinigami and Keneō, disapproving. Only Kuchisake grinned from ear to ear. He lifted a hand to send Maddy a little wave, as if they were old friends, and mouthed the word *Hi*.

"We have to finish the game," Owen said. "Getting the prizes— it's the only way she can get out of his body."

"And cross over to our world!" said Emerson. "Keneō told me

their little plan. The prizes are going to help them open the gate. Maybe she forgot to mention that part."

Maddy huffed a breath. She looked to Dax's face and found confirmation.

Izanami was finishing what she'd started—what they'd stopped the last time they'd played the game. She was opening the gate to their world, and using the prizes of this game to do it.

"We don't have a choice," Owen said miserably. "Look at him. Look what she's doing to him!"

A new horror raked through Maddy. Owen knew what Izanami would do, and he was helping her anyway. But what else could he do? If it had been Dax, she would have done the same thing. She was here, doing the same thing.

"Get the cards, Dax," Izanami ordered from her hands and knees.

"You cannot trust him, empress," said Shinigami quietly, helping an unsteady Ian to his feet. "The cardmaker's son lies. He had the second piece of the tomoe and lost it."

"I was protecting it for you, my empress," Dax said, dipping his head. Maddy wasn't sure whether or not to believe him. His words sounded too earnest.

Ian's eyes narrowed.

Dax's hand cupped Maddy's waist, sliding down. It was an intimate move, and it felt as wrong as it did right. Dax wouldn't hurt her.

Would he?

His hand found her hip pocket, his lips a breath away.

"Do not worry, mortal. This will all be over soon."

She slipped a hand from his cold grip as he reached into her pocket and slapped her hand over his, locking it against her side. He shifted, pressing her to the wall with his hips. Hiding the others from her view.

"You don't scare me," she said. "You're Dax. My Dax."

"I belong to no one but the empress," he hissed.

Emerson moved toward her—Maddy caught a glimpse of her friend over Dax's shoulder. But Kuchisake had cut in, blocking her path.

"Let them have a moment. We should not intrude." He giggled. "Unless they ask us to."

"Maddy, just give him the cards!" Owen begged.

She couldn't look away from Dax's stare.

"Don't do it," shouted Emerson.

"Please," Owen begged. "We can all go together. Finish this together, like before. We'll figure it out, we just need Ian."

"What do you think she's going to do to Ian once she finishes the game, Owen?" Emerson shot back. "You think she'll have any use for him when she takes over the living world?"

Owen's face pinched. "He's going to be all right."

"She told you that, huh?" Emerson shot back as the spider tapped across the floor toward her. She dodged out of the way as it leapt, slamming into a wall with a crash. Rising, it shook like a dog, a puff of white dust rising from its hairy body.

Dax chuckled. "The chaos. I can *taste* it."

Maddy's teeth clenched. The strain pulled her in all directions. Dax, out of his mind. Owen, fighting for Ian. Emerson, trying to dodge past Kuchisake.

Maddy didn't know how to stop the empress from crossing over without losing Ian.

She didn't know how to save Ian without losing their world.

All she knew was that she wasn't leaving this room without Dax.

"You want the cards, fine. Take them," she told Dax. "Take them, and help us. We need you."

His smile flattened. "Help you?"

"You're not going to hurt me. You love me."

He tilted his head.

"Quit wasting time!" said Shinigami. "Get the cards."

Dax's hand tightened around her hip.

Her hand gripped his.

"Take them," she said. "We can finish this together. All of us. You, me, Emerson, Owen, and Ian. The Foxtail Five, remember?"

Her heart was pounding. Her gaze stayed steady on his.

Slowly, she lifted her hand, giving him the freedom to reach into her pocket.

"They're yours," she said. "I trust you. You won't give them to the empress. You won't betray us."

His throat bobbed as he swallowed.

He was still in there. Still him. She could feel it.

"Remember," she willed him.

She pulled out the card on top. She remembered the kanji Owen had read. Valor.

If there was ever a time for courage in the face of danger, it was now.

"I trust you," she said again.

A sharp bite of cold against her palm made her flinch.

Dax pulled away. Her mouth formed a small *O* as she registered the cool, smoldering embers eating the paper from the bottom of the valor card.

On the outside steps behind Izanami, a green flame gate began to grow. Through the shimmering mirage, soft light poured in. A sparkling wash of silver.

The card burned, every eye darting to Maddy's hand, where a single-edged katana appeared. It had a gentle curve, and was light in weight, but nearly the length of her leg. There was no hilt or heavy grip like in the medieval swords she'd seen in movies. Instead, the sleek, silver blade seemed to melt into a base, the handle embraced by plaited jade cords and finished with a golden tassel that tickled her wrist.

A flash of silver caught her eye, and when she peered down at the bottom of the weapon, she found a curved silver comma, embedded in the hilt.

It was the exact shape of the black stone they'd gotten in the first challenge in the coils.

The second prize.

Her arm bobbed as she tried to balance the sword, and she nearly fumbled it to the floor as the last of the card disappeared.

Dax backed away, his wicked smile back. "The root of all honor and bravery," he said, then laughed. "I told you I would get you the second piece of the tomoe, empress, and here it is. Valor."

A weight filled Maddy's chest as her stare lifted from the katana to Dax.

Any sign of familiarity was gone. He was yōkai—empty and cold—and he'd gotten exactly what he wanted.

"Give it to me," Izanami wheezed.

Before Maddy could pull the katana to her chest, a rope of steam cut through the air and snatched it away. In a blink, it was thrust into Ian's open hands, carried by the steam from Shinigami's teapot, drawn from the fold of her kimono.

"The second prize—" Izanami began, but the katana shimmered in her shaking grip, and changed again into a small metal bar, the length of Ian's palm. Blue, and rounded at the ends.

Dax's pocketknife.

"Is this a trick?" Shinigami said. "This is not the second piece. This is nothing more than a child's blade!" Ian's cheeks stained red with anger.

"Aka Manto's son lies, I told you," said Shinigami. Keneō with his many-faced mask stepped to her side, one edge of his lips pulled into a grimace.

"Where is the second prize?" Izanami asked. "What have you done with it?" Her words trailed off into a wracking cough, and she dropped the knife to the ground. It fell with a soft clunk at Ian's feet.

Maddy's breath came faster. She didn't know what had happened—why it had been a katana one moment and a pocketknife the next, but if she could get it, if she could give it to Dax, he would remember who he was. He could help them.

"Izanami?" Owen grabbed Ian's shoulder as the empress crumpled into Shinigami's side. "Ian!"

His face was white. His eyes had rolled back.

This was Maddy's chance.

Twisting out of Dax's grip, she sprinted across the floor, past the giant spider's thrusting legs, diving toward the knife on the ground.

"Wake up!" Owen was shouting. "Ian! Can you hear me?"

Keneō and Shinigami were so distracted by their fainting empress that they didn't see Maddy's hand close around the pocketknife until it was too late. As her fingers skimmed the cool metal, it heated. Vibrated. The blade stretched out from her grasp, silver and gleaming. The handle extended the opposite way, the comma-shaped stone winking at her in the dying light of the giant's eye.

"A trick!" screeched Shinigami, and the giant spider screamed in response.

Maddy stared at the weapon in shock. When the empress had touched it, it was a pocketknife. When Maddy held it, it was a sword. None of the other prizes changed from person to person. How was it possible that she could bear valor when others could not?

She didn't have time to figure it out. Shinigami left the unconscious Izanami in Owen's arms, and turned the spout of her small teakettle toward Maddy. A figure just like her appeared in the steam that came from it, her black eyes wide and her mouth a gaping hole. Another old woman appeared to her left, and then two more, and soon there were a dozen steam Shinigamis, all racing toward Maddy. Maddy leapt up. She swung the sword, and the two closest turned to gray smoke as soon as the blade touched them.

"You have no valor." The closest Shinigami thrust her arms forward, but Maddy swung the katana downward, making the old woman jerk back to protect her wrists. Steam rose from her shoulders, her hands, her head.

She hissed in fury, a sound more like a boiling kettle than a human.

Kuchisake clapped his hands. "Madeline, you look like a lioness! Fight me next!"

"We need to get out of here," Emerson called, springing up just as Keneō swung his knife her direction. "Come on! The gate's closing!"

Maddy couldn't see it over the giant spider's flailing legs. It walked toward her on its back four, the front four waving wildly at her with pointed, clawed tips.

Maddy didn't think. She grabbed the hilt of the katana, the cords creaking in her fist as she rotated her forearm to spin the blade. It made a whirring sound as it split the air. Power thrummed up her arm into her chest. Holding it felt electric. Felt right, like the familiarity of long laps in the pool.

The metal caught a ray of light, brilliant and lethal, and Maddy gasped at the surge of energy through her limbs. She felt like she could take on the giant himself then. Like a warrior, the experience of a thousand battles shooting up through her grip into her body.

She stabbed the spider in the abdomen, and with a garbled cry it crashed against the floorboards.

Kuchisake, teeth and jaws bared through his monstrous mouth, threw himself upon her. His nails were knives, long and jagged blades that cut through the air. She fought back with a skill she didn't know she possessed, cutting down his fingernails in a sharp slash to send them clattering across the floor.

"Maddy!" Emerson's scream drew her attention to the gate, which was quickly closing. Emerson and Owen were dragging Ian's body toward it.

Maddy meant to run toward them, but someone leapt on her back. She swung the sword over her shoulder, catching Keneō between the shoulders. He fell with a scream into one of the steam Shinigamis, which dissolved into a cloud.

With a wide sweep, she arced the blade around her body, clearing everyone from coming too close. But as she turned, one last figure appeared before her.

"Dax," she breathed.

He dropped to the ground, sending a hard kick that took her out by the ankles. She fell onto her back, keeping ahold of the weapon. His fist came down like a hammer, breaking through the floor beside her head.

"Dax!" she shrieked.

"Give me the blade," he said.

"I will," she promised. "I will. Just stop—" She rolled as he stomped the ground beside her hip, breaking another hole in the floor.

"Stop!" she shouted. She didn't understand why this was happening. Why the knife that he'd always carried had become a prize in this game—a blade suitable for royalty.

"The empress needs the prizes."

"The empress doesn't give a damn about you!"

"I belong to her," he said as she popped back to her feet.

He threw a punch and she had no choice but to duck to avoid his inhuman strength. More quickly than she thought herself capable, she turned the katana, slamming the hilt against Dax's belly.

He blew out a harsh breath as the wind was knocked from his lungs. His hands closed around hers—around the sword's handle.

"Wrong," she said. "You belong to me."

He shuddered.

Looked at his hand gripping the hilt of the katana.

When his gaze rose, his eyes were his own.

"Maddy?" he murmured.

She could feel the change in him. The softening of his voice. The way his body curved forward, rather than stretching against his bones like his joints might break.

"Dax," she said, as his fingers squeezed hers.

"Maddy." He looked down at the knife, out at Kuchisake and Keneō and Shinigami, gathering themselves for another attack. "What are you—"

"Take the knife." She tried to give it to him. "If you hold it, you'll know who you are. You can help me."

"No." He shook his head. "No. I can't. It's yours now. I made it so that only you can hold it."

She didn't understand. "Dax—"

"Listen to me," he said, one hand rising to cup her cheek. "I'm dangerous. You have to stay away from me. This can protect you from them. It's lucky, remember?"

"No," she said. "I came here for you."

"You'll leave here without me," he said desperately. He leaned in and pressed his lips hard to her forehead, bringing every emotion to the surface of her skin. "You are everything, you know that? *Everything.*"

"Wait . . ."

"Go."

He pushed her back without another word. She felt as if he'd torn her heart away. She needed another moment, a million more moments, to talk to him, to have him back, but one of Shinigami's steam warriors grabbed him around the shoulder, throwing him against the far wall. He slammed into it in a storm of dust and splintering wood.

"Dax!" she cried as a wall crumbled down atop him.

"Maddy!" Emerson was standing halfway through the glowing green gate now, Owen and Ian already inside. "We have to go!"

She had been here before. She had stood at the gate and said goodbye to Dax, leaving him behind in the horror of this world.

She would not do it again.

She hopped over the spider's flinging legs and dove to the closing gate.

"Take this," she told Emerson, shoving the katana into her hand. As soon as it touched Emerson's palm it turned back into the small, blue, foldout knife. "It's powerful. You'll see." She grabbed the final card from her pocket, and pressed it against Emerson's chest. "The last card is wisdom. If there's anyone who can solve that, it's you."

"What are you talking about? We're doing this together!"

"We will," she told Emerson, squeezing her fingers. Prying them free. "It's okay. We're right behind you."

"Maddy, think about this. He needs the knife. He'll kill you."

"No," she said. "He won't."

The gate closed.

Silence.

She spun toward where Dax had been buried by debris, but before she could run to him, the ground rumbled, a quake coming from deep beneath her feet. She stumbled onto her hands and knees, looking to Kuchisake but finding him just as confused as she was.

Then a white, bony fist shot up from the floor, fingers spreading on the broken wood at her feet.

The last thing she remembered was the giant hand of a skeleton closing around her ankle and dragging her down into the steaming coils of Hell.

OWEN

"Is he breathing?" Owen pressed his fingers to Ian's throat, searching for a pulse. His hands were shaking too badly to find it. The three of them had landed in some kind of gel, a thick, sticky substance that looked a lot like the glitter glue he'd spilled all over himself making a poster for Pride last year. It surrounded them on all sides, a glittering sphere the size of a city block.

Emerson kneeled on Ian's other side. She leaned over his face, her ear to his parted lips. "He's breathing." She fell back on her heels, making a *squick* sound. "He's just unconscious."

"Are you sure? How do you know he isn't in a coma or something? He could have a concussion. How do you know there isn't internal bleeding?"

"I'm not a doctor!"

Owen shoved his glasses up with the back of his hand. His face was damp with sweat, and the frames slid back down his nose immediately.

"Ian, can you hear me?" He patted his pale cheek lightly. His hands were glimmering from the slick substance on the ground, which he transferred to Ian's pale cheek. "Ian! Wake up, okay?" The empress had said Ian's body would fail if they didn't complete the tomoe, but they needed more time.

"Owen," Emerson said, sitting back on her heels. "Owen, where are we?"

He glanced up, finding her staring down at Dax's pocketknife and the final card in her cradled hands. His gaze rose behind her, up the thick gel walls, all coated in glimmering specks of light.

"Maddy?" he whispered. She wasn't with them. There was no one else in sight at all.

"She stayed behind," Emerson said quietly.

His jaw tightened. He didn't have to ask why. He knew.

Dax.

He lifted his hand to examine the silvery glitter stuck to the back of his hand. A gentle whisper filled his ears. Soft and comforting. A woman's voice, humming a tune he recognized. "Do you hear that?"

"Drums." Emerson lifted her head. Some glitter had gotten on her cheeks and the tips of her hair, and it was so opposite her normal hardcore presentation that he almost smiled. "It's one of Trinity Poor's songs, but like . . . the Sunday morning, don't-play-too-loud-because-everyone's-hungover version."

"A heavy metal song?" Owen shook his head. It was the song he and Ian had listened to at The Bean before the empress had taken him over. The sweet melody of it made his heart swell. Soothed the knots between his shoulders. Slowed his galloping pulse.

"I sent this song to Ian," he said.

"I doubt that," she snuffed.

It occurred to him they might be hearing different music.

"Do you think this is the next challenge? Wisdom?" He stood, and his feet slipped a little. He laughed, then scowled, because there was nothing funny about this place. It was a sparkling prison, and Ian was still unconscious on the ground before them.

But it was peaceful here. A deep, settling peace filled his body like hot chocolate on a cold night. He had the sudden urge to take Emerson's hands and slide around like kids on an icy pond. He could feel the hot grip of urgency loosening around his throat. The song calmed him; the air, just the right temperature, soothed him. Even the gel between his toes served as a balm for the burning sand and icy ground he'd tromped over.

If Jigoku had been a nightmare, this was the best kind of dream.

"Owen?" Ian's eyelids fluttered open.

Not *mortal*, said in a petulant tone. *Owen.*

"Ian!" He dropped to his knees with a squish, taking Ian's hand. "Hey. You're awake! Are you okay? What hurts?" His brain caught up with him a moment later. "Is she . . . is she gone?"

"No." Ian let Owen pull him up to a seated position, his back and hair now glowing with silver specks. "She's quiet."

"Can she hear me?"

"I don't think so. She's just . . ."

"Offline?" Emerson suggested, watching him carefully.

"Yeah," said Ian. "Offline. Where are we?" His voice crackled.

"I don't know," Owen said. "But nothing's tried to kill us yet, so that's a good sign."

"I know that song," Ian said. "It's from *West Side Story*."

Owen and Emerson exchanged a look.

"No," said Emerson slowly. "It's metal."

"It's the song we listened to at The Bean," Owen insisted.

"No." Ian shook his head. "I've been listening to the soundtrack for a week. 'Maria.'" He hummed along with it for a moment, and sure enough, he had the tune right.

"I didn't send you that," Owen said.

Ian looked down at his glittery hands. "I'm going through all your shows."

Owen's chest warmed. "You are?"

"And watching Maddy's swim footage. And videos of people playing *Assassin 0* online." He glanced up at Emerson. "That green fog—the choke—it gets everyone."

"Yeah," she said, her cheeks pink and gleaming. "It does."

Owen's heart pounded in relief. At least for now, Ian was okay.

"We got the second piece of the tomoe," Owen said, pointing to the pocketknife in Emerson's hand. "Something's wrong with it, though."

"He changed it," Ian said. "Dax did. Only Maddy can make it the prize."

"How do you know?" Owen asked.

"You saw it," said Emerson. "When she held the knife it was . . . a prize. Now it's just a rusty old blade."

"Why would Dax do that?" Owen asked. "He needs that knife to remember who he is."

"Maybe it was more important for Maddy to have it than for him to remember," Ian suggested.

Owen frowned. "Do you think this is Meido?"

"It doesn't look like any place in Meido I've seen," Emerson scratched the back of her neck. "Nothing's dead."

"Could be a trick," Owen said, as the glitter pulsed like a gentle strobe light around them. He yawned. The music was making him sleepy.

"Maybe," said Emerson. She turned back to Owen and Ian. "But it feels different, right? I feel . . . nice."

"It's definitely a trick, then, because you are many things, but nice is not one of them."

Emerson shoved him.

"I feel nice too," said Ian. He tried to stand, but winced and sat again.

"Whoa. Easy," said Owen, supporting his back with an open hand. "No quick moves." Ian's spine rounded against his palm, bringing a knot to his throat. His gaze kept darting over Ian's face, his hair, the back of his shirt, peppered with shiny flecks. No injuries that he could see.

"I'm all right," said Ian.

"You've been possessed by an ancient empress. Literally no one would be all right."

Ian cracked a smile. "You're worried about me."

Owen huffed. "I'm just stating the facts."

"He's worried," Emerson said, tucking the card and the knife into her pocket.

"Of course I'm worried! You could have died! Multiple times!" Owen refocused his efforts on picking pieces of glitter out of the back of Ian's shirt. There was a lot of glitter, so the task was probably a useless endeavor, but it gave him an excuse to touch him.

"I've got a pretty good bodyguard."

The knot in Owen's throat grew tighter as Ian gave his hand a weak squeeze.

"Where's Maddy?" Ian asked, looking around.

Emerson and Owen exchanged a wary glace.

"She stayed back to go after Dax," said Owen.

Ian scowled. "Is he . . . himself?"

"No," said Emerson.

Ian exhaled. "I don't know how much time I have until the empress comes back," he said, his voice heavy. "Her plan is to open the gates to Meido."

"We know," said Emerson.

"You have to stop her," Ian went on. He was still leaning against Owen for support, the past trials taking a toll on his energy. "She's coming for revenge. She thinks everything in our world belongs to her. She's going to destroy it to punish him."

"Who?" Emerson asked.

"Izanagi," Owen said, sitting back on his heels. "Her husband."

Ian nodded. "We can't let her get through. She can't be allowed to remake the tomoe."

"Then how do we get her out of you?" Owen asked. "She said the tomoe has power. She can use it to get her body back, then she won't need you anymore."

"Her body back?" Ian repeated. His sad smile made Owen's stomach tighten. "No. Owen, she's not getting her body back. We destroyed her. This is all she has now."

Owen stared at him, the voice in the distance growing quiet.

"What do you mean?" he asked.

"She's going to use the tomoe to make this body strong enough to hold her power."

A buzz filled Owen's ears. "But what about you?"

Ian didn't make sense. He looked to Emerson, but she looked like he'd just told her someone had died.

No one was going to die.

"Ian," he said. "*What about you?*"

"I am already gone," he said.

Owen pulled away from him. His legs felt numb. He fell into the gel behind him, sinking two inches. The song played again, but this time it was taunting him.

"No," he said. "You're wrong."

Ian closed his eyes.

"Why bring us along if she just needs you?" Emerson asked. "Why not kill us and be done with it?"

"Because she needs a mortal to play the game," said Ian. "These challenges were made by her husband. He loves the living—as much as she loves the dead. He sees the best in us. He wants her to see the best again too. To work alongside mortals and see what we can do for those we love."

The word was a dagger to Owen's heart.

"Then why make us help the skeleton in Jigoku?" said Owen. "I tried to do the right thing for those mortal players, but it didn't solve the challenge."

"Because the challenges for the pieces of the tomoe are about intention, not just action," said Ian. "Helping our fellow mortals, that's easy. But helping someone like her—like Gashadokuro—it shows her she can be saved too. Even demons need help."

"That's why the card turned for Maddy at Kuchisake's house," said Emerson. "Because her intention was valor."

"Her heart was pure," said Ian with a nod.

"Well my intention is to save you," said Owen. His ribs felt like they were contracting around his lungs. "So tell her that. You're not going with her, and that's it."

He sounded like a child not getting their way. He didn't care. Izanami didn't get to win Ian. That wasn't the game he'd agreed to play.

"Owen." Ian reached for his hand, his eyes wet. "You have to stop her."

Owen pulled away.

"*No.* Whatever you're thinking, it's not going to happen. We're not going to leave you here. We're not going to sacrifice you to the game, pure-heartedly and with good intention. Wrong answer. Try again."

Ian coughed, his body clenching in pain. "I don't want it to be this way."

"Great."

"But there isn't another option."

"There is *always* another option," said Owen. "Tell him, Emerson. Tell him we aren't doing this."

Emerson hesitated.

Owen swung his glare toward her. "You're kidding me, right?"

"We can't let her open the gate," she said quietly.

Owen pushed up to his feet. "I can't believe I'm hearing this." He'd never been really mad at Emerson before, but now he could barely stand to look at her. "None of us would leave *you* here."

"This is different," said Ian, using Emerson's shoulder to push himself up. "We can stop her. There's poison inside me, Owen. We can stop it from spilling all over the world."

Owen crossed his arms, shaking his head.

"When we get the third piece of the tomoe, the final passage will open home. I don't know how much time we'll have. Seconds, maybe minutes. You have to . . . you have to use the sword and kill her. You'll have enough time to get out before the gate closes."

"Stop," said Owen. "We're not having this conversation."

"I've had a lot of time to think while she's been playing puppet master, and it's the only way."

Owen refused to listen to this. He couldn't believe Emerson could. Turning, he stalked away. Desperation was twisting his muscles, wringing his insides out. He wanted to scream.

He walked until the wall sloped up, too slippery to climb. He caught his reflection in the shining surface before him. Thin-rimmed glasses. Pink-tipped nose. Quivering lower lip.

He couldn't say goodbye to Ian again.

He would not kill him.

Absolutely not. Not a chance in hell, Meido, or whatever this place was.

On the glossy ground, his reflection changed. His glasses were gone, this jaw wider, his face older. Gone was his uncertainty and sadness, but his grief remained.

Izanagi.

Owen startled, stepping back. When he looked again, it was his own face. He shuddered, exhaling relief.

"Owen."

He turned to find Ian.

"Hi." Ian gave a small wave.

Owen shoved his hands in his pockets.

Ian stepped forward, the jewel in his hand making his palm pink. "You all right?"

"Great," said Owen flatly. He sighed. "Are *you* all right?"

"Never better." He stepped beside Owen, bumping him with his shoulder. "We've done a pretty bang-up job so far, huh?" He lifted the stone, but Owen looked away.

"I can't do it, Ian. I can't do what you said." He felt empty inside, clawed raw.

"You think I want you to?" Ian gave a morbid chuckle. "Owen, I'd give anything to go back home. With you." He tripped over the last part, returning the stone to his pocket.

A flash of hope lifted Owen's shoulders, only to have reality smash them back down. He and Ian never talked about their feelings for each other. When they were kids, before the first game, Owen had always been too shy. Then after the game, when Ian had come home, Owen's entire focus had been being a good friend. Helping Ian heal.

This wasn't fair.

"Then you will come home," Owen said, his voice thick. "It's settled."

Ian smiled sadly. "You've gotten stubborn."

"Says the guy who says killing him is the only way."

"Has it ever occurred to you that I'm doing it for you?" Owen turned toward him.

"Maybe, for once, you could let me save you," Ian finished.

The twisting emotion inside Owen frayed and broke. The tears broke free. He couldn't remember the last time he'd cried—really cried, not just acting for a show. It was awful. It hurt everywhere, and the snot was not a good look.

"It has to be you," Ian said, and Owen knew that he wasn't talking about Ian's request to kill him.

He couldn't speak to say no. He couldn't yell at Ian for saying something stupid. He couldn't scream at Izanami for putting him in this situation.

All he could do was nod, because it was what Ian needed.

Ian raised a finger, his eyes bright with unspoken questions. When Owen nodded, he wiped away one of his tears, circling his jaw to the end of his chin. The warm wake of his touch remained, even after he pulled away.

"I, um," Owen started, as Ian stepped closer. He was taller than Owen by a couple inches, but some of that height was Ian's unruly dark hair. He grinned, and raked a hand through it, as if he knew it would drive Owen wild.

It crushed him.

"Yeah?" Ian said, his gaze dropping to Owen's lips.

"I just . . ." His thoughts were spinning off in all different directions. "I didn't mean it when I kissed Izanami. That was a total accident. I mean, not an accident, really. But it's like the emperor got in my head or something?"

Ian had gone still.

"Wow," Owen said. "Can we forget I said that?"

"We can file it under End of the World Rules."

"End of the World Rules?"

"Yeah. People do weird things in the face of certain doom." He inched closer.

"Weird things . . ." Owen swallowed.

"Wild things," Ian whispered. "Brave things."

Ian leaned down and kissed him.

His mouth curved into a smile against Owen's lips, and it was in that moment that Owen's heart broke.

He didn't stop it. He let it happen. As Ian's hands found his chest, and knotted in the top of his shirt, he felt the last of his shield shatter and melt, liquid metal surging under his ribs, spreading lower, searing away the chill.

He grabbed Ian's face and pulled him close, kissing him the way he'd never kissed anyone, the way people did in movies. He tilted his lips and pressed deeper, every secret he'd held, every hidden want breaking through in an uncontrollable surge.

I am not letting you go, that kiss said.

I will not let you die.

Ian pulled back, looking up at him with a puff of breath. "Owen."

Owen couldn't speak.

Ian smiled. "Wow."

"What?"

"Something's different. *You're* different."

"I'm not," said Owen. But Ian was right. He felt different. Like the curtain had been pulled back, the stage lights shut off, and he could see every single seat of the theater before him.

The empress was not going to win this game. He was going to win. Because he was the player, he was in control. Ian would survive this, and they would go home, and they would live.

He wasn't unafraid. The opposite. But it propelled him. It strengthened his resolve.

"Yes, you are." Emerson had approached, and was shaking her head with either wonder or disapproval—it was always hard to tell with her. "You look like one of those people who lift cars off an injured child."

"Like you could land an airplane when the pilot passed out," said Ian, nodding.

"Paint the Mona Lisa blindfolded."

"Headline your own one-man show on Broadway."

"Okay that's a stretch," Owen said, his neck warm. "The rest, totally feasible."

"Final form," Emerson whispered. And when Owen raised a brow, she said, "It happened to Maddy, too. Didn't you see her wielding that katana? She was . . ."

"A total beast," Owen agreed.

Emerson nodded. "Everyone's leveling up."

"Why?" Owen asked.

"Boss battle," she muttered. "It's coming—the end of the game. Can't you feel it?"

Owen shuddered. He *could* feel it. It was like watching a storm build on the horizon. The gathering of clouds. The wind that came before the rain. The electric smell in the air. Even here, in this wondrous place, there was a sense of foreboding.

"Oh, I feel it," said Ian.

Owen's skin prickled. Ian's lips were curled in a vicious smile. His gaze had narrowed, and his back was straight. He looked dangerous.

"Izanami," Owen said, stepping to Emerson's side.

The empress clapped slowly, sauntering toward him. "Such bravery, mortal. And here I thought you were just a lovesick puppy, following your master around."

"Leave him alone," said Emerson.

"Or what?" asked Izanami. "You'll kill me? You don't have it in you." She turned to Owen, smiling wider. "Either of you."

"You should not be here." The high voice cut through his thoughts with the sharpness and sudden velocity of a thrown spear. When he spun around, a woman towered over them, her kimono so bright and gleaming he could hardly stand to look at it. Her face was warped with fury as she pointed to Ian.

"The empress of death has no place in the heavens."

DAX

He was hungry.

It consumed him. An emptiness in his soul, pulling at the fibers of his half-mortal body. His senses were sharp. The tree shadows had razor edges. The waves churned in the river, miles away. The steps and dull throbbing heartbeats of a band of old players, moving near the palace, banged in his ears, accented by a furry spider leg brushing the ground.

His head jerked from side to side. He was too stimulated. Unable to filter it all and so accepting it all. Absorbing it into his body. Growing mad with the scents and sounds and sights that overwhelmed him. He knew what would tame it. What would quiet his mind.

Fear.

He'd tasted the girl's in Kuchisake's house. It was bitter and pure, and cut straight through the rest. He longed for it. He *needed* it.

Death wafted in on the breeze, and his head jerked toward the direction of the scent.

The hunters had been tracking him since the giant's eye had been half shut. It was a sickle now, the light it gave dim and eerie, casting long shadows through the woods. He slipped in and out of them, his feet moving silently over the cold ground.

"Dax?" sang a sinister voice. "Where is my dearest friend?"

Dax swung into a tree to perch on a branch. He rubbed his wrist, pressing his fingers against the prickle beneath an old scar. Below, Kuchisake strode through the dead crackling leaves, each step like cannon fire in Dax's ears. The old yūrei's jade kimono was open loosely over his chest, the end dragging behind him.

"Our time is running thin," he continued, a giant spider following in his wake. *Click-click, click-click.* The creature's steps pulled at Dax's focus. "Won't you come out and play?"

"If you reveal yourself . . ." called a low voice, distorted by the mask of skin he wore over his face. It made a squelching sound as he adjusted it. "I will start by peeling your chest rather than your eyes and the pads of your fingers." The click of Keneō's cane against the ground preceded him.

"Such generosity!" said Kuchisake.

"It is better than he deserves," Shinigami grunted. The knot of her hair was loose and littered with dry, broken leaves. Dax could see each piece of debris. Each strand of hair. Too much too much too much. "He has joined with the mortals. Betrayed his empress. He deserves a million lifetimes in Jigoku for such dishonor."

Her words rebounded in Dax's head. He hissed a breath. What fools these yūrei were, believing him possible of such deceit. He would never betray Izanami.

The pain in his wrist turned to a throb. It was an odd sensation. Heat chafed his chilled body. Drew too much of his attention. If it continued, he would have to cut off his hand to be rid of it.

Below him, the footsteps went quiet. It was time to find a new hiding spot.

He swung down, and came face-to-face with Aka Manto.

The cardmaker must have been part of the group, keeping far enough back to catch him by surprise. Sucking in a gasp of surprise, he leapt into the air. Aka Manto caught him around the throat on the way up, slamming him to the ground with enough force to shake the trees. His teeth were bared. Bits of web clung to his hair.

"Ouch," said Dax.

Aka Manto's jaw flexed. "Where is the knife? What have you done with the piece of valor?"

Dax bucked, kicking Aka Manto in the side. The man slammed him down again, making pebbles jump from the ground.

He welcomed the pain. It distracted him from his screaming senses.

"Look at you." Aka Manto growled. "Young yūrei minds are

always clouded by a hunger. Fight it. You must tell me what has happened to that blade."

Dax's mind didn't feel cloudy. It felt like a bucket of broken glass shards, shaken and slicing him raw. He needed to stop it. To taste terror again. To streamline all his warring thoughts into one sweet song.

"Focus," ordered Aka Manto. "If we do not get the second piece of the tomoe back, I can't help you."

From the direction of the river came the sound of quick footsteps—spider steps—and Aka Manto's head jerked up, strands of dark hair falling into his eyes.

"You have found him!" cried Kuchisake, appearing upside down over Dax's head, his sliced smile stretched wide. "Shinigami! Keneō! Aka Manto is here, and he has his son!"

Son.

The word cut through the hunger. Dax was no one's son. He belonged only to the empress.

A boy's image cut through his mind. The empress was wearing a mortal suit. Where was she? What had happened to her? He couldn't remember. He couldn't think past now, now, now.

"Aka Manto." Shinigami appeared in the shadows beside them, Keneō beside her, leaning heavily on his cane. "I see you've escaped the spider's web."

Dax raised a brow at the man still pinning him to the ground.

"Were you going to be someone's lunch?" he wheezed.

Aka Manto's top lip curled back in a snarl.

"The empress was displeased to find your father had broken free from Jigoku. He was meant to serve a thousand eternities there for his interference with the game." Kuchisake sighed wistfully. "I have a hunch he kept the gate in your mother's village so he could torture you both. Love is such a wondrous thing."

An image of a woman in pink scrubs filled his mind. She smiled with white teeth and soft eyes. A slash in his chest, and she was gone.

"My son has betrayed the empress," Aka Manto said, a muscle pinching at the corner of his mouth. "I must see that he undoes what he has done." His hand squeezed tighter around Dax's throat, making him writhe and pant like a mortal.

Shinigami, Keneō, and Kuchisake closed in like a pack of wolves, hungry for a kill. The old man pulled apart his cane, a long, silver blade coming free. Dax clenched his teeth, ready for it to slice him to ribbons. He welcomed it, desperate for relief from their loud voices and the scrape of their clothing against their skin and the crash of the river hidden behind the naked woods, but instead the point pressed to the side of Aka Manto's throat.

"Why should we trust you?" asked Keneō, adjusting the mask of skin over his face. "You used your cardmaking magic to give away a piece of the tomoe, and now your son has done the same."

"Lower your weapon, Keneō, or I will remove your head from your neck," said Aka Manto calmly.

"Then you will have to face me," Shinigami told him. "So many lies, after all our years of friendship."

"I have not lied," said Aka Manto.

"You said Dax had the blade in his possession," said Shinigami. "That he would keep it safe for us until the gate could be opened. But instead, he gave it away. To a *mortal*." She spat the word.

Dax groaned. Words, words, words. Why argue, when they could hunt mortals? Sip on the potent fear in their breath? Ease the pressure in his head. Dax looked up at the man now pinning his body down with his knee. He struggled to get up, but Aka Manto's weight was unforgiving.

"We will get the blade back," Aka Manto said.

Dax opened his mouth to object, but as Aka Manto's fist tightened, only a groan came out. Another image pressed through Dax's mind—a small, foldout knife. Blue on the outside, silver on the blade. His hand curled into a fist at his side.

He remembered what it felt like.

For a moment, his mind cleared.

He *remembered*.

Then the spider moved, its legs tapping, and the blood from Kuchisake's face filled Dax's nostrils and everything was *loud loud loud*.

"How?" asked Keneō. "You saw what it did when the empress touched it. Your son turned it into a weapon for mortals alone! How will any of us take it now?"

Keneō's blade dug into the side of Aka Manto's neck, bringing a black droplet of blood to his skin. Dax focused on it, his hunger surging.

"The card can be undone," said Aka Manto quickly. "Whatever magic he placed on it can be reversed."

"How?" asked Keneō. "Speak quickly, or I'll make your throat into bracelets."

"The girl must die." Aka Manto stared into Dax's eyes as he said it. "Her hold on the prize ends when her life does."

"But she has been taken by Gashadokuro," said Shinigami. "The skeleton has dragged her back into Jigoku."

The empress's nightmare realm. The word sent a shudder through Dax.

"Then we shall find her." Kuchisake stepped forward and opened a small satchel from inside his kimono, producing a green flame.

"You have the passage!" said Keneō.

"Enough to get my friend Dax there and back," said Kuchisake. "But little more."

Shinigami contemplated this a moment, then nodded.

"The second piece is in the possession of the mortal girl with Izanami. If you undo the card magic binding it, then the blade will be with the empress when she finishes the third challenge." Shinigami nodded, her wrinkled scowl accentuated by the shadows of the giant's sleepy eye.

Kuchisake blew gently on the flames to make a small ring, hovering weakly in the air. Behind its flickering, the spindly fingers of dead branches danced in the waning light. From the gate's blindingly white interior came screams of pain and mortal terror.

Dax breathed it in, the sound feeding his twisted yūrei soul. Yes. This was what he needed. No food or drink in the mortal world compared to the pure drug of a mortal's fear.

Aka Manto dragged Dax up. "I will see that it is done."

"How can we trust you?" asked Keneō. "After your son has shown such dishonor?"

Again, the word *son* cut through Dax. He wanted to grab Keneō's knife and bury it in the skin-monger's chest.

"It is the only way I can reverse the shame of his acts," said Aka Manto.

Silence prickled between them.

Finally, at Shinigami's nod, Keneō lowered his knife.

"Very well," Shinigami said. "Do not delay. We will gather the forces of Meido at the empress's palace to await the opening of the gate."

Dax grinned, imagining all the tengu and yūrei and kegare spilling from Meido into the living world. The fear the mortals would have.

His hunger spiked, sharper than ever.

The green portal was small, but it was enough. Ducking low, he stepped through the ring of shimmering fire, finding himself in the dark, on a tree branch no thicker than his thigh.

It took a moment to gain his bearings—enough time for Aka Manto and Kuchisake to follow. The wooden limb was thick enough to hold their weight, but the trunk thickened the higher it went.

The tree was upside down.

"The sky," whispered Aka Manto. "It's gone." The branch shook as he adjusted his feet and glared into the darkness below.

Whatever had once existed there had been ripped away, revealing a jaggedly cut hole to the floor below. Through it, he could see what looked like the remains of an earthquake, chunks of stone and rock hanging over a wooden floor, covered with broken benches and shattered teacups. The hot air made Dax's cold skin itch, and he scratched at his arms.

This place was . . . familiar.

"We have returned to the upside-down woods," said Kuchisake, skipping down a tree branch to peer into the hole. "It looks a bit worse for wear, if I'm being honest."

"Gashadokuro." Aka Manto's gaze darted to the side, where the light was brighter. "Where is the skeleton?"

"Gone, I think," said Kuchisake. "I don't see him in the coil."

Dax didn't know about a skeleton, but he could see the odd shape of their surroundings. The sloped floors, broken and spilling into one another. The rising clouds of steam.

A spiral. They were on the side of a very damaged spiral.

His head gave a sharp pang.

"I've been here," he said. The rough bark of the tree pressed into the palms of his hands. The hot air made him itch. Someone was screaming on a level above them, and it filled him with a rush.

"We were here together!" Kuchisake told him. "You brought me to meet your father. You said it was the greatest moment of your yūrei life."

He vaguely recalled an upside-down house, filled with spinning cards, then shook his head. He did not want to be troubled with memories. He was a servant of the dead empress, soulless and empty. He did only her bidding.

"Where is this mortal girl?" His wrist was aching again. He rubbed it.

"You mean our sweet Madeline," said Kuchisake. He leaned closer to Dax's ear. "Are we here to rescue her? Even if she is already in pieces, I think she would appreciate the gesture, don't you?"

Dax pulled away. "We are here to kill her."

Kuchisake chuffed. "Good luck with that, my friend. You saw her with the katana. She is fearsome without the weapon. With it, she will have all our heads."

Another flash through the hunger—the girl swinging the sword like a warrior. His chest heaved with unexpected excitement.

Aka Manto led a path not down or up, but across the limb to another nearby tree. There, he crossed the bouncing branches and made his way toward the gnarled, upside-down trunk. As they made their way through the trees, Dax's scar grew less irritated. Soon, it didn't hurt at all.

He looked down at his wrist, scowling. He didn't want the pain of it, but being without it struck a chord of wrongness in his chest. There was a security with that burn. It grounded him, and without it, he felt untethered. Like he might go and go until he was so mindless he was only a creature trapped in the present, without any experience to guide him.

It shouldn't have mattered. He was a weapon. All he needed to serve the empress was his cunning. But the more that scar eased, the more lost he felt.

He stopped, and while Aka Manto and Kuchisake carried on, he turned back the way they'd come. Silently, he traipsed through the branches until he arrived at the place where they'd appeared, over the hole in the floor. His wrist was burning again, the scar pink and itchy. He pressed his thumb against it, reveling in the heat that flooded up his wrist.

It prickled as he leaned over the hole.

Something was pulling him this way. Calling him, in his blood.

Was it the girl he was meant to kill? He could remember her fear now. The sweetest scent he'd ever breathed in.

He dropped into the hole in the ground, landing on the broken boards in a cloud of steam. His wrist felt raw.

He smiled and rose to his feet. Then he let the pain guide him.

EMERSON

The woman before them glowed, her skin pulsing with a delicate luminescence, as if there was a light under her glass-like skin. Emerson was struck with wonder—looking at her was like watching fireflies dance across the grass on a summer night. Like seeing the reflection of the moon on the ocean. She wanted to stare at each mirrored patch of the woman's kimono, trace every reflecting hue of green and blue and silver and gold to its source in the world around them. She wanted to run her fingers through the woman's glossy black hair, woven in an intricate twist of loops and knots, pinned together with glossy pearl clips.

"Wow," she whispered. Her desire to be close to the woman wasn't sexual, but ran through the deepest part of her, a balm to her deepest wounds. Being near her made Emerson feel better. Quieter. Peaceful.

"Yeah," said Owen, equally as awed.

"Amaterasu," growled Izanami. "Mortals, meet my husband's plaything."

Emerson glanced at Owen, who raised his brows.

"You do not belong here, Empress." Even Amaterasu's voice was like chimes, enchanting Emerson so much she nearly missed the angry tilt of her brows. "You bring kegare to the heavens."

Kegare. Emerson blinked, trying to clear the fog from her mind. She knew the word from her last time playing. Kegare was pollution. It had tainted Meido, and spread like a virus around the world, infecting everyone inside.

"I made these heavens, in case you forgot," Izanami answered.

"Heavens?" Emerson asked. "This isn't Meido?"

Amaterasu laughed, and beside her, Owen grinned, his eyes

glassy. His reaction made Emerson more aware of her own, and she elbowed him in the side. He sucked in a quick breath.

"This is as much Meido as I am the emperor's plaything." Amaterasu opened her arms wide, the sleeves shimmering with asymmetric fragments of mirror. "This is a place of purity and goodness. Can't you feel it?"

Emerson's eyes closed. She could feel something wondrous happening around her. The gentle joy of the woman's—Amaterasu's— presence.

But there was something wrong.

Emerson was wrong.

She didn't belong here, with the soft light and the gentle drumming music. The sweet scent of seawater and the soft gel ground that might have sucked her in if she would have let it. Opening her eyes, she caught her reflections in Amaterasu's sleeve, and startled at the sharpness of the faces staring back at her.

Her eyes looked too big. Her nose, pointy. Her skull, misshapen in the funhouse mirror reflection. She touched the prickly ends of it, making sure her head was still round.

"This is where the purest souls come to rest." Amaterasu lifted her hand, where a bit of gel, filled with sparkles, gleamed. Emerson stared at it, making out each individual piece of glitter like a star in the sky. There were millions of them. Millions upon millions, filling the ground and the sloping walls and the ceiling.

Were those souls?

She quickly lifted one foot, then the other, wondering if she was stepping on someone. *Lots* of someones. She cringed.

On the ground beside her, Owen had lain down and was making a snow angel in the gel.

"Owen," she hissed.

"Keep your wits about you," cautioned Izanami. "The guardian of the heavens will make you idle. It's how she convinces mortals to stay."

But even as she said it, Emerson blinked back a wave of fatigue. Why couldn't they be idle for a moment? They'd been running nonstop. They'd barely had a chance to breathe.

"All who come to me, come willingly," said Amaterasu. "But it seems not all who reach the heavens are worthy." She gave the empress a pointed look.

"We have come for the final piece of the tomoe, Amaterasu," said Izanami. "Wisdom."

The mention of the piece reminded Emerson of the card and the folded knife she'd tucked into her pocket. She inhaled deeply through her nose, focusing on their task. This wasn't a place to rest. They were still playing the game.

Amaterasu scowled, but somehow even that was blindingly beautiful.

"You shall not have it," Amaterasu whispered, hugging her kimono tightly around her. "Nothing good can come of you having the power of the tomoe. The artifact was broken and taken from you for a reason."

"Which is what, exactly?" Izanami asked, giving a wracking cough that made the woman shudder. "Because my husband was a coward? Because he was selfish and disloyal?"

"Because he protects the living as I protect the dead," Amaterasu answered.

"I protect the dead," said Izanami, stepping closer.

"You twist them into monsters," she said. "Make them live unnaturally long lives, until they're nothing but fear-hungry demons."

"And you trap your souls in ooze until they're clean to your liking," answered Izanami, kicking a bit of glittery goo across Amaterasu's slippered feet. "We both have our ways."

"This is a place of rest," Amaterasu whispered heatedly. "The souls must be pure before they can be absorbed back into nature."

"A world I created them to be a part of just as much as my *glorious* husband," said Izanami. "Or have you forgotten that part?"

"You wish to bring death to the land of the living." Amaterasu shook her head. "You shall not. You *must* not. There is an order of things. A place for every soul in every phase of existence."

"And what of my soul?" Izanami said, harshly enough that she buckled forward, arms crossed over Ian's stomach. Whatever was happening to her was getting worse, and Emerson worried deeply for Ian's fate. "I was trapped in Meido for an eternity. Locked in the dark while he rolled that boulder over my escape—a gate that must never open. You will never know that betrayal."

"I know it," she said quietly. "I was born of his tears when he left you."

Emerson swallowed thickly, watching Amaterasu glimmer as her head bowed forward, and wondering if she'd been wrong about the light under the woman's strange glass skin. If it wasn't skin at all, but the surface of a tear, shifting and changing with every movement.

When Izanami said nothing, Amaterasu sighed.

"He knew you would come."

Izanami lifted her gaze.

"He asked me to help you see reason, but since there is clearly no chance of that, here." She slipped the kimono off her shoulders, the glossy surface of her naked body moving fluidly as she gathered the mirrored robe and tossed it at the empress's feet. "Here is your precious challenge. A broken mirror, shattered by your dear husband. Only one possessing great wisdom can put it together."

Izanami fell to her knees, hands ghosting over the broken pieces of mirror, bound by threads as clear and thin as fishing line.

"You have until the light fails to complete your task," Amaterasu told them. "If you're still here when I return, you'll join the rest of my souls. I think, Izanami, that it will take a very long time to make you clean."

With that, she melted into the gel at her feet, her body suddenly nowhere and everywhere, all at once.

Emerson blinked, her head clearing. She pressed the heels of her hands to her forehead. Her thoughts felt sharp again. Her breath scraped her throat.

"What was that?" she asked.

"The protector of the heavens has that effect on people," grunted Izanami. "She uses it to soothe souls into submission."

Owen sat up. Then stood, wiping the gel off his clothes. His cheeks were flushed. He gave Emerson a look that told her they weren't going to speak about the snow angels.

Emerson touched a small piece of glitter on her fingertip. "So all of these specks of light are actually souls?"

"Souls. Prisoners," Izanami muttered, her hands still roaming over the kimono. "Prisoners of flesh. Prisoners of time. You trade one cage for another from the moment of your birth. Why should your afterlife be any different?"

"She said they go back to the world," said Owen. "After they rest."

"When she deems them clean enough," Izanami said. "Maybe that is a moment. Maybe it is an eternity. Only she can say."

I think, Izanami, that it will take a very long time to make you clean. The idea of being contained indefinitely in ooze made Emerson shiver. "But you get to be free because you're the empress."

Izanami spread out the kimono carefully on the ground, the sleeves off to the sides. It appeared as though she was looking for something on the reflective fabric.

"Has it not occurred to you that when I open the gates, you too will be free? When you live in death, there is no fear of it. No disease. No heartache or grief. Your existence will be eternal."

"So you're doing us a favor?" Owen asked, incredulous. "You're killing everything we know, and we should say thank you?"

"It would be a start," Izanami snapped back. "Now help me fix this! We don't have much time before the eye closes."

Emerson thought of the giant's eye drooping shut in Meido. She couldn't see it here in the heavens, but she knew they were running out of time.

"The game ends when the eye closes," Owen moved beside Emerson, glancing down at Ian. "The tomoe won't work after that. It's game over."

Emerson hesitated as Izanami ripped free the pieces of the mirror, the clear thread snapping as she laid them out on the sticky ground before her. There were hundreds of shards of glass. Even if they could puzzle it out, there were simply too many pieces to fit together.

The task was impossible.

"Maybe the wise thing to do is to fail," she whispered.

"*What?*" Owen turned to face her, his eyes wide. Below them, Izanami was muttering quietly to herself, trying to smash two pieces together without luck.

An uncomfortable ball of heat settled in Emerson's gut. She moved her feet, making a squishing sound. "It's the wisdom challenge, right? That means learning from what we know, what information we've been given. Well, we know what this asshole wants to do, and we know how to stop her." She motioned to Izanami, who gave a frustrated roar.

"Get down here!" she ordered Owen.

"You can't be serious," Owen said quietly to Emerson.

The ball of heat was getting hotter, making it harder to breathe. "We can't let her win."

"We can't let Ian die!"

Emerson hugged her arms against herself, her gaze darting to the rounded confines of their glittering prison. She didn't know what to do. Maddy had given her the knife and the card. Told her that if anyone could solve a wisdom challenge it was her. But would Maddy approve of her failing on purpose?

Not a chance.

Maddy would want her to find another way. They had to save Ian, just like Maddy had to save Dax, but how was she supposed to do that? Ian's fate was inexorably linked to Izanami's success. Izanami's success meant death to the living world. If they helped Izanami win, Ian would be gone, his body never again his own.

Ian was the only one who knew what she had to do, and he wasn't even here to stand with her.

"Get that thought out of your head," Owen told her.

He dropped to the ground and began helping to try to match pieces. Everywhere Emerson looked, her own distorted image stared back at her. She couldn't look at herself without feeling ashamed.

Izanami coughed, then gasped, curling into a ball beside the gathered shards.

"Empress!" Owen caught her as she fell to the side, helping to settle her on the soft ground. As she sank deeper, bits of light coated her sides, souls lulled by Amaterasu's aura.

"We have to hurry," Owen said, leaving her side to return to the puzzle. "Ian's not going to make it much longer."

"Owen," Emerson said, her voice breaking. She hugged herself tighter, feeling like she was about to break apart. How much she longed for Amaterasu's warm presence now. She felt as splintered as the glass.

"*Owen*," she said again. He was going to hate her. He would want her dead, and so would Maddy, and if Dax ever became Dax again, he would surely haunt her to her grave.

She was reeling.

She was going to be sick.

To stop the empress, she had to let Ian die.

It was easier this way, she told herself. Easier than winning this challenge, and taking the piece of valor and killing him as he'd suggested. This would be a kinder death.

Who was she to decide how another—a friend—was to die? She wasn't Izanami. She wasn't Amaterasu.

She backed away. Turned. Pressed the heels of her hands to her temples. The music didn't quiet. It was meant to soothe her but she didn't deserve soothing. She was the bad guy now. The villain of this awful game.

"Help me," Owen pleaded. He was standing beside her. "I need you. *We* need you. There has to be a way to solve this. To fit it all together. We've done harder challenges, Emerson."

She cried, unable to face him.

"He's one of us," Owen said. "He's not a pawn in this game. He's a person. He's our friend."

She wanted to scream.

"We don't have to be on opposite sides," Owen said. "Please. *Please.*"

"We've always been on opposite sides," she said, everything inside her as sharp as the glass on the ground.

"What are you talking about?" He moved in front of her, forcing her to look at him. To meet his gaze. He grabbed her shoulders, giving her a small shake.

"You have Ian," she said, her words hitting with a punch. "And he has you. And Maddy has Dax. And I have no one. Don't you see? I've always been on the other side. The *out*side."

"I don't see," Owen said, lowering, so that his face was the same height as hers. "What about you and Maddy? You two are best friends."

"Then where is she?" Emerson shouted. "She isn't here. She's with Dax, because when it comes to making a choice, she'll always choose him, and you'll always choose Ian, and no one will ever . . ." She gasped, the words choking her. She thought of Maddy, saying that she loved Emerson, that she'd come here for her just like for Dax, but then when the time came, Maddy had left her. Left her with Dax's knife, and a stupid card, and this impossible decision.

"I choose you," Owen said. "I choose you both."

"Don't say that," she said. It would break her, because it wasn't true. He would leave her, he would hate her, just like Maddy, and then she would be alone.

She was always meant to be alone.

The knowledge slashed at her until she could barely hold herself up. Why did it have to come to her? Why did she have to be the odd one out, the remainder, forced to make the big decision because she wasn't in the kind of relationships they were? She wished for ignorance, to blissfully sit by and feel unaffected while couples paired off. Not to care that she was a third, or fifth, wheel.

She wanted love. Just not all the kissing, the touching, that people often thought went with it.

"Emerson," Owen said, softer now. "You and me and Ian, we've always been on the same side."

She pinched her eyes shut.

"It's okay," he said with a small laugh. "Look around. We're on the inside of a glitter bottle. The three of us. Does that seem like a coincidence?"

She didn't want to do this right now, but there was no stopping it. The rush of feelings, potent and scary and new. The thoughts she never let herself delve too deeply into. She'd never put a label to what she was. She told herself it was because she didn't think about it, but she did. She thought about it all the time. If she would ever want to be touched the way she so clearly didn't now. If romance would ever mean something more than words and gestures. If people would think she was weird if they found out. If her parents would be sad if she never got married or had children. If she'd be sad.

If she would always be as alone as she felt in this moment.

"It has to mean something that we're here now," Owen said. "That the smartest person in our crew is holding the wisdom card."

She staggered a breath. "I don't feel very wise."

"But you are," he said. "It's not something you choose. Just like all this." He motioned around him to the glitter, and she felt a tug in her chest. A loosening of that heat behind her collar.

She met his eyes for the first time, the deep brown pools pulling her in.

"You know how I got here?" she asked, wiping her tears away with the back of her hand. "I got sucked into your closet."

"My closet?" He grinned. "And you're surprised you're covered in glitter?" He wiped away another of her tears. "It looks good on you, you know."

She gave a watery laugh. She didn't feel like she looked good. She felt like all her rough edges were on display. Like her skin was as translucent as the top of a lake. Like she couldn't hide because there was nowhere to hide, but also that she was done hiding because it was exhausting pretending like she was fine, and like she didn't care, and like being alone didn't bother her.

But also, she could hear the faraway drums, the soft pound of a metal song meant to soothe her knotted muscles, and maybe it was just because she was here, in this place. Maybe it was the leftover calm that Amaterasu had bestowed upon her. Maybe it was just Owen, looking at her like she wasn't broken. But she felt strangely okay. Not like she was an avatar running from the deadly green mist in *Assassin 0*, but like she was playing a new game, where she was the hero and the choke didn't exist at all, and she could breathe.

She lifted her hand, and looked at the way it sparkled. "It does kind of look good."

Owen smiled. "Yeah it does."

"So, what? This is my coming out party or something?"

He gave a lopsided smile. "Coming out is such a heteronormative concept. You don't have to define who you are to me, Emerson. You don't have to justify it to anyone."

Her mind cleared. It was like he'd pulled free the knot laced around her ribs, and she could finally breathe.

She didn't have to justify who she was. Not to Owen or anyone else.

Not even to herself.

She was a scientific person, a natural skeptic. She questioned everything, looking for order, looking for sense, even in this place. But as much as she'd tried to understand herself, to fit into a box, she couldn't. And maybe that was okay. Maybe it was more than okay. Maybe that was exactly how she was supposed to be. She turned, taking in the reflective pieces on the ground. Seeing her face in a different way in all of them. The different views were distorted, some of them strange, but all her.

All pieces of a puzzle.

As soon as she thought it, the edges of the shards of mirror began to change. The sharp pieces rounding into curving lines that would interlock and fit together. The teakettle puzzle photo Owen and Ian had sent her in The Bean was no different. She could see how each section connected. How the curved lines wanted to be together. Her fingers itched to touch these mirrored fragments now, to make it whole.

She knelt, far enough away from a slow-breathing Ian to give herself space, and began to build.

With Owen beside her, she took one piece at a time and fit them together. The nose pieces went together, unchanging in their reflection of her face as she moved them into position. Her eyes were wide with fear in some pieces, narrowed in anger in others, or cast down in shame. Her mouth was a thin line, or a wide smile. Halfway through a laugh. A tight grimace.

They were all her. Different pieces of her. Different feelings. Different moods. Different Emersons.

The same Emerson.

As the sections became one, she felt a searing inside of her, like a wound beginning to heal. At first it itched, then it burned, then it soothed, like Amaterasu's voice. She worked faster, some of the pieces coming together on their own, as if pulled by magnets to their rightful places. Her fingers moved fast, and she didn't think about what she was doing. Her hands knew the way.

Their time was waning. The globe around them was darkening—even if she couldn't see the giant's eye, this day would soon be done. She would find a way to make this right—to stop Izanami and save Ian. If the sword of valor could kill the empress, maybe this last challenge would give her the knowledge she needed to save her friend.

Finally, there was one piece left. A slice of her left cheek, flushed with embarrassment.

"What do you see?" Owen asked her.

Emerson looked at the oval mirror, the size of her monitor at home, and smiled. The reflection didn't show that same smile, but a hundred others—bitter, relieved, wary, and joyful. There were so many masks here, so many people she'd been and tried to be, like the players in her RPGs that never quite fit.

But this mix of them all was perfect. She was a constellation—each star alone nothing compared to the form they combined to make.

"It's me," she said.

The last piece seared to the others in the mirror, making a smooth, glossy surface. The last broken part of her healed, straightening her spine and smoothing the lines between her brows.

This was wisdom, she realized. Seeing herself for all she was, for the first time.

And . . . liking it.

She didn't mind if she was alone anymore. If Maddy went after Dax or Owen went after Ian. They still loved her, and she loved them, and if it was just her, that was okay too, because *she* was okay.

She was a thousand different reflections bound together.

Everyone she had been and needed to be. Everyone she would one day grow into, then shed like a skin to make something new.

She was not broken, she was a mosaic. A glittering, rainbow collage.

"Damn," said Owen.

She glanced over, but he wasn't looking at the mirror. He was smiling at her. "You just look very . . . lead actor."

"Final form energy," she whispered, remembering how Maddy had looked when they'd first come back to the game. When they'd arrived by choice, rather than being dragged here against their will. How Owen had looked ready to take on the world after kissing Ian. "I told you we're leveling up."

"The glitter helps," he said.

She laughed.

"Where is it?" Izanami struggled up beside them, wide, hungry eyes moving over the finished puzzle. She snatched the card from Emerson's pocket, holding it in Ian's shaking grasp. "Where is the third prize?"

Emerson reached for Dax's pocketknife. For a moment she didn't know if she would open the blade and drive it into Ian's heart, or hand it over. She glanced down at the mirror, but where her face had been a moment ago was now Ian's. It was broken into just as many pieces. Some of them young, some older. His hair was short, and then ragged. His eyes were clear, and black from rim to rim.

In some fragments, he was an oni, with red skin and sharp teeth.

In others, he was the empress.

But the pieces didn't come together like they had for Emerson. They flickered, one to the next to the next, like a light being turned on and off on different parts of Ian. It filled Emerson with a sense of wrongness. An urge to make it stop. The pieces of him—Ian, Izanami, oni—would never fit together. They were never meant to.

She moved closer, the knife in her fist, but as she came over the mirror again, it was her face in it. Her neck, her shoulders.

Around her neck was a pendant on a thin chain. A circle, divided into three swirling, comma-shaped pieces. One black, one gold, one gleaming like the mirror.

The tomoe.

She understood then.

She was not supposed to kill Ian. She was supposed to remake the tomoe, and then use that great power to save them.

"Emerson," Owen whispered. Then he grabbed her shoulder and gave her a shake. "Emerson, you did it!"

The card in Izanami's grasp was burning. The smoldering embers lit Ian's face, his sallow, sickly skin and bulging eyes.

Emerson's heart hammered against her ribs.

The light was growing darker. The flecks of glitter, dim.

She'd solved the challenge. She knew what she had to do—to get the tomoe—but how, she wasn't sure.

"Look!" Owen pointed behind them, to where a green gate had appeared over the shiny ground, the flames shimmering like the souls around it.

Through it, Emerson could see the river, and the bridge near the cave.

Home.

Nerves trembled through her.

Izanami crawled toward the mirror, the last of the card in her grip burning away to a golden stone. The final piece of the tomoe. The last prize.

"At last," she said, then reached into Ian's pocket to draw out a black stone the size of her fist. Izanami set it on the hard surface of the mirror, where it began to vibrate and jump. She pushed the second piece against it, where it made two thirds of a circle, and left a visible gap for the third. She reached a hand toward Emerson. "Quick, give me the knife."

Owen sent a wary glance at Emerson.

"Give it to me!" Izanami ordered. "The only chance of saving your friend Ian is to save me."

The only chance of saving their world was to kill her.

Opening her fist, Emerson let the knife fall into Ian's outstretched hand.

This was it.

They were out of time.

Izanami placed the pocketknife on the mirror between the two pieces of the tomoe. Emerson held her breath, imagining it extending into the katana like it had with Maddy. Spreading into a bright blade with a long, graceful handle.

But nothing happened.

The prizes grew still. The knife did not change.

"No," said Izanami, turning on her. "We need the katana. We need Madeline."

A shadow fell over them.

"Your time is up, empress. It is time for you join the souls, and be purified, so you can finally be rid of the filth that coats your soul."

Amaterasu rose from the gel, sparkling and glorious, and Emerson felt her worries instantly calmed. The guardian raised her hands, and drops fell from them like tears, glistening with the lights of countless souls.

"Stop," Izanami shouted. "Owen!"

Emerson looked to Owen, but he was entranced by Amaterasu, looking up at her with a gentle smile on his face. It took another moment to realize he was sinking into the gel.

And still another after that to realize she was following him under.

MADDY

Maddy scrambled up a slick metal surface, surrounded by hot water. It lapped at her feet, burning through her shoes. She clutched her arm to her chest. Her wrist was broken, hand dangling limply. Her leg had been too—twisted inward in a way that had brought a surge of bile up her throat. But somehow it had fixed itself, and she'd been able to flip onto her stomach before she'd slid off her metal island.

She reached the rounded top, perching herself on her hip before she slid down the other side. Her gaze darted off to the steaming amber water below, to the twisting floors of the building overhead. Her breath came faster. Her heartbeat, in punches.

The coils.

They spiraled above her, floors broken through at random intervals. Dirt and rock and waterfalls of liquid spilling through the gaps. The fire that had circled one of the central floors had climbed to others as well, burning brighter than ever. Heating the room until each gasp felt like swallowing flames.

The skeleton had grabbed her. She remembered that now. Dragged her down through the earth and dropped her. She'd fallen, fallen, fallen, finally colliding with this metal island. Her leg. Her back. Her skull. Everything had cracked and broken.

But now . . .

She looked down at her arm, straight again. She turned her wrist, testing it.

She was healed.

Where had the skeleton gone? She couldn't see it. Was it back up in Meido? On one of the lower floors, making mayhem? Its absence created pressure inside her to move. She didn't want to be here when it came back.

She rose to a crouch, jaws tightening as a burning tree fell from above into the water beside her with a loud hiss. Chaos reigned around her, screams coming from above. A crash, as one of the levels collapsed on the floor below it. People were knocked free, their arms pedaling uselessly as they fell into the amber water around her. Throwing her weight to the side to avoid a downpour of broken teacups, she slipped down the side of the island. Her hand reached out, grasping a solid, protruding beam.

A key.

She used it to hoist herself back up. The lock—that's where she'd landed. The bottom corner stuck out from the hot water, the keyhole filled by the golden prize Emerson had grabbed in the chamber in those caves. The skeleton had used it to free itself.

With that freedom, it'd trapped her again.

A splash came from behind her, and she turned to find another burning tree sinking slowly into the water. This place was caving in on itself.

She needed to get out of here.

Up. Up was out, that's what they'd said before. She needed to find the river, then she'd go back to Meido, then she'd find Dax, and they'd follow Emerson and Owen and the empress-infested Ian to the next level.

She choked on despair. It was so far. So *much.*

No. She would not give up. One level at a time. That's how she'd get out.

There was a sand dune ahead, under a broken floor. If she could swim to it, she could climb onto the level above, bypass the portal between levels. It wasn't close—a pool-length, at least, and the water would be boiling. But she was a strong swimmer. She just needed to move fast.

Her heels squeaked against the metal as she slid down.

She touched the water with one finger, drawing back with a pained grunt. The pad of her finger was red and already blistering.

She stood, her feet sloped. She'd dive, push out as far as she could. Make this a sprint—the fastest she'd ever done. She imagined a pool, the yellow lane lines bobbing in the water in place of the broken teacups. The black line along the bottom marking her lane. She was standing on a starting block, not a lock, and the screams were her whistle.

One harsh, deep breath, and she dove.

Her fingertips hit the water first. Then her arms, her face, her body. The shock was delayed, but when it hit, it was all-consuming. Pain stabbed through her skin, through her flesh and muscles. Instead of screaming, she kicked, keeping her eyes closed, driving her body as hard as she ever had.

One breath, one stroke.

One breath, one stroke.

It hurt. Everything, everywhere, *hurt*. She started to pant, small whimpers slipping out of her lips. She was boiling alive.

Push through, she thought. This was a test, only a test. But tolerable turned to too much in a breath, and she knew she was in trouble.

She wasn't going to make it.

Desperately, she turned back toward the starting block where she'd begun. The water seared her skin. Blisters rose on her hands and exposed forearms. Her nerves spat fire through her body.

One leg stopped kicking, even as she willed it on. It twitched and writhed, then numbed and turned to dead weight.

"Help!" she screamed, still three strokes away from the lock behind her. She didn't know who she was calling for. There was no one here to help.

She heard a splash behind her.

Looking over her shoulder, she searched for movement, but only found debris. Floating cups. Tree limbs, half ablaze.

She hadn't seen that before. She thought of turning toward it but the water was churning beneath her. Something was coming up from beneath.

Frantically, she pedaled toward the block, dragging her leg behind her. Welts split her arms and back. The pain was nearly blinding.

Hurry, hurry, hurry.

Something skimmed by her ankle. A soft touch, but it might as well have torn her boiled skin. She screamed. Kicked. Swam.

A splash behind her. She was grabbed by the back of her collar and dragged backward through the water. Dropped on her back on a hard, hot surface. She couldn't think. The wood scraped her raw arms, the back of her neck. The hot air seemed to slap at every raw wound. She looked up but the coils were too bright, and the shadow over her blinked in and out of focus.

The dune. She'd made it to the sand dune. She was on a broken table over it, low and wide, like the tea table in Shinigami's hut. Gold shone all around her, making her eyes burn.

A voice cut through her agony. Cold, but familiar.

"I'm here to kill you, mortal. But it seems you've already done the job."

She would know his voice, his face, even void of all humanity, anywhere.

Dax, she tried to whisper, but her throat burned. He stood over her, looking down, his face wavering in her vision. When he reached for her, there was no kindness in his touch. He grabbed her braids in his fist. Jerked her head up. Her head slung limply to the side.

Please remember, she thought, teetering on the edge of consciousness. Through the haze, she could see Dax holding his left wrist, his thumb pressing to the tender skin over his veins, and her mind began to drift.

"Three days ago I saw you in the grass beside the ocean," she whispered.

"Last words? How sweet."

"You told me that you loved me but you'd never take me broken." Her heart was erratic. Her thoughts growing fuzzy. "I saw you after breakfast trading stories with your friends."

Dax scowled as he stepped back. "Where did you hear that?"

"You laugh, but now . . ." She gasped. Everything hurt. It was too much. "But now I can't." Tears filled her eyes.

"Stop." Dax clutched his hands over his ears.

"Now I can't." she gasped.

This was it.

This was the end.

Darkness came, stealing her vison.

"Because I know the way it ends."

A tear slipped down her cheek. One more verse. One more, and at least she would know that she'd tried, even if she'd failed.

I'm sorry, Emerson. You were right. You're always right.

"That's enough," he said, grabbing his wrist. "Stop it!"

"You hold me but don't see me," she groaned. The vibrations of her words pummeled her raw throat. "You never let me go. I hate myself for missing you. I hate that you don't know."

Her breath stopped.

Her heart stopped.

As her body failed, she closed her eyes, and swam.

"That I'm haunted," Dax murmured. "All I ever want . . ."

The last word she heard was her name.

She came alive with a gasp. Her back arched, fingers digging into the wooden planks below her. The air clouded around her, white and bright. Was she dead? Was this what happened after?

Sitting up, she swung her legs off the table. Her shoes crackled against the broken teacups on the floor. She checked her arms, her face. Her skin wasn't burned away. It felt soft—damp with perspiration, but unburned. She'd been healed, and Dax . . .

"Maddy!"

Someone was yelling. She rose, broken ceramic crunching under her shoes. She peered through the steam. "Dax?"

He appeared a moment later, his hair wet, his clothes clinging to his body. Then she was in his arms, and he was holding her close, so tight she could barely breathe, but she didn't care. He was cold, and he cooled her hot skin, and she curled into him, her head on his shoulder, her hands fisted in the back of his shirt.

"You're here," she breathed.

"I'm here," he replied.

She pulled back, just enough to look into his dark eyes. His skin was too pale. His body, chilled. "You're still . . ."

"Yūrei," he said.

"You know me?" she asked. How was this possible? "Do you have the knife?"

He pulled her close again. "I have you. That's all I need."

Her hands rose up his spine. Curled around the back of his neck.

His bones stuck out, too sharp, like his jaw, and his teeth. She didn't care. He was him again. He was Dax.

"My wrist burned when you sang—more than before. Then . . . my head was cleared. I remembered. Like how you remember a dream. The words of the song, then your voice. Then everything. Every single thing. I remember all of it."

Heat built in her throat, making it hard to swallow.

"I'm glad," she whispered.

"You're out of your mind for coming here," he told her.

"You going to lecture me?"

"That was it. That was the lecture." He stroked a hand over her hair, weaving his fingers through her braids. Her knees bumped his legs. His hips pressed to her waist. She inched closer. There would be no space between them. Not a breath. Not a whisper.

"I thought I died," she murmured. He squeezed her tighter. His hands on her shoulders. Her arms. Skimming over every place he could touch. The steam was pressing in around them. A cocoon of heat. A boy of ice.

"You did," he said. "But you came back. I could feel you, here." He pressed his thumb to her scar. "I knew you were still close. I could feel you even when you weren't close."

"You die to advance," she said.

"What?"

"That's the way you go to the next level. You die."

He flinched.

"Could we skip that?" he asked. "I'd rather not watch my girl-friend boil to death again if it's all the same."

She looked up at him. "Girlfriend, huh?"

"Soulmate?" he offered. "Love of my undead life? My boo. Get it? Because I'm a ghost."

"That's funny."

"I thought so."

She touched his chin. His bottom lip. His jaw. His nose brushed over hers.

"Wife," he whispered.

Everywhere they connected, goose bumps rose on her skin.

Warmth blossoming against his cold. The scar on her wrist sparking in a different, pleasant way.

"You remembered."

"I never forgot. It was just . . . hidden. *I* was hidden. But you found me."

"And you found me."

She closed her eyes as his cold cheek nuzzled hers. She pressed her chest against his, reveled in his cool breath on her lips. There was something familiar about his scent. Her brows pulled together.

"Why do you smell like—"

"Death." He cringed. "Sorry."

She laughed. "No. Peanut butter?"

"Oh." He grinned. "I made some."

"Is this a ghost hobby?"

"Kind of? Turns out I'm a cardmaker." He gave a short laugh. "I use my music to make cards like the ones we used in the game. You should see it. I made a guitar. Well, a lot of guitars. But only one I can actually play."

He was talking faster, like he was excited.

"Dax," she said. "That's incredible."

"It's a handy trick," he said. "You're incredible. And warm. And . . ." He pressed a kiss to her temple. "I'm not sure how long I have."

She could feel it too. The ticking of the clock. How long would he know her without his knife? She reached around his waist, pulling him as close as she could. "We need to finish the game. If the prizes can make something powerful enough to bring Izanami back, they can bring you back too."

He pulled away, but she didn't let go. "Maddy, even if you could get the tomoe from her, I'm yūrei. You can't bring me back from what I am."

He believed it. She could see it in his face, in his eyes. Resignation.

"Oh, Dax," she said. "If I can find you in another world, I can do anything I want."

She leaned closer, and kissed him.

At first he was too shocked to respond, but then he melted into her. His mouth was cold but passionate, his fingers tunneling through her hair. She gasped as his teeth skimmed her lip, and pressed closer, chest to chest. His heart echoed each beat of hers, and made her more desperate to save him.

"If I lived, I would live for you," he whispered in her ear. "But since I don't, you should know I exist *because* of you. Not even death can keep you out of my heart."

She exhaled in a rush, tingles on her skin.

The ground beneath them began to rumble. The broken teacups clattered against one another, then jumped with a booming crash. Another followed, sending a landslide through a hole in the ceiling from somewhere through the steam to Maddy's left. Dust filled the air, blending with the steam, making her choke.

"What is—" Her words were interrupted by a roar so loud Maddy was forced to clap her hands over her ears. When it was done, a great gust of wind blew through the coil, clearing the steam and dust. Still gripping Dax, Maddy turned just in time to see a flash of giant white bones dropping from above down the center of the spiral. They landed with a thunderous explosion, knocking Maddy and Dax off their feet and onto the tea table where Maddy had awoken.

"Gashadokuro," Dax said.

Maddy's breath came faster.

The skeleton.

They needed to go up, to get out before the monster began a new tantrum, but before she could rise, a fist the size of a desk punched through the ground beside them, bony fingers unfurling skyward.

Dax moved faster than Maddy could see. He was over her in an instant, his body flattening hers against the table, blocking her from the cups and stones that pummeled his back. The ground gave way as the fist pulled back, dragging the table into the hole it had created. Maddy's stomach lurched into her throat as they fell together, down, down, down, a roller coaster with no track, toward the water below.

"Free falling," Dax whispered. *Sang.* His voice against her ear, somehow steady. She opened her mouth to scream, but there was no air in her lungs. Dax's arms were around her, beneath her, pinning her to the length of the table. Through the corner of her eye she could see the amber water. Smell the harsh scent of burned rice tea. She was going to boil again. She was going to die.

The table was suddenly burning. She twisted against it, but Dax held her closer. The flames were cold. She didn't understand. They were going to hit the water. Did he know that? Maybe it's what he wanted. He was yūrei again. Did he even know her?

She closed her eyes and gripped him with all her strength as the last of the board burned away.

I love you.

She willed him to know.

I love you, I love you.

She landed, expecting water. Heat. A hard smack.

Instead, she sank into a bed of soft feathers.

Her eyes shot open. Dax stared down at her, his eyes dark with worry, his mouth strained. White feathers puffed up above him, falling like snow. Above him, around him, fire and death and danger, but there, with his chest hovering above hers and his hand still firm behind her back, she was safe.

The feathers curled around her, arching up into a bowl, and from the center reached a white sail, shimmering with the same white down.

A boat made of feathers.

A laugh burst from her. He'd made this. A cardmaker, he'd said. She didn't understand exactly what that meant, but the table had burned like the cards in the game, and then this.

She stared up at him in awe.

Behind him, a crown of pointed bones appeared, melded to the skull of the giant skeleton. Her eyes went wide, her mouth dry.

Dax turned, following her gaze. He flipped onto his back, shoving her against the side of the boat behind him. The water sloshed against the hull, hissing as it made contact, boiling and churning as the skeleton kicked out a leg to make a wave that made the boat spin. The feathers held, and Dax rose, his balance untouched by the rocking, as if he weighed nothing.

Gashadokuro leaned over them, dragging a scream from Maddy's throat. Boiling droplets splashed onto her face and outstretched hands as the skeleton's pointed crown slammed into the first floor of the coil, knocking it free in chunks. His pale jaw clapped open and shut, his sunken eyes smoldering black with fury. Instead of shadows, the water swirled around him in a steaming, churning cloak as he rose to his feet.

"Mine," the skeleton boomed.

The word felt sharp, a hook, implanting in her chest. Her limbs felt suddenly weak with fear. The water shifted around them, rocking them hard from side to side. Something bumped against the bottom and then the wet, white bone of the fingertip curled over the edge.

The skeleton was going to sink them.

Dax's chin dropped. His hands were loose at his sides but his fingers were moving like a gunslinger from an old Western, ready to draw. The sight of him, even from the back, gave her chills. He was a predator now. A yūrei.

"Sorry," said Dax. "Her soul already belongs to me."

The vow from their wedding echoed in her head in the wake of his words: *It is a promise that cannot be undone. Even in death your souls will belong to each other.*

He lifted his hand, his wrist outturned, and showed Gashadokuro his scar. The skeleton leaned forward, peering at Dax's arm, and let out a roar so powerful, waves formed around him, higher than the boat's sides. His arms lifted as he punched at them, but Dax dodged out of the way, shoving him backward in a tidal wave of boiling water.

More hands appeared on the sides of the boat, but though they tried to pull it down, it would not sink. Maddy gripped the edge, kicking at the finger across the hull. It retreated, but another quickly replaced it.

"Dax!" she cried as a hand hooked around her shoulder, pulling her backward toward the edge. Dax spun, a blur of movement, and before she could blink, the hand was in pieces at the bottom of the boat.

She grabbed a pinky, still wiggling, and hoisted it over her shoulder like a bat.

"Thanks," she said.

He grinned.

She swung, and he ducked. The pinky collided with a new hand, knocking it off course, and it rammed through their feather sail, sending white down through the air.

"The gate!" Dax shouted.

"What gate?"

Gashadokuro attacked with a vengeance, arms shooting from its sides to grab at Dax. He fought them off with a speed Maddy could barely register, his body a blur as he broke one wrist after another.

"Watch out!" he shouted, as the skeleton heaved the giant metal lock from the water and slammed it down. A wave sent them careening toward a blackened tree, half submerged, and the feather sail got caught in the branches. Hot water splashed into the bottom of the boat, burning Maddy through her pants. With a cry, she pushed up the siding.

She looked frantically around but saw no gate, no green flames.

A hand grabbed her around the waist, and she cried out, dropping her bone weapon into the water.

"Dax!" she screamed, but he was scaling Gashadokuro's leg, nimbly crawling between the knobby bones of its knee to avoid the creature's swatting hands.

Before she went over, a man jumped onto the boat from the charred tree the sail was tangled in and dragged her free from the skeletal fist. With a speed equal to Dax's, he chopped and crushed the hands reaching toward them, until the bottom of the boat was filled with shards of bone.

The man turned to her, eyes dark, hair in a knot. Much of the fabric of his ragged kimono had been burned away, but his skin was untouched by the heat. He was slim, and tall, but it was the firm set of his mouth that struck her.

"You're Dax's father," she said. His mom, Vera, had said he was from this world. Maddy had had no idea that Dax had found him.

He bowed.

"I saw him with you," he said. "I heard what he said to Gasha-dokuro."

Maddy didn't know how to answer.

"You came back for him."

She nodded.

"Anytime now!" Dax shouted. He had climbed higher, so far up that Maddy had to crane her neck back to see him. He was standing on a rib bone, yanking at one of the many arms that protruded below the skeleton's shoulder.

A flash of green drew her gaze into the tree. In the branches, a man was standing, a small green flame flickering over a pouch in his hand.

"There is only a little left!" he cried. "We must be quick!"

Kuchisake.

Confusion made her scowl. The last time she'd seen Kuchisake, he'd been attacking her. Now he was going to help them? She didn't trust it.

"Maddy, go through the gate," Dax shouted, just as one of the skeleton's swiping hands caught him behind the knees and knocked him down the creature's chest. Maddy's heart stuttered as he caught himself on the pointed end of the creature's sternum, and kicked at a hand reaching toward him.

Gashadokuro screamed, its upper arms thrashing through the coils, raining down stones and trees and screaming people.

"I'm not going anywhere without you!" Maddy shouted back.

"You have to get out of here!"

The boat shook and rocked, waves from the debris tossing them from side to side.

"Go," Aka Manto told Maddy as the feathers finally began to split. Water filled the bottom of the boat rapidly, pulling it down into the lake of tea.

She didn't have a choice. Her hand in Dax's father's, she climbed onto the tree limbs. They cracked under her weight as she clambered through them toward Kuchisake.

"Hello, my love," he said, in a way that either meant he was happy to see her, or ready to kill her. "I knew our Dax wouldn't murder you. I knew it!"

"Aren't you clever?" she muttered.

He giggled, then motioned toward the small ring of green

flames. It was the size of a tunnel slide at a playground—she'd have to crawl to get through.

Dax. She turned to find him in two of Gashadokuro's fists. The creature had grabbed Dax's arms and legs, pulling them outward to tear him apart.

Fear iced through her.

"Let him go!" She scrambled back toward what remained of the boat.

"No." Aka Manto blocked her. She moved to bypass him, but he grabbed her arm. He gave her a gentle look.

"He's risked everything," he said, then glanced back at Dax. "Do not let it be in vain."

Then he crouched low. With a surge of power, he leapt from the tree, shattering the branches, and landed on the thick sloping arc of Gashadokuro's pelvis. Scrambling up the boulder knobs of his spine, Dax's father wove though the skeleton's ribs, his movements so fast she could barely track them.

With a roar, the monster released Dax, who fell onto the ruined remains of the feather boat. He looked up at the skeleton, who was now punching his own rib cage to rid himself of the speedy yūrei.

"Aka Manto!" Dax shouted. "Leave him!"

"You must not let the empress open the gate," Aka Manto called to Dax. "The final piece of the tomoe awaits in the heavenly eye. Izanami will be there. Use the knife to end her. It is the only way to protect what you love."

"Aka Manto!" Dax shouted. "Jun. *Dad!*"

It was too late. Gashadokuro dropped into the boiling tea, taking Aka Manto with him. The hot pool was swirling now, a funnel dragging what remained of the boat toward its center.

"We are out of time," Kuchisake said. "We must go now!"

Maddy waited until Dax reached the tree, and then dove into the passage gate. Cold leached into her as she tumbled forward, rolling into a tree on the soft, mossy ground. She was up in a shot, watching the gate as the dusk around her faded quickly to night.

Kuchisake rolled through after her.

"Where is—" She heaved out a breath of relief as Dax fell through the closing gate. She grabbed his arm before he hit the ground, and in an instant was pressed against his cool, hard chest.

"I'm sorry," she said, recalling the horrified look on his face when Aka Manto had gone down.

He only nodded.

She pulled back only to find herself in Kuchisake's arms.

"This is nice, isn't it?" he asked as blood from his mouth dripped into her hair.

She pushed back with a cringe. Below her feet, the ground moved, throwing her off-balance. She reached out to steady herself on a large boulder, taking in their new surroundings. Thick fog. Gray moss and dead grass. The land stretched out before her, long and narrow, before dropping away into the fog. Were they on an island? She couldn't see the water around them, if there was any.

The ground moved again.

Not the violent tremor of an earthquake, but something steadier. A subtle shifting. The air blew in her face, bringing the dead scent of Meido with it. She couldn't see anything beyond the cloud, but she braced, ready for whatever this next nightmare would bring.

When she glanced back, Dax was facing Kuchisake. Tension prickled between them, straightening Maddy's spine. She heaved a heavy breath into the cold air, and it misted in front of her lips before the breeze took it away.

"I have to stop her," said Dax. "If Izanami gets through, she'll kill everything I love."

Kuchisake was quiet for a moment, then nodded. "If it is what you love, then it is what I love, my friend."

Dax slowly reached out a hand. "Friends?"

Kuchisake lifted it to his lips, and kissed it.

Dax shook his head, giving a mildly annoyed groan. "My father said the piece of the tomoe was in the heavenly eye. How do we get there?"

Kuchisake's gaze lifted to the tree Maddy had rolled into. Not a tree at all, she realized, but a thick column covered with rocks and vines and stones, leading to what looked suspiciously like a giant ear.

She gaped at the ground below her. Not an island surrounded by fog, but a shoulder in the clouds.

"We're on the giant," she whispered.

Dax huffed, then raked a hand through his hair. "The heavenly eye. It's the giant's eye?"

"And it is nearly closed," said Kuchisake. "You must hurry if you're going to get in."

Hope exploded like a firework inside her. They'd escaped Jigoku. Now they just had to get to Emerson and Owen, and solve the final challenge.

They were going home—all of them.

"Shinigami and Keneō will be waiting for our return at the empress's palace," said Kuchisake. "I will hold them off as long as I can."

"I bet you will," Maddy muttered.

Kuchisake turned to her, his grin, for once, pulling straight.

"It is my duty to protect those I've bound in eternal union," he said. "Izanami is my empress, but there are more sacred honors to uphold. What kind of friend would I be if I bound you both to each other forever, only to help another pull you apart?"

Maddy couldn't quite believe what she was hearing. But there was earnestness in his tone she hadn't heard before. A truth she couldn't entirely doubt.

"Thank you," said Dax.

Kuchisake smiled, his mouth torn at the edges. "Such a wonderful game we have played."

Dax gave him a half smile.

Then Kuchisake walked off the shoulder of the giant into the clouds, and was gone.

Wordlessly, they turned toward the boulders and trees that made up the giant's neck and climbed, using rocks as stepping stones and vines of hair as rope. They rested in the cave of its ear only to catch their breath, then traveled a thin wrinkle of stone up the side of the nose to the single, nearly closed eye.

The white sliver was thin enough that they would have to slide on their bellies to get through.

Maddy took one last look outward into Meido. From here, they could see all of it—the gray, snaking river, quiet with night, the tengu sweeping dangerously over the dead woods. The bridge that had once broken under their weight, and Kuchisake's palace, so far below, the giant spiders that guarded it only tiny black dots.

She took Dax's hand.

Together, they waded into the gelatinous light of the giant's eyeball, and slid into the heavens.

OWEN

This was nice.

Like taking a bath in Jell-O—but really warm Jell-O that glimmered and smelled like jasmine. His mom's jasmine tea. He could hear her laughing as his ears went under, the way she did when he did that scene from *Spaceballs*. God. He hadn't done that in forever. Since just after his dad had died. It was the only way to make her smile. Owen could see it when he blinked now, behind his closed lids. Her smile. *That* smile. The way her nose would get red and she'd wipe her eyes because it hurt to think about him. It hurt Owen too, but he'd keep going, keep pushing, running the bit about being your "father's brother's nephew's cousin," and she'd laugh and laugh until her tears changed to happy, and all his uselessness melted away. This he could fix. Not his dad's cancer or the bills she couldn't pay or the uncertainty, but he could make her laugh.

Another laugh joined his mom's, deep and familiar. He knew it even now, years and years later. His dad was here. They could run those lines together. Owen could hear him calling, the lights pulsing with his voice, *Owen, Owen, Owen, look at you, son. Look how big you are. You're taller than me already. Let me look at you. Let me hear that bit your mom loved. It's okay now, son. It's okay, it's okay, tell me everything. Tell me who you are. Tell me who you love. Tell me. I've got all the time in the world to listen.*

Then a fist in his hair, dragging him up.

"Don't you fucking bail on me now."

Emerson glared at him, glitter in her short hair, on her nose, on her cheeks. She was pretty. Did she know she was pretty? It was nearly dark now, apart from the sliver of light on the far sloping wall, but she glowed. She looked like sunshine.

He should tell her.

"You look like sunshine," he said.

"Unbelievable." She gave his hair another yank.

"Ow!"

"The knife didn't change. The tomoe won't come together!" She jutted her chin toward a flash of green. "And our gate is closing!"

His thoughts returned slowly. The ground glowed in a rainbow of colors. The rounded wall, the curved ceiling. A sphere of glitter. He saw the green passage gate, shrinking before his eyes. It was the size of the cave mouth now. The place where this had all begun. He wanted to go back into the Jell-O. "Emerson, my dad is here."

Her face changed then, and the wince pulled at something inside him. Tightened the strings that had gone slack.

"We're not done," she told him. "I saw what I need to do. The mirror showed me. We have to complete the tomoe. That's how we beat her. We take the power for ourselves, then we free Ian, and go home."

The game. The pieces of the tomoe. *Ian.*

His gaze shot to Izanami, kneeling over the two curved pieces of the tomoe and the pocketknife on the mirror. He looked down at his body, all submerged in the shining gel except his head and shoulders where Emerson had pulled him out.

"Wouldn't you rather sleep?"

The gentle female voice made him instantly bleary again. He closed his eyes, the warmth pulling him back into its welcoming embrace.

"Fight it," Emerson said.

A million lights were calling him.

The sliver of light was paper thin.

Darkness was coming.

He was slipping, sinking, every muscle that had been strained finally relaxing. Peace. That's what this was. He wanted to tell Emerson how beautiful it was. He wanted to tell Ian, to show him. *You don't have to be afraid.*

Emerson had let him go. She stood, and he reached for her weakly, wanting her back. They could be close here. Forever out and free. Nothing left to cause them pain. But she faced the glowing woman with shining, glassy skin, like a warrior.

Unease flexed his muscles.

Amaterasu raised her hands, and spindles of warm light pressed through the air toward Emerson's heart. She tried to step aside, but her feet were stuck in the gel. Amaterasu's golden threads circled her, trapping her arms against her sides. She opened her mouth, but the sweetest music came out, making Owen's eyes blink heavily.

"We're not done," Emerson said again, this time through her teeth. This time, for Amaterasu.

Owen flinched, his descent paused. His dad's voice grew loud again. *It's okay, buddy. It's okay, it's okay.*

Owen's chest clenched.

It felt like goodbye.

He pressed up, his strength returning. His dad's voice fell silent, ripping tears from Owen's eyes. Pain filled him, soul deep. It felt like he was being torn. Tested. Like he was *alive,* a dozen threads tugging all different directions. He thrashed until he got to the surface of the gel. Tiny pulsing lights covered him, making him glow like Emerson. He reached for her, but Izanami caught his eye. She'd fallen over the mirror and the pieces of the tomoe, hacking coughs raking through Ian's body.

He made his way toward her on his hands and knees, dragging through the thick ground. He grabbed Ian, pulled him against his chest.

They were too late.

The game was ending. Ian's body was failing.

Should he take him through the passage gate? Would he live there any longer than he would here? Owen glanced at it, now the size of an oven door. He could feel home slipping away.

"It's okay," he said, terror sharpening his wits. He grabbed the knife, opened the blade, shut it again. How did it work? Why didn't it change like it had for Maddy? What had Dax done to it?

They needed this last prize to make the tomoe.

Ian's breaths came in shallow sips.

"It's done," Izanami panted. "We've failed."

"No." Desperation rocked through him. This wasn't the end.

He dropped the knife, pulling Ian closer. Squeezing him as he shook. But even though he denied it, he could feel the truth pulling at him. The gel ground softening beneath his knees.

"I don't want to be alone."

Owen didn't know if it was Ian or Izanami talking, but he didn't let go. If this was it, he would be here for the end, and through it, to whatever waited on the other side.

"You're not," he said, longing for the peace he'd felt just moments ago. "I'm here."

He looked up to Emerson, and his breath caught.

She was leaning toward Amaterasu, her arms at her sides, her teeth bared. Snares of golden thread surrounded her, but she didn't sink as he had. She didn't buckle under the sweet chiming words of the guardian of the heavens. She pushed back, her eyes open, as fearsome and powerful as Amaterasu was lovely.

"*I'm* not done," Emerson said, and then thrust her arms out to the sides. The bindings fell away, flickering like sparklers on a dark night. Amaterasu gaped at her, her skin shivering, growing brighter. But Emerson did not back down.

She was magnificent.

"I'd listen to her if I were you," came a hard voice through the dark.

Still gripping a trembling Izanami against his chest, Owen twisted, finding Maddy beside him, her body aglow with glitter, her clothes tattered and wet. At her flank, a shadow moved. None of the gel clung to it, not a single speck of light.

Owen didn't realize it was Dax until Maddy lowered, and the gleam from her body lit his face in a prism of colors.

Owen swallowed a breath. Dax's mouth pulled into a grim line. His body was bony and lithe. He moved like an animal, stalking his prey.

Was this his friend, or a demon?

Maddy picked up something off the ground. As she rose, the object in her hand glowed silver, and then burst out from her fist with a high whistle.

The katana.

"Who . . ." Amaterasu balked, then narrowed her eyes on the weapon. "Valor."

Hope surged through Owen as Maddy lifted it over her shoulder, but the guardian raised her hands again. Gold light shot out, thick ropes now, cutting through the air toward Maddy.

"It's time for you to rest," Amaterasu told her, but her voice no longer sounded like chimes. It was strident, and set Owen's teeth on edge. Maddy sliced the katana down, cutting through the ropes that trapped Emerson. They broke like cut hoses, spraying golden light that flashed inside of the sphere. Amaterasu screamed, her voice making Owen dizzy, but Maddy only lunged closer, meeting her bursts of light blow for blow.

"Stop," Owen said. "Stop!"

They needed the final piece of the tomoe. Maybe there was still a chance to fix this.

The passage gate was the size of a manhole cover.

A cold hand closed on Owen's shoulder, and when he looked up Dax was staring down at him with an unblinking gaze.

Fear crashed over him. Owen scrambled backward, recalling too clearly how his old friend had acted at Kuchisake's house in Meido. He pushed Ian behind him, using his body as a shield.

"It's me," Dax said, raising his hands in surrender. His palms were pale, making the scars from old burns stand out brightly.

"Prove it."

"Your name's Owen," Dax said quickly, his smile sharp, and his voice too low to trust. "You're an actor, and a hypochondriac, and your deepest fear is that everyone will realize I'm better looking than you."

Owen huffed. "Now I know you're lying." He took Dax's extended hand, and he pulled Owen up with ease. "But whatever helps you sleep at night."

"I don't need to sleep. I'm already dead."

Owen grimaced, turning away from the passage. "We need the final piece of the tomoe." They couldn't leave without it, otherwise Ian was as good as gone.

"Maddy has it in the knife." He glanced over Owen's shoulder at Ian. "What about the empress? We can't let her cross over."

Maddy screamed as she swung the sword back, glitter flying from the end of it. Emerson had circled behind Amaterasu, and was holding her in a headlock. They were sinking, all of them, into the gel. Maddy was knee-deep, trying in vain to step out. Amaterasu was melting into the ground, translucent and shimmering, and taking Emerson with her.

"She won't if we have the tomoe," Owen said quickly. Emerson had said she'd seen it in the mirror. If they had the power, they could overpower the empress. Get her out of Ian.

"Sounds reckless," Dax said, with an approving nod. He lowered, as if ready to spring. "Only Maddy can unlock the piece from the handle of the katana. Get the other pieces ready. We won't have long."

"What are you going to do?"

Dax grinned. All sharp teeth. "Be a hero, what's it look like?"

He leapt, landing between Maddy and Amaterasu. At his feet, the gel wicked away, as if he repelled it.

"My turn," he told Maddy, as the guardian bared her white, sparkling teeth at him.

"Go!" Emerson shouted. "Maddy, the last piece!"

Owen slid onto his knees in front of the mirror with the two pieces still atop it. He tried to align them, but they were jumping again on the glass.

"What is that?" Emerson asked, frowning down at the mirror as she dropped to her knees beside him.

Thin lines striped across the glass. Then music notes, flittering across the space like butterflies, until finding their places on the staff.

"That's Dax," Maddy said with a grin, taking her place across from Owen.

Owen glanced over, finding Dax facing off against Amaterasu. The ropes of gold stretching from her hands were locked in his grip, and he leaned back, dragging her closer in a game of tug-of-war.

"You bring death to the heavens," Amaterasu shrieked. "Darkness. Kegare. You disturb the souls at rest!" The light surged inside her, making her brighter, a star whose rays were swallowed by the black hole that was Dax.

"Despite all my rage . . ." His voice was a rock and roll growl, and he twisted the beams around his wrist for more leverage. "I am still just a rat in a cage."

"Is he singing?" Owen asked.

"Just wait," Maddy said.

The corner of the mirror Emerson had made for the wisdom challenge had started to burn, embers eating away the glass. On the far sloping wall, the giant's eye was finally closing—the light leaving the corners and working inward, toward the middle.

"We need the third piece!" Owen snatched the two existing sections of the tomoe.

"What do I do?" Maddy held the katana in her open hands, blade on one palm, handle on the other. Between them, embers ate up the mirror and the musical notes on it, leaving no ashes behind.

"There," Emerson said, pointing to a silver semicircle at the base of the grip. "That's it!"

The third, final piece of this puzzle.

Maddy braced the knife against her thigh and pushed on the piece. It popped free. A silver comma. A perfect match for the black and gold prizes in Owen's hand.

"Dax!" Maddy shouted. "Wrap it up!"

"Yes, dear!" Dax yanked hard on the bright cords of light, and Amaterasu was thrown forward. But before she landed in the gel at his feet, a glass wall shot up before her, severing the cords with sparks of light.

"What is that?" Owen asked. But as he looked down, he understood.

The mirror below them burned away, the notes with it. Gone, like a card in the game.

In an instant, a glass box formed around Amaterasu. A prison of mirror pieces, like the coat she'd worn before, but without the fibers connecting the shards of glass. Instead, each piece was soldered together, smooth like the puzzle. She bumped against the sides, nearly knocking it over, but the cell held.

Dax's song filled Owen's mind—*still just a rat in a cage.*

"Did Dax . . . make that?" Owen asked, eyes wide.

Maddy was clapping excitedly. "Yes! Isn't he great?"

Emerson nodded, a small smile curving her lips. "Yeah," she said. "He is."

At the far edge of the sphere, the last of the sliver's light disappeared. Owen glanced at Ian, still on the ground. Was he breathing?

The passage gate was a rabbit hole, floating in the air. Taunting him.

Owen thrust out his hands, the two pieces on his flattened palms. Emerson arranged them beside each other, making room for the final piece. Dax kneeled beside her.

Behind them, Amaterasu wailed in her mirrored prison. "Your filth taints my souls!"

"Do it," Emerson said.

Maddy pressed the silver piece into place.

A blinding light shot upward. A punch of pressure. The force of it threw them backward to the slippery ground. Owen's ears rung as he registered Maddy and Emerson across the circle on their backs, pushing up, and Dax, unaffected, staring skyward.

Get up, Owen told himself, though his head was pounding with the force of a thousand drums. This was it—the moment Ian needed him most. He had to be ready.

As his eyes adjusted to the brightness, he could make out Ian's silhouette framed inside the column of light, arms outstretched. Her stare was wide in agony.

"Izanami!" Owen screamed, reaching toward the light. It took all his strength to push against it, and even then, he could not get close.

Dax turned, following Owen's voice, but it was too late.

Izanami threw herself into the light, snuffing it out with Ian's body. The light went dark—the entire sphere went dark, every soul blinking at once.

The green passage gate had closed.

"What have you done?" wailed Amaterasu from inside her mirrored prison.

The souls glowed again, revealing Ian standing in the center of the ring of light.

"Ian?" Owen whispered. "Are you okay?"

He lifted his face, and as an eerie glow spread across it, Owen knew.

This was not Ian. He could see it in Izanami's hard glare. Feel it in the chill that struck through Owen's veins. Izanami loosened her grip, and the tomoe shone. Black, gold, and silver. The three pieces together at last.

"Get it!" Emerson shouted.

Owen leapt to his feet, but not as fast as Dax. He pounced onto Ian's back, his forearm crushing his windpipe. Teeth bared, Izanami flicked her finger, and sent him flying across the sphere.

Emerson lurched forward, Maddy with her. They snatched at Ian's wrist and arm, but he spun and sent them crashing into Amaterasu's reflective cell.

Izanami turned then, facing Owen. She inhaled deeply, and he could see, even in the soul light, that Ian looked healthier than he had since his return from Meido.

The tomoe had made him strong for *her*.

Terror cracked open inside him.

"Please, Empress," Owen said. "Let him go."

At his feet, the katana waited. Would it let him pick it up?

It has to be you.

Ian's words echoed in his mind.

It has to be you.

Owen felt like the world had turned to slow motion. All rational thought had fled with the light. This was still Ian's body, and Ian was still alive in there somewhere, and even if he could lift the knife, he could never drive it home.

"He would have only disappointed you in the end, Owen," she said. His name on her lips stung.

She thrust her hand toward him and the world went upside down. Pain exploded in Owen's side, in his head and his wrist as he slid across the gel. His glasses were gone, knocked off his face, and his last blurry sight of Izanami was her grim smile as she waved a hand, opening the passage flames. They were larger than any he had seen for a challenge, braided tendrils of green fire arching into the glowing sphere. The crackle snapped and popped over his nerves.

Then the gate was gone, and Izanami, with the immortal power of the tomoe, was finally free in the living world.

MADDY

Everyone was talking at once.

"Why didn't you take the tomoe?" Emerson shouted at Owen.

Dax grabbed Owen's glasses off the ground and shoved them toward him. "Are you okay? Are you hurt?"

Owen put his glasses back on, staring at where the green flame passage had just winked out. "She's going to open the gate. Shit, what do we do?"

"Let me out!" howled Amaterasu. "Let me out, let me *out*!"

"Quiet!" Maddy shouted. She pressed the heels of her hands to her temples. "This isn't the time to argue. We need a plan, fast."

"She's right," said Emerson, her face aglow with specks of light. "We need that tomoe if we're going to keep her from bringing hell to earth."

"And save Ian," said Owen.

"And Dax," added Maddy, her arms stretched out to her sides in frustration before dropping to her sides. "We don't even know where Izanami went."

"Yes we do," Dax said.

They all turned to face him. The giant's eyeball was quiet now, but for the banging of Amaterasu on the inside of her mirrored cage.

"The entrance to Meido can move, but it's been stuck at home for years." He looked to Maddy. "Since my dad first met my mom. He was in charge of keeping the gate hidden from the empress's husband, but . . ."

Maddy rose, reaching for his hand.

"When Aka Manto fell in love with my mom, he was punished in Jigoku. The gate stayed where it was." Dax's head fell forward. He was probably thinking, as Maddy was now, about how his father had taken on the skeleton.

"The cave," Emerson said. Her thumbs pressed to her temples. "The boulder."

"The what?" Owen asked.

"Deep in the cave, there's a boulder blocking the tunnel. That must be the entrance to Meido." She dropped her hands. "It was like the boulder in the coils that locked me in that room."

"Jigoku. Izanami's nightmare," Owen said. "Every floor was something from her real life."

"Please tell me that's not sympathy I hear," Emerson said.

Owen scowled. "She's not this way by accident. Her husband really screwed her over."

"Is that what she told you?" Emerson shot back.

"It's what she showed me!" Owen spun on her. "In the mirrors, in Meido. I saw them together. He loved her. And she loved him. They had a whole life together. And then he . . . he just gave up on her."

Silence stretched between then.

"Why did you see that?" Maddy asked. "Was it part of a challenge?"

"We were looking for you," Owen said. "Izanami said that the mirrors show you what you need to see."

"And you saw their love?" Dax sounded doubtful.

"And her betrayal," said Owen.

"That doesn't make sense," Maddy said. "If the mirrors show you what you need to see, why show you that? Them? When we were playing the last game the mirror showed us what we needed to get to pass the challenge."

"Our dishonorable acts," said Dax.

She nodded.

"Izanami didn't know why the mirrors were showing that," Owen said. "She thought the emperor might be punishing her."

"It's the emperor's game," said Dax.

Maddy paced between them, her feet slipping on the gel. It didn't make sense. "Why would the emperor make challenges to keep the empress from rebuilding the tomoe, then show you how much he loved her?"

Owen shrugged.

"Does sound fairly sadistic for the supposed good guy," said Dax.

Emerson, who'd been quiet, slapped her hands against her thighs. "She's right. That's it! He wants her to know he loved her. He wants her to win."

"What are you talking about?" Owen asked.

"Let her think." Maddy lowered, lifting the katana from the ground. It didn't hum in her grasp. Didn't sing power through her veins. It was just a sword now. A powerful weapon, but just a blade with a handle, and she felt clumsy wielding it.

"The challenges haven't exactly been in the empress's wheel-house," said Emerson.

"Benevolence, valor, and wisdom," Maddy said. "No, not exactly."

"The emperor knew that if she'd go after the tomoe, she'd need to demonstrate them," Emerson went on.

"She'd need a mortal to, anyway," Owen said. "That's why she dragged me along."

"He made her depend on a mortal," Emerson said, excitement making her talk faster. "Yes!"

"Still not following," said Dax.

"The empress saw what the emperor—the creator of this game—wanted her to see. He's not stopping her from coming back," said Emerson.

Maddy's chest tightened. "He *wants* her to come back."

"He hates her," said Dax, lines creasing between his furrowed brows. "That's why he locked her in Meido."

"No," said Owen, raking a hand through his hair. "He loves her. He only hates what she's become. That's why I had to see their love—so I'd know what they had was real."

"He's using the challenges to remake her into who she was before," said Maddy, glancing up at Dax.

"Like she's remaking the tomoe?" Dax blew out a stiff breath. "That's poetic."

"He's trying to save her," said Maddy. She held Dax's gaze, feeling both more determined to get him home and guilty for not letting him be who he was.

A yūrei.

A cardmaker.

But that's not what he wanted, was it? He wanted to come home, with them. To live a normal, mortal life again.

She had never asked him.

She'd come back because she'd wanted him home. But what if this was his home?

She would have to let him go.

They stared at each other, the glimmering light accenting Dax's dark eyes and his hollowed cheekbones. Her chest ached. She pulled her gaze away, focusing on the sword in her hands.

"So how do we stop her?" Maddy asked. "She obviously hasn't changed."

"He would have disappointed you in the end," said Owen.

She lifted her chin.

"That's what the empress said to me. He would have disappointed you—*Ian*. Like the emperor disappointed her. She doesn't know he's trying to fix things."

"So we tell her?" Dax shook his head. "Even if we could find her she wouldn't believe us."

"She'd believe *him*."

They all spun toward the mirrored cage, where the voice had come from. Their reflections showed them in fragments.

Maddy's skin prickled. Amaterasu was still now, and had been listening.

"The emperor?" Maddy asked.

The guardian was silent.

"How do we find him?" Emerson asked.

A beat passed, and then Amaterasu said, "He lives in each of you. In every living thing. You just need to summon him."

"How?" asked Dax.

"Her tears," said Owen. "At the palace, I saw a memory in the mirrors. He said he could never turn away from her when she was crying."

"Will that work?" Maddy asked Amaterasu.

"It might," said Amaterasu. "But she will still have the tomoe's power. She will outmatch him if it comes to a fight."

"Him," said Maddy. "But not all of us together."

"The cockiness of mortals," said Amaterasu. "I will see you again soon if you don't end up in Meido."

As a soul, Maddy realized, glancing to her feet.

"We need to go," she said. "Izanami might already be opening the gate."

"How?" said Emerson. "The passage is gone."

Owen looked to Dax. "Showtime, pal."

Dax's eyes widened. "What does that mean?"

"You just made a cage out of a mirror. Make us a gate home!"

Dax looked suddenly nervous. "It doesn't work that way. The passage, it only works for mortals. Kuchisake had some flames left, but he carried them in a skin pouch."

Owen cringed.

"You made a boat out of feathers," Maddy said, stepping closer. "You made *peanut butter*."

"Right, but those—"

"You made new clothes," said Emerson, closing in on his other side. "Don't think we didn't notice."

Dax tugged at his Green Day tee, clinging to his chest. "I'm not skilled enough. My dad—he was stuck in Jigoku for years. Don't you think he would have made a passage gate out if he could have?"

"He's not you," Owen said. "And he doesn't have us."

Dax's shoulders slumped.

Maddy touched his cold face in her hand. "You made the knife turn into a sword of valor just for me. You chased me through the darkest place in the universe and remembered who you were. Dax, you can do this."

He looked away. "Even if I could, I can't go with you, Maddy. Not like this. My dad, when he crossed over, he changed. He wasn't himself. If I go to the living world and I join with the empress again. If I hurt you . . ." He kicked at the gel at his feet. "The knife isn't mine anymore. It won't keep me real."

"Look at me." She pulled his gaze to hers, and summoned the strength she'd felt holding that katana. "You're not going to forget who you are, because you're going to be with me the whole time. With all of us." She ran her thumbs over his sharp cheek-bones, remembering when they were softer, knowing they would be again. "That knife never made you real, Dax. It was how much we believed in you."

"Maddy," he murmured.

"You can do this," she said, pressing her forehead to his. A hand touched her back. Owen. He wound his arms around them. A moment later Emerson was there too. They held on to one another, surrounded by souls in the eye of a giant, willing Dax to know what she had all along.

That they loved him.

That she loved him.

"If I'm hugging you, you can at least try," Emerson muttered.

He gave a wet chuckle. Then he squared his shoulders and closed his eyes.

"Stand back," he said.

She stepped aside as he took off his shirt, laying it on the slick ground at his feet. A surface, she realized, to make a card. She backed away, giving him room, holding the grip of the sword in her hands. Ready.

"You can't leave me here."

Maddy turned toward the mirrored prison. Amaterasu wasn't banging against the walls, and her stillness put Maddy on edge. She glanced back to Dax, his eyes closed as he knelt over the shirt. Owen and Emerson were on either side of him, watching him.

"I think I can," said Maddy.

"Who will tend to my souls? Keep them calm? The worthy do not deserve an interrupted eternity."

"The worthy." Maddy snorted. "Meido had the worthiest soul there was. And now he's here, and your little lights won't go near him."

Dax was singing now. She couldn't make out the words, but she could hear his rough voice spinning out a melody.

"His soul was never in Meido."

Maddy turned slowly toward the prison. Her own face reflected back at her from every angle, unsettling and strange.

"What does that mean?" she asked.

"Get me out of this prison, and I will give it to you. Then your little yūrei can live again."

Maddy's heart skipped. Dax's soul was here?

He could go home.

"You're lying," she said.

"About my souls? Never." She sighed. "It has been here being purified."

She hesitated. The notes were appearing on Dax's shirt as they had on the mirror before it became this prison. Owen was pointing to them, as if Emerson couldn't see for herself.

"If he had his soul back, what would that mean?"

"He would not be reabsorbed into nature with the rest of the souls." Amaterasu huffed. "He would live again."

Maddy's hands began to shake.

"But know that once he takes it, he will be as mortal as you. As susceptible to death as all of your kind."

"Maddy!" Emerson shouted.

A green circle was rising in the air over Dax's burning shirt. The passage. It stole her focus. He'd done it. He was giving them a way home.

Would he want to live again and leave that behind?

"Maddy!" Emerson shouted again. Owen was already ducking through, disappearing into the shimmering portal.

The world was waiting.

Izanami was waiting.

Maddy turned, and swung the knife as hard as she could. The glass prison shattered, sharp pieces flying out in all directions, implanting into the gel from floor to ceiling.

The guardian stood before her, her hand outstretched, a small light glowing in her palm.

"Get out," she said.

Maddy grabbed the speck of light, so soft and warm, so slippery she nearly dropped it. It pulsed in her hand, sending waves of light up her arm, and she gasped at the sudden surge of emotions inside her. Joy and love and warmth, but fear too. A cold, chilling dread that made her teeth grip. She needed a box for it. A safe. But all she had were her tattered clothes and the sword he had gifted her.

She looked down at the handle of the katana. The empty spot where the final prize had been. Mouth dry, she pressed the warm speck of light into it, and then tore off the end of her ripped sleeve and wrapped it tightly over the hiding place.

With the sword in her grasp, she ran for the gate.

"What happened?" Dax asked. Emerson was already through.

She kissed him, her eyes closed, hoping this would not be the last time. Then she grabbed his hand and dragged him through the barrier.

EMERSON

Before them lay darkness and the stench of death. Emerson could taste it, bitter and rotten on the back of her tongue. Bile surged up in her throat as she reached out her hands and clasped Owen's warm fingers.

"Where are we?" she whispered.

"I don't know," Owen answered, his glasses reflecting the eerie green glow from the passage behind them. "Maddy?"

"Here." Emerson turned back to see her standing with Dax in the threshold to the heavens. But it wasn't the Dax she'd seen moments before. He was changing, his eyes turning black from lid to lid, his teeth sharpening to points. As he stepped away from the passage, his back rounded with a crackle, as if his spine was breaking to form new vertebrae, and his fingernails extended to claws.

"He's good," said Maddy, resting the katana over her shoulder.

"Sure," said Emerson.

The passage closed, bathing them in darkness. She could feel Dax moving, slinking through them, his body a part of the shadows. Terror clenched her jaw. He was like Maddy when she'd come into Owen's mirror in the bedroom, half butterfly. Still Dax, but demonified.

"The cave," he whispered, the sound chilling.

Emerson jerked back involuntarily, her heel knocking into a can on the ground. He was right. This was the cave—she could feel the familiar dread pitting her stomach, the scent of mildew in the air. Behind the shrinking green flames she could make out an uneven circle of light—the reflection of the city off the river. *Home.*

"Dax, wait," Maddy said, but she was cut off by a blast of cold air.

"Children sneaking in the dark," came a woman's grainy voice. "Have you come to join us, or to watch the world burn?"

"Shinigami," Dax hissed.

Emerson sucked in a cold breath. If Shinigami was here, then Izanami had already opened the gate between Meido and their world. She ducked low, grabbing a handful of rocks. A pathetic weapon compared to Maddy's blade, but better than nothing.

The only thing blocking Meido from the living world was them.

"We can't let anything pass," Emerson said quietly.

A rock fell from the wall at her side, and when her gaze shot there, she could make out Dax's dark form climbing up the side of the tunnel on his hands and feet like one of Kuchisake's spiders.

"We fight them back, then get the tomoe," said Maddy, bracing the sword before her.

"Save Ian, shut the gate," said Owen.

"Yes," whispered Dax from somewhere above them. "Time to make an empress cry."

Emerson moved shoulder to shoulder with Owen and Maddy.

"We've come to see Izanami," she called. She couldn't spot the old woman in the dark—but she kept her gaze roaming, and listened for any sign of movement.

"See her you shall." A man's voice had joined Shinigami, his giddy tone threatening to puncture Emerson's courage. "When I sew your eyes onto her new kimono."

Keneō.

She didn't see the strike coming until the blade was a breath away from her cheek. The glint of silver hovered there, stuck in space, stalling her heart. It was Keneō's knife—the one he tucked inside his cane. As she followed the length of it, she found a boy in a Green Day shirt blocking the old man's swing.

Dax smiled, his teeth sharp.

"Careful," he said.

Emerson's breath staggered as she glanced to the man who'd attacked her. His mask of faces was warped with fury.

Before she could take another breath, Dax struck out into the dark, bounding from one wall across to the other. With a roar, Keneō sliced at him, turning so quickly that bits of skin from his mask flew off to land on her arm and neck with juicy slaps. She peeled them off, her stomach lurching.

"Missed me," Dax sang.

"Traitor!" Shinigami screeched at him. On instinct, Emerson ducked. A whoosh of fabric came from above her. A puff of cold steam. She looked back, but the door Dax had made from the heavens was gone now. All that remained was a circle of city light off the river from the cave's exit.

If Shinigami, and Keneō, and any of the empress's creations got out, it was game over.

"Don't let them get by!" Emerson shouted.

"Where are they?" Owen shouted. "I can't see anything!"

A crash and clatter in the dark raised Emerson's defenses. Her hearing sharpened. Her skin prickled with the sudden influx of cold air.

Shinigami manifested before her, her arms spread wide, as if she meant to trap all of them in a deadly embrace. Emerson flung a handful of rocks at the woman's eyes, but they went through her, as if she wasn't real.

Steam.

Another Shinigami appeared, and another beside her. Soon there were half a dozen advancing toward Owen, Maddy, and Emerson. She couldn't tell which one was real—which one to attack first.

"Not this time," Dax said.

He dropped from the ceiling, landing on a Shinigami to Emerson's left. From her hands, he ripped free a teapot and smashed it against the ground. It exploded into pieces—the handle, the shattered base, the spout all flying different directions.

The remaining Shinigamis disappeared, leaving only one behind. She buckled, her screech sending dust raining down from the ceiling.

"Get her!" Maddy shouted, and Owen dove, ramming the old woman into the wall with his shoulder. It was only a minor distraction. Shinigami threw him back with a sweep of her sagging arms.

Deeper in the cave came a monstrous scream—a bird, too large to be of this world.

Tengu.

"We have to get to the gate!" Emerson shouted.

"Go!" Maddy shouted, scrambling to her feet. "We'll hold them off!"

Never split the party. It always ended in disaster.

She didn't have a choice.

The gate had to be closed. Steeling her nerves, she hurtled forward into the dark. She needed to get the tomoe. She'd seen herself holding it in the mirror in the heavens.

Get the tomoe, close the gate.

Save Ian, kill the empress.

A cold sweat broke out on her back.

Ahead, the tunnel turned, the familiar curve that led to a wide room. A light came into view. As Emerson's eyes adjusted, she made out Ian standing before the massive boulder. The tomoe was glowing, embedded into the boulder behind him. Cracks struck out like lightning bolts around it, and chunks of stone had broken free. Some gaps were large enough for a person to squeeze through, and old players, their faces split into deadly smiles by Kuchisake's long fingernail, were trying to get free. They'd been bottlenecked at every exit, hands and legs and heads pressing through. Above them, from another fissure, a hooked beak jutted out, then a flash of inky Tengu wing.

"Izanami!" Emerson shouted, charging toward her. "*Empress!*"

Izanami's hand shot out to the side, freezing Emerson in place in a wash of shadows. Terror gripped her. Every muscle locked, her fingers stretched. Not even her eyelids could blink while the empress had Emerson in her hold.

Izanami faced her, no sign of Ian in her cold stare.

"You have come to try to stop me?" she asked, lifting Emerson off the ground with a flick of Ian's hand. "You? A pathetic mortal, all alone?"

The word echoed through her, threatening to break open healed wounds.

Emerson fought against the empress's cold embrace, but had no control over her own body. Her gaze darted down to her feet, a foot off the dirt. Landed on a black handle embedded in the dirt. A knife. Her kitchen knife—the one she'd dropped when she'd come here the first time, looking for Maddy. If she could reach it, she could defend herself.

"I'm not alone," Emerson muttered through her locked teeth.

"And yet none of your friends have come to help you." Behind Izanami, the tengu were screeching. The horde was pushing. Light from the tomoe in the boulder burned Emerson's eyes, but she could not squint to protect them.

"It is not like Jigoku this time, mortal. No one will return to save you."

Fear pierced Emerson's chest. Memories of the boulder rolling closed after she'd grabbed the golden key. The sound of Maddy's footsteps running away to get help.

The fear that she wouldn't return.

The empress was right. This was the last level with the final boss, and Emerson couldn't beat her on her own. She needed help. Not her friends, not this time. But the only person Izanami would hear.

"He wanted you to win." Emerson fought her invisible bindings to no avail. "We figured it out. The emperor set up the challenges knowing you would get the tomoe."

Izanami tilted her head. "Is that so?"

"He loved you," said Emerson. "He wants you back."

Izanami's laugh cracked off the low ceiling. "And what do you know of love?" She moved closer, and with Emerson off the ground, she could meet her gaze, eye to eye.

Emerson pressed against the hold, straining her arms. Reaching for the knife.

She couldn't move.

"Have you ever felt the hand of a lover, cupping your face? Felt them moving over your body? Seen yourself reflected in their eyes?" Izanami scoffed. "You know nothing of love."

Screams echoed against the narrow walls. What was happening behind her with Keneō, Shinigami, and her friends? Was Dax holding them at bay? Was Maddy hurt? Emerson raised her voice as loud as she could, her vocal cords vibrating in the locked column of her throat.

"Maybe you're right," said Emerson. "Maybe I don't know that kind of love. But I know other kinds. I know about risking everything for someone you care about. I know how it feels when they don't show up for doughnuts and some stupid nail polish you bought as a joke."

"What are you—"

"I know what it's like to look in the mirror and not recognize yourself, and then one day for that to change, and to realize all those pieces you didn't like have come together to make something amazing."

"Oh enough!" said Izanami. "I don't have time to listen to this exploration of the mortal mind!"

"You can't look in the mirror, can you? Because you won't see yourself, ever again. You'll see Ian, and you'll know how much we loved him, and all you'll think about is how you don't have that. But you could."

"Stop talking."

"It could be like it used to be."

"Stop!" Izanami was clutching the sides of Ian's head.

"He loved you," Emerson said. "He wants you to remember."

Izanami threw down her hands, lunging so close Emerson could feel the cold breaths of air on her cheek when she spoke. "I remember his dishonor. His cowardice. His back, as he ran from me through the darkness and sealed this gate behind him." Izanami flung an arm toward the breaking boulder behind her. "I remember losing everything."

Her voice broke.

Emerson's breath hitched as her invisible bonds pulled tighter. She was going to be torn apart. Bright flashes filled her eyes, but through them, she could see Ian's face, wet and streaked with tears.

"Where are you now?" Izanami whispered. Not to Emerson. Not to anyone but the cold air.

The crowd broke free from behind the empress, the split-faced players rushing out into the cave. One knocked into Izanami from behind, throwing her to the side, but she was caught.

Owen held her against his chest, his arms wrapped around Ian's shoulders, his chin notched against Ian's neck.

Emerson could not turn her face to look at them, only move her eyes. Desperation coursed through her as Izanami stumbled back, looking at him in horror.

Owen inhaled slowly, chest lifted, chin high. Gold flecks shone in his eyes, magnified in his glasses, and his shoulders seemed broader as he stepped forward into Emerson's line of sight.

"Izanami," he said, in a deep voice that was not Owen's. "You have summoned me, and I am here."

MADDY

They were being overrun.

Dax, even with all his speed and strength, was not able to hold back both Shinigami and Keneō. Emerson and Owen had made it through, but without them more players were pushing by. Even as Maddy cut at them with her sword, they got up and hurled themselves past her.

"What do we do?" Maddy cried, swinging the sword in a wide, reckless semicircle, the warmth of Dax's soul pulsing through the sleeve she'd tied over it in the handle. It knocked down three players, but more crawled over their fallen bodies, their tattered clothes ripping as they clawed forward.

A tengu screeched in anger, the sound making Maddy's ears ring. The monster was barreling down the narrow hall, bouncing from one side to the other. It bowled into three more players, knocking one into her. The bird's teeth snapped open and shut viciously, its empty eyes wild and trapped.

"Get down!" Dax leapt toward Maddy, knocking her out of the way of the giant bird. It swooped by only to crash into the ceiling and slam into the ground with an explosion of gravel. Its body blocked the tunnel, but only temporarily.

"Cut the wing!" Dax hissed, throwing himself back at Shinigami. "Maddy, the wing!"

Maddy raced toward the tengu's flailing wings, stomping hard on one to break the bones. The sound made her stomach turn, but at least the beast would not fly.

"There you are," sang Keneō, appearing through the horde. He snatched a handful of Maddy's braids in his fist and she gasped in surprise, dropping the katana. It clanged against the ground, just out of reach as he dragged her hair to his face and sniffed it with a giggle. She struggled, kicking back with her heels, throwing back her elbows. Her scalp strained under his grip.

He swung his knife toward her gut.

She cried out, tensing her stomach for the blade, but the knife never connected.

She was knocked to the ground, a sharp, furry leg scraping her cheek. When she looked up, Keneō's body was still standing, but his head was gone.

A spider, each leg longer than Maddy was tall, stood before her. Eight red eyes swiveled toward her, filled with the same hunger for violence they'd just shown for Keneō.

"I'm here, my love!" A hand gripped Maddy's shoulder and hauled her up.

"Did you miss me, Madeline? Because I so missed you," said Kuchisake, his smile stretched from ear to ear.

Maddy grinned as his army of spiders flooded the cave, rising like a tidal wave to cover everything in their tracks.

OWEN

Owen burned. A bursting star in reverse, shards of light searing together. His body was not built to hold such power. White hot flames licked every nerve, scraped every muscle. The power that thrummed through him was infinite.

He was the emperor.

Izanagi.

But Owen, too.

Eternal and mortal, in one.

"You have remade the tomoe," Izanagi said through Owen's mouth. Owen could feel the words vibrate through him, like he was just a string on Dax's guitar. Izanami circled them, predators in a world of prey.

She was beautiful, even like this. Beneath the mortal's skin, Izanagi and Owen could see her shimmering power. Dark waves on a moonlit night.

"Despite your best intentions," she said.

Her petulance pleased the emperor. Drew a rumble from Owen's chest.

"My intentions were that you succeed," Izanagi said. "That you remember the virtues you once possessed. If you lived again, it had to be with a pure heart."

She grunted. "I never forgot those virtues. I knew them, even in the darkest of nightmares, husband, because they failed to serve me. Benevolence, valor, and wisdom are for the weak. I would choose ambition, fury, and vengeance any day."

"That was not our intent in the beginning."

She laughed. "Was it your intent to betray me?"

"Never."

"So then, my emperor, it appears things change." She stopped pacing, squaring Ian's shoulders.

"You cannot bring death to the living world," Izanagi said, and Owen agreed so deeply, he could feel their intentions braid as one.

"But I already have." Her hands lifted. "You feel it every day, husband. Every moment. Sickness and old age. Suffering and apathy. There is no peace in your realm. My roots have leached through the soil of your world into every living thing you've touched. Now I will simply finish the work."

Emerson fell, released from Izanami's hold. She scrambled out of the way.

"I cannot allow it," Izanagi said.

"You cannot stop me, my *love*." The word was bitter. The resentment carved at their will. Even now, the emperor ached for her, just as Owen ached for Ian.

"Owen, watch out!" Emerson shouted.

Izanami raised Ian's hands, and inky black shadows shot from his spindly fingers. Owen and the emperor dodged aside as one as the burst struck down half a dozen players, coating them like ink and flinging them into the walls of the cavern room. With a frustrated scream, Izanami struck out again, her darkness splashing across the room to the ceiling, covering the light of the tomoe. Overhead, the tunnel groaned and a chunk of earth gave way in a spray of rocks and dust.

"You do not want this," the emperor said, making Owen dodge out of the way of the falling debris.

"You dare tell me what I want? After you locked me in that prison?" She bounded off the wall beside the boulder blocking half the gate, scooping up a player to fling toward the emperor. "I hate that everyone thinks you are the hero—the god of *life*. If you hadn't banished me, I would be beside you. If you hadn't tried harder to see past the kegare . . . if you had stayed with me . . ."

New strength pulsed through Owen as Izanagi caught the player and set him down. He rushed after the others.

"I made a mistake, Izanami," the emperor said. "I was a coward."

Memories pelted their collective mind. A thousand sunsets with

Izanami's head against the emperor's chest. The awe of watching her breathe stars into the night sky, blown like sand in her palm. She had been magnificent.

They had been magnificent together.

Grief filled Izanagi. Filled Owen, too. A well of sorrow deep enough to hold the sea.

"You are a coward still!" Izanami hissed, spinning to slam Ian's fists against the wall. Thunder boomed in the cavern, making it shake and tremble. A sheet of rock slid free, crashing to the ground with a spray of dirt.

"It's going to crush us," Emerson shouted through the cloud of dust. "The cave's about to collapse!"

From farther down the corridor, Owen could hear the screams and crashes of battle. It would all be over soon. The cave would fall, and the gate would close again, destroying all in this tunnel.

There was no other way.

"You have betrayed me," Izanami raged, her shadows surrounding Owen and the emperor. Throwing them against the ceiling. Owen's bones snapped, the pain fleeting as Izanagi's power knitted Owen back together.

The emperor knew he deserved every bit of her wrath, and Owen absorbed it, because he had no choice but to do so.

"You are an emperor of lies," she cried now, hurling him to the ground again. In an instant, she was over Owen, her hands on his throat.

"And you are my empress," Izanagi whispered through the straw of Owen's mortal throat.

Izanami did not see Emerson behind her, a kitchen knife in her hand.

She did not see Emerson drive it into the boulder, prying the tomoe free. Or how the rock trembled as the artifact fell into her hands.

Izanami was still pouring her rage into her husband as Emerson dropped the knife and lifted the tomoe over her head, the three pieces sizzling with power. She threw back her head and screamed. The air shimmered, throwing a sparkle over the dark, before the black poison of Izanami's power was ripped away like a curtain and sucked through one of the cracks in the boulder.

With a roar, the empress shoved off of Owen's body, spinning to face Emerson. She lifted her hands, rage clawing Ian's fingers. Bruises blossomed under his eyes, veining out down his cheeks. Lips drew back over bared teeth.

"Go back," Emerson heaved. "To Hell."

With a shriek, Izanami rushed toward her.

But the emperor and Owen were faster.

They dove across the ground. Grabbed the knife. Rose.

Izanami caught sight of them and turned, her back to the boulder.

"Wait," Izanami cried. "My love."

They drove the blade into her heart.

Izanami gasped.

Ian gasped.

The emperor and Owen wept.

They held the blade where it was, embedded in the cold stone of her heart. They pinned her against the boulder, the cracks still open, the tengu and players now desperately trying to cling to the rock. Meido was pulling them back, away from the boulder and the cave and the living world.

It has to be you. The words echoed in Owen's mind. In Izanagi's soul. Neither wanted this. Both knew there was no other way. The tomoe was doing Emerson's will now, sealing the cracks of the boulder from the farthest points inward.

"I'm sorry," the emperor and Owen said. "I see you now. I am not afraid of what you have become."

"Please," begged Izanami. Blood sputtered from Ian's mouth, painting Owen's burned, tattered shirt.

"Kegare," the emperor said, and Owen flinched. "It taints me now too."

Izanagi released the knife's handle, pressing Owen's fingers around it, against Ian's chest. Feeling what remained of the heart beneath grow uneven, and faint.

"It's time for us to go," the emperor murmured.

"Owen?" Emerson was still holding the tomoe, but it was turning to dust in her hands. "We need this for Ian. For Dax. Wait! Emperor!"

It was too late to help them.

The mortals were on their own now.

The blood on Owen's chest and hand grew bright. His skin flashed golden with Izanagi's power. The emperor looked up from the wound to Ian's face, warped with fear, and the tears that came from his eyes.

"We will be together again," the emperor said.

He leaned forward, and kissed the empress.

The power leached out through Ian, making his veins bright. The black bruises drew back like blood in a syringe.

The empress smiled, and it was filled with such longing it made Owen's heart seize.

Then Izanami was dragged from Ian's mortal body back through a crack in the wall, her gleaming shadow gripping the tainted soul of the emperor she loved. They were there, and then they were gone, and Owen and Ian fell to the ground in a pile.

"You did it," Ian whispered up at him. Owen held him tightly against his chest.

Then Ian's bleeding heart stopped, and his head rolled back, and everything Owen had fought for was gone.

DAX

The gate was closing, swallowing everything that belonged inside it. He could feel the pull in his blood, a magnet too strong to resist. It gained power with each passing second, spiders and bodies of fallen players hurling through the air into the black.

Shinigami was gone. What remained of Keneō had been gulped down into Meido as well. Even the tengu did not have the strength to resist.

It was time for him to be gone too.

Clawing into the dirt, he crawled behind a chunk of fallen rock. Meido's call seemed to reach through the stone, dragging him toward his fate.

"Maddy!" he shouted, his yūrei voice a hiss. He was different here, ugly and monstrous. It should have made it easier to leave.

It didn't.

"Dax!" She ran toward him, unaffected by the pull. It was just the dark creatures Meido wanted, not the living. On the opposite wall, Kuchisake was wedged into a divot, bracing himself with his hands and feet.

"We go together!" he called over the roaring wind with a wild grin. "You and I to the very end, yes, Dax?"

At least he wouldn't be alone.

Maddy crashed to her knees before him, cuts and bruises on her face. He stared at her in wonder—this mortal girl who had taken on an army of monsters with only a sword in her hand.

"Dax, look. She gave it to me. She had it in the heavens!"

She stabbed the blade of the katana into the ground and unwound a piece of fabric tired around the handle. In the space where the final prize had been was a pulsing white light. Gently, she pulled it free, cradling it in the palm of her hand.

He stared at it in wonder, his chest giving a sudden lurch.

"Who . . . what is . . ."

"Amaterasu!" she shouted. "Dax, it's your *soul*."

His soul.

Hope slammed through him with a force of a hurricane. It left no room for doubt. He didn't need to breathe, but still, his throat clenched, and he scratched at it, trying to free the lump that had risen there.

"Do you want it?" Her voice was small. She was uncertain, he realized. She didn't know this was all he wanted in the world.

If he had a soul again, he would no longer be yūrei. He'd be mortal.

With a living soul, he'd be *alive*.

"Help!"

Emerson.

Dax turned, careful not to look too far over the stone. Emerson and Owen were dragging Ian through the cave, his arms hanging limply over their shoulders. Debris and bodies flew past them down the tunnel, making a straight path impossible.

Maddy helped them lay Ian on the rough ground. His lips were blue, his face ashen. There was a stab wound in his chest.

"He's not breathing," said Maddy.

"His heart," said Owen. "The emperor did it. I . . ." He looked at his own hands, covered in blood. "I did it."

Dax met Owen's gaze, the panic so potent it he could taste it.

If Owen had done this, he wouldn't have had a choice.

"The gate is closing," Emerson said, tears running down her dusty cheeks. "The emperor and empress are gone."

"Can you help him?" Owen asked desperately. "Dax, please help him."

Maddy closed her hand around Dax's soul, meeting his gaze. Her eyes wet with tears.

He looked to Emerson, who already knew the truth.

"He's gone," Dax said.

If he'd had a beating heart in this world, it would have broken.

"The tomoe," said Maddy. "Maybe it can bring him back."

"It's dust," Emerson told them, looking at her empty, open

hands. "It disintegrated to close the cracks in the boulder and seal the gate shut."

"The soul," he said, pulling Maddy's hand toward Ian's chest.

"Dax," she said brokenly. But she opened her hand. Nothing happened. Nothing changed, not even when Dax took the light from her hand and tried to press it into Ian's chest. His friend's body wouldn't accept the soul.

There was nothing they could do.

They huddled around him, a collective pain spilling free from all their wounds. A mortal panic dredged up from the base of Dax's yūrei soul as the pull to Meido grew stronger. He recalled the day that Ian had stopped beside the old field where his apartment had stood before it had burned. How Ian had handed him the knife.

How they had become the kind of friends who saved each other.

A cold hand closed on his shoulder. When he looked up, he saw Kuchisake, braced against the pull. He pulled a small card from his obi—one of the cards he'd been hoping Dax could turn into a severed head—and pressed it into Dax's hand with a small nod.

Dax opened his mouth, and through the raging wind began to sing.

"The bravest of us all. The one who bent, the one to fall."

He saw the room in Jigoku where he'd first met his father.

Could I make a car? An airplane? A person?

Not a person. Not fully. I have tried.

"All I need is a part, not a puzzle, just a heart." He sang louder, fighting the wind. He wished his father were here now. He was dragging away now, his back pressed against the rock. His ribs cracking against the pressure.

"The card," Owen said. "It's burning. Look!"

"Not a mortal to bring back, just the missing piece he lacks."

The card burned away.

Ian opened his mouth and gasped.

Dax fell over him, exhaustion leaving him unable to hold on. Owen grabbed his arm. Emerson his leg. He was slipping through their fingers.

"Dax?" Ian whispered.

"Do me a favor," he said. "Quit playing cards, huh?"

Ian's heart beat against his ear. Steady. Healthy.

Then his own heart answered.

A soft, uneven throb. Then a boom, louder and louder in his temples, until he could feel the punch of it through his entire body. He sat up. His back straightened. His gums numbed as his pointed teeth evened out. His vision went blurry as it compressed to a normal width.

He strength waned, *changed*, making him aware of his bones, and his gurgling stomach, and a pulse, slamming through his ears. The wind from Meido had stopped pulling him; he couldn't even hear its howl. He felt suddenly fragile. Finite. *Mortal.*

He looked down and found the pulsing light in his hand digging into his palm, spreading a golden glow up his arm and through his chest. Down his legs. Out the ends of his hair. Maddy was crying—happy tears. And Emerson and Owen joined her. *Final form,* Emerson shouted, and they all repeated the words with a cheer. He didn't know what she meant exactly, but he felt better than he had in all his memory. And then they were all hugging, and he was in the center of the circle, feeling them bruise him in a dozen different places with their enthusiastic embrace. Alive.

Alive.

Alive.

He stood. His feet were steady on the ground.

A cold hand fell on his back, and when he looked up, Kuchisake was there.

He didn't say a word. With the wind whipping his jade kimono, he smiled, ear to ear.

Dax nodded at him.

Kuchisake bowed his head.

The wind took him without a sound, and then Dax, Maddy, Owen, Ian, and Emerson ran. They ran like when they were children, sprinting away from a game in the dark. The tunnel collapsed behind them, falling rocks clipping their heels.

Bursting out of the cave, they fell onto one another on the rocks as the entrance coughed dust over them. They stayed there a long time, clinging to each other under a starry sky.

Five mortals who'd played the emperor's game, and won.

IAN

Ian walked alone down Foxtail Avenue in the waning summer light. The tall buildings around him cast long shadows, the bright stripes between them drawing his eyes toward the setting sun—a golden light blanketed with wispy clouds. Not a giant's eye.

He fought the urge to look back over his shoulder to make sure no one was following. He'd been working on that with his therapist—a woman named Darcy who had him practicing his exposure to various triggers out in the community. This week marked the first night he'd been able to sleep with the lights off.

At the intersection in front of Owen's town house, he waited for the walk sign, then crossed. He glanced up the steps to the front door, but didn't stop.

Hurrying down the sidewalk, he wove in and out of the trees, decorated with fairy lights for summer, past the restaurants that had opened their doors to outside seating. Even as a kid, he'd loved the city in the summertime. The surge of cheers from the soccer stadium behind the music hall. The cheesy horse-drawn carriages and bachelorette parties on the street cars. The kids jumping in and out of the water fountains at Washington Park, their cones of Graeter's ice cream dripping over their stubby fists to the concrete below. He could smell the sweet Cincinnati chili in the air from the Skyline on the corner. The volume of life had been daunting since his return, but he was getting used to it again.

Finally, he reached the corner, and pushed into the cool air conditioning of The Bean. The bitter scent of coffee greeted him as he waded through the crowd to the booth in the far corner where his friends were already sitting.

"How's he doing?" Ian asked, sliding in beside Owen. Their hips bumped. Owen smiled down at where they touched and grabbed Ian's hand.

Their fingers wove together, making Ian's strong heart skip a beat.

"Amazing, as always," said Maddy. She was making goo-goo eyes at the singer on the far side of the room. Dax had a steady crowd on Tuesday nights, with regulars who dropped enough in tips for him to buy them all ice cream later.

A woman with silver hair was sitting close, her eyes never leaving him.

Vera had not missed a single set since Dax returned.

Maddy rested her chin on her woven hands and sighed.

"I bet him ten bucks he wouldn't play death metal," said Emerson.

"That's ten bucks lost," said Owen as Dax switched to a harder strum of his guitar. "I heard him practicing earlier."

Emerson scowled.

Owen and Dax had moved into an apartment together a month ago after graduation. It was near the university where Owen's mom taught—where he'd be going in the fall with a major in theater. Dax was still studying for his GED with Ian and Emerson. They had plans to take the test together in September.

Across the room, Dax caught Ian's eye and lifted his chin. Ian waved back.

He'd heard Dax practicing the song too—last night, when he'd been studying at Owen's.

Owen had been helping Ian study *a lot* lately.

"So what are we doing tonight?" Emerson asked, as Dax's low growl twisted into a line of what was definitely heavy metal. Ian grinned. He didn't really get Emerson's music. He far preferred the acoustic stuff Owen had picked out for him. But he loved pretending to be a metalhead to make Owen sweat.

"Kissing my boyfriend?" Maddy offered.

"Gross. Pass."

Ian laughed at Emerson's scowl.

"Packing," said Maddy. She and Emerson were going to be moving into an apartment near the university together next month when classes started.

"Boring," Owen told her.

The barista, a man with tattoos up his forearms, swung by their table, picking up their empty glasses. "You could always play a game," he said, nodding to the stack of board games on a shelf against the wall by the bathroom.

They looked at one another across the table with wide eyes.

"No."

"Absolutely not."

"We're not really game people."

"No puzzles either."

The barista shrugged. "Suit yourselves."

The tension faded as he walked away, and Ian slid back on the leather seat, resting his head on Owen's shoulder. He closed his eyes, the sound of Dax's voice blending with his own beating heart. It didn't matter what they did tonight, or what they did tomorrow, or any night after that.

Because finally he was home.

ACKNOWLEDGMENTS

First of all, let me commend you, reader, for surviving this treacherous game! I know at times it was likely terrifying, and definitely gruesome, but you did it. Thank you for going on this journey with me, and for giving a story like this—dark, twisted, and often uncomfortable—a chance. You are the true heroes.

I am enormously grateful to my editor, Ali Fisher, who helped me bring this nightmarish world to life. From Meido's deadly challenges, to my warped interpretation of Jigoku (Japanese Buddhist hell), to the sparkly goo of heaven's eye, you helped make every trial, pain, and joy *more*, and for that, I am thankful.

Thank you to my agent, Joanna MacKenzie, who has faced every storm with me. If I had to play this game with anyone, you can bet I'd chose you for my crew (sorry!). Thank you to my amazing team at Tor Teen—Saraceia Fennell, Khadija Lokhandwala, Isa Caban, Anthony Parisi, and Dianna Vega, who brought this story to the world in grand fashion. You are the Dream Team, and I'm honored to be in your circle.

Thank you to Matthew Meyer for all the beautiful illustrations on yokai.com, which I have spent countless hours perusing. This art has been such an inspiration.

Thank you to my sensitivity readers, who have delivered such thoughtful notes, and from whom I have learned so much.

And thank you to my friends—those I know online, who have offered such support in these wild times; my mom friends and Jazzercise friends and oldest friends who knew me before I ever wrote a single book—I rely on you every day for my mental health; and my author friends, Lish, Chelsea, Molly, Jeannette (STET, B*TCHES), Cory, August, Jess (SCONE CAMP FOREVER), Katie (who is just family at this point), Mindee (who reminds me what it's all about), and Sara (who still possesses half my brain). I love you all.

Finally, thank you to my family. I'm so grateful to have you all in my life. Jason, I'd find you even in the pits of Jigoku. Ren, I'd protect you from every demon. You both have all my heart.

ABOUT THE AUTHOR

Anne Gregoire Photography

Critically acclaimed young adult author of more than a dozen books, including the Article 5 trilogy, the Vale Hall series, and *The Glass Arrow*, KRISTEN SIMMONS's writing is inspired by her work with trauma survivors as a mental health therapist. She currently lives with her husband and son in Cincinnati, Ohio, where she spins stories, herds a small pack of semiwild dogs, and teaches Jazzercise. To learn more, join her circle on Instagram at @kris10writes or visit her website and sign up for her newsletter at kristensimmonsbooks.com.

www.ingramcontent.com/pod-product-compliance
Lightning Source LLC
Chambersburg PA
CBHW011449170626
46816CB00009B/2599